An Amazing Aptitude

by

M.A. Moone

Other books by M.A. Moone

The Lord's Bit
Grits to Granola

Chapter One

New Haven, Connecticut
Fall, 1989

Tucker Jones, smiling diffidently to the others, slipped into his curved-back conference chair just before their president, James Whipple Tyler III, strode cheerily into the room passing out gruff, hearty greetings. Their boss was seemingly oblivious to the fact that ten of the eleven waiting people were carefully stifling an inward groan as they smiled their acknowledgements. These ten senior managers had come to recognize that the cheerfulness of the morning's salute was a clear measure of the toughness of the forthcoming session.

Today they were to begin preliminary discussions about the possibility of expansion into yet another third-world country. The heartiness of the smile and the spring in the step of this particular entrance bespoke of a grueling morning. Ten pairs of carefully manicured hands began to nervously sort and prioritize the papers lying on the conference table before them. Only Tucker sat with a cleared space. No papers, pencils, pens, recording devices or even a cup of coffee cluttered his area of the table. Hands clasped loosely in his lap, he became invisible: a silent presence, whose purpose in the room was known clearly only to the still grinning man sitting confidently at the head of the polished table.

It was a fact known throughout the company that James Tyler was apt to cancel meetings if Tucker Jones was, for some reason, unavailable. There had been great speculation among senior managers as to Tucker's function. Some who believed they knew, said Mr. Tyler was like a thoroughbred horse and Tucker was the stable goat—a calming influence.

Actually, now that Tucker had been with the company for more than three years, office speculation had

1

moved on to other areas and the topic of his function was seldom discussed. In fact, his pleasant, respectful demeanor to all in the elevators or in the hallways— regardless of company rank, had gained him rather a cult following among the same employees who had wondered endlessly at his lack of an official title and lack of ranking in the company hierarchy.

It was this air of mystery regarding Tucker's function that provided part of his status. He was close to no one, did not exchange office confidences, go for drinks with co-workers or attend company functions. At one time or another, all the office vamps had tried to engage him in mild flirtations, but to no avail.

The mahogany desk in his office would often be empty for two or three days at a time—but if there was a management meeting, you could count on Tucker to slip quietly into his chair opposite Mr. Tyler. Just as you could count on Mr. Tyler to catch Tucker's eye and give the slightest of nods before even the briefest of meetings began.

Tucker's first contact with the firm of Zitec Global Development was as an intern from Yale University doing a project for his Master's Degree in Business Administration. He had been assigned by personnel to Clifton Eldridge, one of the toughest, brightest and most senior of the vice presidents.

Clifton remembered giving him high marks for his projects and writing a concise, positive summary to the supervising professor regarding Tucker's grasp of the problem and the efficacy of the solution—but he was as surprised as any of his colleagues when Mr. Tyler had escorted Tucker into the conference room one morning and announced: "Ladies and gentlemen, this is our newest hire. I believe you all know our former intern, Tucker Jones. He will be attending our management meetings from now on."

This was a well-polished management team. Astonishment was not one of the expressions they allowed themselves. To a person, they sat quietly, faces pleasant and composed, thankful their boss couldn't see that their minds were in disarray as they scrambled for understanding of this unprecedented event, while for the first time noticing that a twelfth chair, Tuckers chair, had been pulled to the

2

other end of the table—directly opposite from Mr. Tyler. Only those with the quickest wits were able to murmur polite words of greetings.

Tucker had responded to each with a quiet, confident smile and a nod, before slipping into his waiting chair. Mr. Tyler paused for a moment, watching the scene and then walked on to his end of the table, sitting to survey the group. He matched their bland and pleasant expressions with his own, nodding the first of the brief, ritual nods to Tyler before beginning the meeting. That was it-- the full introduction and the full lack of explanation.

After the meeting some stopped in the executive lavatory and others went on to confer in their own private offices, but no one in the group seemed able to enlighten them further. Clifton, as the young man's former supervisor, was talked into asking Mr. Tyler, better known to the group as "Whip," in both public and private conversation, for more details.

Clifton was a good choice as he was not only the most senior manager, but also the only one capable of besting their boss on the golf course. Since both men had a healthy sense of sportsmanship and competition, they found time to play together at their country club as often as possible—were, in fact, playing the day after Tucker's appointment. As curious as the rest, Clifton promised he would.

"Say, Whip," Clifton said in his usual forthright manner as he turned to his bag, "are you going to tell us anything further about Tucker's role in Zitec?"

It seemed a simple direct question to Clifton and not at all out of line. They generally talked a little business as they moved from hole to hole. But even before the words were completely out of his mouth, Clifton knew he had just crossed some invisible boundary. They were no longer Whip and Cliff, golfing partners; they were James Whipple Tyler III, President, and G. Clifton Eldridge, Vice President, just as their respective office doors said.

His boss didn't exactly do anything noticeably dramatic—but Clifton had worked with him for fifteen years. The long pause, the big, bright grin and the mild, "Why do you ask, Cliff?" instead of a direct answer to the question, were detour signs warning of dangerous ground. Clifton

3

paused for the briefest of moments, knowing this was the time for absolute truth and conciliation in as few sentences as possible—and then a quick change of topics.

"I guess it was simple curiosity, Whip. The introduction yesterday was quite brief and after the meeting there was some wondering going on in the executive john. I told some of the fellows I would ask." He ducked his head. "I apologize if I'm out of line. If you feel like you need to tell me that you're the president and can hire whomever you choose, for whatever reason, go ahead, but I already know it. I've worked for you long enough to know you have a good reason for what you do."

Steel blue glances met and then locked—neither man wanting to break away until each could see respect and trust still written in the other's eyes. Finally, Whip said, matter-of-factly, "Yep, I'm the president and you're still the best vice president I've ever had; only you're holding up the game."

The tension flowed away. They grinned comfortably at each other before Cliff selected his new number one wood, walked to the tee and proceeded to play some of the best golf of his life.

Generally, when the two played, their small talk was divided between business and world events. On this day, there was no talk; concentration was absolute. To strangers, they might have looked like brothers, both tall, gray hair thinning, bodies starting to sag and paunch, though Whip was the rangier and bigger-boned and showed the decay of time less. They also played like brothers, having the same way of studying the course, the same willingness to risk a tricky shot, the same covering of emotion whether the ball cooperated or not. However, most in the club knew them and were apt to give way to their fast-paced game; watching with silent approval, the preciseness, the determination and the aura of competence generated by the men.

They battled the full eighteen holes, but in the end, it was Clifton's day to win. "By God, that was our most splendid game yet!" Whip exploded as his final putt rimmed the cup and dropped into the hole.

They stood for a moment, arranging their bags, feeling supple and relaxed, looking back over the smooth

4

and restful green of the course. Then with a mutual sigh, they headed for the clubhouse.

As they walked, Clifton allowed himself a small smile and his thoughts to wander. *I'm not the president of Zitec and don't believe I want to be. But it is enjoyable to work for this man who is a winner even when he loses. So Tucker Jones is to remain a mystery, but I can live with it. He certainly seems to be a good addition.* He nodded to himself. He'd just played to win and had beaten a worthy opponent who evidently liked working and playing with a winner. He certainly could live with that. "Well, Whip," he chuckled, the smile on his face stretching to a grin, "The good news for you is that the winner buys the beer, eh?"

The mystery of Tucker Jones' function at Zitec had an uncomplicated explanation, but one that Mr. Tyler recognized should be kept under wraps if it was to benefit the company. That simple explanation, known only by his wife, Midge, was that Tucker, besides being delightfully well-mannered, had an unusual talent. That talent was the ability to remember, if he really concentrated, almost everything he heard. The gift of almost perfect auditory recall coupled with an amazingly logical and objective mind made him of extraordinary value to his employer.

How James Tyler discovered and recognized the worth of Tucker's talent was also simple. Yale's MBA interns were invited to attend management meetings if the agendas were appropriate. The agenda of the meeting Tucker attended focused on clarification of company policy. By simple coincidence, Mr. Tyler and Tucker exited the room together and the president politely, though somewhat off-handedly, asked the intern what he thought of the meeting.

Tucker, with a truly puzzled expression on his handsome face, said, "I found it confusing, sir."

The unexpectedness of the response caused Mr. Tyler to pause in midstride and give the young man a steely look. Truth was, he was also feeling a little confused by the meeting, but had been unable to clarify the cause. He came to a full stop like an old locomotive discharging its steam and turned his full attention on the young man in front of him, immediately liking the way the youngster stood quietly, his gaze level.

5

"Well, Mr. Jones," James said, coming to a sudden decision, "if you have five minutes, I'd like to hear what you have to say about that confusion."

Later that same night, he said with quiet satisfaction to Midge, "That five minutes, which turned into 30, by the way, is likely to be the most productive half hour of my career. This lad is exceptional! When I asked what confused him about the meeting, he told me in one concise sentence, looking me straight in the eye."

"'Sir,'" he said, "'at the beginning of the meeting, you clearly defined the task of the meeting: 'to operationalize the company's short term goals,' but as nearly as I could determine, only two people in the room understood what the term 'operationalize' meant—instead, five people discussed company philosophy and three failed to speak.'"

James took a healthy sip of scotch and smiled at his wife. "So, I got on the horn and called Dale Simons, who is still chairing the business department at Yale and he actually raved about the kid. Within the hour, I called young Tucker in and made him an offer." He beetled his brows. "A generous offer, I might add...expecting him to fall all over me with gratitude. Instead, if you can believe it, he thanked me very nicely, said he believed in Zitec's mission of helping third world countries become more self-sustaining and told me he'd give it serious consideration. I couldn't believe it! What presence of mind for a youngster! Really, Midge, I'm convinced this is an exceptional young man!"

Midge Tyler leaned back in her Queen Anne armchair and smiled as her husband leaped from his chair, set his tumbler on the mantel and began pacing the carpet in front of the fireplace. She had not seen him so happily animated for years.

"Now," he was stumbling over his words in the rush to get them out, "get this. I didn't take the time to introduce the management team by name and while Tucker didn't know the names of the two people in the room who seemed to understand what the word operationalize meant, he could actually recall their conversations nearly verbatim when I pressed him to do so. He also pointed out exactly where the meeting got off track and the times direct questions brought answers that had little or nothing to do

6

with the original question. Don't ask me how he could do that. It was amazing! I couldn't do such a thing. I don't believe anyone else in that room could even come close. Lord, I hope he takes the job. It would be like having my own secret weapon and for damn sure; it would make me do a better job of running the place."

He suddenly stopped pacing and waving his arms and spread his stance, glaring at his wife. "Can you think of one reason a man wouldn't want to come to work at Zitec...especially when he was offered a position that put him as the right-hand man to the president of the company, when he hasn't yet graduated?"

Her eyes were twinkling and a chuckle escaped before she could compose herself enough to answer serenely. "No, James, I cannot. It would seem to be an honor to work with a company that does as much for the world as Zitec does. Now sit down and calm yourself a bit while I go check with Charlie about dinner." She rose from her chair, lifted the tumbler from his hand, freshened it from the crystal decanter on the drink tray, handed it to him with a kiss on the cheek and left him sitting, deep in thought.

James admitted to himself fully for the first time, that what he learned from Tucker had shaken the confidence he had in himself as a leader. What the young man said seemed elemental, that he himself should have defined exactly what he meant by "operationalize," or at least recognized the dissembling going on, but, he hadn't. Now, he was more than a little anxious that Tucker might refuse his offer. He sat reviewing their conversation and was once again convinced that Tucker was NOT trying to make points with a president—the lad had sifted the meeting through his mind and could not find a logical progression. That was what had caused his confusion. Tyler found his clarity of communication quite refreshing. Taking another sip of scotch, he frowned and cautioned himself once more not to count on the young man until he had signed a contract. But, he was counting on it; so much so that he knew if it didn't happen he would be terribly disappointed. He sighed. The ball was in Tucker's court. He had given him a week to make up his mind about the job and if the turmoil he was feeling tonight was an indicator of his state of mind while waiting for Tucker to decide, it was going to be a long week.

Mr. Tyler need not have worried. At the very moment he was sharing with his wife, his feelings of awe about Tucker's ability to relate conversations verbatim, the object of his consternation and hopes was sitting at his computer typing a letter of acceptance to the terms and conditions of employment offered at Zitec Global Development.

Tucker Jones came on board as James Tyler's right hand man only two weeks after he graduated, with honors, from Yale University.

Chapter Two

What Midge and James did not know about Tucker until much later was the fact that his pleasant demeanor and well-trained mind were the result of tremendous determination and rigid self-control. The fabric of his personality had been woven in fear to protect himself from pain since early adolescence.

He had not always felt the need for such protection. His early years, though somewhat unconventional, were very happy. His parents were gentle, intellectual, but distant people who had developed few of the skills necessary to parent a child. Fortunately, on some level, both had recognized their inability to nurture and had, at Tucker's birth, hired Mary and Ethan O'Shea, a middle-aged, Irish couple with an infinite ability to nurture, but an inability to have children of their own.

The O'Sheas arrived within a week of Tucker's birth and took over much of the day-to-day management of the estate as well as the loving care of Tucker, who as soon as he was able to toddle, became Ethan's shadow.

Ethan cared for the grounds, repaired and maintained the house and served as chauffeur from time to time. He kept both the Lincoln and Jaguar running smoothly under fresh coats of hand-rubbed paste wax. He also, on sunny days, pulled the Aston Martin out of its canvas cocoon in the garage and gave it an unnecessary wash and wax before taking Tucker for a spin down to the local gas station to have its tires checked.

Tucker knew, as soon as he was old enough to understand, that the car had been his grandfather's, then his father's and that upon graduation from college, would pass on to him. His father had retired it from use several years after he was born just to make certain he would be able to deliver the gift in pristine condition.

The Aston's chrome and leather gleamed from Ethan's attention and Tucker would sit quietly sniffing, holding chubby hands in his lap those early years, watching Ethan's already gnarled hands gently coaxing the gears to do his bidding.

In later years, he sat in Ethan's lap and carefully steered the car down the driveway, imagining, in detail, the day he would first take it for a real drive.

Though Ethan gave careful attention to the care of the three sleek automobiles, his real love was the garden and the grounds. The joy of turning the earth and watching plants take root and thrive was a never ending pleasure for him and for the sturdy, red-cheeked boy, ever helpful, at his side.

Mary's job was to do everything in the way of housekeeping at the big house, with the exception of dinner preparation. She cleaned, mended, shopped, did the laundry and fixed a light breakfast and lunch, but well before dinnertime she went home to the caretaker's cottage. Then the gleaming, ultra-modern kitchen became the honored domain of Tucker's mother.

Just as Mr. Jones' passion was for managing the family's investments and keeping well abreast of world affairs, the elegant Mrs. Evan Tucker Jones had a passion for cooking. It gave her a most satisfying outlet for her creativity, an area of expertise, and caused her husband to absolutely adore her. Each evening's gourmet dinner was an event, each course a creation; it was a feast for both the eyes and the palate. Whether it was the soup, salad, entrée or dessert, it was a separate culinary presentation and treated as such. The portions were never large, but always beautifully presented on the family's antique Limoges.

When dinner was served, Mr. Jones received the first offering, Tucker the second. Then Mrs. Jones would bring her own plate to the table and Tucker's job, from the time he was a very small boy, was to help with his mother's chair. When all three were seated and Mrs. Jones had picked up her fork, Mr. Jones unfailingly queried, "Well, well, what have we here?"

Thus began the nightly explanation of the what, where, when, how and the why of each course being selected. It did not seem odd to Tucker that to consume a meal took over an hour and that the main topic of conversation was the adventures of the chef. It had always been so at their dinner table.

Unfortunately, the cocktail hour and dinner was the only time the family spent together and so, instead of attention focusing on their son (unless it was to gently remind him of the need for perfect manners and proper table decorum), the message at the dinner table was implicit: this was Mother's time to shine! It was a great surprise to Tucker, when in later years he dined with other families; to find dinner table conversations did not all revolve around the food.

Conversely, many a school friend's mother was slack-jawed with surprise to hear a child still in knickers identify the herbs and spices of any given dish and compliment her prettily as to their effect on the flavor of the dish.

It was not to say that Tucker's parents did not love him. He realized even then that they did. Much later in his life, he realized how much. The problem was that their respective introverted natures simply did not allow for the expression of feelings. In their own way and with their own level of awareness, they tried. He was given swimming lessons, piano lessons, tennis lessons and golf lessons. To their credit, never a recital, meet or match went by without one or both of them in attendance; elegantly dressed, proper in their manner, constrained in their emotions.

Later, in high school, when he began to excel on the debate team, they had Ethan drive them to wherever he was debating. So, his logical deduction was that they were proud of him. But, never, in those developmental years, did either of them express real joy or anger at his winning or losing. His mother was apt to say, "What lovely lettering on that certificate." or "Won't this trophy look fine on the mantel with the others?"

His father was apt to say, "Golf (or whatever was the activity of the day) is certainly a fine sport! Your mother and I are so glad you enjoy it, son."

That his parents were unable to show feelings mattered, but because Mary and Ethan were the antithesis of his parents, it mattered less. The Irish couple lived their whole lives on an emotional level. If Tucker skinned his knee in a tricycle crash, Mary would cry and kick the offending trike for "damagin' her darlin' boy." When Tucker would recite the events that led to the loss or win of a competition over cookies and milk, Ethan's opinion of the sport rose and fell in a direct relationship to his success. If he won the tennis match it was, "A fine gentlemen's sport!" If he lost, it was "A silly game, not to be taken seriously."

In their adoring eyes he could do absolutely no wrong. He thrived on their unconditional approval and love.

The four adults achieved an odd sort of balance in Tucker's upbringing. Mary rocked him and sang him lullabies, his mother taught him manners. Ethan taught him the secrets of the earth and his father introduced him to masterpieces of literature, art and music.

Both sets of adults had pictures of him on their mantels. Mrs. Jones had hired a well-respected photographer to come to the mansion on regular occasions to take pictures both of Tucker alone and as part of a formal family group. His developmental years were recorded most often in stiff white shirts, bow ties and knickers. Mary, on the other hand, took pictures of a moment in time and had the snapshots, taken with her Instamatic, plastered all over the living room wall in the caretakers' cottage. Her favorite, she often told him, was the one with Ethan showing Tucker how to plant one foot on the shovel so as to be able to push it into the ground, taken when he was about four years of age. Both the man and the small boy were grinning unselfconsciously, dark heads bent to their task.

Another of Mary's favorites showed a side view of Tucker pulling a red wagon full of azaleas down the magnificent, curving drive towards a waiting Ethan. The tall Georgian mansion standing sedately in the background did not dwarf the boy, but instead enhanced his sturdiness and sense of purpose.

The picture was taken when he was six or seven, but it could have been taken during any numbers of years and any number of seasons, for Tucker's father, like his father before him, insisted that the flower gardens flanking the entry gate be planted with blooming flowers except in the coldest of winter months. To satisfy this whim, there was a greenhouse nestled behind the caretakers' cottage. Its purpose was to supply the herbs, spices and vegetables for Mrs. Jones' culinary creations and to provide the

12

glorious array of exotic flowers she used to decorate the house itself. For the outdoor planting there were pots of asters, chrysanthemums, daisies, phlox, geraniums and more waiting for the appropriate season for transferring or transplanting to the flower beds.

Ethan and Tucker learned to plant whatever the temperatures would allow, pot and all. It allowed for easy transfer to and from the green house as well as easy removal of spent plants.

It was when Tucker was twelve that his world fell apart. That was when his parents presented the O'Sheas with two round-trip tickets to visit their beloved Ireland. "It was," Mr. Jones pronounced, clearing his throat, "a suitable reward for twelve years of fine service."

Feeling petulant at being left behind and more than a little worried about how it would feel at home without them, Tucker barely managed to return their flurry of emotional hugs and declarations of how much they would miss him and how much they wished he could be with them, as they got into the taxi that would take them off on their adventure. He was, he remembered thinking, getting a bit old for hugging and kissing…not knowing then, how precious those departing hugs and kisses would become…not knowing he would never see them again.

The O'Sheas never returned. The ferry they boarded to take them to Dublin capsized and sank in the freezing black waters of the North Sea. Of the nearly 500 passengers and crew, only 40 survived hypothermia long enough to be rescued. The Joneses received only one scratchy transatlantic phone call from Ethan's sobbing mother.

Tucker remembered the phone call and the subsequent events clearly--until he buried the memory. Part of what he buried was the fact that it was the only time he had ever seen his parents cry. Even then, they did not cry like normal people. Each sat in their respective wing-back chairs, hands clasped, knuckles white and shoulders rigid, with tears sliding silently from under closed lids.

He had watched them silently from the doorway until his father saw him, rose from his chair with a guilty start and rushed across the room to shut the door. For

Tucker, on the far side of that closed door, time seemed to stand still. He stood, nose inches from the polished mahogany, while the true horror of the phone call washed over him. The people who loved him most, cared for him almost completely, were dead.

These people, sitting rigidly in their chairs, who had seemed to him absolutely invulnerable and all-powerful, obviously were not. They had no words to heal him, no arms to hold him. The arms that used to hold him never would again. He felt fear rise like a living thing, choking his heart, his lungs and his brain. *What could he count on anymore? To whom could he turn?* The two who had been his solace and support were gone. They were dead-- unrecoverable--in some dark, cold, watery grave.

Who would take care of him now? Not his parents. The closing of the door was more than symbolic. He was shut out and convinced that there were no healing answers to his silently screamed questions, but he did not cry, not then. His grief, fear and anger filled him like a black well too deep for tears, too frightening to probe for feelings. He had the odd thought that if he cried, he too might drown.

Turning from the doorway, chilled to the bone, he went to his room where he locked his door and stayed for twenty-four hours. He answered his parent's eventual gentle knocks, and his father's soft-voiced apology, with a tone that sounded polite but resolute, in his request to be alone.

When Tucker emerged, pale, hollow-eyed, but in complete control, he sought out his distraught parents and made it immediately clear that he did not want another couple living in the caretakers' cottage. "I'm nearly thirteen," he impressed upon them. "and I certainly no longer need a nanny. It would be much more efficient to hire housekeeping and gardening services."

His logic, even then, seemed impeccable. His parents were persuaded. In truth, they were reluctant to tackle the arduous task of interviewing replacements, perhaps suspecting that Tucker would find anyone selected, unsuitable.

Once the professional services of housekeepers and gardeners had been secured, Tucker began to try to heal his inner pain by ignoring it completely and soon after, troubles with classmates at school began. Feeling anger was better than feeling nothing. He spent his days in a cocoon of numbness, unless he was practicing his growing talent of being able to accurately remember whatever he heard by engaging his classmates in vicious verbal battles. Then the shell would crack just a little and the bitterness held inside would ooze out in sarcasm, belittlement, or a sneering arrogance. He could turn the most casual of conversations into a raging verbal battle, whereupon he enjoyed reminding his victims of their own exact words, repeating selected pieces of conversation verbatim, and then dismissing their arguments when they could not precisely recall his. He was fond of ending an argument by saying, "If you can't remember exactly what was said, you don't know all the facts, therefore you are not entitled to an opinion."

He would then turn his back and walk away, leaving his classmates to stare malevolently at his stiff back, their rage at being summarily discounted, leaving all but the most verbal of the junior high students speechless. Those who were able to summon their wits said things like, "How'd ya like to hear my opinion of you, asshole?"

Neither he nor they recognized that rage and loneliness were hidden behind his slashing tongue and haughty manner.

At home it was a different story. The anger in evidence at school with his classmates was deeply buried as he entered the beautifully carved, massive front door. To his parents, he still appeared to be the model child: respectful, mannerly and studious.

His school attendance continued to be perfect, but he wasn't really there. Only the tremendous ability to remember what he heard prevented his grades from declining dramatically. Never a gregarious boy, one by one, his acid tongue cost him his friends. By the time he reached his thirteenth birthday, his classmates began to shun him.

Several teachers recognized Tucker's distress, but could not reach him. A few asked him to stay after class and suggested that he consider counseling. Ever polite to adults, he thanked them gravely for their concern, assured them with an engaging grin, that he was well aware of going through some sort of adolescent phase, but felt he would be returning to his normal self in the near future. Few were fooled. His parents were called but he was smoothly able to convince them that the calls were an overreaction and admitted, choking out the beloved names, he'd had a "few bad days because of Mary and Ethan." They believed him. They also believed him when he attributed the fact that he was losing weight and day-dreaming almost continually to "being in the throes of adolescence."

It was the family doctor, Dr. Beemers, who finally blew the whistle. Not having seen Tucker since his last year's physical examination, which was a strict requirement of the school for any student taking physical education, he was shocked by the emaciated youth sitting in front of him on the examination table. Not for one second did he allow himself to be taken in by the pleasant demeanor and smooth, pat, logical explanations about adolescence. He'd known Tucker, his parents and the O'Sheas for years— knew more about the Jones' family dynamics through careful observation than they knew about themselves. But, most importantly, he recognized the vacant eyes, lethargy and loss of appetite as symptoms of depression. The word "suicide" kept creeping into his mind as he examined the bony frame. Casually, he inquired how Tucker had come to his office. When he found the boy had come by taxi, he continued the examination for a moment, then excused himself from the room and dialed the Jones' number from his private office.

"Mr. and Mrs. Jones are not at home, doctor." The woman who answered the phone was polite and professional. Identifying herself as a maid from Classic Care Housekeeping Service, she asked if he would care to leave a message. Instead, he asked to speak to Mary O'Shea. There was an audible intake of air from the other end of the phone line and then the quiet voice said, "But, doctor, the O'Sheas have been dead for six months."

Dr. Beemers placed the receiver gently back onto its cradle, the puzzle pieces regarding Tucker suddenly starting to fall together. He scanned his rolodex and located the business number for Mr. Jones.

When the two men were connected, the doctor offered condolences and asked for details about the O'Shea's deaths, Tucker's response and subsequent

16

behavior. Mr. Jones, after the briefest of pauses, told the doctor the circumstances of the deaths in his clipped and distant way. Questions about Tucker produced a different effect. Yes, they had noticed he was quieter and thinner but had attributed it to his age. Yes, he was spending a great deal of time in his room. If Tucker was having trouble sleeping, he had never mentioned it.

The alarm in Mr. Jones voice grew with each question. The nagging fears that he had managed to suppress the past months were confronting him. Dr. Beemers bluntly expressed his own fears, listed the symptoms he saw as evidence of Tucker's depression and asked for permission to hospitalize him, if necessary, in order to prevent possible self-injury. He did not say the word suicide. Mr. Jones was already losing composure, something Dr. Beemers had assumed was not a possibility.

Mr. Jones sounded frightened as he gave permission to proceed with whatever course of action seemed best. Jeff Beemers hung up and gave himself only seconds to compose himself before striding back into the examination room.

Tucker sat in the exact same position, shoulders hunched, head bowed, vertebrae in his spinal column marching skeleton-like down his back. He finally looked up when Dr. Beemers pulled over his three-legged stool, took Tucker's thin, cold, aristocratic hands into his own warm paws and set about trying to capture the boy within his will.

"Tucker," he said, slowly, searching for words that would work. "Tucker, you've been carrying a terrible burden these last six months. It's time to let it go; time to let others help you with the load; time to share the weight, Tucker."

He emphasized the boy's name each time he said it and squeezed tightly with his hands, giving the message that he would not be ignored. The bowed head snapped up and the doctor, his face inches from Tucker's caught a single glimpse of the raw anguish. But then, summoning his tremendous will, Tucker drew the veil and smiled engagingly. "Aw, Doctor Beemers, I'm all right." he mumbled.

"No, Tucker, you're NOT all right. Your whole world is wrong. You lost Mary AND Ethan, both of whom you loved as much as they loved you. You miss them like hell.

You're sad and you're mad and you're scared. You are in so much pain that you are afraid if you let any of it out, let any of it show, you will lose control and do something awful to yourself or someone else. So, you've stuffed it away, Tucker, my man, and it's rotting you from the inside."

The big, vice-grip paws tightened, containing, controlling and dominating. "Look at me, Tucker. Share it with me. I'm strong. I can carry a part of that burden." Taking a long shot, the doctor continued, "Maybe you felt your folks couldn't deal with their grief and yours too. I don't know about that. I think I can help you, Tucker. Will you give me a chance?"

The doctor's voice was gentle, calm and as compelling as the strong grip. But the duality of strength and empathy, usually a strong therapeutic combination seemed to have no effect on the youngster before him and he was frightened for the boy. He was afraid the strength of will, one of the boy's assets was, in this case, working against him. Intuitively he knew Tucker's secret, but he didn't know what to do about it. He swore under his breath but did not release his grip; he was almost afraid to.

He was a general practitioner on purpose—had not even considered psychiatry as a career. Deep down, he felt he had no right to go stomping around in this young man's psyche. Almost against his will he continued softly. "Tell me, Tucker, have you made your plan?"

Those words had a slight effect. Tucker's back straightened and he looked directly at the doctor, eyes wary, saying casually, "What plan are you referring to Doctor? I don't have a plan."

Beemers tried to hold his gaze and failed. He sighed deeply and prayed he wasn't doing further damage to this frail wreck of a human being. "I believe you know exactly what plan I'm talking about, Tucker. It's the plan to do yourself in. If I know you, you've thought out every detail. What's your plan, Tucker?"

At his words, Tucker snapped to rigid attention and tried to withdraw his hands from the tight grip. He finally seemed to feel the doctor's empathy telepathically pulsing through him. The firm hold was suddenly incredibly painful to Tucker. He felt exposed and helpless, knowing that the doctor had accurately read his mind. A sudden rush of anger at having been discovered washed over him in a wave. He opened his mouth to deny and protest, but instead of words, a scream of anguished rage spewed forth. Dr. Beemers came off his stool like a well-aimed rocket and engulfed him in a bear hug just as Tucker started to go physically out of control. The stool went skidding as Beemers folded the thrashing boy under him on the floor of the examination room. It was like trying to contain a wild thing that had gained phenomenal strength through fear of capture.

Finally, by pinning the boy beneath him, he was able to control the flailing arms and legs. When he could get enough breath, he shouted for his nurse to bring in a sedative.

The nurse, veteran that she was, deftly administered the syringe with rock steady hands while she catalogued the amount of pain continuing to issue unabated from Tucker's being. She reached out and stroked his damp hair, making shushing noises of comfort without awareness of doing so. But, Tucker seemed to hear. A corner of his subconscious gave his mind permission to recognize that he had not been touched in this way since Ethan and Mary's death and with that awareness, the screams turned to moans and the moans into convulsive sobbing.

Dr. Beemers, still puffing, finally loosened his grip as the sedative began to take effect. He sat up and gathered the sobbing boy into his arms. "Call an ambulance please, Mavis," he said softly. "And if there is anyone left in the waiting room, please reassure them that things are under control back here.

She nodded, straightened her uniform, found a tissue in her pocket and repaired the mascara that had slid down her cheeks along a few tears of her own. Giving him all that she could muster in the way of a smile, she left him there on the floor rocking the silent, sedated boy.

Chapter Three

The only sign of Mrs. Jones' agitation, as she sat in the chair across the desk of Tobin Van Castle, was the hand that rose from time to time and adjusted the strand of crystals that circled her throat and one manicured finger that discretely slipped up to capture an escaping tear every now and then when the doctor bent over the admission paperwork.

Mr. Jones, his posture perfect, his body still, sat beside his wife, not daring to look at her, knowing that her eyes would mirror his in both the guilt and the horror of not realizing their son's acute duress. *How could we have not known?*

As if reading his mind, the doctor paused in his taking of their family history, looked at them both and said quietly, "I'm sorry to say that suicide is the third leading cause of death among teenagers."

Evan Jones nodded stiffly at his words. "I am sorry our son is to be included in those statistics." He sighed and closed his eyes for brief seconds as if gathering himself. "Jeff Beemers has been a faithful family physician for many years and we are certain he has advised us well in seeking your help. We put ourselves in your hands, Dr. Van Castle. You need only give us clear direction as to our role and we will do our utmost to comply."

The doctor looked at the devastated couple across from him and realized that only their tremendous love for their son gave them the courage to sit in his office, sharing details of what was obviously a very private life. He tried to maintain eye contact with both. "I know it will be of little comfort to you, Mr. and Mrs. Jones, but most parents do not recognize the symptoms associated with adolescent depression."

Mrs. Jones, her fingers again on her crystal beads, said softly but with conviction, "We thank you for your effort to comfort--but doctor, we certainly are NOT 'most people.'

It will be extremely difficult for either of us to forgive ourselves. In the meantime, Evan and I shall hang our faith on Dr. Beemer's high regard and your sterling work with adolescents. Please continue with your information gathering. As my husband said, 'We are truly in your hands' and grateful to be here."

Tobin realized with some chagrin that he had been put back on task. "Yes, well, after we complete the family history and you add any other salient details you think might help explain Tucker's wish to end his life, I will ask that you tour The Institute of Living which includes treatment of adolescents exhibiting suicidal intention. The institute is now a division of Hartford Hospital, but was established in 1822, the first of its kind in the treatment of mental health. If you agree to his placement there, once Tucker has completed his medical and psychological evaluation, his therapy will begin." He slid a glossy brochure across his desk top.

The doctor picked up his pen. "Once this intake is completed and all paperwork is signed, I will have a preliminary visit with Tucker this evening."

Lying in the last bed in the open ward, psychiatric admitting wing for adolescents, Tucker felt as though he were disembodied. He felt he was looking down at the six beds from some high, safe place where no one could reach him. He liked the feeling. Aided by medication, it had persisted through the nurses who came to care for him, even the one who drew a vial of blood and had him urinate in a cup. He hoped he could preserve the feeling through the visit with the man Dr. Beemers said was coming to help him "think and talk about" his sadness.

He watched a short, slightly pudgy man with a head of blonde curls enter through the security door, smiling and greeting the psychiatric nurses with great familiarity and suspected that the man had just arrived. He was prepared to dislike him at first sight and watched covertly as the man stopped to visit with the nurses, read a chart, visit one of the others lying in a bed identical to his. He saw him reach out a hand and stroke an arm, point a finger at himself and grin, as if sharing a joke and generally spreading a feeling of good will and camaraderie throughout the ward. In truth,

Tucker found himself somewhat disarmed and impatient by the time the man walked up to his bed and stuck out his hand to the wan scarecrow of a youth propped up on pillows. "Tobin Van Castle," he said as Tucker's ingrained good manners forced him to return a firm handshake. "sent by Dr. Beemers and your parents. I'm at your service!"

The last words were said as he plopped down on the edge of the bed, ignoring the raised and warning eyebrows of a nearby nurse. It was obvious that what the doctor was doing was contrary to hospital policy. Why that would be so, Tucker didn't know. But he did know that he liked the conspiratorial wink the doctor slipped him as the nurse turned sharply on her heel with a snort to show her displeasure. Tucker found himself matching the wink without meaning to, intrigued by the air of innocent mischief that surrounded the man. He seemed quite harmless, his blue eyes twinkling.

Without much preamble, Dr. Van Castle began talking—not questioning Tucker, but casually and randomly touching on all the areas of hospital policies and procedures that Tucker had been secretly worrying about. After a bit, Tucker even felt free enough to ask a few questions and share a few of the things he thought he'd figured out on his own. He could tell that the doctor was truly impressed at his quick study and understanding of the award system the nurses used to help each patient modify their behavior.

Despite his secret self-admonishment to stay on guard, Tucker barely noticed when the conversation switched to questions about his interests and hobbies and from there to the doctor saying how tough it was for some kids to grow up feeling good about themselves. As fuzzy as the scheduled medication made him feel, it was still interesting to hear Dr. Van Castle talk about other kids he had known and how they learned to handle their problems, or didn't...he talked about that too, in a casual sort of way. Tucker found himself relating to a lot of what the doctor was saying, able to listen, relieved to know that he wasn't alone in feeling the way he did.

Then Dr. Van Castle stood and pulled two books out of his battered attaché case. "There isn't a lot for you to do here, Tucker, so I thought I'd leave these books in case you felt like reading."

Suddenly, Tucker realized the man was leaving. "Doctor Van Castle," he blurted, "This isn't what I thought...I mean...this isn't what I thought seeing a psychiatrist was about." The medication seemed to have lessened his defenses. He cleared his throat, his eyes suddenly bright with uncharacteristic tears. "I mean we didn't talk about things..." His voice trailed off, but his face bespoke his great anxiety.

Gravely, his blue eyes turned smoky with seriousness, the doctor returned to his bedside seat, turning again, one knee lifted onto the bed, so he could make eye contact. "Tucker, what you and I did this evening is what people do when they want to be friends. It's called building trust. I have the sense that you liked the time we shared and would like to see me again."

Tucker nodded, a brief lowering of his chin, acquiescing against his will. His brown eyes, equally dark and serious, never left the doctor's face as the psychiatrist carefully chose the words he wanted to use to make his point clearly. "If I had my way, we would continue visiting like this for a long time. Speaking for myself, I can say I enjoyed this time with you and am looking forward to our next visit which will either be in the office I use here...or possibly at a private treatment facility, in which case, we would talk in your room. Hopefully, in time, you'd come to trust me. Part of that trust would come from you judging my actions. Am I a trustworthy fellow? That would be what you would have to decide and deciding that sort of thing takes time. When you are absolutely certain that I have your best interests at heart, our working relationship would begin. You would be able to share with me, things you haven't been able to share with anyone else. Together, we would be able to figure some things out and put some other things that have been bothering you, to rest. Until then, we would do just what we are doing right now; finding out about each other, testing the waters so to speak. However, here's the rub: I am assuming that you don't want to remain hospitalized for very long, and it is my job to determine that you are no longer a danger to yourself before I can recommend release."

Dr. Van Castle stood up and looked squarely at Tucker. "My sense is that you are a very private person and that had I pushed you today, or been intrusive in any way, you would have made up your mind not to share with me, or worse, just pretend to share in order to be allowed to return home. So, for today, I just sort of carried the ball to let you have some time to make up your mind about me."

The doctor drew a long breath at the end of his lengthy, but closely followed, explanation. "But that comes a little later. We do have a little time to get to know each other. The next time I come, perhaps we could simply discuss your reading. Don't you think that feels about right?"

Tucker nodded his agreement, amazed at the truthfulness of the man. "When are you coming back?" he found himself asking. He watched as the doctor stretched his back and picked up the scruffy attaché case and put it on the bed before fastening the straps. His smile reached his eyes as he reached up and ran a hand through his curls. "You're going to be stuck with me twice a week until you are released and then it will be once a week in my Hartford office."

He exuded an aura of optimism and quiet capability; a lifeline for those willing to reach out for it. Tucker felt a stirring of hope prick through the deep fog of his despair.

Once the evaluation had been completed and Tucker transferred to The Institute of Living, his parents were allowed to visit. They came every day. Never before had the family spent so much time in shared conversation. All three of them, with Dr. Van Castle's coaching, worked at it. His father talked about the world situation, his mother about her adventures in recipe land. Tucker shared with them what he'd read in the books Dr. Van Castle had left him. He admitted to them he had thought they would be psychology books, but instead they were works of fiction; simple to read books, just right for his state of mind, altered by anti-anxiety medication. With amazing candor, he was able to tell his parents, "I don't think I am really capable of reading anything more challenging right now."

They nodded, smiling in agreement, happy to be enjoying his telling of some of the classic literature for

24

young adults. "You did a wonderful job of relating the story, Tucker, dear," his mother said.

Tucker had realized almost immediately that all of the stories had one thing in common: overcoming adversity. He had pointed that fact out to Dr. Van Castle who simply raised an eyebrow and said, "Soooo...?"

"Well, my three favorites were: *Far From Home, Angry Waters* and *My Side of the Mountain.*"

"Why?" queried Dr. Van Castle.

"Because those guys didn't need anybody. They would have been fine by themselves. They didn't chicken out, even when they wanted to."

"I see," said the doctor mildly. And indeed, he did see. He had assigned those three particular books as part of Tucker's bibliotherapy because all three featured boys who came to grips with the need to trust and depend on others. All three stories ended with the boys reunited with other human beings and feeling good about themselves, a fact, Dr. Van Castle noted, that Tucker seemed to have totally ignored.

"It seems to me that you think those boys did a good job of making it on their own. Would you have felt better about the endings if say, Mafatu had chosen to stay in exile even after he had proven to himself he was not a coward?"

And so the gentle, probing conversation went: perception checks, affirmations of feelings, clarifications of values, all part of Tobin Van Castle's arsenal of tools to help Tucker deal with the loss of Ethan and Mary. Using fictional characters, he convinced himself he was addressing the topics of fear, loneliness, sadness and the masks they wore to disguise themselves, helping Tucker relate to those own feelings within himself. He found professional satisfaction in watching the youngster seemingly begin to engage, once again in living. "You just used a perception check, didn't you doctor?" Tucker might ask with good humor in his dark eyes.

"Yes, I did, Tucker, I want to make certain I'm understanding you correctly...been reading up on therapy methods, have you?" And they would laugh together before continuing, Tucker seemingly very relaxed and engaged as they strolled through the fall leaves or sipped hot chocolate at a small sheltered table.

Van Castle was very satisfied with the progress Tucker was making and was starting to consider releasing him. He was continued to be satisfied until one night, at home, as he sat in front of his fireplace, his feet on a hassock, reviewing his notes. It was then nagging doubts began to creep into his mind.

There were those in his field who believed it critical to strike on the important issues while a client was still vulnerable from the breakdown. It was then, at that moment in time, they were most likely to be in touch with their real feelings. Others ascribed to the practice of waiting until the client had regained some semblance of control and stability; until a trust relationship had developed. That second course of action had been his choice with Tucker. Now, it seemed to him that he had made a mistake; had waited too long. The notes from his first meeting with the boy reflected the fact that he had told Tucker then that they would be talking about "hard things," very shortly and that, at the time, the youth had seemed relieved. That was fifteen sessions ago and Tucker seemed less available, had seemed more wrapped in his web of slick denial during today's session than ever before. *That bit about letting me know he knew the definition of a perception check…was that a ploy to take off the heat? Why didn't I call him on it? What's going on here?*

His notes, when he read them carefully, documented his thoughts. *Changed subject many times…Seems shut down though very interested in exchanging thoughts about the characters in "The Loner." Brittle today…Seems to want to please me…Feels like he is trying to figure out what makes me tick instead of what is going on inside himself…Tucker is able to relate our sessions almost verbatim. His auditory memory must be phenomenal.*

The doctor smiled grimly to himself. *Is it possible that I have been indulging myself? These books are all a part of my own childhood and damned if it hasn't been an absolute delight to discuss them with that very bright, logical, tough minded boy.* With sudden insight, he realized it was time to move out of bibliotherapy and into Tucker's life. Tomorrow he would begin to press the issue of Tucker's life-changing loss—Ethan and Mary's death.

Tobin squeezed the bridge of his nose, one of the few overt gestures that showed his inner turmoil, shook his head as if to shut down his brain and decided to call one of his many woman friends to see if they were up for a quick bite of dinner at his favorite pub.

It was nearing dusk and spitting snow when Dr. Van Castle approached the gates to The Institute of Living. Tucker was his last client of the day. It had been one of those days that had made him wonder about his decision to practice in such a difficult field. *Who in their right mind wants to work with an adolescent population where tracking and understanding what motivated a behavior is like herding cats...where there is no normal...only variations of abnormal?*

He shrugged out of his coat and pocketed his gloves before checking the chart notes at the nurses' station. He found Tucker waiting in one of the room's two bolted-down chairs, as was the bed and the table. A small box of cookies lay open on the table. The book, *Robinson Crusoe*, lay beside it. "Good afternoon, Dr. Van Castle, I thought you might enjoy one of Mother's cookies while we talk."

Tucker was smiling his pleasant, composed smile. He had just finished the book by Defoe, another example, in his opinion, of a man who needed no one. It was a great book, but even Tucker had to admit, living alone for 24 years would have been tough. *I think the doctor is going to be pleased when he hears me say that,* he thought. But he didn't get a chance to say anything. Dr. Van Castle was looking grim. His usual vigor seemed missing. "I see from the chart note that you're still finding sleep difficult, Tucker," he said, ignoring the cookies and sitting heavily onto the remaining chair.

What he didn't say to Tucker was that there was also a note in the chart to downgrade suicide precautions. Convinced that his thesis was correct, he had denied it and initialed his response on the chart. Now, he looked long and hard at the relaxed, waiting boy, seeing him nod. "Yes. Luckily, I had a very good book."

Tobin sighed, almost to himself, and said quietly, "Tucker, I fear I am letting you down." Purposefully ignoring

27

the boy's beginnings of protest, he continued, "It's been good to talk about the books, they've been wonderful analogies about the human condition, but it has allowed us to completely avoid talking about Ethan and Mary. In my professional opinion, that is not a good thing. So, this evening we're going to talk about a new order of business."

The doctor made his voice brusque and at the same time, matter-of-fact while carefully cataloging the trapped animal look that flickered and then was veiled on Tucker's face. More than ever, he felt his hunch was correct. The boy's defenses were building to mask his continuing pain. It was past time to unmask that pain and deal with it. He said as much to Tucker, finishing his comments with the assignment he'd planned to give. "Your task today is to spend time thinking about Ethan and Mary." This time, he said the names slowly and lovingly, as if he personally knew and loved them. "Think about things you did together, things you talked about, their bad habits and their good habits. I suspect it will make you cry. My hope is that it will. You will find, after the tears, will come a sense of peace. Perhaps, you'll even be able to sleep a bit better."

He noted Tucker's frozen face, but continued. "Ask for extra medication only if you feel you need it. Remember Mafatu in *Call It Courage?* Your "shark" is just as hard to deal with. Mafatu proved he was not a coward. You can prove it too. You've going to have to dig deep for your own courage, but I'm convinced you have a considerable amount…and you'll need it to do what I ask. From what your parents have told me, I think Ethan and Mary must have been wonderful people. I wish I could have met them."

He leaned forward and placed a hand on Tucker's knee. "They deserve a place in your memory. You should be able to bring them to mind any time you choose and the memory should bring you comfort, not this horrible pain my words are bringing."

The doctor stopped, pausing for breath and preventing his words from continuing their tumble, giving what he said time to register with the stone silent, chalk-faced boy. He then continued slowly and more softly. "I'll be back, first thing in the morning to see you. Call my answering service if you would like to speak to me before then. When we next talk, I will want you to choose at least one memory to share with me. I want you to make those two people real to me."

He pulled a slim brown volume from his attaché case and placed it on the table. "This is a journal. The pages are blank. I want you to write your thoughts down as they come to you. Some of those thoughts you will choose to share; others will be private. Unless you give permission, no one has the right to touch this book."

Van Castle paused again, letting the silence build, wondering if Tucker would break it and was disappointed that he did not. There was not even the nod of Tucker's head to show the doctor's assignment had been received. With a sigh, he buckled the straps on his case and stood, shrugging into his coat. "So long, Tucker. Good luck. Remember what I said about us wanting the best for each other? Don't doubt me now." There was not the slightest acknowledgement of his words.

From Tucker's room the doctor went directly to the nurses' station and had a short talk with one of the night nurses, telling her what he had done and asking for close monitoring. Then he amended Tucker's chart to read: "give medication upon patient request" and turned, with weighted steps, pulling on his gloves as he stepped out into the softly falling snow. He wondered how he was going to find the stamina to make it to his car.

When Dr. Van Castle arrived at the Institute the next morning, he went straight to the nursing station to check on Tucker's status. The day nurse behind the desk, usually quite willing to flirt, instead gave him a frosty stare. *Hard to do when one's eyes are so soft and brown,* he mused to himself. "He wet his pillowcase with his tears, doctor. Thin as he still is, he wouldn't eat any dinner and refused the medication you said he could have, so what do you think his status might be?"

He chuckled softly, ignoring her murderous look and said, "I think it might mean that he is finally going to start to get better!" With that, he turned with a rush to go check on his patient.

Tucker was sitting in a chair, his complexion wan, but the smile on his face softer and more genuine than the doctor has thus far seen. The journal was in his lap, scarecrow hands folded over it. He said, "I did my homework, Doctor Van Castle. Please take out your notebook, because I am going to tell you about this wall of pictures in Mary and Ethan's house. Most of them are of me..."

The doctor's slow, face-covering grin warmed Tucker like a blanket. "Hurry," he commanded as he pointed to the other chair. "We only have an hour."

Before Dr. Van Castle released Tucker from the Institute of Living, they covered every childhood memory Tucker could unearth. They also talked about his future plans, discussing how it might feel to live in his home without Ethan and Mary, how it would feel to return to school after three months and have his classmates ask about his absence. They role played the questions and his responses a number of times even though Tucker said, "We really don't have to prepare for this, doctor; none of them were actually speaking to me when I left." He ducked his head. "I guess I was pretty hard on some of them."

"Ah!" Van Castle said, "Repair work to do then? Would you be able to apologize to those you wronged?"

Tucker looked at him steadily. "Yes, but I believe actions speak louder than words, don't you?"

They smiled at each other. "Yes, Tucker, I believe that old adage to be true. Now, let's talk about some short term goals."

Tucker easily identified three immediate goals: Graduate from junior high on the dean's list; earn a place on the high school tennis team; and, most importantly, Dr. Van Castle thought secretly, to rebuild friendships with fellow students.

Tucker looked directly at the psychiatrist and said, candidly, "I really don't have any friends left at school you know. From what we've talked about, I guess they got the worst of my anger and now they think I'm a real jerk...which I guess I was."

"Stick with your goals, Tucker," the doctor said simply, "and you'll do fine." He was truly impressed with the young man's ability to understand his own situation. This sense of admiration he shared with Dr. Beemers one evening over a very dry martini. Together they worried about his moving back into a household bereft of adults

30

able to share feelings. Both were impressed with the efforts of Tucker's parents to visit the Institute every day, but recognized the continuing limitations of the lovely, though emotionally-distant, couple.

In the end, Tucker surprised them all by requesting permission from his parents to help interview applicants to live in the caretakers' cottage. He expressed a decided preference for a young couple—preferably sports-minded. "Like, you know, a brother or sister type," he confided to Dr. Van Castle on one of his weekly, post-inpatient sessions.

Shortly after that session, and after Tucker's successful reintegration at school, the doctor began to discuss with Tucker the possibility of terminating their sessions. He was a bit surprised when Tucker, after sitting silently for long moments, blandly agreed, suggesting the termination date be by his upcoming fourteenth birthday.

A warning bell should have gone off in the doctor's head. Unfortunately, it did not. It wasn't until well after termination that doubts began to plague him, often resurfacing after spending time with Jeff Beemers. His unrest came from wondering if Tucker had conned him after all. Had the boy really dealt with his grief, or had their easy parting simply been a cover up for feelings of a second abandonment?

At their last meeting they had faced each other in the big comfortable chairs of the doctor's office, and clasping hands, recounted the ups and downs of the time they had spent together. Both admitted that they would miss each other. Dr. Van Castle had brought his own boyhood copy of *Robinson Crusoe* to give to Tucker. He had inscribed on the flyleaf with his cheerful scrawl:

> *To Tucker: Remember, trusting others isn't as easy as it is necessary. Thank you for the many splendid discussions and for giving me the excuse to become familiar with my favorite adventure stories once again. I'm here if you need me.*
>
> *Sincerely,*
> *Tobin Van Castle*

In the privacy of his bedroom, Tucker reread what the doctor had written and felt hot tears smart, waves of heat wash over him, to be followed by a chill that caused bumps to rise on his still thin arms. Tucker held the book carefully for long moments, forcing himself to sit very still and wait for the sensation to subside. When it did, he rose to place the book on the shelf with the rest of his books, but instead, with a moan, flung open his closet door and threw it in a box that contained his journal and the photos he had removed from the wall of the caretakers' cottage shortly after Ethan and Mary died. Then, very carefully, he refolded the cardboard edges, sealing the box. It was symbolic. As he tried so hard to do with Ethan and Mary, he was once again prepared to bury all memory of his time with Dr. Van Castle.

It was during his high school years that Tucker developed and perfected the persona so mysterious and yet popular at Zitek Global Development. He competed on the tennis, golf and swim teams, and continued to impress everyone with his musical talent, playing popular show tunes when asked at parties. He breezed through his classes and was the county and state debate champion three years in a row. His manners, always good, became impeccable. He dated casually, drank a little with the guys and was voted the most likely to succeed of the senior class. He had plenty of casual friends and no enemies, unless his continuing insomnia could be counted as an enemy.

Dana and David Olsen came to stay in the caretakers' cottage. They were both part-time students at Gateway Community College. Working for the Jones' was made to order for them. They could do all the required work and take two or three classes a term. The young couple didn't take the pride of caretaking for the family and grounds that the O'Sheas had, but were neither lazy nor irresponsible and the Joneses were delighted when the Olsens smilingly told them that they figured it might take them seven or eight years to complete their coursework.

Dana was an accomplished tennis player and after the old courts were repaired, she helped Tucker work on his game. David also put up a basketball hoop at either end of the court and the three of them ended up enjoying shooting hoops though Tucker never suggested bringing friends home for a game.

Often, Mr. and Mrs. Jones would bring tall glasses of iced tea and sit on lawn chairs, watching the flashing bronzed body of their handsome son with special pride. If they noticed that the boy who loved gardening never went near the greenhouse or visited with the Olsens in the cottage, even when invited, they didn't mention it to Tucker, or to each other.

His debate teacher counseled him towards law. His history teacher counseled him towards political science and his tennis coach encouraged him to try for a scholarship at Stanford on the West Coast, which the man smilingly admitted, had been his own alma mater. Instead, just as his father and grandfather before him had done, Tucker applied to Yale University. He was among those accepted early and it proved an excellent match as he continued to be a diligent and talented student...again cruising through six years of heavy classes, playing four years on the tennis team and winning the coveted internship with Zitec; having the chance meeting with James Whipple Tyler III and his subsequent hiring, even before he had graduated with his MBA.

Chapter Four

Tucker had carefully prepared his parents for many months prior to the actual event of his moving from home. His job at Zitec assured, he signed the lease on a condominium in the nearby town of Guilford, mainly because it was near the Guilford Racquet and Swim Club, where he planned to continue his tennis and swimming. There were also trails for jogging. Shortly after graduating, he moved from the secluded estate to his condo, about 30 minutes away.

From the beginning, it was a bachelor's home—high-tech furniture of metal, leather and glass. Other than three large pieces of modernistic statuary, nothing, not even a potted plant, softened the effect. The walls were decorated only with austere black and white photographs. The focal point of the large and airy living/dining room combination was an elegant baby grand piano, a second graduation gift from his mother and father. The Aston Martin, they told him, excusing their own generosity, was really a gift from his grandfather, the Chickering baby grand was from them. Its ebony blackness a stark interruption of the otherwise monochrome of beiges he had selected for his color scheme. His dining room was also his office, complete with computer and peripherals ranging across a long desk. He'd designed and had the desk built specifically to meet room dimensions. Piles of business, economic and computer magazines were stacked with precise neatness on his matching bookshelves. He was happy to dine at a small table under the kitchen window. His walk-in closet was filled with well-ordered clothing and carefully stored sports equipment. He was comfortable and very pleased with the space utilization.

If Mr. and Mrs. Jones were unhappy with his decision to move, they kept it to themselves, seemingly pleased with Tucker's assurances that he would be out to see them at least for Sunday dinner and the fact that he

34

had moved less than 30 minutes away. They were also convinced that Mr. Tyler was a genius to have recognized the talent of their son so quickly. "Too bad Ziteck Global is a privately held company," Mr. Jones said to his wife. "We might have added them to our portfolio."

"That would have been a splendid idea, dear," Mrs. Jones said as talk of Midge and James Tyler started to join traditional conversation at Sunday dinners. It was quite clear to both his parents that Tucker was satisfied with his choice in both his job and his life style. He had quickly established his new routines, spending long hours at the computer, working out at the club and devoting himself to Zitec both professionally, and due to Mrs. Tyler's invitations, socially.

Midge Tyler's original dinner invitation was issued out of pure curiosity. She really wanted a chance to meet the young man who had the power to make her usually unflappable husband pace the floor and slop scotch from his glass as he gestured. Her curiosity had turned immediately to awe. She watched covertly as he charmed a roomful of strangers with his attentive listening, knowledge of world affairs and wonderful manners so innately ingrained that they seemed to be practiced unconsciously by her husband's protégé, so handsome in his beautifully tailored tuxedo. She instinctively had the strong feeling that there was something about him that needed a bit of mothering...she couldn't quite put her finger on how she knew it, but she did. Perhaps it was because she knew the long hours he worked for Zitec or possibly it was because he was so readily available to come to her last minute parties, both formal and informal. Whatever the reason, she soon convinced herself that what he really needed was a good and loving wife...and that there was the perfect candidate for him among the unmarried daughters of her many friends. All she had to do was provide the opportunity for him to meet them and nature would do the rest. Tucker soon became a regular at her lavish, but casual, weekend parties.

In fact, he was so often with them on weekends that invariably his absence invoked a "Where's Tucker today?" from one or more of her guests. He was exceedingly popular among all ages. With the daughters because it was clear he would be a superb catch: twenty-seven, wealthy, single and quite attractive with his thick dark-brown hair, square chin and gentle, attentive, brown eyes. The matrons were taken by his courtly manners and diffidence and the men by his air of respectfulness as well as his remarkable skill of active listening.

As time passed, Tucker continued to be pleased with the world he had built for himself. Insomnia was still a problem for him, but he had lived with it for so long it had become part of his life. Some nights, when sleep failed to find him, he would get up, slip into his sweats and running shoes and jog the genteel neighborhood under friendly streetlights. Cruising along, hearing the familiar slap of his shoes on the silent sidewalks, listening to the evenness of his breathing, the strong pulsing of his heartbeat and feeling the perspiration trickle its way down his back were wonderful balm to an agitation he couldn't name.

Visits with his parents also went well. True to form, dinner conversation was mostly limited to Mrs. Jones newest culinary creations, although his mother would sometimes say, "Enough about my recipes, darlings. I would so enjoy hearing about Tucker's weekend with the Tylers!"

Then Tucker would describe his experiences, being certain to include what interesting dish Charlie, the Tyler's cook from Shanghai, had concocted.

Dana and David moved on and another couple now occupied the cottage. Tucker was on pleasant speaking terms with them but did not make the effort to really get to know either of them. He was affable, quick to chuckle, gracious in his manners and always, always in control…until the morning, after long hours at the computer, his back went out.

That morning, as Tucker bent over to slip his shoe horn into the heel of his Bally loafer and felt his back catch, he was merely irritated. He'd had it happen before and was always stiff and sore for several days. He'd been troubled with a stiff neck and shoulders for years, but like his insomnia, it was simply something to be endured, expected even, with so many hours in front of a computer.

Two hours later, sitting behind his desk at Zitec, his irritation had turned to a mixture of humiliation and anguish. Muscle spasms had turned his back into a battlefield. His nerves were screaming for relief from the base of his skull to his sacrum. He wondered if it was going to be even possible to rise from his chair. He considered summoning help several times, but found himself unwilling to pick up his phone.

Tucker sat immobilized, at a complete loss in trying to decide what action to take. He didn't have a doctor; he had never needed one. The only doctor he could think of was the doctor of his youth, Dr. Beemers. Carefully, he lifted an arm towards the phone book in his top desk drawer. Gently, he pulled the book out and with as little movement as was possible, began to scan the "Physician" section of the yellow pages. With a feeling of great relief, he saw that Beemers was still listed at the same address. Gingerly, he touched the buttons, gasping into the phone as another tremendous spasm gripped him.

The nurse who answered the phone recognized both his name and the pain in his voice. "Can you get yourself here, Tucker? We'll work you in if you can," Mavis said in her calm, professional voice. He assured her that he could and hung up the phone and with the same careful movements called for a taxi, all the while dreading what he knew must come next.

It was time to move; time to get up from his chair, put on his coat and leave. He sat, gathering courage, still unwilling to summon help. He could see the whole scenario in his mind and was disgusted by the images. Peggy, the secretary he shared with Mr. Tyler, would over-react--have everyone rushing to his aid, asking questions, feeling sorry for him. He could see himself hobbling, bent over between the desks, all eyes upon him and the images horrified him. He'd be damned if he's subject himself to that degree of humiliation!

Grabbing the edge of his desk, he forced himself erect as a stabbing, shooting pain forced a low moan of agony from between clenched teeth. Pausing, he steadied himself and waited for the black dot in front of his eyes to stop swimming quite so furiously. It took him only seconds to decide he could not put on his coat.

With his clammy shirt clinging to his back and a sheen of perspiration covering his bloodless face, Tucker Jones slowly exited from Zitec Global Development, through the inner sanctum of carpeted, empty hallways to the busy, noisy outer offices, shuffling one step at a time towards the elevator and hopefully, the promised cab, without causing a single ruffle in the business of the day.

"Holy shit, Mister, I hope I'm taking you to the emergency room!" the cabbie shouted above the traffic's roar.

Tucker gasped out Dr. Beemer's address and sank gratefully into the back seat, feeling the waiting cushions help support the spasming area; the cab driver's anxious prattle buzzed without meaning, around his head. He sat, totally absorbed in his own anguish, trying hard not to move. Still, the spasms hit with a fierce randomness that made him groan from time to time.

When the taxi screeched to a halt in front of Beemer's office, the cabbie jumped from the cab and went to summon help. While he was gone, Tucker slowly pulled out his wallet and extracted two twenty dollar bills, leaving them on the seat beside him. Then he reached for the door handle, but when he tried to exert the downward pressure necessary to open the door, a thunderbolt of pain struck and the black dots again circled and exploded behind his closed lids. With another groan he carefully lowered his hand and simply waited, literally unable to lift a hand to help himself.

Then, Mavis was coming down the walk, the cab driver behind her pushing a wheel chair. She opened the cab door, leaned in, to scrutinize his face and said, "Oh, dear, Tucker!" with such sincere sympathy that he had the sudden urge to cry.

"Now, this nice man has agreed to help us get you into the wheel chair. Your part is to do absolutely nothing. Let me move your legs…" With quiet competence the nurse took charge. Tucker did as he was told and was able to make the transition with only minor spasms.

"Tucker, dear, the doctor will have the final say, but my guess is that we will need to call an ambulance. The most we can do for you here is a fast acting injection for the pain."

Tucker did not even try to nod his head in answer. The only thing he said as the cab driver pushed him through the clinic doors was, "Thank you...money is on seat..." before closing his eyes and absorbing yet another spasm.

Tucker had little memory of his visit to the clinic. He vaguely remembered the rumble of Dr. Beemer's voice and Mavis administering an injection while he still sat in the wheelchair in a waiting room filled with people. His next fully conscious moment was in a hospital bed. He knew he must have come by ambulance, but had no memory of the ride. He felt very groggy and as though he had a terrible hangover, but decided immediately that the spasms had stopped...there was pain, but it was manageable.

He slowly turned his head and found his mother sitting in the bedside chair, her head turned towards the window, looking out at the gathering dusk, a book lying closed in her lap.

"Hello, Mother," he said softly and she jumped, startled, then turned to smile at him.

"Hello, dear. Your father called Zitec and informed them that you had been hospitalized." She paused, looked puzzled and then continued. "...and Dr. Beemers said to tell you when you woke that he is very tired of sticking hypodermic needles into you and putting you in an ambulance. He said to tell you that it was very upsetting to his other patients."

Her voice, well-modulated and crisp, made her sound like she had memorized bad script. Tucker had to translate the message, adding Dr. Beemer's gruff and hearty inflections to realize that it was a joke. He wondered if she was feeling a sense of relief to have delivered the message verbatim and decided that she was.

He smiled softly at her. "Thank you, Mother." His smile widened. "I can understand his concern, can't you?"

"Why, no, dear, I cannot. I mean...well, twice in fourteen years just doesn't seem very often to me. A hand fluttered up to the lovely strand of graduated pearls at her neck, her brow knitting with care and concern, she looked at Tucker, puzzled by the smile on his face.

"Mother," he said, "I believe Dr. Beemers was making a small joke. That is his brand of humor, don't you think?"

She paused, looked at him wonderingly and then suddenly her face cleared. "Oh, Tucker! Of course he was joking! How very silly of me! I think I must have been too preoccupied thinking about you to hear properly…and my goodness, how ARE you feeling? Those should have been the very first words out of my mouth."

He sighed, ignoring his headache. "I'm not going to move around to find out. Just lying here, I can feel soreness in my back but much of the pain is gone. Now it's my stomach and my head; one feels queasy and the other stuffed with cotton."

"Yes," she nodded. "The nurse said you've had enough muscle relaxant and narcotic in you to have those side effects. She also said she would be happy to give you something for nausea if you needed it. All I need do is push the button on the side of your bed." She leaned forward and pushed the red button with a jaunty gesture of accomplishment.

She sat for a moment, smiling at her son, and then her face knit itself into another frown of concern. "Tucker, dear, what did you do to hurt your back so?" I want to call your father now and I know that is the first question he will ask me."

Tucker closed his eyes, feeling suddenly drained. "Tell him…tell him I have been very negligent about stretching between long sessions at the computer and when I was bending to put on my loafers, my back reminded me rather sharply of my error. As unglamorous as it sounds, I believe that's what happened. I'm fairly certain the doctors will do an examination of my spine and that will determine the validity of my theory."

Tucker opened his eyes again. "Thank you for being here, Mother. It was good to see you sitting there when I woke. Now, go call Father and tell him I am fine, but sleepy. If he is thinking of coming this evening, please tell him that tomorrow would probably be better. I'm certain I shall be better company by then."

The nurse came in and checked his IV drip, elevated his bed, and put a small cup to his lips. "Here you go. Bottoms up!" she said with professional cheerfulness. "This should manage the nausea. We don't want you going in for an MRI with an upset stomach, do we?"

When she had gone, Tucker forced his eyes to focus on his mother. "In fact, Mother, why don't you toddle on home and over cocktails, you can tell Father the news and thank him for alerting Zitec for me. I can't seem to keep myself awake and there is no sense in your keeping vigil over a son who has merely done something to..."

Margaret Jones watched Tucker's eyes close and his breathing even out. He looked so young and vulnerable! She had the momentary impulse to reach out and smooth his rumpled hair, but instead, stood abruptly and straightened the skirt of her soft wool suit. *Tucker is correct,* she decided. *It is time to go home, finish dinner preparation and have a cocktail with Evan.*

After a last look at her sleeping son, she tiptoed from the room, stopping by the nursing station to find out if and when the MRI had been scheduled. *Evan will want that detail as well,* she thought.

The following several days revolved around the MRI and physical therapy. Tucker was soon able to rise and move without pain. He called the office with an update and asked to be put through to Mr. Tyler. "Sorry, Tucker, Mr. Tyler isn't available, but I'll let him know you called. In the meantime, take care of yourself," she had said pleasantly.

In the end, nothing seriously wrong was found. The prescription was physical therapy, pain medication as needed and an elastic back brace that looked suspiciously like a girdle.

Dr. Beemers had a different opinion. He thought that something was seriously wrong, but not with the young man's back. He just didn't know if that something was permanent.

During the week he had made it a point to take time out from his busy schedule to drop by Tucker's room for short visits. Casually, without seeming to pry, he uncovered, thread by thread, the fabric of Tucker's adult life and was appalled. This seemingly affable, successful, charming, young man had apparently built an invisible, airtight barrier around his emotions. Beemers shook his head. He could see how much like his father Tucker had become. But he suspected Tucker would fail in becoming a replica of his father. The O'Sheas had taught him to feel and laugh, embrace and cry those many years ago. Dr. Beemers decided Tucker's back had just reminded him that his long-barricaded emotions could not be held in check forever. The doctor scratched his burly head and wondered to himself if he had ever known a patient so obviously out of touch with his feelings...and so oblivious of the fact.

He considered his own course of action very carefully. Being a straight-forward sort of man, his preference would have been to confront Tucker with his observations and recommend that he get back into therapy, but he rejected that option almost immediately. To use Tobin Van Castle's jargon, 'Tucker's denial system was simply too strong.' *But, if not confrontation, what approach to take?* Certainly he could not appeal to Tucker's parents. *For one thing, Tucker is an adult now...and for another; Tucker's folks think their son is perfect, just as he is.*

Beemers tussled with the problem as Tucker's impending release from the hospital loomed. Finally he gave up and called his old friend, Tobin Van Castle, and invited him for a drink at Lyon's Gate, their favorite pub.

Dr. Van Castle was no longer in private practice. He had accepted a position at Yale University and was busily teaching, supervising doctoral students, pursuing potential romance and writing a book.

As they sat in front of a pub fire, stretching their legs to the heat, nursing their beer and catching up on each other, Tobin thought his friend, Jeff, was showing the aging effects of pressure. The older man looked overworked and was definitely overweight. Although, Tobin reflected, he probably looked much the same to Beemers. Suddenly his ears pricked and he leaned forward when he realized Jeff was asking if he remembered a former client, Tucker Jones.

Yes, he nodded. He did indeed remember Tucker Jones, and in fact, still wondered about him from time to time, nagged by his own self-doubt. He listened carefully as the doctor sketched out the details of his recent contact with Tucker and the ensuing observations and nodded solemnly when Jeff had finished.

With a deep sigh, the psychiatrist pinched the bridge of his nose and then fixed his bright blue eyes on his friend. "You know, Jeff, as I look back on my relationship with Tucker, I get this gut wrenching fear that there was something I missed with him," he admitted sadly. "I remember that I ALMOST let him snow me when he was at The Institute of Living. He was so damned smooth and personable…not to mention so vulnerable, that I almost failed to confront him directly about his buried feelings. When I finally brought the issue forward he seemed to make real progress. He was able to talk about his Irish surrogate parents."

Jeff Beemers had been listening intently. "Ethan and Mary O'Shea," he said quietly.

"Yes, that's right, Ethen and Mary. I asked Tucker to write down his memories of them to share with me and he kept such a journal for several months." Tobin spread his hands, studying their backs and then looked up at his friend. "Then, he really seemed fine…had reintegrated nicely at school, rebuilt friendships and even helped his parents select replacements for the Irish couple who went down in the North Sea…so we terminated treatment. But…" His blue eyes showed doubt. "During periods of reflection, his name and face come to me and I wonder if there were issues we never unearthed. Our termination sessions went smoothly and he seemed quite content…but I wonder sometimes if it was real or all part of his façade."

Dr. Beemers sat quietly, respecting the admission. Psychiatry was such an inexact science; success in treatment so hard to measure; it took a strong person to stay in practice. He wondered if his friend's switch to the classroom had anything to do with too many such reflections. Finally, he sighed and leaned forward for a sip of beer. "It's hard to say, Tobin. He appears to be pretty isolated. I understand that only his parents came to visit him while he was in the hospital, no work colleagues, no girlfriend, just parents."

"Have you seen him on a regular basis, then?"

Beemers shook his head. "Nope. I hadn't seen him since his last sports physical nine years ago. It's strange, I know he's pretty screwed up and out of touch with his feeling, but even knowing what I know, I really like the kid.

He's so bright and has enough charisma to charm most people right off their feet."

Tobin said, "I think you're telling me that he knows the rules for being a warm and loving human being, he just can't feel the emotions that go with that sort of person."

"Right! Exactly! For a long time I couldn't decide whether to even suggest he might profit from additional therapy. Finally, I very casually suggested that he might want to get in touch with you for a recommendation of someone you might think of as a good fit. You should have seen his reaction! Closed up like a clam."

Together, they pondered what might be at the core of Tucker's struggle. They agreed that the unresolved issue the sessions had not unearthed was at least partly Tucker's loyalty bind. At some point in his adolescence he had perhaps decided, either consciously or unconsciously, to become his (living) father, not Ethan, his surrogate father (deceased). His exceptional will allowed him to carry out his plan. But, in order to do so, he had to deny the part of him that Ethan (and Mary) had nourished.

Van Castle agreed with Dr. Beemers' intuitive notion that he would reject counseling, if getting in touch with his feelings made him feel as though he were rejecting his father.

The psychiatrist also reminded his friend that the Jones' family pattern was to resist change…so that to suggest anything very radical would probably be abhorrent to him. Unfortunately, as Dr. Beemers had suspected, Tobin Van Castle had no magic cure to suggest.

It was Mavis, Dr. Beemers' matronly nurse of many years, looking at him over half-glasses, which he noted perched ever closer to the end of her nose as she moved past the age of 40 and on towards 50, who solved the problem of just how to possibly help Tucker Jones.

Just as he was leaving the office for one last visit with Tucker before releasing him from the hospital, she snorted and said, "If Tucker were my son, he'd get a hot bath and a rub down every night."

After a second, Beemers laughed, feeling like the iconic light bulb had gone off over his head. "Mavis, you are a genius," he said, leaning across the counter and pushing

44

her glasses back up her nose. "That is exactly what that lad needs and I think maybe I know how to arrange it."

He headed out the office door with a bounce in his step. Mavis had given him the key for a therapy that might work for uptight Tucker Jones, son of Mr. and Mrs. "Coldfish" Jones. Touch therapy! He didn't believe humans could survive intact without being touched.

His mind whirled. He wouldn't tell Tucker his recommendation today. He'd have him make an appointment at the office the following day and tell him there. He needed time to think about how to present this new idea and to make the phone call that would set it up.

The following afternoon, when Mavis escorted Tucker down the hall, it was not to the examination room, but to Dr. Beemers' office where the man sat behind his desk looking slightly foreboding and more professional than he usually looked, the polished cherry wood desk lending its own status and dignity to his comments.

After confirming that Tucker's back felt fine and that his back support was in place, Beemers leaned forward and dropped the hammer. "Tucker," he rumbled gravely, "as well as you feel now, you will find what I'm about to say hard to believe…but I can almost guarantee that your back will continue to plague you unless you begin taking care of it immediately. I know you stay physically active and I want you to do the back exercises the physical therapist gave you, but you need more than stretching exercises if we're really going to fix the problem."

The doctor pulled his note pad towards himself with a flourish and whipped his pen from its holder as though he were drawing a sword from a scabbard. He beetled his bushy brows and glared at Tucker as though whatever protests he might mount would best be left unsaid. Then he dropped his head and wrote down a name and phone number, saying mildly, but with conviction, "This is the person I recommend to all my patients with jobs that are hard on backs."

The doctor knew he was stretching the truth more than a little, but he wanted to make his point. "Once a week, make time in your schedule—twice a week would be better and daily would be best, but knowing you, once a week would be reasonable."

45

Tucker took the piece of paper; just looking at the name made him feel a little uncomfortable. He grinned lazily at the doctor. "Kathryn McCall. What is she—a physical therapist?"

"No," said the doctor, trying to keep his voice matter-of-fact, "she's a massage therapist."

Tucker's reaction confirmed the doctor's worry. He was going to refuse. Beemers could see it in the way his back stiffened, while his grin stayed in place and his eyes went blank.

"Ah...no...doctor, I don't think so," he protested. "A massage therapist?" He was already beginning to shake his head when Dr. Beemers, who had already played this scene in his mind a dozen times, dropped the hammer a second time.

"Well," he said gruffly, allowing just a touch of ice to coat his tone, "I must confess I am unused to having a patient challenge a prescribed course of treatment." He lifted his eyes to Tucker's, locking in his gaze, the ice in his voice now extended to his eyes. "I am sorry to say that you have no choice in this matter if you wish to remain a patient of mine."

I'm playing poker in its rawest form, the doctor thought as he paused, letting the feeling of rejection he was sure his words would cause, sink in. Then his voice turned soft and sad. "We've been through a lot together, Tucker..." He let the words hang and give Tucker time to understand the true impact of what he was saying. He felt his shoulders sag and he wasn't acting; suddenly he felt himself to be an old and disappointed man.

Tucker's eyes darted around the office. They looked anywhere other than at the doctor. He felt both trapped and betrayed, his thoughts leaping about, looking for an escape route. Finally, his mind centered on one thought: *Lose Dr. Beemers, one of the only threads connecting to his boyhood? Not likely!* With effort he met Dr. Beemers' quiet gaze, noticed that the ice was gone and felt immense relief. With a sigh, Tucker picked up the square of white between two fingers and said, "Okay. Okay, Dr. Beemers, I'll give it one try."

"No!" barked Beemers, pressing his victory, "Eight sessions constitutes a valid try. Call Kathryn today and set up the sessions. Please schedule an appointment after you have had four massages. I want to measure the muscle tension in your back. This is serious stuff, Tucker, as you can tell by my demeanor. If we can prevent a reoccurrence of the terrible pain that brought you here, it would certainly be worth it," he said as he stood and escorted Tucker from the room.

The doctor watched the straight back fondly and waited until Tucker turned to give a half-hearted wave at the exit before he walked back to his desk to sit for a moment, savoring his success. *Tucker's treatment is now out of my lap and into the capable hands of a very Irish, Kathryn McCall.* He reached for the phone, knowing at this time of day he would more than likely be talking to her answering machine. "Kathryn, he said at the beep, "Dr. Beemers here. You can indeed expect a call from Tucker Jones. I just wanted to remind you that he has been coerced, by yours truly, into making the appointment and is unsure of the benefits of massage. Please be tolerant and patient. This is a very fine young man."

Chapter Five

Tucker's first day back at Zitek had its ups and downs. For the first time he learned that Mr. Tyler had refused to hold any meetings of significance in his absence but, uncharacteristically, refused to see Tucker. One of the women in the secretarial pool confided, "We're sure glad you're back, Tucker. Mr. Tyler has gone from barking to booming all week. It has us all jittery."

Tucker had just nodded and said, "Sorry about that, Sandy," before giving her an engaging grin and heading for his office, a perplexed frown on his face. He felt the first stirring of anxiety.

That night, over cocktails, James stood in front of Midge's chair with his hands behind his back, looking up at the ceiling and then back down at her before he gave a sigh and said, "I was still too angry to face him, so the whole place feels like it is on hold!" He began to pace. "But, really, I'm not angry with him as much as I am disappointed with myself. What did I think the boy was…a life raft? So, okay, here is this young man with incredible talent…did I immediately convince myself that he would be perfect to groom as my replacement at Zitec?"

Midge nodded her head slightly, but continued to sit quietly, knowing the tirade wasn't over. Her husband was merely thinking out loud.

James walked over and put an elbow on the mantel next to his drink. It seemed to anchor him. "Well, as it turns out, I may have made a serious error in judgment, Midge." He turned frustrated eyes on her. "It seems he's not a man, he's a GODDAMNED MACHINE!"

With those words, he began pacing, waving his arms to punctuate his emotions. "This kid has been here now how many dozens of times? Have you ever seen him belly laugh, or act rude, or get angry? Have you ever seen him over-eat, or get drunk, or fail to be gracious?" He stopped in his tracks and turned again to face his wife. "Wait! Wait! I've changed my mind. He's not just a machine, he's a robot! That's what he is, a GODDAMNED ROBOT!"

Midge Tyler had been married to James Whipple Tyler III for thirty-eight years. She rose from her chair and went to freshen his drink and noticed when she did her hands were trembling. There had been tragedy in their lives...the loss of a son. Other than visiting his grave, it was something they seldom spoke of or made reference too, and even after all these years, thinking of his death brought tremendous pain. Her husband wouldn't say it, but she intuitively felt that his rantings were not based on an employer's disappointment in an employee, but a father's disappointment in a son. She was, in fact, recognizing those feelings in herself.

"I think," she said softly as she put her hand on his chest and handed him the scotch, "what really hurts the most was that he felt it necessary to conceal the fact that he was injured from everyone at the office, including you. Help was all around him and he couldn't allow himself to reach out for any of it —not from you, not from Peggy or Cliff, not from anyone. If his pain was as Mr. Jones described it to be, it was excruciating and yet he felt the need to hide it. That poor, poor boy!"

He turned to look at her in awe. She had voiced what was at the core of his anger: that Tucker had not asked for his help. He took his drink in one hand and covered her hand on his chest with his other, engulfing it, feeling the tremble.

The festering hurt had been exposed and she had lanced it with her words of sympathy for Tucker. He felt some of the anger drain away and could feel the hurt more clearly now that Midge had voiced it. He looked at his wife, sipping his scotch, lost in thought. "You know," he finally said, "these last three years have really flown past without my realizing it. But as I think back, I cannot remember Tucker expressing a strong opinion even once. I find myself wondering what that means."

Deep in thought, James sank back in his chair. Drink forgotten, he puzzled out why their relationship had worked so well, even better than he'd dared to hope. Things really had never gone better in the company. He

49

was certain his own management and decision making had improved. Tucker provided him with a verbal and written debriefing summary after each meeting; the verbal one almost always immediately; the computer printout, several days later. It came to him that Tucker's style of presenting the information in such a logical and objective fashion allowed him to draw his own conclusions more decisively...or were they simply Tucker's conclusions left unstated? He honestly didn't know the answer to the question and once he had puzzled it through, he wasn't sure what he should do with his new perceptions of Tucker Jones. His first angry thought had been to dismiss the man. Luckily, he wasn't a knee-jerk sort of a guy and fortunately, Midge had helped him recognize that it might be an irrational over-reaction to his own disappointment, not any lacking in Tucker's job performance. To fire a man simply because he wouldn't rely on a co-worker, himself specifically, was neither logical nor fair. He sighed, took another sip of his drink, sifting his thoughts, unused to the feeling of being indecisive. It made him uncomfortable...*and,* thought Midge as she slipped from the room to see about dinner...*very, very grumpy.*

Tucker awoke the next morning with a sense of impending doom and tried to analyze its cause. He frowned when he thought of the day ahead. He had finally made an appointment with the massage therapist—after nearly a week of procrastination. Then, only the knowledge that he had to face Dr. Beemers the following week had made him do it. *Today I'm going to have to leave work early to keep the appointment.* He frowned again as he focused on his real concern. There would be no problem with his leaving work early, flexible hours were part of his original agreement with his boss...*but Mr. Tyler's reaction wasn't at all what I expected.* He realized then, that part of his foreboding had to do with that reaction, or rather, the lack of reaction to his return. *Why hadn't either of the Tylers called him when he was in the hospital?* There had been get well cards and a bouquet of flowers waiting on his desk when he returned to work. Everyone seemed happy, even relieved to see him back...except Mr. Tyler. *Perhaps,* Tucker pondered, lying with his hands under his head, staring at the ceiling, *he's angry with me for not asking permission before leaving for Dr. Beemers.* That line of thought didn't really make sense and Tucker, quite logically, knew it. Still, the thought of his boss being angry with him was so discomforting he dismissed the whole notion, feeling incredibly uneasy.

To Tucker, it felt as if his thoughts were encoded on one of those old- fashioned vinyl records, going around and around with the needle down. It wasn't as if Mr. Tyler didn't know where he was; his father had made certain of that. He'd called in as soon as he was physically able and every day thereafter, but Peggy always pleasantly informed him that there were no messages and would he please just take care of himself.

He sighed, threw back his duvet and rolled on one side before rising. His back really felt fine but he did his prescribed stretching exercises. He would never forget the pain. His own vulnerability continued to haunt him. He decided keeping his appointment with the message therapist was the right thing to do. He had faith in Dr. Beemers. *If the doctor feels this is the right course of action, the least I can do is give it a fair try*

For Tucker, the sense of foreboding grew stronger as he entered Zitec, rode the elevator to the top floor, and walked through his office door, back brace in place. There was a note on his desk, written in Peggy's careful hand:

1. Phone Mr. Tyler
2. Meeting at 10:00

He read the words several times, waves of relief washing over him, cleansing the dread from his thoughts. *How could I possibly have gotten myself worked up like this? It must be a residue from the pain medication.* He consciously relaxed his neck, did a few neck and shoulder rolls and then picked up the phone. *Things are back to normal,* he thought with the beginnings of a smile.

Mr. Tyler, sounding quite jovial on the phone, asked after Tucker and requested his presence A.S.A.P. Familiar warning bells went off in Tucker's head at the tone and the dread returned. That was the tone of voice that made executives squirm in the plush upholstery of their curved back conference chairs. He knew it well and it came to him that he might be about to lose his job. He cradled his phone, looked around the tastefully decorated office and got woodenly to his feet, marshaling and controlling all outward signs of emotion.

Resolutely, Tucker closed his office door, smiled at Peggy, Mr. Tyler's personal secretary and his, the rare times he needed her services, walked around her desk and knocked softly while turning the ornate handle on the massive door—just as he had done so many times before.

Mr. Tyler stayed seated behind his desk. Tucker took his usual chair and waited. The older man looked at him steadily for a long moment and then said softly. "Welcome back, son." Tucker's throat closed. He found he couldn't speak, only nod. Of all the things he had expected, sympathy wasn't on the list. With great difficulty he kept his face controlled while he absorbed the awareness of how much he had come to respect this man, and how much that simple statement of welcome meant to him.

"Tucker..." Mr. Tyler leaned forward and clasped his hands on the desk, "I have some things to say to you that are important to me. Things that should have been said a week ago, but things I only figured out last night."

The older man sat quietly for a moment, took a long breath to steady his resolve and said, "I didn't see you yesterday or the day before because I was hurt and sometimes hurt comes out the wrong way and sounds like anger."

So far, so good, James thought to himself, *Midge would be pleased.* He looked steadily at the young man sitting silently, expression pleasant, across from him. "You let me believe, or rather I guess I chose to believe, we were not only working partners, but friends. When I found out that it wasn't so, there was a part of me that wanted to hurt you the way you hurt me."

Watching closely, searching Tucker's faces as he never had before, Tyler was amazed at the minute glimpses of emotions that flickered and were immediately extinguished. He wasn't certain, but he thought he saw fear, sadness and perhaps an expression akin to vulnerability. A less careful observer would have seen only a bland-faced young man relaxing in a chair, saying in a

52

carefully modulated voice, "Hurt you, sir? I really don't understand. I would like to think that we ARE friends."

"Oh no," the gray head shook adamantly, "indeed we are not. By definition, there is trust between friends. Friends turn to each other for help. I trusted you, but obviously you didn't trust me. I'm willing to bet big money that you don't really trust anyone. At least you don't trust anyone in this company or you would have asked someone for help the day your back spasmed."

Mr. Tyler, having said his piece, leaned back in his chair, lengthening the distance between the two of them, giving Tucker time to digest his words.

Tucker too sat back. He felt more uncomfortable than he ever had in his adult life. He felt exposed to the point of nakedness and very, very misunderstood. He started to explain, defend himself, but the image of Dr. Van Castle sitting on his bed in the psychiatric ward, explaining the concept of trust between friends shut him down. Instead, he said simply, his eyes looking straight, if not quite steadily into the steel of the older man's, "I don't know what to say, sir."

James leaned forward again, pain etching his face. "There is no need for you to say anything right now, Tucker. I do hope you will take some time and think about this conversation. Think about your reasons for not asking someone from Zitek for help. Decide for yourself if it was because you don't trust anyone here enough to allow them to see you as less than invincible." He cleared his throat mightily. "Let me make it clear to you that this has nothing what so ever to do with the role you currently play in Zitek Global. My feelings stem from personal, not professional regret. You are doing just what I hired you to do…and that, I certainly appreciate.

Tyler did not allow himself the maudlin pleasure of informing the young man that he felt the disappointment of a father who has groomed an unworthy son to take over the family business. That was another truth, thanks to his wife, he had faced himself with last night over dinner. He did say to her, seemingly as an afterthought, "Oh, by the way, Clifton will be sitting in on some of our debriefings from time to time."

That bombshell and the fact that his boss had unconsciously stressed the word, 'currently,' when he had talked about Tucker's role in the company were signals to the young man that something important had changed. He felt a staggering sense of loss as he left Mr. Tyler's office and walked, holding himself militarily erect, head unbowed, back to his own office, carefully closing the door.

He had told Mr. Tyler he would think about his words. The trouble was—he couldn't think. He felt numb. When he heard Mr. Tyler say those words about trust and friendship, it had produced a visual image of Tobin Van Castle so strong he could almost smell the man's after shave. He had banished and buried all thoughts of the man for fourteen years and yet, suddenly, he was forced to consider what it meant that two of the most important men in his life had given him the same message. He also needed to think about why Mr. Tyler had been so hurt because he had handled his back injury by himself. He ground his teeth in frustration in the silence of his office. *All this time, I thought he valued self-sufficiency.* He tried to do a check on his feelings like the psychiatrist had taught him to do and found the only feeling he had was being totally perplexed and puzzled.

Tucker shrugged, trying and failing to bring his whirling mind under some control. Mindful of his back, he carefully sat down at his desk. His back muscles were clearly signaling his tension. He shook his head in disgust, remembering his afternoon appointment with the massage therapist. *On the other hand, perhaps I do need a back massage…that and a little appreciation now and then.* From what he could figure, he had been trying to do exactly what the people in his life expected him to do. He sighed and dropped his chin. *For some reason, Mr. Tyler overreacted. Perhaps, when he had time to think of what he'd said, he will apologize.*

Thoughts continued to buzz like trapped bees in his head without order or resolution. He lifted his chin and exhaled sharply. He had a synopsis to read in less than an hour and a brain that was refusing to concentrate just when he felt it was critical to prove his worth to Mr. Tyler yet again. Resolutely, he pulled the sheaf of papers towards him and began to plow through the paragraphs. Slowly, but surely, his thoughts zeroed in on the marching black lines and columns. He finished reading at 10:25, carefully and precisely ordered the pile of papers, combed his hair and walked to the conference room. Quiet murmurs of welcome greeted him as he slipped into his chair. As it had with Mr. Tyler, the sympathy felt quite unnerving. He was relieved to realize that Mr. Tyler's view of him wasn't held by all. *What is Mr. Tyler's problem? I do a good job for this company and I intend to prove it again at this meeting.* He managed a smile and sincerely thanked the group for their concern and assured them of his recovery, despite a throat that remained desperately dry. His grave, attentive demeanor gave little hint of his resentment.

Mr. Tyler strode cheerfully into the room, greeting his employees with hearty good humor and then went directly to his chair to call the meeting to order.

Once again, Tucker's tremendous will served him well. It was an important meeting. Zitec Global Development had been exploring the possibility of broadening its base of operations to include South America. Several important contacts had been made. According to the synopsis he'd just read, the market seemed unencumbered with serious competition. The economic risks would be tied to the state of the world economy; which seemed to be turning its head toward South America these days, looking for opportunities on the rapidly developing continent, as the various governments seemed, at last, to have moved towards stabilization. Zitec had an international reputation of being able to work within the cultural and political framework of developing nations and had, according to the research team, been given encouragement by ambassadors from 5 countries: Argentina, Brazil, Chile, Columbia and Venezuela. It was heady stuff, since the ambassadors' interest had been seconded by inquiries from prominent South American Industrialists.

This meeting had the potential to be pivotal in the decision-making process and the group treated it with extra attention, feeling quite pleased with how quickly they appeared to be progressing towards resolution. Comments were concise. Questions were probing. The research team had apparently done its work. Mr. Tyler took a more passive role than usual, his eyes roving over the group, pausing occasionally to catch a point. Every so often, his glance would rest on Tucker, sitting quietly, listening intently, absorbing verbiage with great concentration...until at last, at 12:30, Mr. Tyler thanked them for their hard work, made a few summary statements and dismissed them with a smile. He too felt satisfied with the meeting and wondered if he really needed to hold the usual follow up session with Tucker. Things seemed very clear and he was feeling an odd reluctance to meet with the young man. For a moment, he seriously considered canceling their time together and then decided firmly that it was important that Tucker and he continue on as before. *That is what I told him we would do this morning and so we will.*

By the end of their debriefing, James thanked God for his own wisdom. As usual, he wasn't certain how, but Tucker's careful and objective analysis of what was said, how conclusions were reached and the number of times direct questions were evaded or only partially answered, had him jotting notes furiously on his note pad. One big item that jumped out at him was the fact that no reference checks had been done on the South American businessmen supposedly interested in Zitec's help in learning to incorporate American manufacturing technology and business techniques...yet, many of the facts presented had been based on the information presented by these people. Who really knew if the expressed interest could translate into actual working capital?

As usual, after one of the debriefings, Tyler felt settled, in charge and more certain of his direction. The question of whether he was reaching his own conclusions or whether the conclusions had already been reached by Tucker, but left unsaid, was still a mystery. It surely felt as though they were his own decisions, and for now, that was good enough.

He thanked Tucker sincerely and complimented him. "I don't know how you do it, but, by God, you do make my job easier!"

Tucker let out a deep breath unknowingly held. Those were important words and he savored them. "Thank you, sir. I am glad it was helpful." They smiled tentatively at one another and clasped hands briefly, but long enough for the older man to feel the cold clamminess of the young man's hand and register anxiety as its cause.

"By the way, sir, I plan to be gone for the rest of the afternoon, unless you need me," Tucker said a trifle too offhandedly, knowing Mr. Tyler didn't need him, but looking for a good excuse to reverse his decision once again and cancel his session with the massage therapist.

"No, Tucker, things haven't changed," Tyler said, this time convinced in his own mind, "you're still free to come and go as you see fit. You are doing exactly the job you were hired to do. You are a damned fine asset to this place and we're lucky to have you!" He cleared his throat as if to say more, but then simply nodded to Tucker in way of dismissal.

By three o'clock, a reluctant, but determined young man sat in the Aston, familiarizing himself with the directions to Kathryn McCall's office, which he learned was in her home in Milford, before nosing the car into traffic. Directions were just one more thing he found easy to remember.

He soon found himself in a well-kept neighborhood of modest homes and it was easy to find the house as there were numbers both on the houses and on the curbs. Parking the car, he walked down the sidewalk to the house, looking for the office entrance, remembering the woman on the phone had mentioned it was on the left side of the house. He walked briskly, ready to take the plunge and get the whole distasteful experience over with.

He thought of Dr. Beemers and how he had absolutely insisted, to the point of refusing to be Tucker's doctor, that this was the treatment of choice. *I wonder if he comes here for massages,* Tucker wondered. The picture of the graying, portly man, pipe in mouth, big frame stretched out on a small table made him smile. That smile was quickly replaced by a frown as he saw the ludicrous picture of himself on the same table. The conjured image rattled his usually calm demeanor and he reached the office door genuinely agitated.

He stopped and looked around. Something was vaguely familiar about the look of the place. To the rear of the office was a garden of sorts. He could see flowers peeking through the boards of a weathered fence...something tugged at Tucker's memory, something that he could not allow himself to recognize until many visits later. There was a small, professionally done sign by the door that said simply:

Kathryn McCall, Licensed Massage Therapist
Please let yourself in.

Tucker read the sign and nearly turned on his heel. Face grim, he wondered what sort of place it was. *Let myself in? In to what?* As he stood there undecided, the door suddenly opened and a tall, elderly lady with tight, gray curls and a younger woman dressed in a white uniform were standing there. He stepped quickly aside, innate good manners coming to his aid, covering his anxiety with a smile.

"Hello," the three of them said simultaneously. Then the younger woman patted the older woman's arm and said, "Goodbye, Mrs. Downing, see you next week. Remember your plan to leave the heavy lifting for your son, please."

Mrs. Downing smiled conspiratorially at Tucker and said, cheerfully, "But, if I didn't have aches and pains what excuse would I have for indulging in this weekly massage?"

Tucker found himself smiling conspiratorially back. "I wouldn't know," he said, "but I would wager you'd think of something." He heard Kathryn chuckle as they watched the old woman walk smartly down the sidewalk.

Slowly, they turned to look at each other, sizing one another up. She saw a tall, slender man of perfect, almost military posture, a careful expression in his brown eyes, shoulders wide under a beautifully cut suit coat.

He couldn't get past a general impression of auburn, curly hair in a severe, but unsuccessfully controlled braid, large flashing green eyes and a sprinkle of freckles.

"Tucker Jones, I assume?" she said gravely and held out a hand. Again, his good manners forced a pleasant acknowledgement and a firm handshake. He was confident she had no clue as to his inner turmoil as he followed her through a small waiting area and into a room whose main

58

piece of furniture was a long table covered by a rumpled white sheet.

Handing him a big white fluffy towel, she smiled, "Dr. Beemers said you have a very stiff back, so I am going to put you in the steam cabinet before I put you on the table." She pointed to a door with one finger. "Please go into the changing room and slip out of your suit."

It was all Tucker could do to keep from bolting. Kathryn saw the color leave his face and his jaw clench. He appeared to be having some inner struggle. "No," he croaked and then when she looked at him questioningly, he said more strongly, "NO! I came here to have my back massaged—nothing more. No steam bath...just a back massage."

It was Kathryn's turn for surprised silence. She remembered Jeff Beemers' call. For him to place such a call was very unusual—this was evidently a special case. *What was it the doctor had said about this fellow? Something about his not being convinced of the benefits of massage?* She shrugged and smiled. "Okay, I can do that," she said, carefully dropping her smile so he wouldn't think she was poking fun. "I'm not used to doing it this way," she said as humbly as she could. "How should we proceed?"

He stood looking down at the top of her coppery braid feeling overly tall and more than a little out of his element. "Well, I'll just take off my jacket and shirt and sit on the edge of the table so you can work on my back...his words trailed off as he noticed her starting to shake her head.

"No!" Her tone was adamant. "You can hang onto your britches, but you'll have to lie on the table, otherwise, I'm too short." She busied herself putting the towel back on the stack, careful not to look at Tucker, hoping he'd comply.

Tucker found himself struck by the lilt of her voice which carried more of a cadence than an accent. When she finally looked at him, he nodded in acquiescence, seeing the logic of her statement and went to the changing room while she busied herself changing the sheet.

A stray thought popped into his head as he removed his jacket. *There is absolutely no resemblance between this disheveled looking woman and any of the well-groomed women I have dated, or rather, escorted, in the past several years.* Carefully, he hung his shirt and suit coat on a provided hanger. *Rather like comparing daisies to orchids,* he thought sourly as he reluctantly moved towards the table.

Kathryn noted the cold eyes and grim mouth. *Oh brother,* she thought, *he acts like he's having a tooth drilled, not a massage!*

Cautiously, Tucker stretched his lanky frame on the table, fists clenched. *Oh brother!* She thought again. *Go easy here, Katie me girl or he'll bolt and run.* The image of a dentist's office, a place she hated unreasonably, flashed through her mind again and she remembered how relieving it had been to have the dentist spend a few minutes talking to her, telling her that he would explain each thing he was going to do before he actually did it. *Perhaps such a technique would work with this stone-faced gentleman.*

She approached him, holding a warmed bottle of massage oil down so he could see and said, "Here is the oil I'll be using—but first, with your permission, I am going to slip a towel between your back and your britches and then fold it out of the way. I'm thinking it would be good to protect the fabric from the oil."

Tucker raised his head, glanced at the oil and nodded briefly. Kathryn took the nod as permission to proceed. She noted that his eyes remained open while she carefully tucked the towel and then poured the oil into her hand. "I'm going to start with your lower back now," she said, keeping her voice carefully neutral, gently spreading the oil with deft motions. Her eyes widened slightly as she rubbed. It was like massaging granite. She could feel the stony ridges marching up and down both sides of his spine. *No wonder Dr. Beemers encouraged him to come,* she thought.

After a bit, she realized he was not breathing and although the room was comfortably warm, his skin was cold to the touch. *Like rubbing a corpse, I'd think. I wonder what causes these ridges? With the thought,* she realized that she was starting to think about the man and what his problems might be--instead of the musculature and stopped herself—years of professionalism guiding both her train of thought and conduct.

60

"Mr. Jones, please try to relax enough to breathe now, if you can," she said mildly and again lapsed into silence, her fingers beginning to sort out the puzzle of the taut muscles. Here was a challenge!

She soon forgot about the imagined troubles of Tucker Jones and warmed to her task. Supple fingers poked and probed the bunched muscles. The cool skin began to warm under her touch. The breathing became more regular and the hands relaxed. His eyes were closed, but not clenched as they had been. Her fingers were gentle, then firm. At times she called her palms, thumbs or knuckles into play and slowly it felt as though he might be accepting her touch. She began to work upward until finally she reached his shoulders and encountered a tremendous mass of unsupple trapezius and sternocleidomastoid muscles. Slowing her hands, she began creating a new rhythm—softly, softly, convincing the knots under her fingers that she meant them no harm. Fingers wide, she swept the area with a circular motion. "See," her fingers whispered to the same corded muscles that had so appalled Dr. Beemers, "see, it's perfectly safe to relax a little." And slowly, bit by bit, there seemed to be a difference. Kathryn worked the points of his shoulders, the base of his neck, the base of his skull—would have like to follow the corded muscles right up onto his head—but a deal was a deal and after returning to the broad shoulders to ask the knots for just a little more release, she stopped and gently rubbed the excess oil on his back onto the towel she'd used to protect his trousers. These strokes were brisk and carried the air of finality. She then spread the towel on his back, placed both hands firmly on it and spoke for the first time. "Take a few minutes to lie there. I've loosened your muscles a bit. Give them a chance to get used to this new state of affairs. Now, I'll be leaving you to go and change a sprinkler." She permitted herself a small satisfied smile at his nod and his deep, relaxed breathing.

Tucker heard the door open and shut softly as he lay on the padded table considering. *I certainly tolerated this better than I expected...except when she first put her hands on me...that was most disquieting. I wonder why? Why did it bother me so much? She's an odd person. No one I know calls trousers britches.* He found himself lying on the table feeling reluctant to move and gave himself a few more minutes. *It was good when she explained what she intended to do before she did it. It certainly made me feel more at ease…but then she's that sort. I believe, she would be a comfortable person to be around.* His thoughts drifted until he sighed deeply, and forced himself to move from the table.

Slipping into his shirt, Tucker recalled his plan to blank his mind while on the table under the woman's touch. It had been impossible. Images from his past kept up a kaleidoscope of images. Purposefully, he had allowed the image of Dr. Van Castle to remain but he had floated away to be replaced by one of Mr. Tyler. In his mind, they were sad and he was sad. He suddenly felt as though he might burst into tears. He shook his head with resolution. *What I need to do is go home and do what Mr. Tyler told him to do…think about things.* He put on his suit coat, lost in thought, barely registering the fluidity of his muscles.

Kathryn returned carrying a glass of apple juice. She smiled and handed it to him. "I've another client waiting, but I thought you might like to sit and sip this in the little garden off the waiting room."

Tucker was touched. It seemed an incredible act of kindness. He nodded his thanks, picked up his jacket and walked through the door into soft afternoon sunshine, glass in hand. He knew he was not himself, but he was not prepared for his reaction to Kathryn's creation.

Her garden was a square courtyard, bordered by a tall, gray, weathered, wooden fence. Old bricks laid a welcoming walkway to a small table and three chairs. Old fashioned nasturtiums and lobelia combined to make an undisciplined riot of orange, gold and violet borders, flanked by phlox, stocks, day lilies and bellflowers. Spent daffodil and tulip spikes peeked out here and there. Pink roses climbed the fence in some places, ivy and deep purple clematis in others. A soft spray of water drenched tiny violet-like flowers under the deep, dusky purple of the smoke tree in the corner. He remembered then that Kathryn said she had to come out and move a sprinkler. Tucker let his gaze rove, amazed at his ability to recall each flower name.

He walked slowly toward the table, the juice glass wrapped in his long fingers, completely forgotten. The garden seemed to reach out and draw him forward. He sank into one of the old wooden chairs and allowed the color and odors to soak in and wash over him. Thoughts he had not allowed himelf to have; memories he had sworn to forget; began to seep into his mind. Images of other sun-drenched summer days with himself as a laughing boy helping a solemn, kindly man, their backs warmed by the sun, as they planted borders of flowers much like these, in the endless beds of his parents' estate would not be denied.

His eyes softened and a smile ghosted on his face. There in his mind was a cheerful woman with the camera— begging for smiles and poses, hugging them both, bringing them warm scones and cold lemonade. The loving images, he realized then, had been with him while he was on the massage table, but he had blocked them as he had always done, allowing only Dr. Van Castle and Mr. Tyler to surface in his conscious thought. *But not here, not in this garden!*

Here, the other two would not be blocked. He closed his eyes and tolerated the pain as he continued to allow what was now a flood of memories to bombard him. For some reason, here in this small garden, he felt strong enough to allow the memories. He found he could even think their names, see their faces. "Hello, Ethan. Hello, Mary." He whispered the names softly, eyes closed, allowing their features to become sharper, more defined, until they seemed to be in the garden with him; the images so real he could almost feel Ethan's work-roughened hand ruffling his hair.

Time passed unnoticed, the memories of the O'Sheas strong upon him until a door slammed suddenly from somewhere within the house. His eyes jerked open and he looked wildly around before sinking back into his chair and picking up his juice. The pain in his chest was gone and he felt deeply at peace, just as Tobin Van Castle told him he would, all those years ago.

Slowly, Tucker allowed his eyes to rove the garden once more, gathering minute details, storing them away. Then he reached into his inner coat pocket for his checkbook and pen. After he wrote Kathryn's check, he turned it over and in his careful hand, wrote: Thank you. I'll call for another appointment. He placed the check under his empty glass and with a deep sigh, rose to his feet and walked from the garden without glancing back.

Chapter Six

Tucker's tremendous control of thought and emotion served him well as he threaded his way home from Kathryn's through heavy commuter traffic. He kept both hands firmly on the wheel, squinted to keep his concentration and felt as though he had accomplished something very difficult when he turned into the underground parking of the condominium building, nosed into his parking space and turned off the key.

"Not yet. Not yet," he said softly to himself. He climbed from the Aston and walked to the elevator doors. *Not yet.* His mind continued its mantra as he was whisked upward. Tucker could not remember wanting to be home as much as he did now; wanted to be behind closed doors with the world shut out.

With a sense of great relief, he walked into his living room, set down his attaché case, walked directly to his stereo and selected Vivaldi's *Four Seasons CD for his player.* As the lilting string section introduced the season of spring, Tucker poured himself an uncharacteristic scotch, his boss's drink, and sank into his stylishly sculpted, beige, leather chair. *Now…he thought, now you can think.*

He took a sip of scotch and tried to think about his day, but instead found himself thinking again about the "mind-banished" Dr. Van Castle and the time they had spent together when he was a teenager. He was surprised that the remembering caused so little agitation and only the remnants of anger. He clearly remembered the time when just hearing the word psychiatrist brought on feeling of being horribly trapped and exposed. Now, his gift of auditory memory allowed him to recall so much of what they had talked about that he could replay their conversations almost as if they had been recorded. *'Hopefully, in time, you will come to trust me. Part of this trust will come from judging my actions. When you are absolutely certain that I have your best interests at*

65

heart, our working relationship will begin.' Tucker closed his eyes and thought. *Those words were so important to me then, and I suspect they are important to me now.* He sat up and put his scotch on the side table, thinking about what Mr. Tyler had said about him not trusting anyone and then cradled his head in his hands, reviewing, thinking, considering…

Looking objectively at himself, Tucker knew Mr. Tyler's words to be true. But he wasn't entirely convinced that it was all bad, either. *For example, I did trust Dr. Van Castle completely and look what happened. Out of the blue, he tells me I'm about to be terminated.* He took a gulp of scotch, feeling the old anger rekindle. *That man didn't have a clue how much I needed him! He allowed himself to be duped by a mere boy and discontinued the visits that were my life thread of support…gave me a book instead of friendship.*

Tucker shook his head sadly. What he had learned, what Dr. Van Castle's real gift had been, was teaching him what he already suspected. *People can't really hurt you if you don't let yourself get close enough to let it happen.* He let out a low, sad sigh. *But, Tucker, admit it; not trusting seems to have brought on its own set of problems.* He listened quietly to the music for a long moment and then stood, shaking his head as if to clear his thoughts. It was past time for him to get to work on summarizing the oral debriefing and he still had not eaten.

He decided that eating would have to wait. The meeting had been complex and he needed to get his analysis and summary down while the events and the players were still fresh in his mind. But instead of turning on his computer, he pulled stationery from a drawer, addressed an envelope to Dr. Jeff Beemers and wrote a three line note that said simply:

> *I had a massage today. I believe it was helpful. Thank you.*
> *Afterwards, I thought of Ethan and Mary. I thought you would want to know.*

Tucker signed his name and looked at the words, Ethan and Mary, for a long time before he sealed the note.

Now why, Tucker wondered, *do I think Dr. Beemers would want to know I was thinking of Ethan and Mary?* He shrugged…and then he grinned. *That's two notes of thanks written today, if the one on the back of a check counts.* He couldn't quite put his finger on what pleased him about today's thank you notes and made them different. He often wrote thank you notes, had, in fact, personally gone to a stationery store, selected an expensive quality note paper and had envelopes tastefully embossed with his new address just for that purpose.

As he sat, sipping scotch, an odd thought came to him. *The difference being, I wanted to write those two notes. I wasn't being polite. I wasn't being dutiful…I was expressing what I was feeling…and I expect both Beemers and Van Castle would find that fact interesting.*

Two hours later, his stomach growling, the summary ready for a final edit, he headed for his kitchen. Luckily, his mother always made a little extra for him on Sunday. It was like having his own gourmet frozen food section. He simply had to open his freezer door, select the neatly wrapped container at the top of the stack and pop it into his microwave. While he waited and sipped his now watery scotch, he pulled a piece of paper out of a kitchen drawer and wrote in heavy black letters across the top:

THINGS I NEED TO THINK ABOUT

While he ate, he made his list:

1. People I care about
2. People I don't care about
3. Things I care about
4. Things I don't care about
5. Things I am good at
6. Things I am not good at
7. Ethan and Mary

He thought long and hard about the list as he tidied his kitchen, then snatched it from the table, crumpled it into a ball, slam dunked it into the waste basket by his desk and with a shrug, turned on his computer. Vivaldi had finished, it was time to get some serious work done. *Writing that list was a really stupid idea,* was his last thought before he began to edit.

The next morning, Tucker awoke to the realization that he had slept a bit better than usual. As he came fully awake he began to remember the events of the previous day and his first inclination was to block the thoughts; remembering made him very uncomfortable. He realized, since his back ordeal, it felt as though his neatly ordered world and neatly ordered mind were both failing him. He felt the compelling need to get himself back on track. *I wrote a list while dining last night, for God's sake!*

He lay, for a moment, fretting. Worry, like a sludge blanket, weighed him down. Then, like a small life raft, scenes from a sun-dappled garden and a massage woman with unruly, copper hair came into focus. He concentrated on the image and a smile twitched like a tic in the corner of his mouth. *What was it that Dr. Beemers said about how often I should really have a massage?*

Of course, Tucker, being Tucker, the words came clearly to mind. *He said, once a week is okay, but twice a week would be better and daily would best. This is Wednesday. Maybe I should call for a Friday appointment...*

Tucker rolled out of bed and began doing a series of exercises recommended by his physical therapist. As he rolled carefully down, vertebrae, by vertebrae until he touched his toes, he remembered that he'd had trouble concentrating on data in several sections of his summary while he was editing the evening before, so decided to stay home and work it out. He also wanted to do some poking around in his data file on past discussions of similar topics and do a search for current articles on acquisition and development of commercial buildings, funding sources, other countries involved, other firms involved, profit margins, and stability of political systems. These were areas already covered in yesterday's meeting, but still, he liked to verify facts.

At one o'clock he called Mr. Tyler to tell him he was transmitting the report. The call was unnecessary and Tucker knew it. Mr. Tyler was faithful about checking his electronic mail file for incoming data, especially that not available for retrieval by secretarial staff.

Even as he pushed the button to connect to Mr. Tyler's private line, Tucker was asking himself why—and realized with sudden insight that he wanted to hear warmth in the older man's voice; to know there was more than a computer link between them.

James Tyler had spent time, on and off, during the day, thinking about Tucker and was surprised when the call came. Immediately, his mind cataloged the new behavior. Gravely, he thanked Tucker for the information and for the call. There was a long pause on the phone and he could hear Tucker clearing his throat. "By the way, sir, I've been thinking about our conversation..." Another long pause while Mr. Tyler waited patiently. "Well, sir, I mean...what I want to say...is that our relationship means a lot to me, so I tried to make a list of things to think about but...ah, it's proving difficult, sir."

Mr. Tyler sat back in his chair. He found himself struggling to find the words to respond. Today, as he'd been thinking about Tucker, he'd convinced himself that adjusting his personal feelings about Tucker to meet what he now thought to be the true nature of the young man was his only course of action if he was to continue to benefit from Tucker's unique set of skills. Last night, he had in fact, said to his wife, "Maybe we've been seeing too much of Tucker socially. Let's get this relationship back onto a more professional level." She had given him a long look, but had said nothing.

Now, he identified in Tucker's voice the one quality that had been missing...confusion. The boy, for the first time in his memory was uncertain. *Well, well,* Mr. Tyler thought to himself with surprise, *I was able to rattle his cage after all.*

"Tucker..." he said, pausing, willing his voice to stay neutral, but failing, "aw, hell, son," he blurted, "the last thing you need is a list! You've got it all within you, boy. You need to think about only one thing: who or what has made you so distrustful. Once you get that figured out, then you can start to deal with it."

The long pause at the other end of the line made the old man nervous, but he had long ago learned the value of silence and allowed his message to lie between them quietly. Finally, there came a worried, "Thank you sir. I will, sir," and the connection was broken.

At their respective desks, the two men sat staring at their telephones for long minutes, unaccustomed emotions flooding them both.

It took Mr. Tyler only a few minutes to come to grips with his; sorrow for Tucker and absolute disgust with himself. He had made the lad into some sort of super hero; someone who would lead his company onward and upward, once he, "the king," had decided to turn over the reins and retire. When he discovered the flaw in the image of Tucker he'd created, he had taken it personally, felt betrayed, felt absolutely justified and quite virtuous when he'd dressed the boy down. Now, he sat in his silent office, hands flat on his desk, wallowing in his own feelings of quilt, ruminating over the phone call. He'd been pretty direct...but he had said exactly what he'd wanted to say...and Tucker had actually thanked him. Then Tucker's words came to him. If he remembered correctly, Tucker had said how much their relationship meant to him.

"By God!" He sat up straight, smiling hugely. That phone call hadn't really been about the report; the report was only the excuse for the call. The crux of that phone call was Tucker letting him know, as best he could, that he, James Whipple Tyler III, was important in his life. The old man grinned and reached for the phone.

"Midge, dear," he rumbled into her ear, "I don't know what we've got going this weekend, but do try to include Tucker, won't you?"

On her end of the line, Midge's eyes widened and she looked at the telephone receiver in surprise. It was certainly not like her husband to be capricious. The firm message last night had been to reduce social contact with Tucker. Now, it seemed something must be planned for the weekend. "Certainly, dear! Remember, Dawn will be here as well; so we might do something with the boat."

Dawn, the daughter of Barbara, her best friend from college days, had come east to visit Tufts University. She was staying with them, but currently had gone to Boston to meet with faculty there and was including a sightseeing trip up the Eastern Shore on Friday, before returning to stay with them for the weekend. Midge hadn't really made any

70

real plans, suspecting the girl would want to spend her remaining time with them on Long Island Sound, indulging in her passion for sailing.

She hung up the phone and stood staring at the instrument, realizing she was feeling awash with relief. Their phone calls to one another were often like this, short, crisp and businesslike. She knew he'd fill her in with details about his change of heart over cocktails this evening. It was one of their married rituals she liked best, the cocktail hour. Not for the liquor but for the communication. It was something they had started as newlyweds that had developed into a nightly occurrence. It was then they shared their day's events with each other, laying out problems, strategies, solutions—just talking, gossiping, keeping in touch with each other. "Talktails," she'd started calling them when yet his bride. She was never bored with what went on at Zitec and he never seemed bored by her stories of volunteer work and household management. They were a team—a flying wedge of two and the hour they spent together each evening had been a cementing factor in their marriage.

Before the advent of Tucker, her husband had often bemoaned the fact that his board meetings didn't seem to run smoothly. "Off track," was his term to describe how it felt. These last three years, she'd not heard that refrain. She'd heard instead, "Tucker said this"…and, "Tucker thinks that…" Midge took a deep breath and felt her spirits rise. She had been so very disappointed that Tucker had not called James to help him when he was having those terrible muscle spasms and she agreed with James that he didn't seem to trust enough to allow them to see him vulnerable and needing help. But, after thinking things through, she found herself feeling even more "motherly" towards him. So, she was greatly relieved to think that a slender thread seemed to have been thrown across the breech between her husband and the gentle-eyed young man.

Absentmindedly, she poured herself a cup of coffee from the carafe on the dining room sideboard and wandered about the house, touching this, straightening that, plumping pillows and picking up last evening's newspaper that was still littering the area around her

71

husband's chair. They were small tasks that Clarice, her housekeeper, could easily have done, but somehow they helped her think. Robot-like, she went about setting small things to right, her mind furiously planning. The weather was so glorious, a weekend on the motorsailer seemed a natural and she was pretty sure it was exactly what Dawn would want to do.

Midge began sifting through friends, wondering who might be available on such short notice. *It will have to be a mostly Friday/Saturday event as Tucker will want to spend his Sunday evening with his parents.* Her hand stilled on the cushion she was plumping as her mind went off in a new direction.

She had never met Tucker's parents, but had friends who knew them socially. They were described variously as, intellectual, aloof, unfailingly correct and always gracious in their behavior. Her friend, Althea, in trying to describe Tucker's mother said that the only true animation she had ever witnessed from the woman came over hors d'oeuvres and dinner at the Bartelsons. The story, as she recalled Althea's telling of it, brought a twinkle to Midge's eyes.

They had been lunching together, having just finished a hard morning's work cataloging donated items for the forthcoming, "Save Our Spaces," auction. It was a favorite cause for both of them. The considerable money generated by the S.O.S. auction and other fund raising events, went straight into an interest bearing account to buy suitable land in New Haven to be reserved for the development of pocket parks. Midge, Althea, and a third friend, Emory, had remained active and invested in the mission for more than 25 years, becoming lifelong friends in the process.

On that particular day, as Althea slipped into her storytelling mode and began her tale about the Joneses, Midge remembered that she had been especially interested. The mystery of Tucker Jones had already captured her and she hoped to have some light shed on what made the young man such an enigma.

It seemed the Bartelsons had thrown one of their famous, intimate dinner parties for a mere 20 people to introduce their new chef, fresh from studying in France.

Tucker's parents were two of the 20. When Althea had called to R.S.V.P., Sue Bartelson had told her the Joneses too, had accepted. The capable hostess had been both surprised and delighted that the reclusive couple was coming.

When Mrs. Jones walked through the door the night of the dinner, Althea said she knew immediately that something was up. There was a spring in her step and a sparkle in her eyes, a far departure from her usual seemingly shy, demure demeanor. "Now, don't get me wrong, Midge." Althea had leaned forward earnestly over her cup of tea. "Margaret Jones is a lovely person, a wonderful listener…she's just not…well, not what you'd call dynamic…or vivacious. But, that night, something about her was really different. It was as though the dinner party was to be a grand treasure hunt…and she had the secret map!"

Althea warmed to her story. "And there was something else, Midge. I'd seen her at other parties where she skipped hor d'oeuvres entirely and simply picked at her dinner…and that was simply not the case. I mean, she seemed to position herself to be in just the right spot to take the first canapé out of the kitchen. Then she would take little nibbles, sniffing, chewing, nodding or shaking her head—totally absorbed, like a food tasting judge at a county fair. She did the same thing at dinner. It was hard not to stare, once I'd noticed. And I don't think I'm the only one who did."

Althea paused dramatically, took a sip of tea and said, with laughter in her voice, "Well, when the facts came out, the young woman who passed herself off to the employment agency as having studied at Cordon Bleu in France had actually been in the Joneses' employ for several years—as a domestic! She'd learned to cook, first by watching Margaret and then trying out the recipes on her husband who was also employed by them."

"By the way," Althea informed Midge, "everything you've ever heard about Margaret's cooking is absolutely true. I, personally, know of no one who passes up those infrequent invitations to one of her dinner parties."

Midge leaned back, enjoying both the story and Althea's enjoyment of the telling. She smiled, "This is getting to be a very good story, Althea."

73

Althea returned her smile and continued. "So, evidently, after a time, this young woman started asking Margaret questions, which she was quite happy to answer. Then, one day, when Margaret came into the kitchen at an unexpected hour, there sat this woman copying her recipes like crazy! In most households, she would have been fired on the spot. In the Joneses' household, that was not the case. Margaret was actually flattered and evidently took her on as a student, impressed by how much she had learned just by watching and asking questions."

Midge let her eyebrows arch in surprise, but kept very quiet. She did not want to distract Althea from the conclusion of her story. Picturing Margaret Jones teaching an employee the art of gourmet cooking caused her to look at the woman in a slightly different light. She tucked the thought away to digest later and found herself wondering if Tucker had been taught to cook.

Althea sighed, "I forgot to tell you that this couple was working for the Joneses only until they finished college. After graduation, they left the Joneses' employment. At that time the woman decided what she really wanted to do, instead of pursuing a job in her field, was to become a chef."

Althea paused and took another sip of tea, much like a speaker standing behind a lectern might do, both to wet her throat and to build suspense. Then she nodded, as if to herself and said, "She knew she wasn't likely to gain employment without credentials from some prestigious school of culinary art, so she faked it; wrote herself glowing letters of recommendation, one of them supposedly from Margaret, and took them to an employment agency. In this day and age, she probably wouldn't have gotten away with it, except for the fact that Sue Bartelson called the agency on the very same day, desperate for a chef to cook for an already arranged dinner party. The employment agency said they had a seemingly suitable candidate, but had not had time to check references, since many of them came from France."

"But, Althea, what she did was forgery!" Midge found herself a bit shocked.

"Well, yes…but you know how persuasive Sue can be! She implored the agency to let her give the woman a try...and of course, hoping for a whopping commission, they agreed."

Althea spread her hands, smoothing the linen tablecloth, smiling in remembrance. "The party was such a success that the Bartelsons hired the woman on the spot and scheduled a second party—announcing it as an introduction to their new chef...Dana Davis. It was to this party Margaret and Evan, along with the rest of us had been invited."

Althea drew her story to a close. "You see, Margaret knew about the subterfuge because the employment agency had already called her to check the reference letter she had supposedly written."

Althea smiled wryly. "It must have been an odd conversation, with HER trying to talk about the woman's skills as a domestic and THEIR wanting to know about her ability to cook. It was only after she hung up the phone that she put the two together and came up with the probable fact that Dana Davis was seeking employment as a chef and had forged her signature on a letter of recommendation Imagine her surprise when that invitation came. By the time the party rolled around she had decided that she wouldn't squeal. I mean, after all, she knew the woman could cook! But unfortunately, the employment agency was thorough in their reference check and within several weeks, had concluded that Dana Davis was a fraud. They called Sue, most apologetically. Sue confronted her new cook who immediately burst into tears and admitted the whole thing. Then, Sue called Margaret, who confirmed the story. When Sue asked her why on earth she had kept the knowledge to herself once she had received the dinner party invitation, Margaret acknowledged it was her own vanity: a certainty she could teach someone with Dana's talent to cook far better than any cooking school 'And frankly,' Margaret said to Sue, 'after our wonderful evening, I feel quite vindicated. Haven't the two parties gotten rave reviews? Isn't Dana far more reliable than your last cook who had to be let go for excessive tippling?'"

Althea threw back her head and laughed. "Sue said Margaret was quite adamant and firm in her conviction that it was up to the employment agency to do their homework. In her mind, it was simply her job to be sure Dana passed muster and…she added that she had worked very hard at the party to determine just that fact. 'After all,' she said to Sue, 'do you want an excellent chef or one whose only qualification was that of studying at Cordon Bleu?'"

Midge was thoroughly entertained by the story. "And what was Sue's response?"

Althea grinned. "Well, she wasn't entirely convinced, so then Margaret somewhat curtly reminded her that many go to learn to cook properly, a lesser number go to learn to create, but only a handful actually succeeds in either. Her logic was so impeccable that when Sue related the conversation to her husband after a particularly delicious dinner, he banged his hand flat on the table and absolutely roared with laughter. 'By God, whoever would have guessed that mouse-like Margaret Jones was a pragmatist? Call the employment agency,' he boomed. 'Give them their full commission—keep Dana, but count your silverware!'"

"Sue said it had been his final word on the subject and she was really quite relieved not to have to let the woman go. Besides, she had called Margaret again and was reassured that 'other than copying my recipes and faking her credentials, the woman appears quite above board!'"

At the end of her long reminiscence with Althea's story, Midge found herself still holding onto a pillow in her living room. She wondered if Evan Jones had noticed his wife's odd behavior at Sue's dinner party. Althea had told her that the man absolutely doted on his wife and seemed very proud of Tucker. She had also said they seemed to be an extremely well-informed couple.

Giving a sigh, she thought, *The Joneses seem to be the perfect family.* Still, there was something puzzling about Tucker, and traditionalist that she was, she guessed it had something to do with his upbringing. Suddenly, she found herself wanting to meet the elder Joneses very much…something she and her husband had decided against, not quite knowing what it would mean to become friends with the parents of an employee. *Perhaps I should revisit that decision with James.*

She gave the pillow a final thump, thinking of Tucker. She really liked the young man and she thought the feeling was returned. Of course, after what James had said, she wasn't certain Tucker had real feelings. *But then,* she thought to herself, *if he doesn't have feelings, why is it that he is the one to always volunteer an anonymous donation when I go looking for money to support one of my causes...especially those having to do with children?*

"Remember the condition, Mrs. T. This is just between us," he always reminded her as he handed over the check.

Always, she winked and said solemnly, "Absolutely...just between us." And she'd kept her word. Even her husband was in the dark regarding Tucker's philanthropy. She smiled to herself. *There's a mystery about this boy that needs unraveling, and I'm just the one to do it!*

Meanwhile, the object of her thinking still sat hunched by his phone, staring bleakly at its sleek, high tech lines as though it might at least give him some answers—if only he could think of the questions. He hadn't meant to have that last part of the conversation with his boss. Somehow, the words had just slipped out, something he never allowed words to do. But, he could hear the sincerity and caring in the older man's tone and for some reason, felt a nameless anxiety come over him. Nervous fingers drummed a staccato rhythm on his desk while he tried to calm the growing agitation. Thoughts continued to slam into each other without logic or order and he wondered for a moment if he were going to "lose it."

"NO!" he said loudly, shattering the stillness of his living room. "NO! THIS WON'T DO!" He jumped to his feet. *I have to get out of here!* He stood, frozen in the ready position, like a boxer waiting for the instruction from his coach as to where he should go. Suddenly, like a whisper in his ear, the answer came from somewhere deep inside: *To the garden...you need to go to the garden.* The thought washed over him and he took a deep breath and then another as his thoughts quieted. *Yes! That is exactly what I need to do. I need to go and sit quietly in Kathryn McCall's garden to figure out what just happened.*

He picked up the phone. Before the dialing could catch up with his rapid pushing of buttons, he slammed the receiver down. *What is she going to think? One massage doesn't give me carte blanche to her garden. She'll think I'm presumptuous or worse yet, she'll think I've come unhinged.* Tucker sagged back into his chair, his mind starting to jumble once more, when Dr. Van Castle's clear, boyish voice cut through his mounting panic. "Tucker, learn to ask for what you want. Decide if the motive for wanting is okay. Then, take a minute to rehearse the request in your mind. Write it down if you want to. Do whatever you need to do so that you have confidence that your request will be clearly received."

"All right! All right!" Tucker said into the silent room, the conviction in his voice growing. "Here, Dr. Van Castle, is what I want. I want to go to the garden because there is something very restful there; something that makes me feel relaxed and peaceful. I want that feeling again. I usually get that feeling from running, but I can't do that right now so, even if I have to schedule another massage, I want to go."

Tucker found he was smiling slightly, the picture of the short, vital man clear in his mind. He ducked his head and admitted. "The truth is, I wouldn't mind having another massage, Doctor. What do you make of that?"

He sat back in his chair, his smile stretching to a grin at his own antics. He never talked aloud to himself. Not ever! He was glad there was no one to hear him now. He tried to think what it was about the back massage he enjoyed but found himself thinking instead of the color of Kathryn McCall's unruly hair. The color seemed to defy description. It wasn't red. It wasn't brown. Rust came to mind, but the things that he had seen that were rusty couldn't begin to compare with hair that had glints of gold and copper. *Actually, it reminds me of something. I wonder what?*

He thought a little longer over this seemingly important, but unsolved problem of assigning a name to Kathryn's hair color before picking up the receiver. After three rings, he heard the recording on the answering machine. "Hello. You have reached the answering machine of Kathryn McCall, massage therapist. I am sorry not to be able to take your call, but please leave your name, number and message after the tone. I will get back to you as soon as I can. Thank you."

Tucker was immensely relieved. He should have remembered that she had an answering machine taking her calls. He had gotten it when he called the first time. It was clear to him now that she couldn't allow a telephone call to interrupt a massage.

When the familiar beep came, he was ready with his message. It was much easier for him to make the request to a machine and it would also give her time to think about it...and turn his loony request down if she chose. "Miss. McCall," he said crisply into the receiver, and then wondered if she really was a "Miss," "this is Tucker Jones at 783-8739. I am calling for two reasons: The first is to schedule another back massage and the second is to thank you for the use of your garden and..." He paused, swallowed audibly and continued. "I wonder if I might come and simply sit in it, your garden, I mean...on occasion. I, ah, found it very soothing. Thank you."

Tucker realized that his crisp tone had deteriorated a bit as he talked, but strangely, he didn't seem to mind. The dice had been rolled. It was out of his hands. The feeling was familiar...similar to how he felt upon accomplishment of one of Dr. Van Castle's many "assignments." Getting up from his chair, he began pacing about the living room. *What does it mean, that after all these years I am starting to think about Dr. Van Castle?*

Briefly, he thought about calling the doctor to reestablish contact and found that the thought was very agitating and consciously changed his focus by noticing that the cleaning service had neglected to return his magazines and objets d'art to their precise spots. He straightened the magazines, carefully aligning their corners to those of the end table. He finger combed the fringe of the beige and ivory Persian carpet, squared the three large, free-form sculptures on the book case precisely as he liked them and aligned the toast-brown throw pillows on the couch with military precision. Then he stepped back and looked around the room, pleased with what he saw.

The burnished ebony glow of the wood in the baby grand piano added just the touch of richness the area required. He walked to it and sat down. He had not allowed himself to play other than pop and show tunes for some time. His fingers drifted over the keys, remembering days when he had played, Bach, Beethoven, Mozart and, of course, Vivaldi, for hours, blocking out all thoughts, concentrating hard enough to block the pain that the music itself carried out the open windows of parent's home.

Tucker sighed, suddenly exhausted by the day's events. He'd call to check in with his parents pretty soon, but for now, he would just relax on the couch. The computer could wait a bit. He selected a CD placed it in the player, stretched out and closed his eyes to the soothing strains of Beethoven's Moonlight Sonata.

Chapter Seven

Kathryn scheduled massages with 20 minutes between clients. That way, even on a day when she was booked straight through, as she often was, she had time to change the massage table and answer the calls left on her answering machine, tend to household tasks, talk with her daughter, and a myriad of details that demanded her attention daily.

This day, she went to the front of the house and pulled the hose over to drip under the rose bush by her front door and then took her calls, listening to Tucker's voice with some surprise. *Why on earth does that up-tight man want to come and sit in my garden?*

She nibbled her lower lip and began tucking escaped strands of hair back into her braid, a sure sign she was thinking hard. *He's deceptive, that one. He can look relaxed, even with that finishing school posture and he moves like a dancer, all fluid-like and graceful... but, those back muscles are telling a different story. It's like he's two people—one who likes to sit in my garden and leaves his thanks on the back of a very generous check—the other as stiff and tactilely defensive as ever I've seen.*

Kathryn remembered the stony ridges under the flesh of his back. They were a challenge to her skill, and she did love a good challenge. She checked her book and sighed as she penciled his name in the Friday afternoon opening she'd hoped no one would want. An early start to her weekend would have been welcomed, especially since the weatherman had promised a continuation of the sunny weather. She paused, keeping track of her fast disappearing time and still continued poking at her braid, trying to decide whether to put him off until Monday and whether or not to give him permission to use her garden. *It's such a strange request.* Kathryn rewound the tape and listened again, looking for clues.

The voice started out sounding very crisp and businesslike. That is how she remembered him; crisp, sure of himself and very uptight! She rewound the tape and listened again. No clues...except perhaps his voice grew less self-assured when he made the request to use the garden. *This is so strange,* she thought again. *He's obviously a well-heeled man. Surely, he knows a good many people with gardens much bigger and more finely kept than mine. Surely, if he wanted his own garden, he could have it.* She felt herself becoming a bit annoyed until she remembered that he had used the word, her very word, no, actually, her mother's word to describe her little patch of grass and flowers...garden. That was unusual. Most people would have called it a 'yard.' *Perhaps,* she thought reflectively, *it is reminding him of something or someone special. Besides,* she chided herself, *why are you comparing your garden so unfavorably to grander ones? Bigger doesn't necessarily mean better. You've worked hard on that space, Kate!* She smiled, thinking back to the five years it had taken her to turn the space from dirt and weeds to what it had become—a feast of color and texture. She enjoyed taking a glass of something out to just sit and be still when she found a moment.

Kathryn stopped poking at her hair, suddenly feeling a bit small and mean. *For heaven's sake,* she thought, putting hands to square hips, *the man said he found my garden soothing. That's a compliment! Besides,* she thought, *the words ring true. I, myself, find it soothing. If it gives me a sense of well-being, why not Tucker Jones? What person could be so selfish that they wouldn't share?* She reached for the phone. "Mr. Jones," she said without preamble, when he picked up the phone and said a sleepy hello. "this is Kathryn McCall." She tried to match the crisp professionalism she'd heard from him on her answering machine. "I can schedule you in at 3:20 Friday afternoon or on Monday at either 11:20 or 3:20."

Tucker cradled his receiver, trying to gather his thoughts. Her tone threw him. It was so unlike the voice he remembered. *I've probably offended her by asking to use the garden.*

"Mr. Jones?" The crisp voice inquired into the silence.

"Oh, yes, sorry, Miss McCall, sorry. I was just checking my calendar," he fibbed. "Please schedule me for both 3:20 appointments." Tucker looked at the mouthpiece of his phone with amazement. *Now, where did that decision come from?*

"Fine," she said, "I'll schedule you in. And Mr. Jones, of course you may use the garden if it gives you pleasure."

Her voice warmed when she spoke of the garden and Tucker felt an unidentifiable pang as the lilt returned to her voice. It felt as though he had been given a gift.

He grinned hugely into the phone. "You're quite certain you don't mind? he asked. "I mean it wouldn't be an inconvenience to you or your family, would it?"

"Oh, no," she said firmly, "I wouldn't think so." She seemed to be thinking out loud. "My daughter, Allison, is soon to be leaving to visit her father and Jon Bon certainly isn't going to mind an occasional visit, so help yourself. If it does become an inconvenience, you can count on me to let you know."

"Wonderful! Thank you so much, Miss McCall. I might even be over this afternoon. I really cannot thank you enough and I WILL count on you to let me know if I make a nuisance of myself. This really means a great deal to me."

Kathryn found herself laughing at his rush of sentences. "You're quite welcome, Mr. Jones. See you Friday at 3:20. Goodbye, Mr. Jones." His words and the genuine enthusiasm caused Kathryn to stand thoughtfully by the phone for a few seconds, ignoring the tinkling bell that signaled someone in the waiting room. *A strange and complex man, that one,* she thought again. *I hope I don't regret sharing the garden with him.*

At the other end of the telephone line, Tucker sat quietly by his phone, his thoughts skipping and bumping all over each other. For once, he didn't mind. *She's going to let me use the garden. I could go over there right now if I wanted to do so. I signed up for two more massages. Wonder why I did that? I was wrong to have called her Miss. She's been married. Maybe she remarried. Who knows? She probably has an ex-husband, if her daughter is going to visit him. Wonder why her son isn't going too? Jon Bon, now that is an unusual name for a child, but a nice name. Had she stressed the word 'occasionally,' when she'd said he could visit the garden?* He could, of course, even in his newly wakened state, recall the entire conversation, including all the nuances. *No, I don't think so. It seemed strictly straightforward; professional…with only one lilt.*

The lilting tone had come when Kathryn gave him permission to visit the garden. His mouth, of its own volition kept turning up on the corners and one random thought captured the notion that he was actually smiling, grinning really. His thinking stilled long enough for him to wonder how long it had been since he'd felt like his smile came from within instead of being the polite, accepted response to a social situation.

Tucker's thoughts rushed on. He had the mad thought to call Dr. Beemers and tell him he'd scheduled two more massages. He found himself grinning again. *He'll probably feel faint!* As he reached for the phone, he felt it ring at his touch. For a moment, it didn't seem possible that someone could be calling him. He let the phone ring a second and third time, taking a deep breath and slowing his thinking. It was Midge Tyler.

"Hello, Tucker," she said in her usual cheerful voice. "I'm so glad I caught you at home. Do you have a moment to talk, or are you in the middle of some project for Zitec?"

"Hello Mrs. T," he responded, falling naturally into his polite and affable mode—which in this case was easy to do. "You know I am never too busy to talk to you!"

She laughed and he smiled into the phone. He really liked this unassuming, sharp as a tack, bit of a woman with her tousled cap of gray curls and her piercing, clear, blue-gray eyes. It always felt to him as though she were soul reading and finding something worthwhile when they conversed. He often wondered if everyone felt that way around her. "Tucker, I do love it when you flatter me. Listen, dear. James tells me that your back is much better and this weather is simply too nice for a body to be hunched over a computer all weekend and so I'm proffering a rescue."

He chuckled. "Well," he said, somewhat wryly, "if ever a body needed some rescuing, it would be Tucker Jones'. What did you have in mind for him?"

She laughed again, her genuine fondness for Tucker warming her words. "Oh, you know us. It won't be anything fancy—bring boating clothes and we'll think of something to do on the water. In fact, if you're not otherwise engaged, come out Friday evening—I haven't yet checked the tides and that would give us some latitude in case we needed an early morning get away."

"That sounds just right!" he said, meaning every word. "And you, dear lady, are superior to my computer under any circumstances. Thank you very much for thinking of me. I do have an appointment in Mitford that doesn't end until about 5:00 on Friday—would 7:00 be too late to arrive?"

There was a slight pause, then she said, "No-o-o, but in that case, you'd best come dressed for dinner."

A bell went off in Tucker's head. "Come dressed for dinner" meant a dinner party—which meant Midge Tyler had probably found yet another suitable daughter among her circle of friends.

"Mrs. Tyler," he teased, "Are you trying to fix me up again?"

"Why, Tucker Jones, whatever do you mean?" She feigned a tone of injured innocence.

"You know what I mean," he chided sternly. "The last three years I've met more attractive, eligible young women at your home than most men meet in a lifetime. Convince me that it has all been pure coincidence!"

"Why, dear, you've caught me nearly speechless with surprise." A bubble of silver laughter crept into her voice. "And all this time, I didn't think you'd even noticed...so I stopped. Did you notice that too?"

"Mrs. Tyler," Tucker said fondly, "you are indeed a work of art! What is the name of this one?"

"Dawn...Dawn Simpson, and she's darling. I promise. But, Tucker, this IS simply a coincidence. She's our houseguest."

"Don," quipped Tucker, ignoring her protest of innocence, "is rather a masculine name. Does she live up to it?"

"No, silly! She's D-A-W-N, you know, like a sunrise. It's a proper California name for a beautiful California girl. Now, goodbye dear. Don't ask me any more questions. I want you to be surprised. See you on Friday. Do try to look nice," she said sweetly before cradling the phone.

Midge was smiling at her jibe as she cradled the phone. *As if that young man ever looks the least bit less than perfect,* she thought. *How do these things find their way out of my mouth?* She turned, still thinking, and hurried towards the kitchen to find Charlie and fill him in on the weekend plans. *So, Tucker did notice my attempts at match making after all.*

Midge had often wondered as he had never asked a single one of her young friends out on a date. For a while, it hurt her feelings, but then she had briefly assumed that he was already in a relationship—but since he was almost always free when she called to suggest that he come for a weekend, it became evident that he was not. Besides, several of the young women, taking advantage of the liberated generation to which they belonged, had called to invite him out. As far as she knew, he'd generally accepted the invitations and had proved to be a most charming companion, according to the girls' mothers.

A while ago, she'd decided he was probably gay and as an experiment, had invited a very handsome homosexual young interior designer named Alex Adrian to one of her parties and then watched carefully for any chemistry. There was none. There were no secret glances, private exchanges or protracted conversations of any sort. In fact, Althea told her that Adrian, as he chose to be called, stopped right in the middle of a serious discussion about the merits of Oriental versus Persian carpets with two other women and herself. He had been distracted by Tucker's walking past. According to Althea, Adrian had muttered rather to himself, but loud enough for the group to hear, "What a waste!" before continuing the conversation of the importance of knot count, dyes, quality of yarn, and detailing just why he felt a hand-loomed carpet was really worth the price.

Suddenly, Midge felt her face flush. *I wonder if Tucker knew what I was up to. He might have, since he knew about the "fix ups" with all the young women.* She sighed and shrugged her shoulders. *Oh well, obviously he hasn't held it against me. Besides, I've entirely given up on finding Tucker a girlfriend.* Then, she thought of Dawn and felt the stirring of her old matchmaking tendencies. That this weekend's houseguest was a gorgeous, natural blonde from Santa Barbara, California, the daughter of one of her dearest friends, was merely a coincidence.

After all, if James hadn't called and asked me to invite Tucker for the weekend, they might never have met. The fact that Dawn is considering Tufts University for her graduate work and we just happen to live in New Haven and can be of assistance to her has not one thing to do with Tucker. Not one!

Earlier, Dawn had called to report that she was having a wonderful time and that they could expect her on Friday afternoon. She had seemed quite taken with the professors in the psychology department at Tufts.

Midge ran distracted fingers through her curls. Dawn was going to be a bit surprised that a party had been arranged since her call. Then she found herself smiling and admitting to herself that it seemed somewhat providential that the timing of her visit was so perfect, that she was such a wonderful young woman...and that James had called to tell her to invite Tucker for the weekend.

Remembering her first impression of the girl when she gathered her from the airport, she couldn't wait to see Tucker's face when he was introduced. *If good carriage, a lovely, lithe figure and wonderfully warm brown eyes count, Tucker is going to be impressed.*

That her friend's daughter had been well-schooled and lovingly raised soon became evident on their ride home. However, it was also apparent that Dawn was less formal in her manner, more spontaneous and enthusiastic in her responses than young women raised and schooled in the east and that, Midge admitted to herself, took a bit of getting used to.

James had been immediately charmed by her self-confidence and spirit of adventure. Dawn had asked his advice about what to see and what to look for during her tour of the Eastern Shore. *Really,* Midge admitted, *I found it quite refreshing to be around her and so did James. What had he said? Oh yes! 'That girl looks like a suntan lotion advertisement, smiles like an angel and knows almost as much about sailing as I do.'*

As Midge walked into the kitchen, an Asian man, their chef of many years, immediately recognized the look on her face. "Oh, oh, party planning time, eh, Mam? Charlie see your face. Big party coming up quick, yes? You need help with plan, yes?" He paused and the smile left his face. "Mam, you need me to work this weekend?"

Midge, startled from her reverie, stopped in mid-stride at the entrance to the kitchen.

"Oh damn, Charlie! James just called me a bit ago and asked us to throw something together for this weekend, but I'd forgotten! This is your weekend off for the dog races." She paused, thinking hard, respecting his contractual rights. "Oh well, if you have time now, let's put our heads together and plan the food. Then, I'll just have it catered, or perhaps borrow Joseph from Althea."

A frown puckered Charlie's brow. After James had eaten in the restaurant where he worked in Shanghai, he asked to meet Charlie and had offered him a position in their home on the spot. Now, he and this woman had worked together seamlessly for thirty years. Their dinner parties were much admired and he had quite a lot of status among his peers. Immigrating to America was one of the smartest things he'd ever done. But, right now, he was trying to figure out if Midge was serious about asking another cook in to mess up his kitchen, or if she was just trying to work him around. He adored her, but he did hate to be manipulated. He thought fast. He was an avid fan of the greyhound races and had negotiated one weekend off a month, and every Sunday for the sole purpose of meeting his friends at the track and rooting on his favorite dogs. The other three weeks, on his Monday off, he studied the papers and tracked the dogs' records. He had his own system of figuring out which dog might win. It was a system based partly on Chinese astrology, partly on his careful research and partly on intuition. He was successful more often than not. He was also a wise and careful man. The money he won at the track went straight into the stock market. He decided to find out more about the weekend before making his final decision. He wouldn't give up his dogs easily.

Charlie squinted his eyes, sighing dramatically. "What does Captain have in his mind?"

"Oh, Charlie, I'm afraid it is going to be a lot of work...a light dinner Friday night...but then, it must be boat food."

Charlie sighed again, but this time it was not for effect. She had him and she probably knew it, even if she HAD been manipulating him. Mam knew the moment she said the word "boat" he would capitulate. Charlie liked his dogs, but his passion was the sleek 65-foot motorsailer with its powerful twin engines, gleaming teak galley with its brass trim and stainless steel appliances, crisp white sails and the beautiful name, Faith, scrolled tastefully in gold on the stern. He scoffed at others who put clever but tacky names on their beautiful and expensive boats. His boat, for that is how he thought of her, had a name of dignity. It matched her in every way.

They smiled at each other in recognition of each other's thoughts...minds flashing back to Charlie's first turn at the helm...when "Captain," as Charlie called his boss, became aware of Charlie's close scrutiny while he guided the boat to catch the full effect of a capriciously gusty wind. Long Island Sound had been glorious that day with its golden sun and dancing waves. The guests were relaxing on deck or in the salon, partaking of Charlie's excellent "boat food," their happy conversation and gentle laughter punctuating the sound of the swells breaking along the bow of the sleek yacht. Suddenly, Mr. Tyler said an amazing thing! "Here you go, Charlie, take the wheel."

Charlie, who had been deep in the middle of a fantasy of doing just that very thing, leaped guiltily to his feet. "Oh'un, no, no thank you so much, Captain. I do not know how to do what you ask." He felt the need to distance himself from this wonderful temptation, fearful of the consequences if he stayed, and began backing away.

"Now, Charlie, calm yourself." James had said in a mild voice. "I'm not asking you to take charge of Faith; I just thought you might like to feel what it is like to hold the wheel. I'll be right here with you. There is no danger, I can promise you that!"

On that fateful day, Midge had been sitting, watching the interplay with interest. She too had noticed Charlie's growing delight on their sailing outings. She watched the slender figure bowing and backing away from her husband. She couldn't hear the words, but she could pretty much figure out the interchange. She saw Charlie's head shaking a vehement "NO," while behind his back, out of James' sight, his hands curved and clenched as if grasping the wheel. She could almost feel his rising excitement and terror. If there were someone sitting beside her, sharing the moment, she would have leaned over and said, "I'll bet you a dollar James can talk him into it."

She would have won her bet. Slowly, like a violinist approaching a Stradivarius for the first time, Charlie approached the wheel. Her husband showed uncharacteristic patience, she could see he was talking to Charlie, probably telling him things about sailing, keeping him interested, giving him time to consider this new idea.

Finally, after the diminutive cook had finished his cautious approach and was standing near the helm, James, still talking, took one hand from the wheel and gestured for Charlie to grab hold. One gold brown hand seemed to reach out almost in spite of itself, fingers curving over the smoothness of teak and brass.

They stood, sharing the helm. James was still talking, suggesting headings, every so often taking his hand from the wheel and momentarily leaving the slender, tightly gripped one in charge. This went on until Charlie stopped wincing when it happened. And so they sailed, sheets trimmed, Faith cutting a clean crystal swath through the cobalt water, the white splash of Charlie's smile clearly defining the joy of the moment.

Suddenly, Charlie's face turned upward and he said something to James. Midge could hear her husband's booming laugh and saw him raise both hands high and step back. That had been the beginning of Charlie's love affair with the yacht.

Now, some 30 years later, Charlie was just as capable as either of the Tylers at handling the honorable vessel. It was he who was hoisted in the Bo' sun's chair when a line needed to be unsnarled. As often as not, it was also he who held the boat steady and calm through narrow rough water passages.

One day, prior to a sail, he found a plain, square, white box sitting on the table in the salon of Faith. He looked from Midge to James with a question in his eyes.

"That's for you, Charlie," Midge said softly. James added, "Believe me; you've earned the right to wear it. You've got the touch, Charlie."

For a moment, he was so taken aback he thought the lovely box itself was the gift. It would have been a very good box for storing possessions. Bowing low to hide his confusion and uttering a profusion of "Thank you so much" as he picked up the box, he suddenly knew it was not empty. He could feel its heaviness so he sat it back on the table and lifted the lid. Remembering the moment still caused his heart to beat faster...there was so much joy to remember.

He had slowly reached in among the softness of the white layers of tissue paper and lifted out a hat. It was not just any hat, but a real yachtsman's hat, just like the captain's, only, across the front of his hat, just above the bill and bold braid, marched the letters that gave him ownership. "Captain Charlie," it said. He found himself speechless and could only bow and smile. So much joy! So much symbolism in the gift! He believed it was the happiest moment of his life. And from the way Captain cleared his throat and the suspicious moisture in the corner of Mam's eyes, he knew they understood what words could not convey.

From that time forward, when sailing, Captain Whip never called him Charlie again. They called each other simply, 'Captain.'

Charlie signed his third deep sigh and brought himself back to the present. *Go to the races when he had an opportunity to sail and wear his hat? Not Likely!* He smiled in gentle resignation at Midge, who appeared to be still wrapped in similar memories. With dignity, Charlie said firmly, "That Joseph is one very fine fellow, but he does not know "boat food" and he does not know how to help Captain with Faith. I will go to the races next weekend, sail this fine weekend. It is okay. This weekend most auspicious for a party on Faith."

Midge blinked, pulled back to the present by his words. "Oh, Charlie, thank you so much. I truly had forgotten. It has all been so sudden. I do appreciate your flexibility. Besides, it really works out better since this is

Dawn's last weekend with us." She felt her spirits lighten. "Things are going to work out splendidly!"

Charlie put the tea kettle on to boil and got down what Mam called their "magic book," while she hurried in search of paper and her address book. She needed to give Charlie a rough list of whom she planned to invite so he could start thinking about the menu.

They had their strategizing and meal planning down to a fine science. In the magic book were records of other outings, detailed down to who had been invited, what the menu had been, which items had been especially well received, what wines were served, how many bottles were drunk and a myriad of other useful data. Another section of the book listed the names of guests, their food and beverage preferences, whether they took their coffee black or otherwise, how much rough water they could take and other items noted so as to make their time with the Tylers memorable.

Guests had no clue that they were statistics in a record book. Thus it never failed to amaze them when, without asking, the unfailingly polite, impeccably dressed captain/chef, in his Captain Charlie hat delivered their coffee, their morning eggs or their evening cocktail prepared exactly to their preference. Midge accepted their accolades on Charlie's behalf, never hinting at the book's existence, instead merely saying, "Yes, Charlie's memory IS phenomenal, isn't it?"

Now, he poured through the detailed, well-organized contents. There would probably be ten guests aboard. Charlie thought he would know the eating habits of all but Dawn. The list under her name was still brief. The note said:

> Juices, white wine, tea with lemon preferred over coffee.
> Will drink coffee black in the AM only.
> Passed on Chocolate Torte???
> Two helpings of vegetables

The question marks following the skipped dessert entry simply meant that Charlie didn't know if she didn't eat desserts, didn't like chocolate or didn't like that particular type of dessert.

By the time Midge returned to the kitchen, she had decided exactly who she wanted to invite. She worried a bit as she gave the names to Charlie. If everyone, besides Dawn and Tucker, she had in mind could come, it was going to be an easy group to plan for. But, the notice was quite short; in fact, it was short almost to the point of being bad manners. However, these were all old friends and were used to spontaneous parties with the Tylers. Charlie nodded his approval, satisfied as she left to go and make the necessary phone calls.

Her first choice to invite was Althea and her husband, Robert, their daughter, Deborah; and her fiancée, whose name was also Robert but had agreed to answer to Rob when the family was together. it was the first call she made.

Althea was delighted with the idea and agreed, like the good friend she was, to call Deborah and both Roberts to be certain schedules were free.

Clifton Eldridge and his tall, elegant wife with the equally elegant, though masculine name of Emory, she left to her husband to contact. *After all,* she thought as she gave him the instruction to find out and call her back as soon as possible, *this weekend is really his idea!*

Minutes later, returning to the kitchen, she found Charlie already had a good start on the planning. "Let's go ahead and plan food for ten please, Charlie," she confirmed, handing him the guest list. "James will call any minute now. Clifton and he are playing golf this afternoon and I have his promise to ask them to join us."

Charlie had flipped through the section indexed as "guest log" and scanned to see how long it had been since some of the intended guests had shared such an outing. He also scanned down the list of preferred and taboo foods. The taboo list for this group was a very short one. Althea hated mayonnaise; Rob was allergic to mushrooms, deathly so; and Emory wouldn't touch champagne. The list of food preferences was much longer. This particular
group of people, over the years had raved about most of Charlie's "boat food" creations.

"Does Mam have a theme in mind for this happy boat trip?" Charlie queried. "Not much time to do fancy, Wednesday is already casting long shadow."

"Heavens no, Charlie! Let's make this one simple and without fanfare. It's truly a last minute, throw-together thing. Please just do simple things. You could even do it here. There's really no need to cook in the galley. I know how much more trouble it is." Clarice will be back by then and I know she would be glad to help you, if you made things here ahead of time." Midge looked squarely, imploringly, at Charlie as she spoke. She was still feeling guilty about his needing to rearrange his plans.

Charlie, the master of last minute, 'throw together" parties, merely snorted and said, "Clarice already have plenty to do when she gets back. Mam, go play in garden for 20 minutes, give Charlie time to think, please."

Midge accepted her cup of tea and went to do as she had been told. It was a glorious day in Branford. From her patio she could look out over the rolling lawn and see the graceful Faith waiting patiently in her berth at the Pine Orchard Yacht and Country Club Marina. *What would we do without that man to bail us out when we have these sudden whims?"* she mused silently to the white, sun-centered Shasta daisies flanking the stone bench where she sat. She wondered again where Dawn was and if she was in the middle of some grand adventure. Speculatively, she wondered if there was some young man on the West Coast pining for his sweetheart adventuring in the east. Thinking again of Tucker, she hoped not.

Chapter Eight

When Tucker hung up the phone after accepting the invitation from Midge, he was still smiling. Usually, he regarded the telephone as an intrusive technological necessity. Today, it had temporarily redeemed itself. Evidently, he too had redeemed himself. Mrs. T wouldn't have called him without an okay from his boss, of that he was certain. He had been dreading the thought of going to the office. Now, he thought, *perhaps it won't be so bad.*

From the telephone, he had also gotten permission to use the garden. Thanks to it, he had his time planned from now through the weekend. That thought reminded him that he needed to call his mother and verify that he would be with them for Sunday night's dinner. He picked up the receiver and pushed the button that connected him to her private line.

Margaret Jones was happy to hear that Tucker was spending the weekend on the "open sea," as she called it. Secretly, she worried a bit about how much time Tucker spent alone in his condo, ostensibly working on his computer. Outside his club, his weekends with the Tylers seemed to be his only regular social engagement. She knew, from conversations with Althea, that the Tylers were quite fond of him. She also knew that Midge Tyler was forever finding suitable young ladies for him to meet during these gatherings. According to Althea, Tucker absolutely drove young ladies wild. As she listened to his well-modulated voice and pictured his tall form, perfect posture and chiseled features, Margaret found it easy to believe. However, again according to Althea, to this point in time, he hadn't seemed interested in any of them.

She raised one carefully manicured hand unconsciously to finger the pearls at her throat as she listened to her son. He was telling her that he hoped to leave the Tylers in time to be home for their Sunday evening together. This also pleased her as one more example of his thoughtfulness. He was a wonderful young man and that he did not yet have a serious relationship should trouble no one. After all, he was only twenty-seven.

"Now, Tucker," she laughed her low and throaty laugh, "please do pay attention to what their chef has come up with this time. I know he will plan something spectacular. Do bring the details to cocktails when you come. I really can't imagine how the man can 'create' anything edible with all that water sloshing him about!"

Although Margaret had never once tasted any of the food prepared by the Tyler's chef, she was quite familiar with some of his dishes both from Althea and more importantly, from her son.

Tucker, after witnessing years of recipe dissection, was really quite skilled at detecting the "secret" ingredients, a skill of which she was very proud, though she never directly told him so.

After a few more exchanged pleasantries and queries about how the new young college couple was adjusting to life in the domestic service of the Jonses, Tucker rang off and booted up his computer. He planned to work at least three hours and then go and visit the garden. *This certainly has not been my most productive day, but I have all day tomorrow to prepare for Friday's meeting.*

His mind felt crystal clear and he knew he was going to be at his logical best—if only he could sustain concentration. It was not a serious worry since he had come to not only trust, but to depend upon, his ability to block out unwanted thoughts to get even the most difficult of tasks done.

Briefly, as he set his wrist alarm, he wondered if he would even see Kathryn McCall when he visited the garden, then plunged into the collected data set.

At 2:30 his alarm went off and he pulled himself out of the volumes of fine print, feeling fuzzy and distracted. It took him a few seconds to reorient himself, so deep and complete had been his concentration. This was also a feeling he had become accustomed to. Clicking into the word processing mode, he spent the next 30 minutes summarizing his impressions and then happily shut down the machine, stretched carefully and realized for the first time that he had forgotten to eat lunch. He grabbed an apple on his way past the fruit bowl to quiet his growling stomach and munched it while he slapped some Monterey Jack, dry salami, horseradish, mustard and lettuce between two slices of deli rye.

Uncharacteristically, he wolfed the sandwich down. Generally, he was careful to properly set his small table and sit down to eat, no matter how casual the meal. This day, his thoughts were on the mossy rock fountain and the wonderful combination of shade, filtered sunlight and the pure sunshine, all present in one small space. Clearly, it was a garden at its best in the afternoon. He decided, on the spot, to fix a thermos of lemonade to take with him and on a whim included two glasses in his backpack, wrapping both in multi-layers of paper towels—on the odd chance that Kathryn might have time to join him. He also grabbed the rough draft of the summary he'd just completed, thinking he might feel like perusing what he'd written while sitting in the garden. He was humming under his breath, buoyed by an unfamiliar but wonderful sense of optimism.

Suddenly, Tucker stopped in his tracks—the feeling of anticipation evaporating and into its place, crawling unbidden, was a dark and debilitating sense of dread. He'd experienced it many times in the past--before he had learned the trick of blanking his mind. But this time, the trick failed him and the immobilizing questions came flooding into his mind. *"What if it isn't the same? What if this time, there is no magic, no sense of Ethan and Mary's presence, no feeling of peace? What if it just feels like any other place with flowers, stones and bricks; just a pleasant place? Why did I count on this so much? Why did I set myself up like this?* A better way, he decided firmly, would be to sit himself down in his own ergonomic chair in the living room and read the summary right now. *It is absolutely stupid and senseless to get the Aston out and drive at least twenty to thirty minutes in Wednesday afternoon commuter traffic just to go and spend an hour in the back yard of some woman's middle class neighborhood in Milford; a woman who probably doesn't really want me there. I'll see plenty of flowers at the Tyler's' place this weekend, if flowers are really what I want to see!*

Tucker stood, both hands gripping the backpack, lips pressed into a wire-thin line on an iron face. Feeling horribly defeated, he slowly began unzipping the backpack. *Going there is certainly the most illogical thing I have thought about doing for a long time,* he reflected. *It's a good thing I came to my senses. A much sounder plan is to go for my massage on Friday a bit early and try sitting in the garden. I won't count on anything, but it seems logical to give the place a second try.* He concentrated on slowing his breathing, drawing in deep breaths. *Really, there is absolutely no sense in making a special trip over there on some foolish whim.* He felt the familiar sense of melancholy stealing over him. Gone was the sense of optimism, of rewarding himself for a job well done by taking time to go to the garden. The feeling of dread left him as suddenly as it had come, leaving in its place a void. He simply felt foolish, flat and drained of energy. He put the lemonade, thermos and all, into the spotlessly clean refrigerator and headed slowly for his bedroom to lay in the cool darkness, fully clothed; staring up at the ceiling, wishing desperately for the quiet mind that would allow sleep to come.

He tried to identify, put a name to what he was feeling. This was foreign territory to him. For all these years he had avoided even using words that had to do with feelings. He wasn't even sure how to go about what he wanted to do, because he wasn't sure what he DID want to do. He recalled what Mr. Tyler had said about not needing a list, needing a heart instead. Tucker groaned aloud in despair. *If I don't have a heart, why is my whole chest aching right now?* "I am in pain," he said aloud to the ceiling. "Why am I in so much pain?"

"Because," the stark white ceiling seemed to whisper, "it's the only thing you will allow yourself to feel. You're afraid to remember…afraid to feel…afraid to take risks. You used to feel…but then you stopped because it hurt too much."

Yes, Tucker's mind agreed, *I am afraid. I think I am especially afraid of that garden because it soothed me into remembering the time when I COULD feel. It made me feel the presence of Ethan and Mary.* "I'm so afraid, ceiling." he whispered. "I'm afraid to trust myself, afraid of the pain, afraid of being found out, afraid of embarrassing myself or my family. It's fear that rules my world, ceiling, and I don't know what to do about it!"

He lay there, drained but feeling a curious sense of relief at having stated so bluntly what he had carried so long and so hidden inside, if only to the now silent ceiling.

Slowly, his lids fluttered shut and he drifted into a kaleidoscopic world of fragments from the five senses: The taste of Irish soda bread, the fragrance of sun-warmed flowers, sunlight dappled by tree shade, the sound of laughter and the touch of strong work-hardened hands pushing his swing skyward. For once, he allowed the memories to comfort him, lull him into a sleep undisturbed and restful.

When Tucker awoke, the feeling of riding an emotional roller coaster and being totally out of control had faded. Rolling his head slowly from side to side as if to clear it from the day's ups and downs, he found what had stressed him so much too difficult to remember. He felt rested and energized. He rose and looked out the window into the twilight. A jogger passed beneath his bedroom window and he made a sudden decision.

He had not run since his back injury. *But, if I'm careful, do some stretching and take it very easy, I should be all right. Besides, If I am going to start taking risks, I might as well start with jogging as anything else.* He raised his eyes and said, "Am I right, ceiling? Is this what I need to do? Take some risks? What does that mean to take some risks? It sounds like something Dr. Van Castle would say, don't you think?"

Tucker lowered his eyes and laughed nervously, "God, I've got to stop this talking to the ceiling stuff, I'm feeling pretty crazed as it is."

Reaching into his closet where his running shoes were still lined precisely beside his other shoes and his shorts and tee shirts were shelved in ordered piles, he pulled a set from the top of their respective piles and dressed quickly. He stretched carefully, worrying a little about the fading light, but decided he could simply run to his club and finish on the indoor track or just run under the street lights if he needed to. Life suddenly seemed full of options.

It was a delightful summer evening, He decided against the club, though he hadn't used it since his back spasms. Warming up slowly, he threaded his way easily through strolling couples, visiting women and children waiting to be called in for dinner. Oblivious to the many admiring glances tossed his way by the younger women, he settled into his rhythm, taking care to pace himself, concentrating on his heel strike and the balance of his stride. *It's wonderful to be running again,* he thought. *I didn't realize how much I've missed it.*

Once in the park and on the bark chip trail, he allowed himself to pick up the pace, began to perspire freely and felt his breathing start to labor. It surprised him to note how his conditioning had slipped in such a short time and he dropped to a walk, reminding himself of the importance of taking it easy.

As his breathing slowed, Tucker took time to look about and notice that the city had installed night lights over the park trail for the convenience of night time joggers such as himself. They were just coming on. Delighted, he smiled and resumed his slow lope along the trail. Thirty minutes later, he called a halt at the edge of the park and began his cool down walk back to his condo feeling better than he could remember. He promised himself he would go cheerfully to Kathryn, do the back exercises recommended by the physical therapist at the hospital and anything else he could think of, just so long as he could have his nightly jog. He would even call Beemers tomorrow just to verify that it would be okay to do so.

Full of resolution, Tucker headed for the shower when he noticed his message light winking its insistent red eye at him. He flipped the switch and heard the lovely, modulated voice of one of Mrs. Tyler's better looking "set ups."

"Good evening, Tucker, this is Heather Anderson. I have two tickets to the Spring Concert in Discovery Park but no escort. Would you be interested in the position? It's a week from Friday at 8:00 o'clock. Please call me and say, 'Yes.'"

He sighed, thinking that a concert in the park on a night like this would be a pleasant evening. He knew Heather, both from a party at the Tyler's and because they belonged to the same club. He had accepted her invitation to play tennis there and felt she had enjoyed his company.

100

He decided to call her back and accept her invitation—only right now he needed a shower.

It was while he was standing, mesmerized by the hot, driving, jets of water, that he thought, *wait a minute. I'm going to accept Heather's invitation because she seems to enjoy my company? Tucker, how did you make that decision? Did you even think to ask yourself how you feel about Heather Anderson? How do you feel about Heather? Are you just using her to get to listen to an evening of classical music? Do you like Heather for any other reason than the fact that she enjoys your company?*

Soaking his entire head under the blasting spray, he discovered he couldn't muster one feeling about Heather Anderson and the realization shocked him. His anxiety again rising, he began thinking about the other women Midge had been pushing at him these last several years. He could describe all of their physical attributes, could even ascribe personality traits, but he felt nothing about any of them. Many had been quite complimentary towards him. Most had made it clear that they would like to be asked out—but when he thought of them, their personalities and their looks would not remain separated.

Tucker banged his fist against his forehead, wondering exactly what this startling revelation meant. *Here I am, twenty-seven years old, supposedly in my sexual prime and I'm not even remotely interested?* "Good Lord," he whispered to himself, "the scary thing is, I hadn't really noticed."

He didn't feel shocked anymore, just interested. He was finding out some things about himself today. For the first time, he was consciously allowing himself to do some introspection. Carefully, he turned off the faucet, thinking back, trying to remember the last time he had felt interested in a woman. *Really, not since high school,* he decided.

Of course, back then, he hadn't done anything about it, but he could definitely remember wanting to. He blushed, remembering kissing Jane Goodman at their senior party. It had been a private beach and he had gotten up his nerve to walk her away from the bonfire into the star studded darkness. In the shadow of a towering sand dune they had kissed a lingering kiss. Then, suddenly, she had slipped her tongue into his mouth, giving him an immediate and throbbing erection. At the time, it had startled him badly and he pushed her away from him, feeling grateful for the darkness that hid his condition. Embarrassed beyond words, he'd let her think he was offended. She'd called him a prude and several other names before running back to the group.

Now, thinking about it, he groaned and slowly toweled himself off. Almost ten years later and he was still embarrassed. Clearly, he needed help from someone or something. He remembered Dr. Beemer's gentle suggestion about counseling and shook his head vehemently, blocking the thought. Instead, as he stood in the still steaming bathroom, an amazing alternative popped into his head. He draped a towel about his loins and headed for his computer.

Calling up the word processor he selected the "new" function and created a file labeled simply, "FEELINGS."

This document will be in the form of a journal he typed, his fingers flying over the familiar and friendly keys. It is to be the written conversation of Tucker Jones' talks with his ceiling. He grinned at his own foolishness but recognized the seriousness of his intent and typed on. My ceiling says the only thing I know how to feel is fear (of pain). It was a very insightful observation. I think he/she/it is mostly right, but only if we're referring to people. I think...here he paused a long moment before he continued. ...I'm pretty normal in other areas. For example, when I do a good job in a meeting for Mr. Tyler, I feel proud. When I feel hungry, I eat. I felt very happy and quite content while running tonight. Of course, maybe the reason I did was because I didn't allow myself to think about people. What is it with people and me, ceiling? Do you realize the last time I kissed a girl I was a senior in high school? I'll tell you I felt something then and it wasn't just embarrassment!

Tucker's flying fingers stilled. He closed his eyes, lost in thought for long minutes. When he opened his eyes he wrote: So, here is my task: Every evening that I am home, I

102

will spend some time creating this file. I will read the entire contents every day...and every day I will write whether or not I have had a genuine feeling towards a person. Here are some feelings I can name: Fear, anger, sadness, joy, hope...Tucker dropped his forehead, resting on his hands, thinking hard. Finally, he wrote: This is harder than I thought, Ceiling!!! Is ambivalence a feeling? I think I need to read a book about feelings because I know there are a lot more.

Tucker looked back over what he had written. It seemed to be the rambling of about a fifth grader. There was not one thing logical or organized about it. He seriously toyed with the idea of deleting the file and scrapping the whole idea of his self-study plan. He felt absolutely foolish. Instead, he forced himself to continue. He wrote: I am feeling foolish, Ceiling! Then he thought for a while, drumming his fingers on his desk top. *So, here I am, really trying my best and all I'm feeling is foolish and very uncomfortable.* He typed: Why am I feeling so uncomfortable, Ceiling? Then, after another long pause an idea came to him. He continued, fingers again flying. I think feeling foolish and feeling uncomfortable are really ways of saying 'I'm afraid.' I wonder how many of people's feelings...No, I mean my feelings, not other people's feelings, Ceiling...are fear-based. I'm good at knowing about other people's feelings, this journal is supposed to be about MY feelings.

Tucker re-read what he had written. The disjointed, spontaneous nature of his writing didn't bother him quite so much this time. He felt as though he had stumbled onto something momentous. He entered the SAVE command and leaned back in his chair. *In a way, this was easy,* he thought. *Talking to my computer is much easier than talking to a person. I can ramble as much as I want. I don't have to make sense.*

He glanced at his clock and was shocked to see how long he had spent composing such a few awkward lines. Granted, much of the time he had been thinking instead of typing. *Which, I suppose, is just as important. Besides, thinking is something I happen to be good at.* He allowed his thoughts to flick back to Dr. Van Castle and wondered what the doctor would think of this new experiment. Then, he considered, just briefly, asking Dr. Beemers about the man when he called tomorrow.

At the thought, a feeling akin to revulsion swept through him as he finally forced himself to consider whether or not he might profit from more visits with a psychiatrist. This line of thinking felt so aversive that he immediately and with finality, squelched it. Instead, he called his personal organizer up on his screen and wrote himself a memo to call Dr. Beemers about his desire to continue jogging. He also remembered to write in both appointments with Kathryn McCall on his electronic calendar. He then flipped the OFF button and watched the light fade from the screen.

Gradually, Tucker became aware of his surroundings and realized that he was sitting, chilled to the point of shivering, in a damp towel. His stomach growled, reminding him that he had neither eaten dinner nor read the summary he had written earlier. He shrugged. *All right, Tucker, first things first--even workaholics like you need to eat.*

He stood, carefully hitching his towel, grateful that his back still felt fine and headed for his bedroom. As he slipped into his pajamas and robe, he felt hopeful that Jeff Beemers would agree that he could continue to run. He wondered what he would do if the doctor said, "No." *Hold on, Tucker, it's illogical to worry about something only a future telephone call can determine.* He ran a comb through his hair and headed for his kitchen.

Tucker, padding around in his kitchen, was noticeably at home. It was a fact unknown to anyone but himself that he truly enjoyed the tasks of shopping for groceries and preparing his own small gourmet meals. Unlike his mother, who prided herself on creativity, Tucker had refined both the shopping and the cooking to a science.

Once a week, he sat down at his computer and planned his week of eating. Every menu he used was in the computer. He even had the list of necessary ingredients for each recipe cross referenced to a computer generated grocery list. This was fairly easy because he narrowed his choices of food that he might purchase down to a list of exactly thirty. It made shopping more efficient.

He also had, in his freezer, the "treasure trove" of leftovers from Sunday dinners with his parents. He had actually planned on making a pasta dish for the evening, but looking at the time, decided there was little choice but to go the frozen food route. He reached into the freezer and pulled out the top, neatly stacked package.

Tonight's carefully labeled container said: "Osso Buco var." The var. meaning it was his mother's variation of the Italian veal dish. He remembered that it was nicely spiced and quite brothy. Quickly crushing a fresh clove of garlic, he smeared a wooden bowl then tossed in some already prepared chunks of crispy romaine lettuce from his vegetable drawer.

While the microwave hummed, Tucker made a simple salad dressing and cut a hunk from yesterday's sour dough bread. Then he set his single place at the gleaming glass and chrome table; handwoven place mat, cloth napkin, and flatware of simple Danish design that he had personally selected, as he had every single item in the condo when he'd set up housekeeping.

He ate slowly, looking around his well-ordered space, pleased with the high-tech, young bachelor look he thought it represented. Even eating alone as often as he did, his manners had not deteriorated. He made sure of it; always returning one hand to his lap after using his knife; making certain that he did not allow even a single clank of metal against the delicate edge of the white Franciscan bone china dinner plate; carrying each moderately-sized bite of food carefully to his mouth and then chewing each bite thoroughly, mouth closed, before swallowing.

The Osso Buco really was very good with its broth-laden brown rice hinting of saffron and the bite-sized, tender chunks of veal. *I must remember to tell Mother that the spicing was even more perfect now than when she first presented the dish,* he thought as he rose from the table.

Only after the kitchen was put back to sparkling rightness did Tucker pull out the summary. His choice would have been to watch a bit of news, but it wasn't really any big effort to begin the self-critique of this most recent work. His desire to perform well at Zitec far outweighed any need for the news and his ability to be so strictly self-disciplined was one of the traits of personality he gladly admitted to. Besides, today had been difficult. It felt very good to do something so familiar that it was like breathing or practicing good manners. He pulled his chair closer to his desk, turned on his reading light and settled in. He planned to work late, knowing that his nap voided any chance he might have had for a restful night.

Chapter Nine

Kathryn's clock radio began its waking serenade with a jingle designed, she supposed, not only to sell coffee, but to make one want to hop cheerily out of bed at 6:00 AM and rush down to put on the pot.

She stretched under her down comforter and wiggled her toes happily. A cup of coffee did sound good. She had fixed her Silex with a timer set to start the same time her radio went off. As far as she was concerned, as long as there was a cup of coffee waiting, 6:00 o'clock in the morning was a fine time; especially on mornings such as this when the world seemed soft and peaceful in the beginnings of a new day.

Listening to the news for 15 minutes was her way of keeping up with the world. Otherwise, there was not much time in her day. At exactly a quarter past the hour, she slipped out of bed and into her blue jeans, worn soft by repeated washings, the knees permanently dirt and grass stained from hours of working in her flower garden and front yard. She donned a sweatshirt, tied a handkerchief around her wild curls and tiptoed down the hall to let the cat out of Allison's room.

In an hour, Allison's radio would wake her, but for now, she carefully opened the door a crack and smiled at the majestic gray tabby cat waiting impatiently at the edge of the braided rug. The birds had been singing their wake-up songs for more than an hour and he was in a snit to be out of doors.

Together, they slipped down the stairs, Jon Bon hurrying as much as his dignity would allow, tail twitching with impatience. She smiled. He always had been a cat who let one know exactly what was on his mind. She let him out the kitchen door and went to get a mug of coffee to take to the garden.

It was cool enough, as she stood surveying her flowers, that the warmth of the mug felt good in her hands

107

and the steam warmed her face as she drank. Jon Bon was having his customary drink out of the fountain as she set her cup on the table and pulled on her gardening gloves.

Yesterday, she had bought two flats of annuals: sturdy marigolds, scarlet sage and lacy white China asters. Her goal was to get them into the ground before her work day started. But first she had to do something with the drooping foliage of her spent bulbs. She had read in a gardening magazine that one could fold them over and put a rubber band around the tops to minimize their height and keep them out of the way of the new blooming flowers. It seemed such a simple solution. She hoped her new plants would work to further shield the browning leaves. She also noted that she had again let the weeds get ahead of her and shook her head in resignation. *What's that old saying, "So much to do, so little time"?*

Dropping to her knees, she closed her eyes in order to better picture how the plants would look when inserted in front of her trussed up bulbs and among the perennials and annuals already in place. She smiled and picked up her packet of rubber bands. She could see what the finished product would look like very clearly and it pleased her. Working quickly, but stopping every now and then for a sip of now lukewarm coffee, her allotted 45 minutes slipped quickly away. She heard Allison's alarm go off and sighed with resignation. Only about half the plants were in the ground and it was time to go in and start breakfast. Jon Bon strolled over to critique and give a quick brush against her leg. It was his breakfast time too.

Luckily, Allison was also a morning person. By the time the oatmeal had cooked and the toast was up, she was bouncing down the stairs with ribbons, brush and comb in one hand, library books in the other.

Kathryn grinned at the seven-year old elf standing in front of her and reached for the brush. Petite did not begin to describe the tiny, wiry bundle of energy with her own unruly curls and her father's deep blue eyes and sandy hair. With a mother's practiced hands, she began corralling the mop into two pony tails that far more resembled the pom pom on a poodle's tail than any tail Kathryn had ever seen on a horse!

108

With only a little more than a week of school left, Allison, known mostly as Sunny by her friends, was winding up the second grade with her usual flair for detail.

"Now, Mom," she said, scrunching her face against the pull of the brush through her tangled curls, "I think I might be missing one of my library books. They all have to be returned or I don't get a star on my chart that says 'library books back.' You haven't seen any others lying around anywhere, have you?" Without waiting for a reply, she rushed on. "And don't forget you have to sign my permission slip or I can't go on the field trip to the park. Kids who don't bring their permission slips have to stay at school in the first grade room."

The words, "first grade room" were made to sound like some absolutely dreadful place filled with snakes and scorpions, or at least humans on a lower social level. Kathryn pulled tight the last ribbon and went obediently to sign the permission slip in question while her daughter fed Jon Bon and poured herself juice and for her mother, more coffee.

No matter what else was going on in their respective lives, except for Saturday mornings, mother and daughter always managed to sit down and eat breakfast together. Usually, it was a pleasant interlude. However, this morning, Allison was yet again making it clear that oatmeal was not her favorite breakfast and that she would have preferred Captain Crunch or Trix or some other cold cereal touted on Saturday morning commercials between cartoons. It was a very old and long-running complaint and as usual, Kathryn held firm...only on Saturday mornings, while watching cartoons, was Allison allowed to indulge herself.

"You'll thank me when you grow up strong and healthy with beautiful teeth and roses in your cheeks, me darlin' child," was Kathryn's stock reply. To which, Allison would say peevishly, "But, Mom, I already have beautiful teeth and roses in my cheeks. Just ask Miss Roseblat."

Miss Roseblat, second grade teacher at Hathorne Elementary, was Allison's world authority on any subject known to man. "All the more important to keep them that way! Besides, you really don't know what those two missing teeth are going to look like, you know. But, since you are only allowed to eat junk cereal when you watch Saturday

109

morning cartoons, I figure you've got a better than average chance of carrying on the family's pride in having a wonderful smile."

When Kathryn was relaxed or trying to get a point across as she was now, her Irish lilt reverted into a true brogue. "And don't be tellin' me what other parents let their children do, please. I've grown a bit tired of that line and am certain you can be comin' up with something more original and more convincin', if only you'd spend a bit of time thinkin' on it."

It was one of Allison's charms to immediately recognize when the round had been lost. She sighed deeply, picked up her spoon and dug into the hot cereal. Not that she didn't intend to pursue it another time; she just knew better than to rile her mother's Irish temper. That's when Kathryn said things like, "I'll not hear another word of this!" Unfortunately, unlike many of her friends' mothers, her mother meant what she said, and to bring it up again caused dire consequences, up to and including being grounded, threatened with being sent to bed without supper, or a spanking with her hairbrush. Luckily, since Allison had figured all this out, she had been truly grounded only once.

They finished their meal companionably, making plans for their final weekend. It was to be special, since it would be their last for the rest of the summer. On Monday, Allison would be catching a plane to join her father in Texas. "Taking the train to the Bronx Zoo might be fun," Kathryn mused, "if the weather is this nice."

Allison looked up from clearing her place. "That could be okay, I guess. Would I be able to bring friends?"

Kathryn smiled at her. "Just one," she said and watched as her daughter nodded and said, "Well, that's perfect then," and went bounding up the stairs to brush her teeth. Already, the doorbell was signaling that the cadre of children who walked the four blocks with Allison to Hawthorne was at the front door. *What a politician this child is! Where did she learn those bargaining skills?* Allison had been hinting about going to the zoo for months. But now, she pretended to be lukewarm about the idea so she could negotiate bringing a friend.

110

Shaking her head, she went to greet the three giggling girls on her front steps and tell them Allison was on her way. *I wonder which of this lot is going to be picked out for the grand honor of riding the train all the way from New Haven to New York?"* she mused.

An hour later, showered and dressed in her crisp, white uniform, Kathryn checked her appointment book and sighed when she saw every slot was filled. The money was nice, but by the end of the day she would be exhausted. Noticing Tucker's name, she began the habitual chew on her lip. That the man had scheduled two appointments surprised her. *I wonder what caused him to do that...the massage or the garden?* She smiled to herself, remembering how adamant he had been about just allowing the back to be touched. *He's a puzzle, that one.* "He's sure a handsome devil," she admitted out loud. "I'll wager he's broken a heart or two."

The object of her musings was at that very moment lying in bed, objectively reviewing his life and wondering if the self-exploration he was doing via the computer was really worthwhile. He decided, finally, that it might be. He also decided, somewhat belatedly, that he had better call to accept Heather Anderson's invitation to the concert. Good music was something he enjoyed and he planned to pay close attention to his own feelings and reactions. It would be an experiment of sorts. He made a small sound in his nose that he would have been chagrined to know sounded suspiciously like a snort. A real experiment after a hiatus of ten years would be to kiss her...*if I can remember how,* he thought gloomily.

Tucker's thoughts rambled on to Kathryn McCall and his afternoon appointment. She had been very patient with all his demands. He wondered if she had other patients as reluctant as he had been. But, as his note to Dr. Beemers had said...it had been helpful and so he would continue. He remembered that he had also neglected to call the doctor and decided to do it before he left the condo.

On the way to the shower, he began thinking about Kathryn's garden. *Gardens can tell a lot about a person. That place speaks of an owner who loves not only flowers, but gentle peaceful spaces.* From her weathered boards

111

and old bricks, he suspected she also valued old things. *There's not a reason in the world I can't go early and spend some time there, not one!* He was whistling softly as he stepped into the spray. As he lathered his hair, he remembered his concern that the garden would have lost its charm. He shook his head at the irrationality of his thinking. It couldn't change in just two days. If anything was changed, it would only be his perceptions. *The garden itself doesn't have the power to disappoint me, or frighten me, or make me anxious; only my feelings have that power.*

There was that word again, feelings. He thrust his head under the heavy spray and began to concentrate simply on the feelings his hands created on his scalp as he massaged away the shampoo and then on how the hot water loosened his muscles. He was pleased how supple he felt, only a slight twinge in his thigh muscles reminded him of Wednesday's evening run in the park.

As he prepared his breakfast, he though carefully how to phrase his request for the doctor's blessing on his plan to run. He hadn't liked it when the old man laid down the law to him...didn't want a repeat performance of the conversation when Dr. Beemers had told him to either take his professional advice or find another doctor. He didn't want another doctor...just a professional opinion on the feasibility of someone with a back injury like his being able to run. He wanted to do it badly, but not at the expense of a healthy, pain-free back.

He swirled the water boiling in a sauce pan prior to slipping in the raw eggs and it seemed an appropriate metaphor for his mind—swirling smoothly until the bubbles reasserted themselves and messed up the flow. He smiled and dipped in his slotted spoon to swirl the water again, thinking, *Feelings are the bubbles that mess up the flow of my mind.* Then he concentrated on his task. For perfectly poached eggs, one had to gently release the shelled eggs, one at a time, into the gentle centrifugal motion.

Tucker sipped his orange juice, counted to sixty and removed the pan from the gas; the perfect eggs to start, what was probably going to be a very interesting, but hardly perfect day.

He let his thoughts drift to Midge Tyler's invitation and the California "set up." She certainly had not been very

112

disclosing about this woman whose name sounded like a man's. He shrugged his shoulders. *Perhaps there isn't much to say. Mrs. T has a fondness for describing people as 'darling,' including me.* So, that she was, "just darling," could mean any number of things. *And, what is a 'proper California girl'? I have no idea! I don't even know what a proper Connecticut girl is.* He gave up his line of thinking, sighed, set about washing his dishes and then went to make the call to Dr. Beemer's office, halfway hoping the doctor was already seeing patients and that he would be able to make the request through Mavis. That was not his luck.

"Why, hello, Tucker. Yes, the doctor certainly can take your call. One moment please," Mavis said in her unfailingly cheerful, professional voice.

Tucker found his palms were perspiring and that he was gripping the receiver in both hands while he waited to be put through. He had already decided he was not capable of more than asking his question straightforwardly. Dr. Beemers would have seen through any subterfuge.

"Good morning, Tucker. How are you doing?" rumbled the familiar voice.

"Well. I'm really feeling quite well, Dr. Beemers. In fact, I was feeling so well that I took a little run the night before last. I felt fine afterwards, but it dawned on me that it might be wise for me to check it out with you, in case it might be harmful to my back."

There was a pause and then Dr. Beemers said, "I got your note and I thank you for it. Are you going to schedule additional massages?"

Massages? thought Tucker, *I thought we were talking about the feasibility of my running. How did we get on the topic of massages?* He did not say his thoughts aloud. Instead, he said, trying to picture the look on the doctor's face, "Why, yes. As a matter of fact, I have one scheduled for this afternoon and a second for Monday."

There was a pause from the other end of the line and then a soft chuckle. "Well, that's fine, Tucker. Tell you what, this is a provisional yes. Do your stretching exercises before and after you run. Continue your massages and be smart about protecting your spine. Oh yes, and stay off the pavement. Then when I see you next week, we'll take an x-ray of your lower back and see how it looks. We can make a final decision then."

Tucker felt relief flood through him. A provisional yes was much better than a flat, "no," any time. "Thank you Dr. Beemers. That was the answer I was hoping for. I won't take more of your time now, but I will schedule my appointment for next week, if you would please connect me back to Mavis."

"Good, Tucker. I'll look forward to seeing you. Please give Kathryn my regards." With that, Dr. Beemers pushed the button that connected Tucker back to the reception desk.

"Mavis," he said in his easy way. "you are talking to a wiser man."

She laughed. "Are you, Tucker, dear? What makes you think so?"

"Well, for one thing, I've learned to do exactly as Dr. Beemers tells me. I find that when I do, my life runs more smoothly. Right now, he is telling me to schedule an appointment to come in next week. And so, wisely, that is what I am doing."

"Why, Tucker, I do believe you ARE learning a thing or two. Would you prefer a morning at 9:00 or an afternoon at 3:00 appointment? I have one of each left open for next Friday."

"Let's see," Tucker thought quickly, "I guess I would prefer the morning time. I have a Friday afternoon massage and I was hoping to make that slot in Miss McCall's day a permanent appointment," Tucker found himself saying.

"Fine, Tucker. See you next Friday at 9:00 o'clock. Have a good weekend. I can't think of a better way to start it than with a massage by Kathryn McCall."

Tucker pondered the conversation for a moment. Ms. McCall certainly had a fan club at that office. He wondered, briefly, if there was another connection. *How did Dr. Beemers come to recommend Kathryn out of all the licensed massage therapists in the area?* He wondered again if Dr. Beemers had ever used her professional services and then, characteristically decided it really wasn't his business and allowed his thoughts to move on to the fact that he had been given at least provisional permission to go running. Life was getting back to normal. On an impulse he walked over to the gleaming black piano and lifted the lid. He hadn't played any classical pieces for a very long time, only light pieces designed to entertain. He looked long and hard at the keys. It seemed as though they were inviting him to indulge. Slowly, he took his place on the hard bench, undecided, clenching and unclenching stiff fingers, wondering what they would remember. Mozart, List, Brahms...he could see the composer's faces, hear strains of music...

Tentatively he straightened his wrists and curved his fingers over the keys. He could almost hear old Mister Hermann say, "Remember there is a small rubber ball in the palm of your hand. Drape your fingers over it." The image of the old man came clearly and obediently he draped his fingers over the keys. Almost unbidden, his fingers spread and he began to play the scale of chords, slowly first and then faster and faster. He covered the keyboard hand over hand from the lower to the upper octaves and back down. Major chords and minor chords either crashed or rolled softly in smooth cadence from under his fingers. His foot automatically moved to the pedals, increasing the range of emotions he could ask the simple chords to convey.

Finally, his fingering slowed and he let out a whoosh of breath. He was tempted to try a piece, but told himself that he really didn't have time. He looked at his watch. It was 9:30. Mr. Tyler would have come in at 8:00 and would have read the revised summary that was waiting in his electronic mail file by now. He'd probably have some questions or want some clarification on the data Tucker had gleaned from his data base search. So, it was time to be moving if he was to be at the office for their usual 10:00 o'clock meeting time.

Almost reluctantly, he closed the lid on the keyboard. *Truthfully*, he thought to himself, *I am not quite ready to play again. But, I had the desire for a moment. I felt it! It was momentary, but real—that desire to play again.*

For a long time, that desire had not only been missing, but Tucker had even avoided looking or thinking about the beautiful instrument that dominated his entire living space.

He went into the closet and scrutinized his ties. He had five that went well with the soft gray suit he chose to wear. Finally, unable to make up his mind between a formal burgundy with a blue strip and a dove gray with small red fleurs-de-lis, he chose neither and put on a soft pink and gray paisley silk. He shook his head as he tied a careful double Windsor knot. He was a decisive person. To stand for five minutes in front of a tie rack was a waste of time, definitely not efficient time management. That was why he had separated his ties into groups that went with a particular suit, so he could grab any one of the group and look good. Now, he would really have to hurry. Besides that, he suddenly remembered he had not packed for the weekend or called Heather Anderson. He would have to come back to his condo after the massage and be late arriving at the Tyler's, or come back and change and pack before going to the massage, which might mean he could not carry out his plan to spend an hour in the garden.

Tucker slammed out the door and heard it lock behind him just as he remembered that he had left his attaché case and his keys sitting on the kitchen table. Grinding his teeth in frustration, he fished the extra door key from the key holder in his wallet. He had always kept both a car key and a door key concealed among his credit cards, but had never needed either before. As he fumbled with the lock, he hoped this lack of organization was not an omen of things to come. Mr. Tyler was going to expect him to be able to do an in-depth debriefing after today's meeting...and rightly so. *This business of Zitec expanding to South America is far more complex and less well-researched than it first appeared.*

Tucker's revised summary highlighted questions that had not yet been raised--vital questions, ones that were not easily researched. It suggested a need for further clarification of the data already presented by the research team to the rest of the group was in order. *Perhaps I am not researching the correct topics, formulating the correct Boolean search overlaps to call up relevant articles. Things simply aren't clicking.*

Thinking about the problems of the day calmed him a bit and by the time he rode the elevator down to his car, he was feeling less fragmented, if not back in control.

Sinking into the soft brown leather seats of the Aston Martin always gave him a sense of satisfaction. It so suited his image of himself, as it had his father and grandfather before him. The car was not flashy or even especially well-known, except among those who loved a classic, well-machined, powerful and superbly designed vehicle. He carefully fastened his seat belt, readjusted his already perfectly adjusted mirrors, kicked the big engine to life, pushed the button to open the garage door and drove out into the golden day.

He pushed the old car to the legal limit, changing lanes smoothly, accelerating past slower cars, trying to make up for lost time. He had absolutely no desire to keep his boss waiting—ever! Just to cover his tracks, he called Mr. Tyler's secretary on his car phone.

"Peggy, this is Tucker," he said. "I'm fairly certain Mr. Tyler will want to keep our usual 10:00 o'clock, but we didn't confirm it. Am I on his calendar?"

"Yes, Tucker, you definitely are. In fact, he was just out here asking if I had seen you yet."

"Thank you, Peggy. Please tell him I'm about 10 minutes away and only traffic could prevent me from punctuality," Tucker said in a light tone that belayed his anxiety. Promptness was a personality trait Mr. Tyler valued highly, as did he.

With exactly four minutes to spare, Tucker leaped from his car, attaché case in hand, strode through the front door of the building and dashed for the elevator which was conveniently standing empty, door open. At 10:00 o'clock, he was striking a casual, unhurried stance in front of Peggy's desk.

"Nice job, Tucker. However did you do it?" Peggy smiled, eyes twinkling. "He's waiting, convinced when he needs you most you're stuck in traffic. Oh, I might warn you; this hasn't been his best morning."

Tucker nodded, "I'm not surprised," he said simply and then turned to knock and disappear through the big double doors.

Mr. Tyler looked up at the knock and smiled at Tucker's entry. "Thank God, you are a punctual man, Tucker! I was afraid you were stuck in traffic and I'd have to go into that meeting with more questions than answers…just like that revised research summary you sent me."

Tucker settled into his customary chair at the small round table and opened his case, extracting both his logic files and his copy of the summary. Mr. Tyler joined him immediately.

"I think the area we need to focus on is my analysis of current research. Perhaps, we missed some of the key words used by Kelly and Henry," Tucker said without preamble. "It was easy to get a list of foreign companies currently doing business in the South American countries that have the probability of gaining emerging economic nation status. Of those five countries, I eliminated Venezuela and Columbia because of the drug cartel's probable sabotage of any major manufacturing effort. That left Argentina, Chile and Brazil."

Tucker paused while his boss absorbed the information and when Mr. Tyler finally nodded, he continued. "As you can see, Germany and Japan seem to have dominated the field of venture capital. Then I limited the companies to those ventures that had been capitalized in the last five years. You will notice that none of the big investors in either of the two countries appear as players. I don't know what that means, but it seems an interesting question to pose to your team."

Tucker had prepared computer printouts of the overlapping circles used to schematize the information requested of the data base. As always, his boss was amazed at the number of logical approaches Tucker could come up with.

"Sorry about all these pages, Mr. Tyler. They mean very little, because even with all these queries, I couldn't find much. Look." He pointed to the set where he had requested information on all of the countries in South America having deep water ports, significant foreign investment and important non-government, commercial enterprises. The search indicated finding 32 such entries. Next, Tucker pointed to a set that limited the search to the previous five years and that dropped the number of entries to 12.

"Now, 12 entries seem about right, maybe a bit low, but look what happens when we separate the categories of acquisition and development..."

Two heads bent over the graphic presentation of data, slowly unraveling question after question that would need to be asked and satisfactory answers found before Zitec would consider expanding to the South American continent.

Tucker began refolding the computer printouts, satisfied in his own mind that the project wasn't dead but that logic and careful research had replaced staff enthusiasm. Henry and Kelly would have their work cut out for them. He felt more on the right track and evidently, so did the older man.

"Ah, by the way, Tucker," Mr. Tyler paused and fastened his gaze to the wall over Tucker's head. "I know I told you that Clifton would likely be sitting in on some of these meetings, but I've changed my mind. I'm not certain the three of us could accomplish what just the two of us do. I certainly would not want to dilute these sessions. I've come to see them as a necessity."

Tucker looked up from his work and caught Mr. Tyler's eyes somberly upon him. "Yes, sir," was all he said. But, he knew two things for certain: Mr. Tyler had been sincere about saying he was a necessity to the firm and that Mr. Tyler was going to come into the conference room absolutely bouncing with good will in about three minutes...which would mean to everyone assembled that a late lunch, if any, was at hand.

Chapter Ten

While Tucker and Mr. Tyler were preparing for their meeting at Zitec, the Tyler's houseguest, Dawn Simpson, had handed in her application to enroll as a Masters level student in the Boston School of Occupational Therapy. It was her last appointment before leaving the Medford/Somerville campus of Tufts.

The University had been most impressive, both in its curricular offerings and faculty attitude. Somehow, even though the rich heritage of the venerable campus left her feeling a bit awed, it was clear that participatory learning was a strongly held norm, and that fact moderated the feel of Tufts to a campus that fit beautifully into Dawn's view of how she wanted her learning experience to go; a dynamic blend of research and scholarship. Unlike the University of California at Santa Barbara, the classes at Tufts were, for the most part, small. She liked that and she liked the fact that the professors with whom she met seemed genuinely in love with teaching. Interviews had been designed to discover her goals in graduate work. The questions she asked were answered forthrightly and it was clear that each faculty member she had come to visit had read both her transcript and her letters of recommendation. To a person, they had been supportive of her application, giving her a feeling of optimism as she signed the final forms that would send her application to the graduate admissions committee.

She was now free to meander happily south in the rented Mustang convertible. Putting down the top of the peppy, red car, she realized with a pang how much she was counting on admission. Then she paused, shrugged and told herself it was now in someone else's hands; time to let the worry go and begin the last leg of her adventure.

Once she cleared the Boston metropolitan area, she headed towards Plymouth Harbor and the Pilgrim Memorial State Park. She also wanted to go to the Cape Cod National Seashore Park, places James had recommended she see. It took her out of her way, but she wanted to be able to take pictures for her family.

Besides, she couldn't quite get over how short distances between places were. The distance from Boston to New Haven was less than the distance from Santa Barbara to Los Angeles. James had told her that New York, Massachusetts, Rhode Island and Connecticut together were less by half than the size of California.

As she exited Route 3 and headed for Plymouth Harbor, she was blissfully unaware that two and a half hours away, Midge and Charlie, were at that very moment, putting the finishing touches on factors that would control her life for the weekend.

It was a good decision to come east, she thought as she pulled into the parking lot of the monument. It was so different than she had expected--so different from the rolling brown-velvet hills around Santa Barbara. She smiled to herself. *It was watching all those gangster movies and the hordes of people in Times Square watching the ball come down on New Year's Eve that gave me the impression that the East Coast was totally concrete, wall-to-wall people and maybe a dangerous place to live. Thank goodness I listened to Dr. Dravin.*

As she was nearing completion of her degree in psychology, one of her favorite professors at the University of California at Santa Barbara started talking with her about doing graduate work in the East. Casually, she had mentioned his suggestion to her parents. A bachelor's degree in psychology, as much as she had loved the four years of study, didn't qualify her to do much, she admitted. And besides, although she was certain she wanted to work with children, she really wasn't sure a clinical practice was what she wanted. To do something more activity-based, such as adaptive physical education or occupational therapy seemed more interesting.

Her mother immediately suggested that they call her dear friend and sorority sister, Midge Tyler, who lived in in a small town near New Haven, Connecticut, to see what schools might be available in her area.

Dawn had demurred, images of crowded, dirty cities, ghettos and rude people filling her mind. But then, on a whim, she had asked for an appointment with Dr. Dravin, the man who had first planted the idea of broadening her horizons to ask for details.

His strong recommendation had been Tufts University in Boston. He had also laughed heartily about her perceptions of smoke, dirt, wall-to-wall people and crime infested streets. He assured her that she could go to such areas if she chose, but that much of the East Coast was quite rural. She had listened carefully, but hadn't really believed him.

A week after her conversation with Dr. Dravin, encouraged by her parents, she had written to Tufts requesting information, trying to ignore the voice of her own misgivings.

Her father and her mother pushed her to explore other schools as well. She declined at the time, feeling sure, after receiving the literature from the school, that there were several programs she would want to pursue. Child development, social work and occupational therapy topped her list. Now, looking at the unimpressive piece of granite that had once been part of Plymouth Rock and reading the careful interpretation, part of her mind drifted. She was excited about Tufts, but was sorry she had limited herself now that it really WAS too late to explore further. Her parents had given her two expense-paid weeks in the East as a graduation present. The first week she had spent with the Tylers and their wonderful staff-turned-family, Clarice and Charlie. Most of the second week, she dedicated to learning about Tufts and exploring the eastern coast. Now, she was nearly out of time; Midge would be taking her to catch her plane on Monday.

She sighed. A degree in occupational therapy from Tufts was what she now had her heart set on... *But what if I don't make the cut? Why didn't I go ahead and explore other options?* It was totally unlike her not to have a backup plan. She decided she would at least ask the Tylers what they knew about schools in their area.

Thinking of the Tylers also made her smile reflectively. *Thank heavens I listened to my mom when she suggested I use them for a home base.* With a continent between them and no real excuse to travel, her mom and Midge had only seen each other three or four times in the last 20 odd years. But they talked often on the phone, remembered each other's birthdays and sent pictures and cards at Christmas. Despite the distance and the time, the bond of friendship had remained surprisingly strong.

Smiling, she remembered how Midge had scooped her off the plane, ushered her to the baggage claim area, insisted that they find a porter to carry her minimal luggage and then whisked her through the front entry door of the airport with only minutes to spare before her chauffeur carefully maneuvered the purring, champagne-colored Mercedes curbside. There, he skillfully palmed the porter a generous tip, after seeing to it that her bag and backpack had been carefully stowed in the cavernous trunk.

All three were puffing slightly and laughing as the big car carefully nosed back out into the creeping traffic. "Dawn, meet Hank. Hank, meet Dawn," laughed a self-satisfied Midge Tyler.

Hank, one of three chauffeurs employed by Zitec Global Development, smiled at Dawn in the rearview mirror. "Nice to meet cha, Dawn. Ain't this lady a little tornado when she decides to get somethin' done? You ever been in an' outta any airport this fast in your life?"

Dawn shook her head vehemently, unknowingly creating the effect of spun gold floating in the sunlight slanting through the back window of the car, causing both of the older people to catch their breath and remember younger times.

Grinning unselfconsciously, she said, "Never! But I knew from my mom about this lady's ability to organize, so, I'm not surprised."

Midge ran fingers through her short hair, as if making sure it was organized too, pleased with the accolades. They turned to look at each other. Dawn sat quietly while Midge took stock. "You know," she said, "pictures do not do you justice. You are probably the healthiest looking person I have ever seen. You must drink fresh California orange juice every day!"

Hank, taking advantage of his long-standing as a safe and reliable driver for the company and the excuse of his 68 years said, "She ain't only healthy lookin', she's beautiful. Only what he said sounded like "bootieful." His words set everyone laughing again.

"Thank you, Hank." Dawn had said without guile, "It was the luck of the gene pool."

And so it had gone. There was never an anxious moment. She and Midge were soon filling each other in on a number of things interesting to them both.

Dawn had only one moment tinged with sadness at the house and that was soon after she had arrived and realized that the bedroom assigned to her must once have been their son's. The room obviously had been redone, but there were clues that a less perceptive person might have missed. Dawn, being Dawn, noticed everything right away. The first thing was a small but beautiful bronze statue of a thoroughbred horse on the bureau. Another was a built-in desk complete with bulletin board and the third thing she saw as she looked out the window onto the magnificent grounds and vacant stable was the most poignant of the three. Scratched crudely into the hard mahogany wood of the windowsill was a name. "Scotty" it read, carved by a small boy's new pocketknife she imagined. Scott, she knew from her mother, had been the Tyler's only son. He died from an aneurysm of the brain his freshman year in high school. One minute he had been a laughing, dashing adolescent, schooling a recalcitrant thoroughbred over a jump, and the next minute he was unconscious on the ground. She didn't know all the details, only that he hadn't survived. She had still been in junior high at the time. She did remember when her mother got the phone call.

She thought back. Her family had been just starting dessert. In fact she and her younger brother, Cal, were arguing about who had to answer the phone. Their mother had settled the argument by answering it herself. Dawn could clearly remember the whiteness of her face when she returned to the dining room and said to her husband, "Charles that was Midge. Make a plane reservation for me, please." Her voice had choked then, and it took a great effort for her to whisper, "They've just lost Scotty to an aneurysm."

Tears, held firmly in check stood in the corners of her mother's eyes. She squared her shoulders took a ragged breath and said firmly "I must go pack now... And Dawn dear, you are in charge of Cal and Lisa Ann while Daddy takes me to the airport. Please see that the kitchen is cleaned up so Maggie doesn't have to do it all in the morning."

Her dad, without a word, had jumped up to go and do her bidding, but her mom had lingered a moment, given each of them hugs so hard they almost hurt as they sat stone still in their chairs, dessert forgotten. Then, without a word, she left to do her packing. Dawn remembered that her mother had specifically put her in charge of bedtime, a responsibility she usually hated.

"Please see that you're all in bed by nine. It's a school day tomorrow." She had said to the group. Then she looked directly at Dawn. "I'm counting on you, dear." She had given her older daughter an extra squeeze and the younger children a long, "do as I say," look. But this time there had been no problems. Like zombies they cleaned up the kitchen. Their dad, who was leaving a note, dictated by his wife, of instructions for Maggie, the lady who came in days to help, was amazed by the lack of bickering.

"Hey, guys," he had said, "you can relax a little. Mom has got to go and help Midge and James, but she'll be back in a few days and I should be back in a few hours." His words were wasted. There was no relaxing. Things were too topsy-turvy. Someone they didn't really know had died. Thinking about death was scary, but not as scary as watching their parents walk out the door and knowing that their dad would return, but that their mom wouldn't be there when they woke up in the morning.

They stood at the door for their final hugs, waved until their parents were out of sight, and then turned as a unit. Though it was not yet nine, they climbed the stairs toward their bedrooms. Seven-year-old Lisa Ann had tucked her hand into Dawn's at the top of the stairs. Big blue eyes pleading, the little girl whispered, "Could I sleep with you tonight please, Dawn?" Touched, she'd nodded affirmation and then noticed Cal standing stock still, watching them, too proud to ask. Lightly she reached out and punched his arm. "Care to join us, big guy?"

That's how their father had found them, snuggled, pajama-clad, a scatter of intertwined arms and legs. Gently, he had disengaged the two younger children and carried them back to their respective beds.

125

Thinking back, Dawn could remember her mother had been gone for more than a week that seemed more like a month. Things had been running pretty ragged by the time she returned. Dawn couldn't remember her saying much about the trip or the death. But, the first evening back she gathered the three of them around her on the couch; she and Cal on either side, Lisa Ann on her lap. "I don't think Daddy and I tell you three often enough how much you mean to us. We love you so very much and we are very proud of how you all pitched in to help while I was away."

There was something somber and serious in her voice. It wasn't the lighthearted hugging and kissing she usually did and for some reason it embarrassed them all a little. Not understanding, they'd squirmed away and Cal had said, "Aw, Mom!" Dawn wished that at least one of them had said they loved her too.

Now, Plymouth Rock behind her, driving along the in the snappy, red Mustang convertible that Mr. Tyler had insisted she rent, Dawn pulled herself from her musing and glanced at the map. She was doing well! Having learned to drive on crowded, crazy, California freeways, the East Coast beltways, turnpikes and parkways simply seemed different, not undoable…though Boston itself had been a bit of a challenge with all the tailgating and honking of horns. It was no wonder so many of the cars there had scrapes and dents.

Looking at her watch, she decided if she skipped the Cape, there would be time for a long run before dinner if her calculations were correct. That was something else that had surprised her about the East; so much room to run. She had almost left her Adidas at home. It would have been a big mistake. As it was, she had been able to run almost every day, had in fact, cruised the entire Tufts campus. It had been a perfect way to see how much older and more venerable it looked than any West Coast campus she'd ever seen. She liked that; it gave her a sense of the country's history.

She felt the same way about the Tyler's house. It seemed so historic. Laughing to herself, she decided she should probably call a structure that you were chauffeur-driven to, had acres of rolling lawn, a huge yacht moored within view, a stable, and a residence big enough to swallow two of their own generous California ramblers, would probably be called a mansion or an estate, not simply a house.

Whatever it was called, she liked it. That first day when Hank had pulled the car under the porte-cochere and she realized that the unassuming woman sitting next to her was the mistress of all this, she turned and said, cocking an eyebrow, "You sure you have room for me?"

Midge had at first looked slightly shocked. Then she burst into a peal of her tinkling laughter. "My gracious, child, you are your mother's daughter. Only Barbara has a sense of humor drier than my own."

She turned and took both of Dawn's hands in her own, leaving Hank to stand, a willing eavesdropper, holding the open car door. "Yes, dear, we certainly do have room for you. I already have my fingers crossed that you will decide to continue your education in the East and that you will come as often as you like and stay as long as it suits you. You've not yet met James, but my guess is, you two will take to each other immediately, especially if you can talk boats or golfing."

Dawn laughed. "I grew up in Santa Barbara, land of sun, sailing, surfing, swimming, golf, tennis and almost anything else a person can do outdoors. My mother spent the years of my youth worrying because I was such a tomboy and the years of my adolescence worrying because I had turned into a girl."

Midge nodded as she stepped from the car. "I can well imagine," she said dryly. "Young men must absolutely have flocked to your door."

Dawn, standing tall above the gray cap of curls and looking down at the trim figure beside her said in a matter of fact tone, "Oh, probably not any more than they flocked to yours when you were my age. Mom said the only reason you weren't a model is that you forgot to grow tall."

"Model?" The sound of Midge's pleased chuckle floated back as they walked towards the ornately carved front door. "My dear, I never gave that field a thought. They used to call me Midget, you know. In fact, James still does sometimes when he knows I'm in a good mood. Now, your mother was the one! She could've modeled. She also could have had any boy or man in college, but she seemed to ignore them all until she met your dad. Then talk about head over heels! James and I double-dated with them from time to time and we used to tease them that at the end of the evening, they would never have been able to remember who else was in the car."

Now, just thinking about that conversation with Midge gave Dawn a warm but slightly homesick feeling. Her parents were still like that sometimes. She wondered if she would be like her mom, not seriously interested in anyone until she met the man she wanted to marry. *So far*, she thought, *it sure seems like I am.* Though she had a lot of good male friends, had dated a bunch, no one had really ever given her that special feeling she was waiting for. Oh, she'd felt she was close a time or two, had even gone steady for a while her senior year, but when things started feeling too serious, she cut and ran. She shook her head, remembering her reputation of being a heartbreaker. One of the campus clowns at UCSB had put out the word: "Look out for Dawn Simpson. She's a wonderful friend, but a terrible date. She'll break your heart and beat you at tennis all on the same day."

She shrugged inwardly and thought, *Oh well. I am who I am. College was fun and my friends are real.* A group of them still got together on the beach as often as they could manage. *Life has been really good to me,* she reminded herself sternly and then sighed, feeling a bit depressed. Not many of her friends came from families like hers. The homesick feeling hit her again as she pictured things that were going on at home.

For the first time, she really thought about what moving to the East Coast would mean. The only times she had really been away from home had been summer camps as a girl, visiting her grandparents in Oregon, and weekend camping with friends, both in high school and in college. Once, her parents had gone to Europe on a vacation, but she had been a junior in high school and more interested in her friends than family life. Besides, they were the ones who were away from home. She still had her friends, her room and her things about her. This time it would be very different. She would only get to see her family two or three times a year. She felt a tremendous sense of aloneness.

128

Suddenly her throat felt tight and a piece of Dawn was aware that there was more going on inside her than homesickness. She took an exit off the Old Boston Post Road and pulled into a parking lot. She felt confused and drained, but had the overpowering need to stay where she was until she got some understanding of her emotions.

Suddenly, she found herself wondering if it was this hard for her friends to leave home. *It sure doesn't seem that way. Most of them couldn't believe I wanted to live at home through all four years at UCSB when they could hardly wait to move into an apartment or sorority. Maybe,* she thought, *I'm just a bit retarded in my desire for independence. Maybe that is why moving East sounded like a good thing. I mean, once I moved that far, I wouldn't be likely to wimp out and go running home.* She sighed, a second deep, shaky sigh and recognized a ring of truth in what she had just admitted to herself. It wasn't just the opportunity to widen her horizons; it was to place a continent between herself and her family so she wouldn't go running home and embarrass herself. It also explained why she hadn't pursued other Eastern schools. *There is probably a part of me hoping Tufts will fall through.* She lifted her chin and jerked open the convertible's door, as if to deny the picture forming in her mind of herself as a middle-aged spinster still living at home. That was definitely NOT what she had in mind! *I just need to give myself a boost out of the nest, that's all.*

With another bit of insight she realized that just a little while ago she had been thinking about exploring other colleges, not for their superior programs, but because she wanted to be closer to Mr. and Mrs. Tyler. She wanted to substitute one set of parents for another. "No, Dawn, my girl, you are made of better stuff than that! You will go to Tufts, if they accept you, and they probably will, and that is that!"

She lowered herself into the car and sat another five minutes, thinking, unconsciously pulling some of the wind tossed tangles from her hair, then started the engine, remembering the run she had promised herself.

As she drove, she reflected that it felt like she had reached a firm decision about the course of her life...well at least the next few years. She recognized that it would be a

129

major change for her and the whole idea would take some getting used to, but it certainly felt right.

By the time she crossed the Massachusetts state line and was back in Connecticut, her natural optimism had partly returned. As she pulled into the vast circular driveway, it came to her that she was really looking forward to seeing Midge and to be able to bounce her thinking off her mother's old friend...but first, a long, easy run in the afternoon sunshine.

Chapter Eleven

It was a productive meeting and all but Tucker were amazed by their boss's understanding of the issues and by the questions he fielded. But, by the time the meeting let out at 1:00 and Tucker and Mr. Tyler had thoroughly debriefed, it was past 2:00. By the time Mr. Tyler told him details about the weekend, including obscure hints about their blonde houseguest, with whom he was obviously enamored, it was 2:15. Since Tucker's first priority was to sit down at a computer and get a hard copy summarized for his boss, he bolted towards his office telling Peggy to hold all his calls. The complexity of the interactions of staff was a challenge even to his great memory and this was one meeting he wanted to get immediately into a computer's memory bank. At 3:10 he punched the "SAVE" command and then gave the "SEND" command, placing the data in Mr. Tyler's computer. By 3:15 he was jogging to his car, knowing he was going to be rushing for the rest of the day. Something, he reminded himself again, he absolutely hated to do. It was such a graphic reminder of poor planning.

He unlocked the Aston Martin and slid behind the wheel. Getting to Kathryn's on time was doable with a little luck and good driving. What he didn't have time for today was lunch or the garden. Missing lunch wasn't an uncommon incident, but he wished he had time for just a few minutes of sitting and watching the water trickle over the rocks in the fountain. He wondered what the woman would think if he showed up and said, "Never mind the massage; I'll take the garden treatment instead." For a moment he considered it seriously, but then remembered his pact with Dr. Beemers. He felt decidedly agitated about not selecting his preference, but instead of allowing the feelings to develop further, he concentrated on driving.

The man who walked up to Kathryn's office door may have convinced himself that he had tuned out his frustration, but Kathryn, taking advantage of the fact that he was several minutes late, was dusting and straightening magazines in the waiting room, sensed his tension the moment he strode through the door. She paused in mid-swipe with her dust cloth and watched him carefully, while smiling her welcome.

Tucker saw Kathryn and stopped, holding himself very still, seemingly quite relaxed, while he returned her smile. Then, still puffing slightly, he said in his mild, affable manner, "Sorry to be late. No excuses. Poor planning."

Kathryn thought, *this is one strange man. He can look so easy going and sound that way too. Yet I would bet $100 that every muscle in his body is as tightly strung as a steel guitar.* Aloud she said softly, "Oh, Mr. Jones, you needn't be sorry. It's Friday and we all get a little behind by Friday. Besides, I too have had a busy day with not a minute to put the waiting room to rights."

Tucker acknowledged her comments with a slight bow of his head, thinking how strong the lilt in her voice was at that moment. "You know Ms. McCall," he said smiling and meaning it, "I suddenly feel as though I not only have been forgiven, but that I have done you a favor. You are most gracious."

Kathryn, never at a loss for words was surprised to find herself unsure how to respond, but recognized immediately that somehow she suddenly felt gracious! Working on a hunch, she looked him squarely in the eye and said, "Please call me Kathryn. And listen, Mr. Jones, I have a proposal. I don't think you've yet had time to visit the garden. If you'd like, why don't you go sit in it for a bit. I'll make us a pitcher of juice and how about a bit of a snack? I'll confess I've not had time for a bite... Well, actually, I used my lunch break to get some bedding plants into the ground." Grinning ruefully she said, "You'll have a much better massage if I have a bite to eat."

The joyful look on Tucker's face came and went in such a flash that Kathryn later couldn't recall if it was real or just the result of her overactive and very creative imagination.

"Ms. McCall...ah, Kathryn..." Tucker stopped, cleared his throat, and then started again. "Kathryn, do you read minds? My original intent was to come an hour early today and spend time with your flowers. Unfortunately, that

132

didn't work out. Neither did time for lunch. So, actually, I would enjoy a bite to eat very much. I also have a dinner engagement in Branford that starts this evening and includes the weekend... For which I have not packed a single article. That means I cannot dawdle in your garden after our appointment, even though I had been counting on it. So, you see, if we could spend half of our hour in the garden and half in massage I would be a much happier man. He stopped, looked at her and sighed. "I am certain this is an imposition, but I am most grateful and I will most certainly reimburse you for your time."

They smiled at each other. "Go to the garden and admire my new handiwork and I'll join you," she said over her shoulder, already on her way to the kitchen.

Tucker stood for a moment watching her retreating back with a puzzled look on his face. There was something very sturdy and trustworthy about the square-framed woman. Something that allowed him to respond to her offer; knowing somehow that she didn't invite people to share her time if she didn't want to. There was comfort in that knowledge. *Mr. Tyler is like that;* he thought as he opened the door and headed for the garden.

Immediately, he spotted Kathryn's lunch time handiwork and stood, the afternoon sun warming his back like a blanket, noticing how the daffodils were trussed and hidden behind the new plantings. *She really is quite artistic and bold in her color scheme,* he thought. *That she would rather put the roots of tender young plants in the earth than eat, also says something about her.* He took off his suit coat and tie and hung them both carefully over the back of a chair before sitting back to absorb the warmth, the color, the sound and odors. He was grateful for the few moments of solitude that would allow him to master his emotions if the garden had lost its magic to soothe. He let his eyes leisurely roam the small space.

Suddenly, his gaze was arrested as he realized he was not alone after all. Large, aquamarine eyes held him in silent surveillance from under the ferns by the smoke tree. Haunches drawn well under, back straight, head up, tail curled sinuously around front paws, the cat looked very much like statuary placed just so, to surprise garden visitors. He returned the steady stare.

Tucker didn't really know very much about cats, having grown up with neither cat nor dog, but suspected this one was larger than average. He hoped it didn't mind his intrusion and that if not friendly; it was at least not aggressive. It did not seem to be either, he decided, as it sat stone-like, taking his measure; the stone image furthered by the grayness of the coat.

The sounds of Kathryn moving around in the kitchen were barely audible through the wall of the house. He could hear her footsteps and the muffled slam of a cupboard door. Obviously, those sounds also meant something to the cat. His attentive gaze wavered from its fixation on Tucker and he turned a cocked head toward the sounds from the kitchen. Carefully, uncoiling his tail, he stood with a graceful combined stretch and arching of his back. With great but unhurried purpose, he walked over to the table and without so much as a glance toward Tucker, sprang easily into one of the empty chairs and began washing a smoky paw.

The office door banged, startling them both, as Kathryn came into view carrying a tray laden with juice and sandwiches. Tucker jumped to his feet, embarrassed. "Sorry, I didn't hear you. I should have at least held the door," he blurted as he took the tray, set it on the table and deftly pulled out the remaining empty chair.

"Mr. Jones, you do have lovely manners," she smiled as she sat. Then she noticed the very attentive cat in the third chair and smiled again. "I see you have met Jon Bon. I should have known he would be here." She reached for the pitcher and poured two large glasses of orange juice. "The sandwiches are tuna. I don't know how he knows, but we think it's an association of sounds rather than smell; though we aren't really certain. All we know is that there is never a can of tuna opened at this house without his knowing it."

So, Tucker thought with surprise, *Jon Bon isn't the name of a son, it's the name of the cat.*

They looked at the dignified cat waiting quietly, but expectantly in the chair and then looked at each other. Tucker gave a small chuckle. "You had mentioned sharing the garden with Jon Bon, but I assumed it was a son, not a cat," he confessed. "I had been wondering about the origin of the name."

134

Kathryn laughed. "The origin of that name lies in the fertile mind of my seven year old daughter. Who knows how Allison comes up with most of the things she does. But I would wager if you asked her, she would have a logical, at least to her, explanation made up...if necessary, on the spot."

Neither had yet taken a bite and Katherine paused with a slight look of concern on her face. "Listen, I hope you aren't a vegetarian. I forgot to ask you, but decided on my own that you hadn't the look."

Tucker nodded. "You are correct in your assumption. I am not a vegetarian. Tuna is a wonderful food and the bread looks delicious." Tucker took a moderate bite and chewed in his usual slow and proper style, hand in lap, holding the paper napkin carefully in place.

"Actually," he said, once his mouth was empty, "going without lunch is usually not a hardship, but for some reason, today I am famished. I really cannot thank you enough." He smiled and inquired mildly, "Do you do this for all your clients?"

Unfortunately his question was asked just as Kathryn had taken a first healthy bite and was only able to shake her head in mute denial, while Tucker sat with his eyes fastened with fascination on her mouth, watching her chew. Suddenly, the realization that he was staring at the movement of her lips struck him and he reached for his juice glass, ducking his head in embarrassment. *Good Lord,* he chided himself, *you are behaving like an oafish lout today. This woman probably thinks you are an absolute ingrate. Get a hold of yourself! Say something charming.* Instead, he took another bite of sandwich, eyes fastened on his plate.

Kathryn, in fact, had not even noticed his slip in etiquette. Talking about Jon Bon's funny name had caused her thoughts to turn to her daughter's leaving. *Not much time left she thought sadly.*

Leaning back and putting her feet up in the cat's chair, she felt the sun warm her closed eyelids. Absentmindedly, she took a bite and chewed slowly. It was always so hard to have her leave. The house seemed empty in the absence of Allison's cheerful and organizing

135

"busybodyness." She swallowed, glanced at Tucker and said, "Sorry. I was thinking about my daughter. She goes to visit her father in a few days and it always takes me some time to adjust. You were asking, before I started wool gathering, if I made a bite for all my clients. The answer is, of course, no. I do offer a glass of juice, especially for those that have had a session in the steam cabinet and a deep massage. I don't like to send them away to drive when they are so relaxed. It seems to me that the juice should raise their blood sugar level." She shook her head in amusement. "No, the lunch was for me. I was really hungry too. But, you know, I will admit that I had a strong hunch back there in the office that you too were in need of a bite."

They glanced at each other's plates, both empty except for a cat bite of tuna left on Kathryn's, and smiled. He found he wanted to ask her a million questions, but all of them seemed somewhat personal, so he did not. Instead, he said, as he watched Jon Bon politely accept the morsel from her fingers, "I remember some things about flowers from my boyhood. I noticed your treatment of the daffodils and Narcissus. "It is very clever. We didn't do that. Instead, Ethan and I would dig the bulbs as they spent their blooms and replant them in what we called the 'recovery room.'"

Ethan's name had rolled smoothly from his thoughts and from his tongue. *The garden, even with Kathryn's presence is working its magic,* he thought. He looked at her and could tell she was waiting for him to continue.

"Recovery room? What on earth is that?" She finally prompted, clearly interested.

"Oh, it was just a greenhouse behind the caretakers' cottage where we planted things in want of a rest; things no longer in a suitable state for the formal gardens flanking the house and drive; things needing a little extra care. It was sunny and protected with good soil, like this in your garden. So things usually recovered and got rotated back into the landscaping when the time was right."

Tucker's whole countenance, it seemed to Kathryn, had relaxed a bit when he spoke of the "recovery garden." Unknowingly, she had leaned forward, pulling her feet off the cat's chair and tucking them onto her own. "So, you could take all the bulbs and replant them until their foliage had died. Then did you dig them up?"

Tucker nodded "I think so. I think Ethan dug and divided them in the fall and then replanted them out in front in the spring. There seemed to be hundreds and hundreds of them and I can remember complaining to Ethan that it was too much work for their short blooming period. But, he said he planted them so the good Lord would be reminded, come spring, what the color of sunshine was."

Kathryn nodded, charmed. "But," she said, "in a way you were right. It means those bulbs had to be planted two different times each year. I don't believe I've ever heard of such a thing!" She fell silent, trying to picture the setting Tucker had just described. "It does seem a lot of work to avoid a bit of wilted brown foliage, doesn't it? The flowers must've been glorious though."

Tucker closed his eyes, remembering the yellow and cream flowers lining the drive, circling trees and shrubs with their bright spots of color. "Actually, they were quite showy, as I recall."

Something in the way he punctuated the sentence let Kathryn know that the subject was at an end. She was perceptive enough not to press. She looked at her watch and jumped to her feet. "Good gracious, Mr. Jones, our 30 minutes in the garden has turned into nearly 40. If we don't hurry, you are going to end up keeping your hostess waiting after all."

Tucker rose in a much more dignified fashion. "Well," he said, "I suppose we could cancel the massage, although I suddenly find myself reluctant to do so. Let's give it a go and let the rest of the day work itself out."

Even as he said the words, Tucker found himself mentally contradicting himself, though without much conviction. *Things don't just work out. It's planning and careful organization that causes things to work out,* he chided himself. Then, he gave a mental shrug and let the thought go before reaching to help Kathryn load the dishes on the tray. He took one last glance around the garden before picking up both coat and tie then following her into the reception room.

He felt much more relaxed now that he knew the routine and stretched out willingly on the table, waiting patiently while she dispensed with the tray and washed her hands.

"Mr. Jones, I know our agreement is to only work on your back, but last time I noticed that you carry just as much tension in your neck and possibly even your head. Perhaps you could think about allowing me to work on those areas a bit after I'm done with your back, if not today, then at a future date."

Kathryn's request was delivered in a manner that suggested she didn't care one whit whether he availed himself of the additional massage or not. She intended to give him plenty of time to think about it and tried to make it sound like a simple, offhand suggestion. She succeeded.

Face down on the table, feeling only a little anxious, Tucker mumbled into the crisp white sheet, "Maybe on Monday." He couldn't see Kathryn smile as she began to smooth the warm oil onto his skin. *Bit by bit,* she thought to herself, *bit by bit, I'll get him to loosen up.* Then she began to concentrate on the steel puzzle under her hands, aware that her time was limited, but that just getting the man used to having hands touch and work his muscles would be forward progress. *In fact*, she thought, as she worked, *perhaps he is already a little less tense today. Perhaps the garden does help him relax.* She tried to picture him as a boy, planning bulbs in muddy dirt, but found the image incongruous with the man in the pressed suit and perfectly coordinated shirt, socks and paisley tie.

Tucker, lying quietly under the strong hands, tried to concentrate on the poking and prodding going on with his muscles. Much of it verged on being painful he decided as strong fingers found and depressed knotted muscle, holding the pressure for what seemed minutes before releasing, only to apply the pressure a second and even third time. Just when he would be about to protest, the prodding would stop and a soothing kneading motion would begin. When she began rubbing off the excess oil with the towel, he realized his 20 minutes were up and was surprised to find himself feeling regret.

"Now, Mr. Jones, I know you're feeling a bit pressed for time, but please do stay on the table for just a few minutes to give your muscles a chance to get used to feeling a bit more relaxed. They've a memory for such things you know," said the lilting voice floating above his head.

138

He did as she asked, listening to the sounds of her closing for the day, wondering where her daughter was, wondering what she would say if she knew that he was wondering about such a personal thing.

After a few minutes, she released him and handed him his shirt. "Now, Mr. Jones, don't embarrass me by offering to pay for the time in the garden. In fact, why don't you just pop into your suit jacket and be on your way. We'll settle your debt up on Monday."

Tucker sat up, starting to protest and then simply nodded his head while slipping back into his shirt. "That makes sense, if you're sure you don't mind. I'll be, as you so aptly put it, on my way, and then Monday when things are less hectic, we can settle on a fee."

It was only after she let them out and turned the lock that Kathryn realized the man had avoided answering her request that he not pay for the time spent in the garden. She hoped it would not be an issue. To think of taking pay for allowing someone to spend time in her garden somehow made her feel... It was hard to put her finger exactly on the emotion... *Not exactly cheap*, she thought, *although that is a component*. The word 'unworthy' popped into her mind. *Yes, that's it. It would make me feel unworthy-- like being paid for a good deed or an act of kindness.* Her mother always said, 'Some things you do for pay and other things you do to pay back the world for its blessings, and the two shouldn't be confused.'

Kathryn sighed and looked at her watch. She had about 20 minutes before she had to go pick Allison up from her music lesson; time to change her clothes and set a sprinkler or two.

Chapter Twelve

As he pulled away from Kathryn's, Tucker realized that his sense of needing to rush had evaporated. It wasn't that he didn't need to hurry. It was obvious to him that he would be leaving Guilford for Branford just at the peak of rush hour traffic. It was also obvious that he was going to be late and would need to call Midge and let her know. Somehow, it just didn't seem important enough to be upset about.

Remembering his intention to call and accept Heather's concert invitation, he punched her number into his car phone and found himself pleased that she was at home. Generally, he preferred answering machines.

"Hello, Heather, this is a contrite Tucker Jones finally returning your call and saying he'd be delighted to attend the concert and to thank you very much for your thoughtful invitation." His voice sounded slightly bantering, but at the same time, genuinely sincere.

She was a woman who knew what she wanted and generally got it. She hadn't really decided if she wanted Tucker Jones yet, but she was interested. Actually, it wasn't his good looks, his money or his good manners that attracted her. She had enough money, looks in men weren't all that important to her and everyone with whom she associated had good manners. No, what intrigued Heather was his aloofness. She was rather used to men fawning over her and Tucker had not. He had been polite and good company when they had been together, but if he was attracted to her, he was keeping it well hidden. Heather smiled to herself. She did love a challenge!

They chatted easily about the details, about the glorious weather and as Heather had nothing definite or exciting planned for the weekend, she decided to test the waters and move the conversation on to their respective weekend activities, hoping for a spontaneous invitation of some sort. When Tucker said he had been invited to

Branford to sail with the Tylers, she felt suddenly and unaccountably cross that she had not.

After saying a pleasant goodbye to Tucker, she hung up the phone and tapped it with one, carefully manicured fingernail. It would be very easy for her to ring up Midge and get herself invited for the weekend, but she wondered how smart it would be. What would Tucker's reaction be to find her there? She just wasn't sure. However, she suspected if he thought she was interested in him, he would run the other way. *No,* she thought, *stick to your plan. Match his aloofness, pleasant banter and politeness with your own.* Yet, the more she pondered it, the more undecided she became. A sailing weekend might be the perfect opportunity to display her feigned lack of attraction. She could easily picture herself charming the other guests, helping Mr. Tyler with the boat and acting very casual, but kindly towards Tucker. Besides, she had several new outfits, not to mention a new swimsuit, just perfect for a casual weekend of sailing. That thought, and those images tipped the scale. She decided to call Midge and invite her to lunch one day next week, perhaps dropping the fact that she had no particular plans for this weekend somewhere in the conversation.

Midge Tyler was nobody's fool, but she had also been the one to introduce Heather to Tucker in the first place and just might be a willing ally. Only a phone call would tell. Heather paused a moment before picking up the receiver, rehearsing the conversation and its possible outcomes in her mind. If invited, she needed to protest just the right amount before giving in. If not invited, she must be smooth enough to make Midge think the phone call's main purpose was the lunch invitation and the other conversation was just idle chitchat. It absolutely couldn't seem that she was trying to wrangle an invitation if she and Midge weren't on the same wavelength.

One of the things that always surprised Heather when calling the Tylers was the fact that Midge herself usually answered the phone. At her own parent's house, the help was trained with the precision of a professional answering service, to field the calls.

Today, Midge sounded a little harried, but in her usual cheerful mood when she answered the phone.

Heather said as much and Midge, as if on cue said "Oh dear, yes, I guess 'cheerfully harried' would correctly describe my state. James has Charlie and me rushing about, planning one of our famous, last-minute boat parties. We have a darling young friend from California staying with us, though right now she's on her way back from visiting Tufts University and I'm starting to worry because she's not yet here..."

Heather cut in smoothly, feeling that Midge was about to go off on a tangent. "Well, I won't keep you, then. You are going to have splendid weather. I wish I had thought far enough in advance to have something "outdoorish" to do. I find myself a bit envious. However, this call is about inviting you and mother out to the club for lunch next week. I have a tennis lesson scheduled at 1:00 on Thursday, and if this weather holds, we could have a leisurely lunch on the deck before I meet the pro." Heather made up the details as she talked. "I'm calling you first, because I'm pretty sure mother is free, but I wasn't sure about your volunteer work. I know mother would adore playing nine holes with you."

Heather had given special emphasis to the words adore and you which caused Midge to laugh. "Heather, your mother would adore playing nine holes of golf any time with anyone, including me. It does sound fun. Call Elaine and check to make sure she's not already playing. I did have Althea and myself penciled in to do some work at the S.O.S. office, but we can change that. Just let me know."

"Wonderful!" Heather exclaimed. "I'll organize it. How very good it will be to see you again. It's been a long time." Knowing full well that what she was about to propose was highly unlikely, she said wistfully, "I don't suppose Mr. Tyler could come too? It does seem ages since I've seen you both." She let the note of wistfulness turn to sadness in her voice and Midge immediately felt that she had somehow been neglecting this beautiful young woman.

"I'm sorry Heather, but James generally works right through the lunch hour. I know he would really love to see you, but his working day is truly that. Even I am not privileged to lunch with my husband."

"Oh." Heather said, allowing a sad and wistful note to play along the line before continuing in a determinedly cheerful voice, playing her last card. "Well, I will definitely have you both in my thoughts this weekend. It should be glorious sailing weather." That was it. Either Midge would say, "Come along dear," or she wouldn't.... But she did.

"Goodness, Heather, if you don't have weekend plans, please consider joining us. Besides, our houseguest, Dawn, and a few other older folks, there are three other young people you know. Deborah, Robert and of course, Tucker. Charlie and I are just now putting the finishing touches on the menu. Please do try to arrange your plans."

Now that's a sincere invitation, Heather noted to herself with satisfaction. On the other end of the phone line, she relaxed into her most gracious mode, allowing herself to be only slightly coaxed before accepting.

Once off the phone, Midge smiled to herself, a twinkle in her eye. *Two beautiful women for Tucker,* she thought mischievously, and hurried, somewhat nervously, to tell Charlie that one more person would be joining the group. She knew he wouldn't complain. He never did. But sometimes she wondered how close she came to tapping the depth of his patience. In this case, he simply nodded and reached again for the magic book.

"Menu might have to change a little, Mam. Ms. Anderson has long list after name," Charlie said quite matter-of-factly, apparently ready to throw out Wednesday's planning and start over if necessary, even though he should instead be starting on the preparations for the evening meal.

Midge paused, frowning. "What do you mean Charlie? Is Heather one of our picky eaters?"

Charlie nodded and handed Midge the book.

"Why so she is! I'd forgotten that. Good heavens, she's only been to dinner three times and look at the list! She won't eat things with garlic in them? Good heavens!" She exclaimed again. "If that isn't uncivilized, it is at least unusual."

Midge thought fast. There would only be the four of them this evening, if Dawn and Tucker showed up as scheduled. *Good thing, since garlic prawns were on the night's menu,* she thought with relief. Tomorrow morning, there would be a simple buffet for guests as they arrived. No garlic there. But her frown deepened as she looked at

Charlie's proposed menu of "boat foods." A third "Good heavens!" showed the state of her growing agitation. "I've really thrown a monkey-wrench into things haven't I? Practically everything we like has garlic in it. I don't think I ever noticed that before."

Charlie took the book and rescanned the list: allergic to shellfish, no garlic, spicy foods make sneeze, limit salt, no peppers (red, green, orange, yellow), no dairy products, cause rash. The list went on to the back of the page. At the bottom, in a carefully drawn box labeled simply, Miss Anderson liked – – were exactly seven entries: grapes, croissants, yogurt, chicken, salmon mousse, beef bourguignon, coffee.

Midge slapped the book shut and made a quick decision. They had already ordered 15 pounds of cherrystone clams six loaves of French bread to be made properly garlicky and served with a huge salad made of those new, fancy lettuces being imported from California growers and a dozen Maine lobsters. She certainly did not intend to ask Charlie to change that menu. Besides, she thought, Charlie's beef bourguignon had lots of garlic in it, so perhaps Heather wasn't serious about her eating dislikes. *Who knows what goes on in the minds of young people these days!* She thought.

"Charlie, would you have time to perhaps roast a chicken or two and call the bakery and have them include some croissants along with the other bread we've ordered? Other than that, I vote we leave the menu alone"

Charlie, face bland, nodded. Then he grinned mischievously and slipped into a teasing, Charlie Chaplin voice. "No problem, Mam. Charlie call now. All be delivered one hour. Dinner be on time. Breakfast be on time. Guests arrive. Be on boat by 10:00. Captain happy. All fine."

Midge laughed at the idiomatic speech and touched him on the arm, eyes suddenly serious. "Thank you again, Charlie. I know I've said it a thousand times, but I really don't know what we would do without you!"

She turned and walked over to a drawer for her clipping shears, still perplexed over Heather's apparently diverse list of unacceptable foods. *Not that I know her very well,* she admitted to herself, *but she certainly appears to be in robust health, easy-going and thoughtful.* Midge tried

144

to think of other picky eaters she knew and could not think of a one that was not somewhat neurotic. Heather Anderson, she decided, would bear some close watching. With a sigh, she slipped out of the door and into her garden.

Dawn, directed by Charlie, found Midge just walking towards the patio with an arm full of flowers. "Well done, dear, you've arrived and just in time. I was beginning to let myself worry a bit." Midge tucked her flowers under one arm and reached out for a one-armed hug.

Dawn returned the hug and the two women walked arm in arm toward the kitchen entry. Dawn's voice spilling news of her adventures with such enthusiasm and at such a pace that Midge found herself breathless. There was something so infectious about this wonderful young woman's boundless energy and optimism.

"But really, Midge, I've just got to have a run. I'm dying to run. I've been cooped up in that car for too long. Just tell me what time I need to be back, showered and presentable and I promise I will." Dawn's earnestness made Midge laugh.

"Well, many plans have been made in your absence, but I can wait to share them if you can wait to hear. Go and have your run. We do have one houseguest arriving this evening, so we will be dressing for dinner. Count on dining at 7:00, and if you want to join us for cocktails, be ready by 6:00."

"No problem! Absolutely no problem!" Dawn reached over and planted a quick kiss on top of the silver curls and hurried off to get the bag containing her running togs from the trunk of the red Mustang.

Midge sighed, pleased with the demonstration of affection. *That's what Charlie always says. 'No problem'. Really, it's an excellent motto, if not philosophy for life,* she mused to herself as she set the flowers in the sink of the gardening room and went to select a crystal vase.

Tucker called just as she finished arranging the mass of flowers for the sideboard; a proper backdrop for tomorrow's breakfast buffet. It was unusual that he would call when he should be driving his lovely old car up the drive within an hour.

145

Before he had a chance to do more than say who he was, Midge interrupted. "Tucker, dear, why are you calling? Don't you dare tell me you've got to work or that you have some terrible bug and can't come. I won't hear of it! Especially, since I've arranged not one, but two beautiful young women for your weekend's companionship."

Tucker laughed. He could hear the note of real stress under the light tone and rushed to reassure his hostess. "Now, Mrs. T, even if I weren't in excellent health, which I am, the thought of seeing you, not to mention two gorgeous women, would bring me around. It's just that I have been running a bit late all day today. I'm at the condo right now and will take the time to dress for dinner and throw a few things in the boot of the car before I head out. The radio is saying that traffic is in its usual Friday night frenzy. So, this call is to say don't hold cocktails. It's going to take me a couple of hours.

"Oh, Tucker," Midge said with relief, "thank you so much for letting me know. I shouldn't imagine you're going to be able to be here much before 7:00. So, now I can catch Dawn before she goes running and tell her to take her time. See how things work out, dear?"

Midge hung up and hurried to intercept Dawn who was coming down the wide curving staircase backwards, two steps at a time, pausing to do a wide-legged stretch at each dissent. She grinned it Midge, looking up through her bangs. "I do this at home. Hope you don't mind. It really stretches my hamstrings."

"Of course I don't mind, Dawn. You can stretch any string you want to on my stairs. You do it quite gracefully."

Dawn smiled and pointed to the back of her well-formed thigh. "There's nothing like a long drive to shorten this muscle. I tend to neglect it, but I can always tell because then I can't touch my toes." So saying, she reached over and placed both palms flat on the carpet in front of Midge.

My goodness, thought Midge with awe, *if only Tucker could see her now!* Dawn had her hair pulled up into a tight, no-nonsense pony-tail that would have been severe on most women. On Dawn, it merely accentuated her wonderful bone structure and made her eyes even larger

146

and darker. She was dressed in a loose fitting tank top and nylon running shorts in an electric, florescent pink.

Midge sighed. "Dawn, you should present yourself to a sporting goods manufacturer. I'm sure they would pay you to wear their products. I can't believe how becoming you look in such simple togs. Your mother was the same way, you know. Only, I think your suppleness makes you even more naturally graceful in your movements. I mean, no one should look graceful descending two steps at a time, backwards, bent like a pretzel, but somehow you did."

Dawn laughed. "Thank you, Midge. I'll hurry so we'll have time to talk before your houseguest arrives."

Midge waved her hand. "No need. He just called and is running late. He said he'd be here as soon as traffic allowed, but not to hold cocktails. That was what I was coming to tell you, but then I got distracted. Take your time. I don't think he can possibly be here before 7:00. So, you have almost 2 hours to structure as you choose."

Midge walked Dawn out the front door. Dawn knew where she was going, as she had run almost every day before her trip to Tufts. She was headed for the Shoreline Greenway Trail. Midge watched as a young woman settled into a long, loping stride and disappeared down the curving driveway. Then she closed the door and hurried back towards the garden, wanting to clip a few more flowers for the dining room table. She also wanted to do a simple arrangement in the cloisonné vase at Charlie's desk in the kitchen. It had become her way of thanking him for his tolerance and capability when words failed her.

As she went to get her clippers, she mused that Dawn had not seemed the least bit curious whom the houseguest might be. And, for that matter, Tucker hadn't seemed very curious whom the second young woman might be. She sighed. *Perhaps I really don't understand young people and am simply becoming a meddlesome old woman. Gracious! I certainly hope that isn't true. I do so enjoy introducing my young friends to each other.*

When James teased her about her romantic streak she had always replied, "I just want everyone to be as happy as we are, dear." To which he always replied, I think like Abraham Lincoln thought; most folks are as happy as they make up their minds to be." She thought about the old quote as she selected a rose to clip. *Is happiness just a habit? Could one simply make up one's mind to be happy, despite adversity, poverty, tragedy and all those other things?* She shook her head feeling defeated. Her ability to be analytical was too affected by her own good fortune.

She walked into the kitchen, roses in hand, frowning in introspection and stood beside Charlie who was deveining prawns in the sink. "Charlie," she said seriously, "do you have a definition for happiness?"

The cook was quite used to these philosophical questions from his boss and always undertook to give her a straight answer, though often the questions seem to come from left field and he seldom knew what made her ask. He turned gentle, somber black eyes to her and said, "When Charlie thinking of day-to-day conduct he recalls what Confucius teach. But for matters of the spirit one must turn to Lao Tsu." He paused and closed his eyes.

Midge waited quietly. She knew he was looking inward, remembering other times and other, ancient teachings from his past. She marveled at the stillness and serenity in his face as he began to quote:

> "He who stands on tiptoe is not steady.
> He who strides cannot maintain the pace.
> He who makes a show is not enlightened.
> He who is self-righteous is not respected.
> He who brags will not endure.
> According to the followers of the Tao,
> 'These are extra food and unnecessary
> luggage.'
> They do not bring happiness.
> Therefore, the followers of the Tao avoid them."

Charlie opened his eyes and looked at the small, still woman in front of him. "Mam know when one pushes too hard all things go ka-pooy. One must accept. Not resist. Someone in this country once say, 'Success judged by getting what you want.' Happiness is not the same. Happiness depends upon wanting what you get, after it becomes yours."

Midge nodded, unwilling to break the spell. *What an unusual and special man he is; a blending of the best of two cultures, with his Japanese father and Chinese mother.* He'd quoted his obscure Chinese philosophy to her many times before. Sometimes, she understood and sometimes she did not, but it always made her think a little differently and ponder a little longer.

She had found it did little good to question him further. He had said what he wanted to say and he expected her to go away and think about his words. She imagined that was the way he had been taught and that to ask for further clarification in his culture would have been considered impertinent.

Midge quietly left the kitchen, absentmindedly found a vase for the flowers, nestled the single, yellow tea rose bud in the vase on Charlie's desk, and then tucked herself into her husband's big comfortable overstuffed chair to await his arrival, still working around the edges of the meaning of happiness.

According to Charlie, Lao Tsu's teachings, as written in the Tao te Ching, seemed to be saying that all those people she knew who were striving to get ahead, boasting of their accomplishments, working to change the world, weren't happy. *Merciful heavens! It just about describes the majority of our social set!* She chewed her lip, fascinated by where her train of thought was leading her. It wasn't something she expected to resolve. She knew there were no pat answers and would have been disappointed in herself if she had looked for them. It was the philosophical, mental exercises she enjoyed. It was her private side and a nice contrast to the no nonsense, practical part of her that she shared openly with others.

She sighed and put her thoughts away for another day and began to review what organizational tasks needed to be accomplished, glad Clarice was going to be back in time to get brunch organized. Looking at her watch, she realized that James, too, was evidently going to be a little late and decided to go up and change before laying out his clothes.

149

Chapter Thirteen

Dawn, determined not to be late, simply set her watch to buzz in 30 minutes as a reminder to turn around and start back. Then she set off to enjoy her run. She felt loose and her energy was high. She cruised along Lake Avenue until she came to Waterside Road and from there she connected to a service road on the Tyler's Club on Club Parkway. After a short distance on Pine Orchard Road, she turned into the parking lot of the Pine Orchard Fire House and found the trail over the old railroad bridge. As she lengthened her stride, she felt the temperature drop a bit as the canopy of maple and elm trees shaded the trail. The trail was a multipurpose one with bikers and hikers on it. She spotted a faint trail veering from the main trail and on a whim, decided to take it, hoping it might take her to Young's Pond. Her watch went off. Her plan was working beautifully; she would be back with plenty of time to spare. She stopped and turned around, heading back towards the main trail. She had no idea that her careful plan was about to be ruined until the moment her toe caught on a hidden root while she was cruising at good speed back down the leafy path. Tumbling headfirst and landing hard against the trunk of a gnarled shagbark hickory tree, she lay stunned, trying to make sense of what had happened. Never in all her years of running had she ever taken a serious fall and it took a moment for the realization to hit her. When it did, she took a deep breath to steady herself and then took stock of where it hurt. For sure, her left shoulder was going to be at least sore. But, as she gingerly moved her arm she felt the pain subside and was assured that nothing serious had happened to it. Her knee was another matter. She had left tender skin on the rough, hard bark. Her whole left knee was a raw, seeping mess. It reminded her of the worst floor burn she had ever had in all her years of basketball and she knew it was only a matter of minutes before the skin glazed and stiffened. She looked at her watch and groaned.

Her good plan had suddenly gone badly awry. If she was going to get home on her own, she had to get started immediately as there was no way she could run...and a two-mile limp was going to make her dreadfully late.

Once started, she found by gingerly putting only her toe down and keeping her left knee slightly bent, she could tolerate the pain and keep a slow but steady pace. She rejoined the main trail and limped along, eyes downcast, dignity in tatters. There was no one about and she decided they must have gone home to dinner. On she limped. As she reached Pine Orchard Road, she couldn't help but think to herself that if motorists in California saw a wounded runner they would stop and help. Actually, in California she would've flagged someone down, or asked them for a quarter so she could call her mom. For some reason, she couldn't bring herself to do such a forward thing in these elegant surroundings. She limped on, fretting over the passage of minutes, berating herself for her lack of vigilance on the trail and generally fighting off a pity party. Despite her best efforts, tears slid in steady tracks down the grit on her face.

Tucker, in the process of congratulating himself for making decent time in bad traffic, saw Dawn the moment he turned onto Club Parkway. She was obviously a runner in distress, the limp pronounced, the progress labored. He looked at his watch, 7:10. Stopping to help would make him even later, but he knew Midge would forgive him immediately when she found out he had been doing a good deed. He slowed the Aston and pulled up alongside the limping figure.

"Excuse me, Miss." Tucker cleared his throat and waited for her to turn her head to look at him. When she did, he felt a strange sensation in his chest. She had been crying, that was clear from the muddy tracks down her cheeks.

Stopping, eyes vacant, she waited quietly for him to continue. His quick glance told him all about the fall. He noticed the bruise already darkening her shoulder, twigs and leaves caught in the loosened ponytail, and a nasty skinned knee caked with dried blood that he knew had to be painful. He found he needed to clear his throat a second

151

time before he could speak. He smiled. "If you would consider a ride from a stranger, I would be happy to take you wherever you're going."

Dawn looked at the handsome, brown-haired man in a navy blue blazer, sitting behind the wheel of a low-slung, beautifully cared for gray Aston Martin, and said in a voice of detached wonderment, "Good grief! I'm being rescued by James Bond!"

The smile left Tucker's face and his friendly tone turned cool. "Hardly," he said as he got out and offered his arm for support as he helped her to the passenger's seat.

He returned in silence to his own seat and then turned to ask Dawn for direction. She immediately recognized, by his grim look, that she had made some tremendous faux pas. "Listen," she said before he could say a word, "I can tell I've offended you. It must've been my remark about James Bond. Sorry. He's this guy who drives an Aston Martin in spy flicks."

"I know who James Bond is," Tucker gritted out between clenched teeth. "I'm sorry I seem to be over reacting, but this car has been in my family since 1953, long before Ian Fleming ever invented 007 and certainly long before Hollywood got their hands on his books and made a beautifully designed and great driving car into some sort of macho status symbol!"

"Oh dear!" said Dawn, wincing as she tried to turn and look at him. "I put my foot in it, didn't I? I really am sorry--especially since you are the only one kind enough to stop and offer me a lift home. Actually," she paused, "not home. I need to get to that house over there and I think it's just up the street and then a cut to the right on Lake Avenue."

Tucker lifted his gaze to where Dawn was pointing. The roofline of the Tyler's Tudor mansion was visible over the trees. The grimness left his face and he looked at her in sudden recognition, remembering now that Midge had told him Dawn was about to go for a run when he called. "That's the Tyler's house. You must be their houseguest, Dawn."

"Yes, to be more accurate, I'm their houseguest in hot water. I was supposed to be home and all slicked up by 7:00 to meet their other houseguest."

Dawn turned a miserable face towards him. He felt the same pang in his chest he had the first time she had turned her eyes on him and he at once attributed this lurching sensation to sympathy. He thought he'd better clear up the situation. "Well, you may not be 'slicked up,' but you have met their houseguest." He smiled, forgiving her forever for the James Bond remark. "Sorry to be so tardy in introducing myself, I'm Tucker Jones."

"You're the other houseguest?" She looked him over carefully. "What a nice surprise! I guess I was expecting someone more the age of Mr. and Mrs. Tyler." She smiled, started to extend her hand for a handshake, then winced from the pain and said, "Oops! No handshakes from that shoulder for a bit."

Tucker looked at her in chagrin. "Now it is my turn to apologize. Here we sit, when you need to be getting to the Tylers and into hot water all right, not trouble, but certainly a soak in the tub would ease the aches." His eyes softened. "I had better warn you, Midge is probably going to go into a tizzy. She is a bit of a mother hen you know."

They smiled at each other. Tucker eased the sleek car back onto the road. "I know," Dawn said simply.

True to Tucker's prediction, their arrival caused quite a furor. Midge had convinced her husband that Dawn was late enough that he should get into the car and go looking for her. James was in the process of backing the Rover from the garage and Midge was standing on the front steps as the gray Aston coasted to a stop under the porte-cochere.

Jumping out and hurrying to the passenger's door, Tucker said as calmly as he could manage, "I met Dawn on the way here. She took a bit of a spill on her run, but I don't think she's done serious damage."

Midge's hand flew to her throat and she paused for a moment, frozen by the twin feelings of relief and anxiety that washed over her before she sped down the steps and flew around the car to the open door. One look confirmed her fears!

"Oh my dear! I knew something was wrong! I told James it would be so unlike you to be late. He was just coming to look for you. I'll go call the doctor... Are you badly injured?"

153

She paused for a breath as Tucker put a firm arm around her shoulders to steady her. Dawn interrupted quickly, "I don't think I need a doctor. I'm fine, Midge. Well, perhaps not fine, but at least nothing is broken except my dignity." Dawn smiled ruefully, feeling the sting of tears under her eyelids at the look of sympathy and concern on Midge's face. She didn't know why she always felt like crying when someone showed they really cared about her, but it had always been so.

Now, she fought the tears by concentrating on lifting her abraded knee out of the car. Tucker was right there to assist her. He gently helped her stand and supported her as she attempted to walk. Her leg had really stiffened to the point that any extension was quite painful. After watching her take two hobbling steps, her mouth drawn in a tight line, Tucker took charge and against her weak protest, lifted her easily into his arms. He carried her up the front steps and into the house, just as James, who had re-parked the car, came hurrying towards them from the garage. Tucker paused inside the front door, waiting for Midge to precede him and to reassure his boss, but was momentarily distracted by the intimate proximity of the very feminine bundle in his arms. He suddenly felt very strong, very protective and somewhat astonished by his decided attraction to her body odor. It wasn't just a runner's perspiration; there was something more…a citrusy scent he couldn't place. He found himself breathing deeply, drawing in the odor, trying to put a name to it, until she looked up at him with a question in her eyes.

His face flushed in embarrassment, but he laughed easily and said, "I just wanted to show Mr. Tyler you are all right and to get my breathing ready to rush the stairs."

She nodded as if what he said made perfect sense, let her head drop against his shoulder and closed her eyes. She listened to his murmured conversation with James, felt his careful step on the stairs and was glad to be almost to her room. *I am more than ready for a long soak in the tub!* Already, she could hear the water running.

As Midge leaned over to pour creamy white bath oil into the stream of water filling the tub, the vision of Tucker gathering Dawn into his arms seemed to rise from the steam. *Do they have any idea of the perfect picture they made,* she wondered. Dawn was all tan arms and legs; the hot pink of her running togs making a wonderful contrast against the dark blue of Tucker's jacket. Tucker's dark good looks contrasting beautifully with her blondness.

Midge stood for a moment watching the tub fill, eyes closed tightly, preserving the image; crossing her fingers for luck that she just wasn't imagining that an important connection had been made.

Tucker stood on the threshold of the bedroom, unsure of the proper protocol for entering a young woman's boudoir, but somehow reluctant to release his cargo. Dawn felt his hesitation and said softly, "I think if you were to sit me in the chair, it would work best. Then you can leave me in Midge's capable hands."

Gently, he placed her on the edge of the chair and supported her as she found a comfortable position. He could tell from the tentativeness of her movements that she was in more pain than she would admit to. She looked up at him with clear brown eyes. "Thank you so much, Tucker," she said sincerely, and for the first time, Tucker saw the wide smile showing her dimples and snow white, perfect teeth. He felt the lurch again and found himself returning the smile with the same stretch of whiteness; a true grin, very different from the small gently curving smile he usually allowed himself. It was a smile that lit his entire face and made his dark eyes glow.

"Not at all. My pleasure." He said as crisply as he could manage, backing towards the door just as Midge slipped in and took firm charge.

"Dawn, wouldn't you know it, I gave Clarice the afternoon and evening off. But I'm sure we can manage this together. Tucker, dear, go and tell James the details. You can bet he's dying to know. Then go and tell Charlie to keep holding dinner and ask him for some of his smelly ointment. Tell him the one for burns. He'll know what I mean. You and James go ahead and have cocktails... In fact, please have them fix a toddy for Dawn and a scotch for me."

Tucker nodded, and glad to have something further to do, headed for the stairs. His boss was waiting at the foot of the curving baluster, holding tight to the ornate newel post as if supporting himself.

155

"I think we can all relax," Tucker said, smiling from the top of the stairs to reassure the older man. As he descended he said, "Your wife, the mother hen, is now in charge. You are to fix the three of us a scotch and Dawn a toddy. I am to go tell Charlie to hold dinner and to solicit from him some sort of ointment. Then, we are to sit and wait by the fire in a quiet manly fashion while I reassure you that Dawn will recover completely."

Letting go of the post, Mr. Tyler looked at Tucker with relief and sighed. "So, she's not badly hurt then? I was wondering about calling the doctor?"

Tucker shook his head. "We'll let Midge have the final say. Dawn is saying she doesn't need one. My guess is she'll have a sore shoulder and a knee that hurts like the devil, but other than that, she'll be all right."

The two men stood looking at each other. "Messed up your blazer a bit," said James absentmindedly as he reached out to brush some of the dust from where Dawn had been nestled against Tucker's chest.

"It's not important," said Tucker who usually hated to look less-than-perfect and had been known to change clothes several times a day.

As Tucker walked toward the kitchen, he reflected with some surprise that he really meant what he said. He wasn't just being polite. The fact that he had gotten his coat dirty didn't bother him in the slightest. In fact, it almost seemed like a mark of honor.

Charlie looked up, pleased when Tucker walked through the door. He had found Tucker a willing listener on many subjects and quite knowledgeable for one so young. Tucker also knew his way around a spice rack and surprised Charlie more than once by identifying an obscure seasoning in one of his special creations.

"Well, Charlie, sorry to tell you, but Midge asked that dinner continue to be held," said Tucker. "Their houseguest injured herself while out running and will need some time to recover before dinner."

Charlie set down the pan he was holding and gave the young man his full attention. "Missee Dawn hurt too bad?"

"No," Tucker shook his head. "Not too badly. But Midge sent me to ask if you had some burn ointment that

156

she might use. The young woman did skin one knee rather severely."

"Ah!" said Charlie. Wiping his hands on his apron in a worried fashion, he disappeared through the door that led to his quarters.

While he was gone, Tucker looked around the kitchen, unconsciously memorizing details to share with his mother. The gleaming organization of pots and pans matched her own. He glanced at the huge prawns lying in some oil-based marinade and gave the mixture a sniff. *Whew! I can see other spices, but what I smell is garlic and a lot of it,* he decided. His mouth began to water, reminding him how long ago it was that he had eaten the tuna sandwich in Kathryn McCall's garden. *What is it about that garden that appeals to me so much? I talked about Ethan too... And it seemed very natural and not at all painful to do so.* He was standing, propped against the counter letting his thoughts ramble when Mr. Tyler walked through the door and handed him a scotch. He looked very much out of his element as he searched out a coffee mug and reached for the ever-simmering teakettle on the back of the range, just as Charlie re-entered the kitchen carrying a round flat tin covered with Chinese writing. He looked at Mr. Tyler in surprise. The man seldom visited his kitchen.

"Captain, if you don't mind, I am making Dawn a toddy," said Mr. Tyler somewhat apologetically.

Charlie frowned. "No. No alcohol for Missee Dawn," he said sternly. "Not good for now. For now, I will fix her drink." With that he turned in his slippers and disappeared through his door once more, returning almost immediately with a packet of white powder. Into a lovely porcelain mug he poured the contents of the packet, a squeeze of lemon, a sprig of mint and hot water. He took down a small lacquered platter and covered it with a cloth before placing on it the tin of ointment, the cloud-colored cup with its steaming drink and the single rose bud Mrs. Tyler had arranged in his cloisonné vase just that afternoon.

Handing the tray to Mr. Tyler, he said with satisfaction, "Captain, you tell Missee Dawn this makes aches and pains go away quick. Much better than alcohol. Won't feel sleepy, just relaxed."

Touched, and a great believer in Charlie's wealth of knowledge, the big man bowed slightly to the greater wisdom of the slight, erect figure before him and said quite humbly, "Thank you very much, Captain. I certainly will deliver your message."

Tucker watched the exchange with some surprise. He had never seen his boss quite so diffident. He found himself also dipping his head and shoulders in a proper kowtow, honoring the knowledge, feeling grateful to the cook for sharing his skills as an herbalist. "Charlie," he said with heartfelt sincerity, "you are an amazing person. We are in your debt."

James nodded in silent agreement, glad Tucker had found the words he'd wanted to say. It did not strike him as odd that Tucker had spoken for the family. Later, in a private moment, he recounted the conversation to Midge and her ears perked up immediately. "You know," she dared to muse, "it seems as though Tucker may be trying to tell us something." There she let the conversation end, but she did note that her husband's full attention had been captured. He would think about her words, and if she knew anything at all, she knew he would bring the topic up at another time.

Tucker watched, somehow feeling left out as the big man added Midge's scotch to the tray and ascended the stairs. He went to stand in front of the fire to nurse his own drink. He had the sudden urge, as he stood staring at the flames, to be sitting at his computer, dialoguing with his ceiling. The thought made him smile. He would write:

Dear Ceiling, this has been quite a day. I sat at the piano and played chords. For a moment I really had the desire to play classical music. It was a real feeling, Ceiling! I also had a massage and time to sit in the garden. I talked about Ethan and it felt okay. So did the massage. I made a date with Heather Anderson because I really wanted to. I also rescued a damsel in distress.

Mentally he inserted the word beautiful before the word damsel so he inserted it in his text. I rescued a

158

beautiful damsel in distress and it felt really good, even though she got my blazer dirty.

Mr. Tyler found him, one arm out bracing himself against the mantel, smiling into the dancing gold of the fire. He had built the fire, not because the weather warranted it, but because he wanted something to do while waiting for Dawn to return. Now he was glad he had. Tucker, back-dropped by the flames, made a great picture and he stood for a moment to enjoy it. *There seems to be something different about the lad, though I can't quite put my finger on just what,* he thought.

"Well, Tucker, the tray is delivered," He announced. "I believe the ladies will be down in about 30 minutes. At least that is what I am to convey to Charlie," he said sounding like a man who has proudly dispatched an important duty.

Tucker, reverie broken, turned a serious face to the steel blue eyes. "Any word as to how she's feeling now?" He asked.

"No." Mr. Tyler shook his head. "But I would swear I heard giggling as I waited outside the door for Midge to take the tray." With a mischievous twinkle, he said, "I thought sure, given my advanced age and honorable demeanor that I would be allowed to present the tray to the patient ensconced, according to Midge, up to her neck in bubbles." He allowed himself a forlorn look and sighed deeply. "No such luck though. Midge took the tray at the door."

Tucker caught his mood. "Say, I'd like to give that a try myself. Can you think of something else we might take up?"

Mr. Tyler snorted, "Not you, Tucker. With your smooth talking gift of gab, you'd probably get in the door and come back down here waving bubbles at me. No, as you so aptly said, 'we must wait by the fire in a quiet, manly fashion'…as soon as I tell Charlie when we can expect the ladies down, and fix myself another drink."

When his boss came back from the kitchen, Tucker had made his drink and was waiting, quarter in one hand, scotch in the other. As James accepted the drink, Tucker said, "Now, sir, I would like to think we respect each other as fair men. Am I a correct in my assumption?"

"Ah, why yes, son, I would certainly say that is a fair statement. Why do you ask?"

"Oh," grinned Tucker, "I'm just playing a hunch. One of us has to carry Dawn down the stairs for dinner and since, as you noted, I'm definitely the younger, likely Midge will call for my help. However, knowing you, I fear you might, very politely of course, pull rank on me. So, what do you say we flip this quarter to see who gets the privilege?"

The older man was clearly amazed and his face showed it. *There really is something different about Tucker tonight; it isn't just my imagination.* He snorted and then burst into hearty laughter that went blooming through the house. "Now, Tucker," he chortled, "I hate to remind you of this, but you are the one with a bad back. You possibly shouldn't be lifting anything at all, much less a long-legged female. I may be a touch older, but I'm still big and strong…and there's not a thing wrong with my back."

Tucker's eyes twinkled merrily. He was enjoying this repartee. The thought did flash through his mind that for once he had entirely forgotten his back. When he reached out and plucked Dawn off the ground into his arms, his back was the furthest thing from his mind. Happily, it still was.

"Now sir, you force me to play my trump cards. First, you have always told me that experience counts. Having already demonstrated my proficiency at carrying the young lady, I am the natural choice. Besides, I don't believe a man with alcohol in his system should try to carry anyone down steep stairs."

"Alcohol in his system? Alcohol in MY system? Why you young upstart, what's that in your hand if it's not alcohol?" roared Mr. Tyler.

"Ah yes, but sir, notice that only a few small, token sips have been taken. I have been practicing restraint in order that I may be worthy of undertaking such a quest!"

Tucker clicked his heels together knight-like and pounded his chest with a closed fist before dropping to one knee.

Mr. Tyler had never seen Tucker so informal or so playful. *What has gotten into this young man?* He wondered to himself, secretly suspecting that he knew the signs. He almost couldn't believe his eyes when Tucker dropped on a knee. The Tucker he thought he knew would have worried about mussing the crease in his trousers. He laughed again, both amused and amazed, loving the interplay.

"Get off your knee, lad. We'll flip for the honor, if you insist on putting your poor back in jeopardy."

"I do, fair boss," said Tucker rising from his knee and smoothly flipping the quarter into the air.

"Heads!" boomed Tyler as Tucker deftly caught the coin and slapped it on the back of his wrist.

Tucker peeked at the coin. "Care to make it two out of three?" He asked dolefully.

"Hell no!" gloated Mr. Tyler. "Always choose heads when you have the chance, Tucker. For some reason, they come up more often."

"More often, but not always, sir," grinned Tucker, lifting his hand to show the silver eagle, not the head of George Washington, hidden beneath his palm. "Now, you can't say you weren't given a fair chance."

Midge, at that moment, walked briskly into the room looking slightly flushed and quite beautiful in the softly draped deep violet dress her husband loved.

"What on earth is this racket about? I do hope you two aren't in your cups. One of you has to carry Dawn down the stairs."

Flipping the coin once more into the air before slipping it back into his pocket, Tucker smoothed his hair, straightened his tie and winked at them both. "I suppose someone has to do it," he said, heading for the stairs.

Midge looked at her husband in wonder. "Whatever has gotten into Tucker? I've never seen him like this! What happened to Mr. Cool? I could hear both of your voices all the way upstairs!"

"I think it comes from rescuing damsels in distress," Tyler said dryly, then winked and draped his arm over her shoulder, pulling her close for a quick hug. He sighed, thinking of the coin toss, and said something mysterious. "And I was bought off for a piece of silver."

"A piece of silver? Whatever are you talking about, you strange man?" Midge peered up and caught the twinkle in his deep blue eyes. She sighed. "Never mind. I don't care to know." She pointed. "Scoot this chair around and get the low hassock so Dawn can sit comfortably." Midge gathered the throw pillows off the couch and went to find more.

Tucker took the stairs two at a time and knocked gently at Dawn's door.

"Come in, please," came a muffled voice.

He found her sitting, injured leg propped on a low footstool. She smiled and he returned her smile, looking her over carefully. The bruises and scrapes were all covered by a simple but sophisticated summer dress of aqua blue. He walked over and sat before her on the edge of the stool. "I know you must be in some pain, but just sitting there, you look the picture of health and vitality," he said softly, fighting the urge to reach out and wrap the hand lying in her lap into his own two.

It was true. She wore no makeup except lip color, but the darkness of her lashes and the natural color in her cheeks made it appear as though she did. The deep suntan framed by her blonde hair made her look wonderfully fresh-scrubbed and wholesome.

She looked down at his hands noticing the grace of the long, slender fingers and could almost feel the warmth of their touch. Then she looked up and found him scrutinizing her. Smiling, she felt her color rise and was glad that he couldn't read her mind. "No more sticks."

"No more sticks?" Tucker asked, puzzled.

"No more sticks...in my hair." Dawn laughed and pointed to her head.

"Oh," mused Tucker, "those sticks. No." He leaned closer, again examining the frame of gold held back from her face with a blue ribbon. "No." He said again, finally ending his examination and leaning back. "No sticks and no dirt. But how do you feel? Is it all right if I carry you the same way I did before?"

"Yes," she said simply, "that would be fine. We'll just have to be careful of my knee, but my shoulder actually feels much better."

"Right. Now then!" He bent to fold her gently into his arms, catching another delightful whiff of the lemony perfume. "Down we go to dinner."

Actually, Dawn thought to herself, *I could've made it to the top of the stairs by leaning on his arm, just as I did*

162

with Midge... She let the train of thought trail away... *On the other hand, this is much better,* she decided as she rested easily in his arms.

The Tylers were waiting at the foot of the stairs, holding hands, watching with silent approval as Tucker carefully descended the stairs. Something about the way he was holding their beautiful charge made them turn and look at each other for a knowing moment. Midge felt her husband give her hand a fond squeeze that said, *"Yes, dear, I know what you're thinking. Perhaps this time you have done it."*

"Well, Dawn, my dear, you certainly look lovely. How do you feel?" Mr. Tyler asked, as Tucker reached the bottom step and Midge directed him towards the waiting chair.

Dawn laughed, "If you want to know the truth, I think I could've gotten myself down those stairs. But," she said, looking up at Tucker as he carefully deposited her in the chair and propped a cushion under her knee, "I'm really enjoying all this attention."

Midge gave a sigh of contentment as she looked around the cozy room. She was sure it originally had been called a drawing room, a place where the ladies could withdraw while the men sat around the dining room table, to smoke cigars and sip brandy after dinner. Now, it made an intimate study, just right for either James and her, or a small group such as this. She rose, "I'm going to go and tell Charlie we're ready for dinner now, but we'll wait until he calls us.

"Good!" smiled Dawn, "I am really, really hungry for some reason. Please thank Charlie for the ointment and the potion. Tell him I think it has helped a lot."

As Midge left, Dawn turned to Tucker and said sincerely, "And thank you too, Tucker. You've been just wonderful." She laughed ruefully, looking at the two men swirling their scotch and scrutinizing her. She decided it was time to change the subject. "I can't tell you all the misconceptions I had about the East Coast. Except for this," she gestured toward her knee, "it has been a wonderful adventure from start to finish."

"Finish?" Tucker said, feeling some alarm. "Does that mean you're leaving?"

163

"No. I mean yes. Well, actually what I mean is, I'm leaving on Monday, but I've applied for admission to Tufts University beginning this fall," she said, suddenly feeling for the first time, very decided. "Of course, it's rather short notice for them, so I'm not positive I'll be accepted. However, if I am, I'll be moving from Santa Barbara to Boston in September."

Mr. Tyler leaned forward with interest. "Of course you'll be accepted!" There was not a shadow of doubt in his tone. He had assumed she would like Tufts, but what he wanted to hear about was the trip he had helped her plan. "So, you like the place eh, Dawn? I thought you might. Now, how about the red convertible and our sightseeing route? Did you get lost?"

"Absolutely not!" She smiled, eyes shining. "Really, your roads are well marked and the traffic is certainly no worse than that in Southern California. It was all so different than I expected. On the West Coast, Highway 101 is all about the Pacific Ocean. Most of the time you drive right along it. On the East Coast, you have to drive to places to see the water. Here it's more about quaint cottages, monuments recording historic events...I love the fact that the Old Boston Post Road was built so stagecoaches could deliver mail. I mean, the age of everything here made me realize that this is where our country's dreams began." She smiled at James. "It was even great to see what was left of Plymouth Rock. Thanks for putting that in the itinerary."

James nodded. "Did you like the Mustang?"

"Loved it!" Suddenly, her voice lost its animation. "Only, as much as I liked the program and the faculty at Tufts, driving back down I suddenly realized how far I was moving from my family."

Dawn looked at both men, shrugged and said with her usual honesty, "I hadn't ever thought so, but now, I think my family is pretty unusual, or at least I'm pretty unusual. Leaving home still doesn't sound that good to me, though I do think it's time."

Mr. Tyler, touched by her demeanor and her honesty, cleared his throat. "Well, Dawn, I wish more children felt that way about their parents. Tell you what--feel free, if you do end up back here, to use Midge and me for your surrogate parents. I can't tell you how much we have

164

enjoyed your visit and how we would look forward to having you anytime you'd care to drive down.

Midge walked in just as her husband was finishing his invitation. "I suspect you have been talking about things that I am going to have to ask you to repeat at dinner. I should have made a rule that you couldn't talk about anything interesting in my absence! Come to dinner and fill me in, please."

Tucker, who had been listening to the conversation between his boss and Dawn with quiet interest, unfolded his long frame from the couch and went to stand by her chair. "Dawn," he said with merry eyes, "I know how hungry you are. You'll get to the table much faster if I carry you."

"Okay," she replied promptly and lifted her one good arm, thinking how odd it was that Mr. Tyler too had used the word surrogate parents-- perhaps Boston and Branford were just the right distance apart after all.

It was a simple meal featuring Charlie's garlic prawns, a lovely mélange of al dente steamed vegetables, a simple green salad and rice with a subtle flavor that Tucker later decided was some sort of spiced seaweed. The conversation flowed easily. Everyone was interested in Dawn's perceptions of their coast as compared to the coast of California. She told of her meandering trip home from Boston in the red convertible.

At the end of the leisurely meal, Midge slipped away from the table and returned with Charlie, who was laden with the huge silver tray of fresh strawberry torte and a lovely tea service. He deposited his load on the sideboard and deftly began serving, nodding his head in pleasure, while accepting accolades for the dinner. When he set the torte in front of Dawn she said, "Oh yum!" He nodded happily to himself. One more piece of information for the magic book!

Later, in front of the dying fire, they discussed the plans for the weekend. It was only then that Tucker heard who the other guests were. Heather Anderson's name surprised him. What a coincidence, he thought, and then wondered why she had not mentioned it when they talked on the phone. He shrugged and forgot about it as he listened to Midge unfold the plans.

165

Dawn laughed. "Midge, you said you had plans to tell me about as I rushed off to run. I had no idea you'd put together a whole weekend. It sounds like a lot of fun. I do love to sail!" She stopped and frowned, counting on her fingers. "11 people... No actually, 12, counting Charlie... That's a lot to be on the motorsailer. Are you sure I won't be in the way?"

"Midge waved her hand in a characteristic gesture and looked meaningfully at her husband, reminding him that the weekend had been his idea for retrieving Tucker from exile.

"No, dear, you certainly won't be in the way," he rumbled. "Faith handles up to 16 people very nicely. You'll be quite comfortable on the forward deck on a chaise lounge when we moor. In fact, I think it's the perfect way for you to meet a few of our friends."

Midge chimed in smoothly, "Fortunately everyone could come; a happy circumstance, since I didn't even start calling people until Wednesday. And, of course, bless Charlie. This was supposed to be his weekend to go to the dog races, but when I asked him to change his plans, he said, "No problem, Mam." Then he sent me out to have a cup of tea in the garden while he put the whole menu together."

Tucker looked at Dawn. He could tell she was genuinely excited. Her eyes sparkled and she began to ask Mr. Tyler questions about the sail. Her enthusiasm was catching. He had sailed with the Tylers many times, but never had he looked forward to it with such anticipation.

He and Midge exchanged glances and smiled knowingly as the older man recaptured the floor and began to further extol Faith's virtues. *Get the man started and he will be glad to talk about Faith all night,* their looks to each other said.

Midge glanced at her watch, reluctant to see the evening end, but knowing that their guests would be arriving for breakfast at 8:00 and her husband would be making noises about delayed departure several hours before it was actually a real possibility. Suddenly, she remembered Dawn's car. "Darling," she interrupted, "when you're working out your timetable in the morning, don't forget we need to take the rental car back."

"What? Ah, yes. True. Tucker would you help me with that first thing in the morning?" asked James, his mind shifting from pleasant conversation about the boat to his organizing mode. "You know," he said, in the same voice he used to bring meetings to closure, "we really should think about getting some sleep. Tomorrow is going to be a busy day."

Tucker looked at Dawn and smiled, "Are you ready to be carried upstairs?" he asked, trying not to look too eager.

Midge watched silently as Tucker carefully picked Dawn up and then trailed them up the stair so she could help Dawn get ready for bed. As she followed behind them she decided not to over-interpret Tucker's behavior. *Though it does seem he has been especially attentive towards Dawn this evening... Or is it just my imagination?* Perhaps it was simply because Dawn had been hurt and Tucker's natural instinct for kindness had been aroused. Midge sternly warned herself not to get too excited. She had thrown beautiful women in Tucker's path before... Not that it had done any good. *Why do I think it would be different this time? Perhaps because from the look James gave me, he thought so too. If I'm not mistaken, he thinks there's chemistry floating in the air.*

Her smoky blue eyes sparkled. She could hardly wait to get everyone settled for the night so she and her husband could have some time to discuss these young people. It was going to be an interesting weekend. Suddenly, she found herself thinking about Heather Anderson's phone call, seemingly out of the blue, and found herself wondering what the real motivation for the call might have been...*perhaps Tucker Jones.* She sighed with satisfaction. *Yes, indeed, it is going to be a very interesting weekend*!

Chapter Fourteen

It seemed to Tucker, who had found sleep even more elusive than usual, that he had just closed his eyes when he heard the rhythmic thumping at his door, signaling his boss was ready to return the rental car and wanted his help.

"Come in, Sir," he said in a clear voice that belied his lack of sleep.

Tyler strode in, freshly shaven, hair still damp from the shower. His eagerness to begin the forthcoming day was clearly evident by the sparkle in his eyes. "Up and at 'em, Tucker, my lad! The day is going to be a sailor's dream." He laughed at his own enthusiasm. "Faith is champing at the bit and so is Charlie. We've got to get the rest of the stores on board by 9:00 and then we can set sail as soon as Midge gets people fed and organized. In the meantime, we have to drop the Mustang off and pick up the lobsters – so into the shower and let's get on with it."

Tucker looked up at the big man standing there in his white ducks and navy blazer, literally rubbing his hands in anticipation and felt a sudden pang. *Do I look forward to anything that much?* He shoved the thought away and said. "Aye, aye, Captain! I'll make it quick."

In the shower, as he let the rivulets stream down on his head, he thought of Dawn and realized two things: He had thrown himself out of bed without doing his back check and that he was humming "Polonaise Militaire" by Chopin in the shower.

Mr. Tyler had given him the marching orders to go with his music. Hurriedly, he soaped and shaved. As he slipped into his own white ducks and deck shoes, there was a second thump on the door and before he could say a word, Mr. Tyler strode back into the room carrying a cup of coffee. Tucker knowing his boss was hurrying him along without using words, grinned and said, "Very nice! This is what makes your Tyler hospitality so famous. The host delivers coffee to the guests."

James nodded with satisfaction at Tucker's progress in getting dressed and noted the playful tone was still in Tucker's voice. It was the last thing Midge and he had talked about last night before turning out their light. Something was a bit different about Tucker Jones. Whether it was the result of Mr. Tyler's lecture about trusting people, meeting Dawn or something else entirely, they didn't know. Whatever the cause, they wanted to respond to it--nurture the attempts. To that end, Mr. Tyler handed Tucker the mug, clicked his heels and thumped his chest with his fist the way Tucker had done the previous evening. "'Tis the least one can do for a noble knight who rescues fair damsels."

Tucker grinned as he tucked in the tail of his crisp, white sport shirt. "I was pretty gallant, wasn't I? How is Dawn this morning? Suppose she needs another lift down the stairs?"

Tyler nodded and then shook his head, throwing up his hands. "Tucker, I can't answer three questions at once," he chided. "I have just come from her room, actually. I needed to get the Mustang keys so took her a cup of coffee too. I told her to be ready to be carried down in five minutes and she said she thought she could make it herself...thank you very much!"

Tucker looked quickly at his boss. "Now does that seem like a good idea to you, sir? I mean, after all, she is your charge. Don't you think you should lay down the law and say she goes nowhere unless carried...preferably by the man who won the right with the toss of a coin?"

Tyler laughed and shook his head. "Not I, Tucker. That young woman has me wrapped around her little finger; even the thought of laying down the law to her makes me quake. If you want to carry her, let's see you use your silver tongue to talk her into it."

"Well," said Tucker, taking a gulp of coffee. "I rather think I will have a go at it." He thrust his cup at his boss with a twinkle in his eye said, "Follow me, sir, and I'll show you how it's done."

When Tucker knocked at her door, Dawn had been standing, sipping her own coffee, looking out over the

169

deserted stable grounds and admiring the day. Part of her thoughts had been on Tucker and so it seemed very natural that he was the one who walked through the door when she answered the knock with a cheerful, "Come in, please."

Tucker had decided to take a stern tone with her, rehearsed in his mind the words, "Now see here, Dawn, you really shouldn't..." But those thoughts dissolved when he looked at her. She was wearing a gauzy peach-colored, cotton blouse and some sort of baggy shorts that belted at the waist and left no doubt that under the fabric was a very feminine form. Her hair was tucked into a French braid that showed her slender neck to good advantage. He found he was staring at her, hand on the doorknob, effectively blocking Mr. Tyler from the room while he looked his fill.

She smiled and said, limping around the room to show him she could walk, "Oh, Tucker. I was just thinking about you. Look how well I'm walking. Charlie's ointment must really work. Thank you so much for packing me up and down the stairs yesterday. But, as much as I love being babied, I know I can handle them today. I'll just take my time."

Tucker finally tore his eyes from her face and moved into the room to look down at her knee. He could see the shine of ointment covering the rusty patch of abraded skin. He had to admit to himself it looked less angry than it had yesterday evening. He also had to admit that she had great legs.

"Hello, Dawn," he finally said, somewhat belatedly. "Mr. Tyler and I are on our way to do errands and I just wanted to check on you before we left. It is very good to see you so much improved." He heard Mr. Tyler snort behind him. "Coward!" the sound seemed to say.

Suddenly, he grinned at her and threw up his hands in a gesture copied from his boss. "Listen," he said, "I must confess there is a part of me that is disappointed now that my services are no longer needed. I found it rather stimulating to exercise my muscles in such a manly fashion. May I suggest we swing down the stairs one last time, just so I have one more opportunity to feel chivalrous?"

She laughed; a clear, carefree laugh and he heard Mr. Tyler snort again. This time the snort was in amazed respect that Tucker had so smoothly turned the tables.

Now, Dawn was doing Tucker the favor. She wouldn't be able to resist. James shook his head and reached for Dawn's coffee cup. He could see on her face that being carried down the stairs one more time by the lean man with the gentle brown eyes was not adverse to her. He couldn't wait to tell Midge.

"Well, let's get it done then so we can be on our way," he said as gruffly as he could manage while smiling benevolently at the handsome youngsters. "Tucker and I have things to do."

"Up we go," said Tucker softly as he lifted her happily into his arms and headed out the bedroom door before she could really protest. He suddenly felt strong, masculine and invincible. It was an incredible, irrational feeling and he felt a whistle start in his throat as he whisked her down the stairs. *It wasn't that she's a wisp of a thing like Midge,* he thought. *She's really pretty tall and muscular. It's that she feels just right to carry. Not too light, not too heavy.*

"Take me to the front door," she cheerfully directed as he came to the bottom step. "I want to wave goodbye when you drive off in my little red car."

Tucker obediently headed toward the open front door, but took his time holding her before gently depositing her at the top step.

Mr. Tyler handed them back their cups and Tucker the keys to the convertible, then left them standing in a pool of early sunshine while he went to back the Range Rover out of the garage and get final instructions from Midge and Charlie.

Tucker looked down at her as she sipped the last of her coffee. He could see a very light dusting of freckle sprinkled across her nose. "Midge told me over the telephone that you were a 'proper California girl.' Enlighten me, please," he said softly. "What is a proper California girl?"

Dawn looked up to see if she was being teased or if he was being as serious as his tone sounded. It was a funny thing about Tucker, she was finding. Sometimes, his speech and manners seemed what her father would probably call 'old world' in their formality. Sometimes, he sounded normal. Sometimes, like now, she couldn't tell if

171

he was just being polite, making pleasant conversation or was teasing her. She too wondered what Midge meant by a 'proper California girl.' It crossed her mind that people on the East Coast might have misperceptions about her part of the country, just as she had had about theirs. Unconsciously, she used a technique she'd learned in a psychology course and evaded just a bit. "Why, I'm not certain I know. What do you think one's qualifications might need to be?" she said in a light, joking tone, putting the question back to him.

Tucker smiled, not at all offended. "Well, we will just have to ask Midge, won't we? If she means women from California all look like you, I've been living on the wrong side of the country." Tucker was adapt at gentle compliments, was in fact, known among the Tyler's social set for the smoothness of his flattery. However, for some reason, this compliment made him blush. Dawn, too, felt the color rising in her cheeks and bowed her head back over her coffee cup.

"Actually," she said, finally raising her head and looking directly at him, "as a psychology major, I would be interested in a serious answer to the question of whether environmental, geographical and other forces, outside the family's influence, I mean, have a homogenizing effect. Maybe to some extent there is such a thing as a "New York girl," a "Midwestern girl," or other such designations. It's interesting to think about. Really, let's do pin Midge down when we are on the boat. It could be a fun conversation."

When Tucker heard her say the word 'psychology' and alarm bell triggered in his mind. *She isn't a psychology major,* he thought grimly. *She has graduated! That makes her a psychologist. I'm certain it hasn't been mentioned to me.* The dreaded feeling of angst settled unaccountably in the region of his solar plexus.

He had been standing rather close to Dawn, but suddenly he stepped quickly down two steps to get some distance and jingled the keys in his pocket. "Well," he said abruptly, "I'd better get the Mustang turned around and ready to go. Can you make it back into the house by yourself?" He hoped his tone didn't sound as dismissive as he felt.

Dawn looked at him sharply. He hadn't responded to her question and now he sounded very abrupt, angry even. Clearly, she had been dismissed. Her eyes widened and she felt the prick of unwanted tears, but with great effort, she replied with a steady voice, "Of course I can. I'll even carry your cup." She reached out her hand.

Tucker looked down, surprised to see he was still holding his empty coffee cup. Without really looking at her, he walked back and handed it to her. With some dismay, he watched her turn on her heel and limp back through the open door. He could see that he had offended her, but even now he felt suffused by dread. His mouth felt metallic. His dismay with his own behavior quickly turned to anger towards Dawn. *A psychologist!* He thought in disgust. *Why didn't she tell me that last night when we were talking about Tufts? She mentioned a good program, but I am certain she failed to mention what that good program was. She was probably psychoanalyzing me the whole time!* Tucker felt his heart rate accelerate. His chest tightened even more. He felt tricked and somehow, very vulnerable. He realized he was almost physically ill from unresolved anger.

The lack of logic in his thinking didn't faze him, but a strange sense of loss cut through his anger and reduced it to misery. His stepping backwards from Dawn and down the stairs had done more than put physical distance between them. Emotional distance and emotional protection had also been put firmly back into place. The Tucker of old turned on his heel and strode to the convertible, eyes grim, jaw clenched.

It gave Tucker some sort of satisfaction that he was waiting in the car when Mr. Tyler came wheeling around the corner of the mansion and signaled Tucker to follow him. *It's good to not keep one's boss waiting,* he thought smugly, recalling one of the tenants he felt important to guide his conduct in the world of business. Somehow, the recollection, instead of steadying him, only made him feel sanctimonious and hollow. There was an aching feeling somewhere in the region of his rib cage that he couldn't identify. So, in the normal Tucker Jones fashion; he immediately blocked any introspection.

By the time Dawn limped through the dining room and set the coffee cups on the sideboard, she had

173

convinced herself that she was overreacting. *It isn't like me to be so sensitive,* she chided herself. *Maybe I'm still a little rattled from yesterday's fall. Besides, when you get right down to it, Tucker Jones simply isn't my type. He's too polished and way too reserved – – probably a real tight ass when you get to know him better,* she thought grimly.

At that point, her habit of always being truthful with herself took over and she gave a small sigh of regret. *Admit it, Dawn, when he picked you up this morning and you could feel his heart beat, it turned you on a little.*

She walked through the kitchen door to find Midge, Charlie and Clarice busy at their respective tasks. The kitchen table was literally covered with a mound of silver tableware. Counters were laden with boxes of things still to go on the boat.

The previous day, Charlie had stocked the boat's larder with all the non-perishable items. There was wine and champagne chilling. The onboard lobster tank had been freshened and the aerator turned on in anticipation of the arrival of the lobsters and cherrystone clams which, hopefully, James and Tucker were soon to be hauling onto the boat along with the fresh fruit and vegetables.

Clarice had spent her morning making sure each berth had fresh sheets and towels. The three heads were sparkling. The teak wood throughout the salon glowed from her polish. Sitting at the kitchen table behind the pile of silver she had already shined, she was the first to see Dawn in the doorway. A smile lit her face. "Dawn, honey, I heard you took a bad spill. Come here so I can see."

She watched Dawn limp into the room and her eyes squeezed shut in sympathy. "My but that thing looks painful! See what happens when I leave for an afternoon? Something bad happens…that's what! Don't know that this place can get along without me for even a minute."

Charlie and Midge turned in welcome and most of the pangs of distress Dawn was feeling vanished in the face of their obvious pleasure at seeing her. "Hello, Clarice. Welcome back," Dawn said.

"Well," said Midge, "if reports from James are accurate, you and Tucker both got your coffee and though you are better, Tucker insisted on carrying you down the stairs. Is that an accurate report?" She asked as she turned from where she was rolling out a huge mound of dough and came to give Dawn a floury hug.

Dawn nodded and hugged her back, smiling over the petite shoulder at Charlie. "Thank you for all the worrying about me and taking such good care of me," she said sincerely. "You make me feel like part of the family. I can't tell you how much I appreciate it. I am definitely less sore than I had any right to expect...and Charlie, I swear the ointment is magic on my knee. I have had plenty of floor burns in high school and the pain stayed with me for days, just like a real burn. This feels very different."

Charlie nodded, pleased down to his slipper-covered feet to have her so appreciative of his help. *This is one pretty young lady on inside as well as outside,* he thought to himself...and what he was thinking, Clarice said aloud.

"Dawn, honey, you are just about the prettiest white girl I ever did see. I told my husband. I said, 'John, she's pretty on the outside but she's got soul on the inside.' Makes me feel good to be around you, child. When Mrs. Tyler tells me you are leavin' on Monday I said, 'What? Already? Why, she just got here! Seems like she was here no time at all before she went trottin' off to Boston.'"

Charlie looked at Midge who had gone back to her dough. Guests would be arriving within the next half hour and she had put herself in charge of making a huge stollen to accompany the quiche and fruit Charlie was preparing. It was past time for the bread to be in the oven and she knew it. He watched as she scraped the flour-dredged fruit mixture from the mixing bowl into the center of the dough, added dabs of butter and carefully sealed the loaf, working quickly but giving her attention to Dawn. He could see great fondness in his employer's eyes and recalled seeing her look at Tucker in the same way.

"I agree." Midge nodded, responding to Clarice's comments about Dawn, "It really doesn't seem that you've been here any time at all, Dawn. How is it that you wormed your way so quickly into everyone's heart? Even James admitted it to me this morning." She smiled at the young woman ruefully, "It's going to be a sad day for all of us when you get on that airplane."

Dawn walked over and sat down by Clarice who was polishing a lovely silver sugar bowl and dropped her head to rest on the ample shoulder. She sighed and a funny look that Midge couldn't place crossed her face. But when she spoke, the look was gone and there was mischief in her voice. "I can just see me now. The permanent and pampered guest, carried up and down the stairs, morning coffee brought to my room, hair French braided by Midge, bed made by Clarice, sumptuous meals prepared by chef Charles...nothing to do all day but be loved." She gave a little snort. "Sounds more like the life of a poodle than a psychology major, don't you think?"

They all laughed. It was the no nonsense practicality of the girl that seemed so at odds with her glamorous, good looks that particularly endeared her to people.

"Okay," said Dawn, making her voice sound like Mr. Tyler's. "Enough of this warm fuzzy stuff. We've got people coming pretty soon, so put me to work I can do anything but climb stairs."

Clarice promptly handed her the sugar bowl. "Here's a good job for you honey. Sit right here with your leg stretched out a little and finish this silver for me. I'll wash what I've got done and get it arranged on the sideboard." She patted Dawn's good knee with one dimpled hand and began scooping up already polished silver.

By the time the first of their guests pulled up under the porte-cochère a little after 8:00, the fresh fruit platters were chilling in the refrigerator and the quiche and bread were ready to come out of the oven. Midge rose to go greet her guests and then looked down at Dawn, suddenly remembering a forgotten detail. "Oh dear, I told James to remind you to pack for the weekend before you came down. Did he remember to do so dear?"

Dawn smiled. "I'm sure he did," she said diplomatically. "And yes, my big backpack is sitting on my chair ready to come down."

"Good for you! I should have known you'd be organized," Midge said smiling over her shoulder at the young woman wiping down the table where she had been polishing the silver.

176

When Tucker and his boss returned from their chores, all the guests but Heather had arrived. There was a pile of bags awaiting transfer to the Range Rover under the porte-cochere. Midge met them at the front steps. "Tucker, dear, would you please go up and get your bags and Dawn's when you've finished loading this? Dawn said her bag is on the chair in her room." Without waiting for his answer she turned to her husband and said, "And James, would you please do the same for us?"

James nodded happily. Things were on schedule. The boat looked great. He turned and looked over his shoulder to where, a quarter mile away, the sleek vessel with its spire-like masts was waiting at the marina. It was one of his great pleasures to look down the undulating green expanse of lawn that fell gently to Lake Avenue with the Pine Orchard Golf and Country Club marina, St Helena Island and the Sound all visible in the distance. Rubbing his hands together, he bounded up the stairs to retrieve their bags, the younger man in his wake.

Tucker grabbed his two Battenkill canvas bags and hurried down the hall toward Dawn's room. He could hear his boss already charging down the stairs. He still had a hollow empty feeling in the pit of his stomach, although the harried pace Mr. Tyler had set in order to get the car back and the boat loaded had helped him shut it out. But now, as he opened her bedroom door and stepped in, the feeling of a nameless loss washed back over him. Without thinking, he shut the door behind him and stood looking around the room. The room was pin neat, the bed made; bathroom and closet doors carefully closed. Satiny pink slippers tucked carefully under the edge of the bed were the only signs of femininity in the room.

The room assigned to him by Midge Tyler was guest room neutral in decoration. *This room is definitely more masculine than feminine with its rich dark wood and the beige and navy bedspreads.* He wondered briefly at Midge's reasoning in assigning the rooms and then picked up the lumpy, worn backpack on the chair and looked around for other bags to take. There were none. A heavy sweater was lying beside the pack, so he picked it up too, held it to his face and breathed deeply. It was definitely Dawn's. The citrusy spicy smell of its owner permeated the

177

heavy knobby white cotton. Finally, he shrugged and headed down to breakfast. *I'm going to have to ask Dawn if she has additional luggage,* he thought. Then he sighed, realizing the reason he was reluctant to talk to her was tied to the sense that he had acted very unfairly towards her earlier that morning. Nevertheless, the sense that he had been victimized stayed with him as he stowed the luggage in the back of the Rover and the nameless sense of misery settled like a mantle over his shoulders, weighing him down.

The sound of tires on the cobblestone drive diverted him from his thinking. He recognized the black BMW as Heather's and waved a welcome.

Heather smiled as she watched Tucker standing beside the Rover, hands in his pockets, looking very relaxed and definitely handsome. *Yes,* she thought, *I just might spend some energy on this man. He does have a certain quality about him.* She pulled smoothly beside the Rover popping the trunk lid as she opened her door. "Hello, Tucker," she purred as she pivoted in her bucket seat, smoothly extending both long and lightly tanned legs to the ground, pausing for the merest of moments to allow him to take in the presentation, before rising gracefully to her feet.

"Hello, Heather. May I transfer your bags?" He replied, smiling a small but warm smile.

She nodded her assent and when he walked to the trunk and saw the three lovely navy leather bags he wondered again at Dawn's lack of luggage. "I believe you're the last to arrive. So, I'll close the door on the Rover and we can go in to breakfast," he said, hefting her bags on top of the others.

"Wonderful!" She said, tucking her hand in the crook of his arm and matching his stride. "I'm starving!"

The patio off the dining room was east-facing and was awash with early morning sunshine. Dawn, telling herself that she was feeling a little overwhelmed by meeting so many new people, had withdrawn to go and sit in a corner wicker chair in order to finish one last bite of stollen and her coffee when Tucker and Heather stepped, arm in arm, through the French doors and onto the patio. Watching silently and noting the gentle grace and self-assurance of the lovely, obviously very cultured woman on

Tucker's arm, she felt a sharp twinge that she immediately recognized as jealousy. *Good grief, Dawn, get a hold of yourself! Look at those two. They are a couple if you ever saw one.*

Indeed, as they warmly greeted the group and loaded their plates amid cheerful banter, it was easy to assume they had done this together many times before. She looked down at herself. Almost everyone in the room had on either white slacks or in case of the women, white skirts. She was the only one in shorts, baggy khaki ones at that. Tucker's friend was dressed in a tailored white skirt, a navy blue blouse with a crimson sweater tied casually about her shoulders. Her white leather deck shoes were spotless. Dawn looked down at her grungy, once white tennies and shrugged sadly. She'd never paid much attention to her shoes, other than making sure those she ran in gave her good impact protection.

I'm definitely outclassed in this crowd. Thank goodness Mom insisted that we practice good manners and have decent grammar; at least I can fall back on those two things, she thought glumly, wishing suddenly she were anywhere but sitting on this sunny East Coast patio, feeling very much like an interloper.

Finally, looking up, Dawn caught Clarice's eyes hard upon her. *That woman misses nothing,* she thought. *She sees me here, moping in the corner over things there isn't a single reason to mope over.* Dawn forced a smile at her across the room and squared her shoulders. She realized with a start that she had been doing every single person in the room an injustice. Surely, none of them cared what she wore. They had all greeted her warmly and until she had chosen to withdraw, had engaged her naturally in their conversation. With resolution, she put down her cup and got to her feet to go and meet the new person and join the group. She saw Clarice nod in apparent satisfaction and then turn to begin clearing the places of those guests who had already eaten and had gone to sit on the white stone wall bordering the patio where they could look out over the grounds toward the boat.

Heather had not seen Dawn sitting in the corner when she swept happily into the room on Tucker's arm. The fact that the Tylers even had a houseguest had temporarily

179

slipped her mind until she saw the beautiful, athletic looking woman limping across the room and heard Midge say with obvious affection, "Oh, Dawn, there you are. Come and meet Heather Anderson, another of our wonderful young friends."

It took the smallest fraction of a second before Heather was able to compose her face exactly in the expression she wanted and turned slightly in her chair to smile warmly at the woman standing there. She reached out to clasp Dawn's already outstretched hand in both of her own.

"Oh Dawn, I am so pleased to meet you. Midge told me she had a houseguest but she didn't tell me how beautiful you are."

Dawn looked down at the graceful, lightly tanned hands with perfectly shaped and buffed nails, holding captive her own sunbaked hand, with its closely cropped, unpainted nails and felt her knees go weak with relief that they were dirt free. She managed the ghost of her Ipana smile, but felt too tongue-tied to say more than "Hello, Heather. Thank you for the compliment. It's nice to meet you, too."

Fortunately, Tucker, sitting across the table from Heather, inadvertently saved her from trying to think of more banality, by taking the opportunity to ask about her lack of luggage. "Dawn, I put the backpack and sweater from your chair into the Rover. If you have other bags, I'm sorry to say, I didn't find them." He said the words with a crisp impersonalness that caused Heather to smile with satisfaction on the inside, Midge to prick her ears in wonder and Dawn to feel for the second time that morning that the man had, for some reason, built an invisible barrier between them. She took his cue and answered with the same tone. "Thank you for asking, Tucker. I only packed one bag. Perhaps I should have asked someone's advice. I only took what I would've taken had I been sailing on the Pacific."

Midge, looking back and forth between the two of them, felt a frown pucker between her eyebrows and her heart sink. *What on earth?* She wondered silently. *This is not the report that James delivered to the kitchen earlier.*

These two are treating each other the way a shopper would treat a salesclerk.

James had reported with twinkling eyes that he thought there was definite electricity in the air and that Tucker had been whistling as he carried her down the stairs. They both agreed that they had never heard the young man whistle before.

Heather chuckled warmly, releasing Dawn's hand after giving it a small squeeze. *Time for generosity and magnanimity,* she thought. Aloud she said, "Don't worry for a minute, Dawn. I'm sure I brought enough for both of us."

Dawn felt her heart warm at the kindness and fastening her brown velvet eyes on Heather's amber ones, said with her usual straightforwardness, "I may have to take you up on it. In California, it's swimming suits and shorts during the day and sweats at night, and then sweats only when necessary." She laughed a bit ruefully. "In Southern California, packing heavy means taking a sweater."

Tucker said nothing more and had, in fact, turned his attention back to his food, causing Dawn to acknowledge that she was interrupting their breakfast.

Midge broke in smoothly to encourage Heather and Tucker to take their time and to ignore her husband if he came to hurry them. "Really, he said we had until 9:30. You've got 15 minutes." She emphasized her remarks by taking their cups and refilling them with coffee from the silver urn.

Dawn had followed at her heels and also poured herself an additional cup, although she had no real desire to drink a drop. Further, she had even less desire to give herself the usual, "*Snap out of it ninny, concentrate on someone else besides yourself,*" lecture she had used for years to pull herself out of feeling blue. But, by rote, the words formed in her head and she went to rejoin the group on the stone wall.

Loaded to the roof with the luggage and remaining supplies, the Range Rover had already departed by road, Charlie in his Captain's hat at the wheel, Midge beside him; the rest of the group would take a more direct route in Mr. Tyler's golf carts. He was already waiting impatiently behind the wheel of one, beckoning with an arm. "Clifton, Emory,

Dawn...let's get going. I'll take you down first. Robert can bring his family. Then, I'll return for Heather and Tucker."

The assembled group tried not to grin at his impatience. Except for Dawn, they had seen it before, and though they refused to be unduly hurried, they tried hard to meet his leaving deadline.

Tyler's enthusiasm and energy were infectious and as the cart swooped down the gentle slope over the velvet greenness of the manicured lawn toward Waterside Road and then the path to the marina, Dawn felt her mood lighten with the rush of air and the warmth of the strengthening summer sun. *Time to join this party,* she thought with determination and turned to smile broadly at Clifton and Emory. Then she looked back at the other cart. Robert was grinning from ear to ear, enjoying the happy, startled squeals of the women in his family as he maneuvered his cart skillfully to catch up with the floor-boarded pace set by James.

Althea was holding tightly onto her side rail and Rob and Debra were holding tightly to each other. It was a wonderful picture. Dawn turned back and leaned into James in an odd sort of armless hug of affection and said, "You seem to have wonderful friends."

Clifton and Emory in the backseat, hearing her words smiled to each other feeling included in her opinion. Emory, perceptive, introverted, but with a wicked sense of humor, leaned over and whispered in her husband's ear, "She's not only gorgeous, she has good taste."

This was not Dawn's first sail on Faith. That first evening after her arrival a week ago, she and James had taken an after dinner stroll down to the dock and boarded. To her, it seemed huge, made even larger by the silence and the fact that it sat alone in its berth. They toured the airy salon, the sumptuous master suite and the two small but comfortable staterooms. She marveled at the seemingly numerous tucked-away berths that seemed perfect for crawling into to read or dream. But the galley was what impressed her the most. It was superbly organized, complete with all essentials necessary for gourmet meals, including a lobster tank.

She laughed when she first saw it, thinking it odd that there would be an aquarium on a boat. When Mr. Tyler had explained its function, she was properly impressed and turned to him, her eyes shining. "You know, Mr. Tyler, this doesn't seem quite real to me. I've only seen motorsailers from a distance and the yachts I'm used to are like 40-footers. When we'd sail to Catalina Island, we'd see boats like this and make up stories about the people who owned them. They were all movie stars, oil sheiks and gangsters in our stories, not normal people like you and Midge. I mean, this is the ultimate! I can't even imagine what she would be like under full sail. It must truly feel like flying."

"When are you going to start calling me James?" he asked. The big man smiled at her and noticed how she was taking in every detail, her enthusiasm genuine. He thought to himself, *she wants to go sailing, but good manners are telling her she shouldn't ask. Barbara and Charles have certainly done a good job with this one.*

He watched her explore every nook and cranny of Charlie's kitchen. It might be fun he decided, if indeed she could follow directions and knew the nautical terms, for the four of them to take the boat out on the sound. "Have you sailed quite a lot, Dawn?" He asked, probing mildly.

She smiled. "I went through stages. One of my high school boyfriends had a 34-foot Sabre. We got good enough to enter the class races sponsored by the Santa Barbara Yacht Club. So, for about six months, I guess you could say I sailed every spare minute." She looked up at him, suddenly serious. "It was quite a shock to me to wake up one morning and realize that I liked the boat better than I liked the boy. Unfortunately, once I'd realized it, I had to break up with him; otherwise I would have just been using him."

There was genuine sadness in her voice, but it was her innocence and lack of guile that made Tyler feel suddenly older and wiser. He cleared his throat. "Well, dear, you know you did the right thing. I do imagine the young man was devastated. He probably didn't like losing you one little bit."

"No," said Dawn matter-of-factly, "he didn't. In fact, his parents had to put him into therapy because he got pretty depressed." She looked at him and shrugged. "That was the downside. The upside was that he taught me how to sail well enough that I was able to crew for others fairly often."

Tyler smiled. "Well then, if you can take orders and handle a sail, perhaps Midge and Charlie would join us for an evening's sail tomorrow. Faith really does demand a crew of four for a relaxed sail. I do have it rigged so Midge, Charlie and I can handle her, but we stay very busy."

And sail they did! Midge had grown up on nearby Martha's Vineyard and was as capable as her husband. Charlie, absolutely in his element, stood glued to the wheel, giving crisp orders around a permanent mile-wide smile. They all felt a little younger and a little fresher, watching Dawn's lithe body, as she flew to do Charlie's bidding, eyes shining, enjoying the moment with her entire being.

Today, as the golf cart spewed laughing guests, Dawn concentrated on the fact that she was lucky enough to have a final sail on the gloriously different Long Island Sound. She did not let her mind dwell on the fact that today she would be sitting on the sidelines.

She tried not to feel useless as everyone fell to, helping carry the luggage and supplies from the Range Rover on board under Captain Charlie's direction. The state rooms had been assigned to the married couples, everyone else was to pick one of the single bunks. Things were quickly in order and one by one, the guests joined Dawn where she was sitting comfortably, out of the way, on the deck in front of the raised salon.

Deborah sat next to Dawn and sighed comfortably. "I'm sure it's thanks to you, that we all got invited on this last-minute sail. Midge has been raving about you to my mother since you got here."

Dawn smiled at her. "Well, that works for me," she said. She scanned the friendly faces and thought to herself, *Mom always said you could tell people's character by the company they keep. Well it's clear that the Tylers keep wonderful company. I keep waiting for that cool, aloof snobbery towards people from the West that is supposed to run rampant in the East. Where is it? Heather even offered to share her clothing with me.* Suddenly, she broke her reverie and asked, "By the way, what all do you people pack to go sailing anyway?" She asked the question with

184

such sincerity that everyone, after a moment of introspection, broke into hearty and honest laughter; immediately thinking of their own bags and all the things they packed but wouldn't likely use or wear.

Rob leaned forward. "Yes, Deb darling, what do you bring that takes two big cases?"

Not at all nonplussed, Deborah flipped her head and refused to be tied down. "Oh just things a woman needs," she said loftily. Then she turned to Dawn and said, "If you want to know the truth, I bring too much. I have at least four wool sweaters, a raincoat, my own pillow, things like that. What did you bring?"

Dawn smiled and pointed to the stuffed backpack she was using as a backrest. "That's mine. Besides shorts and shirts there's mainly a toothbrush, some cosmetics, a hairbrush, long pants, sweats, my camera and a book."

"Good heavens, Dawn, don't tell James or he'll put us all on luggage rations." chuckled Emory.

And so the conversation went, all small talk, light and without much content, but designed to pass the time gently *and*, Dawn reflected later, *to make me feel welcome and at ease.*

Emory, the watcher, took note that even after the men went to get direction from Charlie and she and Althea walked to the bow to admire the houses and grounds flanking the bay, Deborah and Dawn sat exchanging interests and information, as women will when they really want to get to know each other. She watched as the sun gilded the spun-gold and taffy-colored heads bent attentively towards each other and wondered idly if Heather would join them, or stick like glue to Tucker.

In no time at all, the bumpers had been pulled and the great engine began throbbing its way past St. Helena Island and on out into the wind-whipped whitecaps of the sound.

Chapter Fifteen

Heather had taken the opportunity, while waiting for her golf cart ride, to plan her course of action. She had been taken aback when she first saw Dawn. Not one to underestimate the competition, she knew danger when she saw it. For some reason, there was something very attractive about Dawn's obvious lack of attention to her appearance. *No makeup. No nail polish. Hair done in a simple French braid...and those God awful baggy shorts! She definitely has the natural look.*

It was evident that the California woman lacked Heather's own polish and sophistication. The best plan of action, she decided, was to be wonderfully kind and caring to the injured guest. She already had found out from Midge that Dawn was leaving for the West Coast on Monday. That knowledge and the fact that she already had a date sealed with Tucker the following Friday meant she could afford to ignore him just a little now and make it up to him at the concert. The plan grew clearer in her mind. She had known Deborah for many years and knew she would fall readily into the threesome of happy, chatting, close, young women friends Heather planned to foster. Nodding her head with satisfaction, she decided she would provide a buffer between Dawn and Tucker and at the same time further endear herself to the Tylers by her graciousness towards Dawn. It was evident that they were enamored of her.

The scenario in her mind made her smile. Even though she had not seen a single bit of warmth or attraction between Tucker and Dawn, precautions were always useful. Her relationship with Tucker would be well established by the time Dawn returned in the fall and besides, Dawn would probably be very busy in Boston and not even in Branford all that often.

Heather pulled her shoulder-length, chestnut hair into a low shiny cub at the nape of her neck as the sails rose skyward in white, billowing splendor and the boat leaped in response, cutting cleanly and swiftly on her seaward course. She stood and went to where Deborah and Dawn had tucked themselves out of the way ahead of the mainmast. Sitting at Dawn's feet, she examined the ugly, rusty, red sore carefully.

"I've never been attracted to jogging," she murmured, allowing a look of concern to darken her smooth brow. "Now I know why. My goodness but that does look painful! I saw you walking and wonder if you should. If you need anything, please feel free to ask us." She smiled at Deborah as she included her at Dawn's behest. "We are quite good at fetch and carry."

"Actually," said Dawn, feeling warmth spread through her at the kind offer, "it really doesn't hurt as much today. I know it looks bad when I limp, but I find if I really keep up on my toe, I get around fine. But, thank you both for the offer. I'll be sure and take you up on it if I need to."

Deborah broke in, "Heather, Dawn is coming back this fall if Tufts will accept her application into graduate school."

"Really?" said Heather, a tone of pleased surprise in her voice. That Midge had already related many of the details of both Dawn's painful fall and school plans, she didn't say.

At Dawn's nod of affirmation, she clapped her hands and exclaimed, "That is wonderful news! You'll be close enough to drive down for weekends and I love Boston. Sometimes, Mother and I drive up, just to do the galleries and have lunch. Perhaps, if graduate school studies allow, you'd care to join us one day. Or..." She paused and said in her best matter-of-fact voice, which carried just a touch of ownership, "...perhaps Tucker and I could talk you into a hike in the Maine woods when the leaves turn."

Heather watched Dawn's face carefully for some telltale sign of jealousy or surprise and thought something flickered momentarily, but she couldn't be sure. Deborah, not to be outdone by Heather's offer of continuing friendship said sincerely, "I know you have beautiful scenery on the West Coast, Dawn, but Heather is right. Autumn in the Maine woods is really splendid. I'd love to be a part of showing it to you and Rob enjoys any chance to be outdoors. Besides, he really knows the area. His folks have a cabin on Lake Sebago."

Heather smiled benignly and let Deborah take over the plans. Clomping around in the dirt of Maine held little appeal for her. She actually didn't even own a pair of hiking boots. Her intention had been only to establish the seed that Tucker and she were a comfortable twosome, and didn't really know why she had mentioned hiking.

After letting Deborah rattle on for a bit and watching Dawn's enjoyment of the idea take hold, Heather smoothly changed the subject to one she knew Deborah would love even more. Reaching out, she gently lifted Deborah's left hand, holding the engagement ring so that the splendid marquee-cut diamond caught the sun and sent sparkles of rainbow color dancing in the light. "Have you two set a date yet? Or is it so much fun being engaged that you plan to stay that way for a while?" she murmured in a carefully teasing voice.

Deborah blushed prettily and dropped her heart-shaped face, allowing her taffy blonde curls to fall into a curtain over her blush. The truth was, Rob couldn't begin to draw on his trust fund until he graduated from college and, since he had taken two years off to knock around Europe before starting, he would not graduate until the following June. The nest building instinct was very strong in her and the waiting was becoming daily more difficult. If she had her way, she would have asked her parents for the money instead of the wedding, forsaken a honeymoon and simply eloped so that they would have enough money to live on. She was certain that with careful budgeting, her "dowry" and the job she'd held as copywriter at a small liberal newspaper since graduating from Amherst, would see them through. But Rob wouldn't even consider it as an option and they had both resigned themselves to the year's wait. She sighed and lifted her head and said fervently, "I only plan to let this engagement last another 11 months, 17 days and I don't know how many hours."

Dawn and Heather looked at her in surprise. Immediately, Dawn reached out and took Deborah's ring hand in her own. "Oh, Deborah, you look so much in love. A year isn't so long--not when you have a lifetime to look forward to. Besides, if I'm any judge of the circles you and

188

your parents run in, it's going to take a year to plan the wedding."

"My goodness," thought Heather smugly, *"it's no wonder Tucker isn't attracted to her, she does say the most tactless things."*

But Deborah didn't seem to mind the obvious reference to her family's wealth. She nodded, feeling contrite about her own impatience. "Yes," she said, "I know. And," she smiled wryly, "you sound just like my mother. But it seems like we've waited forever! When I complained, Mother asked me if we had considered living together." Her eyes suddenly twinkled. "My mother and Midge are renegades you know. They are always coming up with something avant-garde to keep all those old blue-blooded volunteers they run with reaching for the telephone. They say it's their obligation to keep the ladies from dying of boredom." She paused. "But, I told Mother neither of us believed in cohabitation without benefit of clergy."

Dawn squeezed the tiny hand. "Yours is the dilemma of our generation," she said thoughtfully. But, though both young women looked at her with interest, she didn't have time to explain her comment as Mr. Tyler, resplendent in his navy blazer and gold braided hat stood before them.

His bulk blocked the sun as he towered over them. "I've come to claim Dawn for the time being. She can't walk very well, but she's got to earn her keep somehow. So, we'll have to let her steer. Besides," he grumbled, "you three have been planted here since we cleared port. Start spreading some of your young sunshine around the deck...captain's orders."

Dawn took his proffered hand and got carefully to her feet, saluting him with a smile of joy. "Aye, aye, on my way, sir...but what about Captain Charlie?"

"The good captain sent me to get you. He said, and I quote, "Tell Missee Dawn honorable captain must turn into honorable cook. Please relieve him of a major happiness."

They all laughed. The message was clearly translated. Dawn was thrilled that the two men had decided she was capable of such responsibility and that, finally, she could do something of use.

189

She waved happily to the older women as she made her way past the salon on the narrow decking. Now, she knew why those ladies were so fair. They worked at it. It seems strange to her that they weren't all out basking in the sunshine; it was so much the lifestyle of Californians.

All three ladies waved, watching her limp past, each with their own thoughts, as they listened to her happy chatter and James' rumbling banter in return. It was obvious that he was there to catch her, should the knee cause her to stumble.

James lifted Dawn up the steps onto the flying bridge and then watched her unselfconsciously return Charlie's polite bow and listen intently as the small man pointed out landmarks and related it to the compass. Dawn's face, in concentration, was beautiful and she assumed command with confidence. Charlie watched her for only a moment before descending the steps and leaving her in charge.

After Dawn had passed, the three women in the airy salon turned without words and looked towards the bow. Both Deborah and Heather had gotten up and moved to where Rob and Tucker were sitting in lazy conversation, legs dangling over the edge, mesmerized by the clean slice of wave action off the bow. Pixie-like Deborah had slipped herself into the protective curve of Rob's arm and the ladies couldn't help but notice that Tucker had turned to smile at Heather as she moved gracefully to his side, the body space just a touch closer than Tucker usually allowed.

Althea was the first to break the silence. "Well, Midge, from the looks of things, you obviously know some things that Emory and I do not. The last I heard, you were looking forward to introducing Dawn to Tucker."

Midge frowned thoughtfully, "I really don't know anything. In fact, I'm very confused. Last night, Tucker seemed quite attracted to Dawn. James even thought there was some chemistry floating about when he saw them both early this morning. I thought so too because Tucker seemed so transformed." She looked fondly towards the lean figure at the bow. "Tucker is such a dear, but he is rather too perfect to be real," she said in way of admission and found both friends nodding in agreement.

"Well, last night, she continued, "he appeared quite, ah, let's say, unbent. Not relaxed exactly, but warmer and more spontaneous. James noticed it too." She frowned. "Truly, I didn't know that he and Heather were forming an..." Here again, Midge hunted for words. "...attachment, I guess. Really, it is strictly a coincidence that both Heather and Tucker are even here at the same time. I invited Heather at the very last minute on Friday when she called to invite me to have lunch at the club next week. I thought it might be fun..." Her words trailed off and the look on her face plainly marked her second thoughts.

Emory listened carefully, smiling at Midge's eternal manipulations and wondering about the spontaneity of Heather's call. "Do you and Heather lunch together often?" she asked casually.

Midge shook her head, catching Emory's drift, but not wanting to admit that she had wondered about the coincidence of Heather's telephone call herself. She knew how Emory loved what she called the "intrigue of human nature." She was just the opposite of Althea, who hardly ever considered that others might have hidden motives. "No, actually, this will be the first time. And it's not only Heather, but Heather and her mother. We're to play golf while Heather plays tennis. Midge related the entire phone call and ended with, "That reminds me, Althea, I forgot to check my calendar, I may have double booked myself. I know we have the S.O.S fundraising meeting on Wednesday. Did we have something else booked for Friday?

Althea, with twinkle in her eye, turned to Midge in surprise. "What? Confusion with your calendar? That doesn't sound a bit like you, Midge. That's my trick. And, here on this beautiful boat, I can't even remember where my calendar is, much less what's on it. Let's deal with it when we get back home."

The conversation drifted onto other things from there, but Emory cataloged the fact that Heather's call to Midge had not come until late Friday. *It seems an odd time for a young woman to be calling an older woman to set up a golfing date for a third party who might or might not be available,* she thought. There was something about Heather that both puzzled her and put her on guard though she couldn't quite determine what. Perhaps, it was because the woman seemed just too perfect. Emory gave a mental shrug, remembering that was also how she felt about Tucker sometimes. Perhaps then, they would make the perfect couple.

Sounds of Dawn giving commands from the flying bridge wafted through the open windows and the mental picture of the three older men vying to do as bidden, brought a smile to her face. Listening to the young woman's healthy, unaffected laughter, Emory couldn't help but think Tucker Jones was making a serious mistake in his choice of women. She thought about saying as much to the others, but they were already talking about Deborah and Rob's plans and the moment had passed. Instead, she leaned back and relaxed, enjoying the coolness of the breeze and the excellent glass of iced coffee that Charlie had just placed before her. She lazily reflected on his talent for remembering what guests preferred in the way of food and drink and watched as Heather, after laying a gentle hand on Tucker's arm, turned from the group at the rail and started towards their table. *Interesting. Very interesting,* she thought to herself before smiling a welcome and patting the chair beside her.

Tucker, on the other hand, was not allowing himself to even consider his conduct of the morning; wouldn't entertain even a single introspective thought about what had made him back down the steps away from Dawn or why he felt overpowered by the feeling of having been deceived; or what was causing him to be more attentive than usual to Heather. Had he not been so out of touch with the fact that feelings, rightly or wrongly, sometimes control behavior, he might have realized that part of the motivation for his behavior came from a desire to make Dawn jealous, a simple, elemental junior high school sort of thing to do. But, instead of trying to understand what was making him feel so out of sorts, he reverted to type; totally blocking any thought that made him feel uncomfortable; controlling his every word and gesture so as to appear as expected...the affable, unfailingly polite and gracious guest.

His behavior played perfectly into Heather's plans. For her, the weekend couldn't be going better. It was she who took her leave of Tucker at the rail and went to converse with the three women sitting comfortably in the shade of the salon and she was particularly pleased when Emory had patted the seat of the chair in welcome.

Later, after Dawn had returned the helm to Mr. Tyler, Heather made her way, aft to ask humbly, if she might also have a try at the wheel. Mr. Tyler was surprised, but pleased at her interest. However, she shortly gave the job back, pleading incompetence and laughing ruefully at her own lack of aptitude. She then stayed to chat with him until it was time to anchor the boat.

As they waited to be served a luncheon of bite-sized, spicy, sesame chicken, served with cellophane noodles and a wonderful crunchy cabbage salad, Heather found opportunities to praise both the chicken and Dawn's handling of the boat in front of the others. "Goodness, Dawn, you made handling the boat look so easy, I was sure I could learn it, especially from someone as competent as Mr. Tyler...but I just lost my courage in face of all that responsibility. I think I had better stick to my tennis and swimming," she declared ruefully as she moved toward the buffet table.

What the young woman had no way of knowing, as she instructed Charlie on which of the dishes to serve her, was the detail in Charlie's magic book. She hadn't a clue that the blandly prepared, skinless chicken breasts that she ignored were on the table especially for her. Neither Midge nor Charlie exchanged glances or raised an eyebrow, but both remembered and looked forward to dinner to see if the garlic, like the spices, would now be palatable to the young guest.

When the motorsailer was finally moored near a small, rocky island in a deep-water cove, it was Heather who encouraged everyone into their swimming suits. She looked forward to Tucker's appreciation of her figure in her new swimsuit, a simple one piece of shimmery, deep blue-- modest, except for the very high-cut thigh that made her legs look even longer.

Suddenly, in mid-encouragement, she allowed her smile and banter to fade. "Oh dear," she said. "Oh, goodness, Dawn, I have forgotten about your knee. Swimming would be difficult for you, wouldn't it?"

Dawn looked down at the ugly knee in disgust, unused to being held back from anything she wanted to do by an infirmity. Then she shrugged matter-of-factly, "I'd be foolish to try it," she said, looking toward Charlie who nodded in confirmation. "But please, go for it. Don't hold back on my account. That is what would really make me feel awful." She looked around at the concerned faces, for some reason, finding herself wanting to avoid looking directly at Tucker.

"Really, I mean it. I am having a wonderful time, in fact..." She brightened. "...I'll get my camera and take pictures of you all going over the side."

Midge, able to put herself in Dawn's place and feeling her distress, took charge and said brusquely, "Dawn is right. It would be a travesty not to have our swim on such a nice day. Into your suits everyone! Dawn and Charlie can hold down the boat."

Elfin Deborah was the first into her suit and over the side. She balanced on the rail for a second, as she had done many summers of her childhood, before jackknifing cleanly over the edge. Dawn captured her at the apex of the dive. Both Tucker and Rob went off the rail shortly thereafter. But Heather had taken the time to take the gold clasp from her hair and re-affix her waterproof makeup before emerging. Dawn looked at her and decided she looked like a model on assignment. "Good grief, Heather! You have a body to die for. You look just like a model. I've never seen anyone make a suit look better. Here, let me take your picture."

Heather smiled and posed, genuinely pleased by Dawn's sincerity. She thought again how lucky it was that Tucker was not attracted to her. *Of course,* she thought with satisfaction, *few men in my circle would be attracted to someone who uses the phrase, 'good grief'.*

To Dawn she smiled and said, "Actually, it's the suit making me look good, but thank you for the compliment. It's the first wearing and one always wonders..." With that, she stepped to the rail, paused, balancing confidently on the sun-warmed teak, allowing both those in the water and those preparing to climb down the rope ladder for a gentler entry, time to admire her. Then, with a last smile for Dawn, she executed a perfect swan dive into the clear, cobalt water.

Dawn limped to the rail, taking last pictures of the laughing, un-self-conscious adults making their way down the ladder and jumping, with gasps of pleasure, into the water.

Midge, the last one over the side, turned her smoky eyes on Dawn. "You are such a dear." She said simply, before turning to follow Emory down the ladder.

Feeling immeasurably comforted, Dawn leaned over the edge and called. "I don't know how you can have a good time without me, but do try."

The group turned and treaded water, lifting arms to wave in salute. It was the gentle banter they all understood and with light hearts they stroked for the familiar outcropping and the young people already nearing the shoreline.

With a sigh, Dawn turned from the rail. She had planned to put on her bikini and lie on a chase, reading her paperback. But suddenly, her suit seemed too revealing and very unsophisticated. She wished she'd brought her one-piece. She limped to the galley to find Charlie. Maybe if she helped him put the luncheon things to right her world would feel better. Her mother had always said, "Nothing cheers one up like doing a good deed."

Charlie, who had witnessed the whole leave-taking, could pretty well predict what was going on in Dawn's heart. It wasn't as if he couldn't hear part of the banter going on between Mr. Tyler and Tucker as he came and went from the kitchen to the dining room just off the study, last evening. He too, found himself surprised at Tucker's jovial tones. He too, thought he felt chemistry and was surprised to watch how differently the two young people were treating each other on this happy day. He'd watched Dawn pull herself away from some sadness while in the kitchen that morning and wondered at its cause. It was still with her now, he saw, as she attempted to turn on her glorious smile and instead found tears beginning to slide down her face.

Charlie didn't panic, in fact, he felt quite relieved. *Yes indeed, it was an affair of the heart.*

"Oh, Charlie, please forgive me. I really am having a wonderful time. I have no idea what these stupid tears are about. It seems like I might be feeling sorry for myself. But that's too silly to contemplate. I really don't mind not being able to swim to the island. Honest!"

"Perhaps," said Charlie, feeling the need to offer comfort, "Missee Dawn missing own big ocean in California."

Dawn looked at him in surprise, touched by his perception and gentle tone of understanding. "Why, Charlie, that might be it. Yesterday, driving back to Branford, I started thinking of what it would mean to move out here and when I thought of how much I would miss my family, it made me cry." She did not elaborate on the depth of her grieving or what she had figured out about its cause. But, she remembered clearly how settling it always felt when she finally figured out what was truly bothering her. In a flash of awareness, she recognized that today's tears were not caused by homesickness. They were caused instead, by her apparently unwarranted and futile attraction to Tucker Jones. She sighed deeply, coming to grips with the unpleasant truth of the matter, unaware that Charlie was watching her internal struggle.

Finally, when she again focused outward, he broke the silence by saying, "If Missee Dawn home in California on such one fine day, how would she spend time?"

"Oh, Charlie," she said, leaning back on the cushion, protecting her leg, "Santa Barbara is just like this, or even warmer on most days. If I had the time, I would probably be at the beach, playing volleyball or surfing with my friends. She looked at her watch. Actually, by this time of day, my friends and I would be lying on beach towels in our bikinis or sitting in short little beach chairs, slathered in suntan lotion, listening to music and drinking beer from a cooler."

Charlie's face brightened. "Missee Dawn go get into bikini and suntan lotion. Charlie find music and one damn fine Chinese beer."

Dawn looked momentarily startled and about to refuse but then saw the look of joyful anticipation in the soft dark eyes and understood he was trying to make her feel better. She looked around the galley and noted that it was mostly in order. She nodded and stood to smile at him. "Aye, aye, Captain," she said, saluting before limping to do his bidding.

By the time she returned, book and suntan lotion in hand, Charlie had music from an old Beach Boys tape playing. He had pulled a chaise lounge to the sunniest spot on the deck and was just popping the top of a beer. "Charlie think no glass for beer on beach. Beach bunnies drink from bottle, right?" He was smiling happily and Dawn laughed right out loud.

"I owe you one, Charlie, you darling man. This makes me feel right at home," she said, taking a hearty pull at the beer which was very cold and absolutely delicious. "Yum!" She said and carefully, protecting her bent knee, sank slowly to the chase.

That was how the swimmers found her as they clambered, laughing and puffing, up the rope ladder to the strains of the Beach boys singing, "Do-o-o you love me-e-e? Do-o you, surfer girl-l, m-y little surfer girl-l?"

Charlie covertly watched the expressions of the others as they caught their first look at the golden girl who looked straight out of a Hollywood set; shining with oil, nose and lips covered with zinc oxide, holding a book in one hand and waving a beer at them with her other, smiling, calling a welcome, with no idea in the world of the sensuous picture she presented. Even in repose, the litheness of her runner's body was evident, muscles well defined, tummy concave in its flatness; the deep tan setting off the florescent, green string bikini perfectly.

"Gracious," said Emery, finally breaking the appreciative silence, and mimicking Dawn's slang, "now there's actually a body to die for!" Her ability to say what the others had been thinking broke the spell and everyone grabbed towels that had been conveniently placed by the rail and rushed happily forward…everyone except Tucker.

The cook watched his face carefully as he continued to stand by the rail, slowly and methodically drying himself. If ever a man was trying to regain composure and control, that man was a red-faced Tucker Jones. Nodding to himself in secret satisfaction, Charlie hurried to serve drinks.

By the time Tucker joined the group, Deborah and Rob were sitting by Dawn, all three sitting sideways on the chaise. As usual, Rob had an arm around his petite fiancé and was leaning forward to share something with Dawn. Everyone but Heather was in the process of pulling up chairs or chaises and leaning back to enjoy the diminishing sunshine. Heather walked up to Tucker and stood closely by his side. It seemed very natural that he put his arm around her.

Chapter Sixteen

For Dawn, lying dry-eyed, but sleepless in her tucked-away bunk behind the galley, the picture of Tucker's arm slipping casually, but protectively, around Heather's willowy waist was forever branded on her mind. She knew she would be able to draw it forth in minute detail any time she so chose. Then she groaned, remembering. She really didn't have to memorize anything. Some devil within had caused her to pick up the camera lying on the table beside her beer and snap their picture. What on earth in her quirky nature had caused her to do that, she had no idea...unless there was an unknown touch of masochism in her soul. She certainly couldn't think of any other reason to take the photo. Then, in her objective fashion, she began to chide herself for having the emotions of a schoolgirl with a new crush. *The guy already has someone. He never even made a real move towards me. Obviously, I got my signals crossed. He was being polite and charming, nothing more.*

His cool behavior on the boat she could attribute to Heather's presence. She'd certainly had guys act like that before around their girlfriends...like they were afraid to be friends, in case it made their girlfriend jealous. She admitted for the umpteenth time that her looks were her curse as well as her blessing. *And honestly, when I think about it, Tucker and Heather seem to be the perfect pair; so self-possessed and finishing-school sophisticated.* That Heather had asked for one of the Chinese beers, but had emphasized to Charlie, when he took her order, that it be served to her in a chilled glass, was one example of that sophistication.

Dawn sighed. She couldn't even remember drinking beer from a chilled glass, other than in a bar. *They are a well-suited pair and I simply need to accept the fact. Of course, I should have taken their picture. I took several of Deborah and Rob. I even promised them copies; so why not copies for Heather and Tucker?* She groaned again.

Even linking their names in tandem made something inside her hurt. With effort, she forced herself to think of something else.

By sheer will of concentration, she thought about the evening. Her mother would want all the details of the lovely mooring spot, the wonderful hors d'oeuvres of cherrystone clams followed by the garlicky, delicious Maine lobsters, all of them fresh from the aerated tank. But for the life of her, she couldn't recall many of the other details. She remembered Mr. Tyler putting the Beach Boys tape back into a sound system, replaying the song, *Little Surfer Girl* and dedicating it to her. She could remember taking several more pictures, of what she could not recall. The wine had been passed and re-passed and there had been lots of shared stories of other sails, the usual talk of politics and the economy, compliments to Charlie on his meal and some discussion of the times people needed to get back to meet other commitments. These were not things her mother would be interested in, but at this moment, it was all she could recall.

Suddenly, she wanted her mother--wanted to throw her head on her mother's lap and bawl her head off under the comfort of her mother's soothing hands. Her mom would be able to help her sort this out and get a handle on it, just as she done a thousand times before. But, her mother was on the other coast. *Okay, maybe this is my first shot at standing alone on my own two feet,* she thought. *I need to not only face up to the fact, but accept it! Tucker Jones is not interested in me!*

It seemed unfortunate, but true and a fact to internalize: For the first time she thought she might be truly losing her heart...and there was no reciprocation. *Stop being such a baby, Dawn! Feeling sorry for yourself and acting like a spoiled brat won't get you anywhere.* Lying wretchedly in the dark, she continued to chide herself. *This is your own fault! If you can't read a guy's signals any better than you did, you're just asking for it!*

She felt a prisoner in her berth--partly because her knee kept her from being able to toss and turn and partly because she could not seem to put the matter of Tucker Jones to rest.

Dawn might have rested more easily, had she known that she was not alone in finding sleep elusive. In his hammock, slung above a snoring Rob, on the after deck, Tucker Jones lay woodenly, staring up into the starlit blackness. He was not at all surprised by his insomnia since it was often a fact of his life. He was surprised at the tremendous difficulty he was having keeping his mind quiet. Over the years, he had perfected the art of keeping an image of a quiet blanket of lightness in his mind. He even thought of it as keeping a blank mind. This ability allowed him to keep at bay the many intrusive nighttime thoughts that used to bring pain and disquiet to an otherwise controlled and perfect life. He'd sadly discovered that he could not play classical music on the piano without experiencing strong feelings, so he had given up playing all but pop tunes. But, he had perfected his blank mind technique...until tonight. Had he been home, he might have risked allowing the thoughts to materialize, might have talked to his ceiling or written what he was feeling in his computer journal. *But not here; not on the Tyler's boat.* Already, he had come close, several times, to losing control of his thoughts and once, even control of his body. He felt embarrassed even remembering when he had climbed up over the edge of Faith and saw Dawn lying on the chaise lounge, only a bikini between her and complete nakedness. His physical attraction had been so strong, only the fact that Charlie had conveniently placed towels for them by the rail, had allowed him to save himself from a terrible embarrassment.

Even in the coolness of the night he could again feel the heat in his face. But with tremendous will, he once more emptied his mind and quietly waited for the night to pass; trying to recall every detail of Charlie's cooking so that he could properly share his weekend outing with his mother. She would be especially interested to know that the Tylers had served a white Zinfandel from California with the lobsters. His parents had generally shied away from domestic wines, but he had to admit, this had been very good, not too dry, not too fruity--very complementary to the sweet lobster meat.

By 6:00 A.M., Charlie was up and preparing coffee in the galley. He saw Tucker roll gingerly from his hammock, trying hard not to wake Rob. It looked as if Tucker's back was stiff and Charlie watched with fascination while the man went through a double series of gentle exercises reminiscent of the tai chi practiced in the country of his father. He was struck by the young man's grace of movement and allowed himself to wonder, for a moment, about Tucker's parents.

Charlie had an unvoiced, secret desire to meet Mrs. Jones. Her passion and talent for cooking was legendary and still growing among his circle of professional peers. But, in addition to meeting the woman, he wanted very much to see her kitchen. Tucker had described it to him once and since then he had longed for a tour as another might long to travel in exotic lands.

What Charlie didn't know was that Mrs. Jones, through Tucker, had kept tabs on his recipes for the last three years and had an equal desire to meet him and see his kitchen. Unfortunately, she could not think how to arrange it in any socially acceptable way.

Tucker, having finished his exercises, took the smaller of his two bags with him into the head just as Dawn emerged from her cocoon. She pulled her cotton sweater on over the same baggy shorts she'd worn the day before and came limping into the galley carrying her elastic band and a comb, barefoot and sleepy-eyed.

She had combed her hair, but the braid crimps from the day before made her look a bit unkempt and disheveled. As if it were the most natural thing in the world, she put an arm around the slight shoulders and rested her head, for a moment, on the top of Charlie's. He was incredibly touched. There was nothing, not one thing in the world he would not have done for her at that very moment. He had seen her give hugs to Mam and Clarice, but this was the first time he had felt included in that spontaneous circle of offhand affection.

"Morning, Charlie," she yawned hugely and stretched. "It's going to be another beautiful day, isn't it?" She limped on into the breakfast nook and snuggled into the cushions, smiling a still sleepy smile. "If you pour me a cup of coffee, I'll squeeze those oranges for you. We

California girls are very good at that sort of thing, you know."

Charlie, face alight with an ear to ear grin bowed deeply. "California girl good at many things. Make this cook smile. Missee drink coffee, talk to Charlie. No need to work," he said as he poured coffee into a thick white mug and handed it to her.

"Oh come on, Charlie, let me help. If I were at home, my mom would have one of us kids doing this very thing."

The little man nodded in understanding, remembering her stated homesickness of the day before and pushed the bowl with its orange mound towards her, also handing her a sharp knife and the juicer.

"California like China, like Japan, like world. Some customs same, some not same, some hard to understand. People different but all the same. It is a good world, but sometime hard to understand everything," Charlie said obscurely as he turned to leave to go to his bunk and retrieve the salve he had brought along for Dawn's knee.

Dawn looked up from her orange cutting in surprise. She'd actually been thinking similar thoughts, not on a global scale, but certainly on a coastal scale; pondering again, the things that influence customs and behaviors. On the West Coast, she never gave a thought to whether she was dressed appropriately, was saying the right thing; was being overly friendly or unsophisticated. She never even considered that her bikini might seem immodest. Here, on the East Coast, she found herself making continual comparisons. This morning, lying in her bunk after a nearly sleepless night, she finally admitted that she was intimidated by Heather and also jealous. Such feelings were new to her. She couldn't remember ever feeling that way about anyone at home. Her thoughts had made her feel small and unworthy and she had made up her mind that the best course of action was to continue being herself...only just a little more reserved.

Monday, she would be on a plane flying back to her own "country." But, if she was going to like living in the East, she was going to have to really examine her own behavior. *Like last night,* she thought. *It seems so natural for me to throw my arms around the Tylers, give them a*

203

good night hug and thank them for the wonderful day. But, I didn't see anyone else do that.

In fact, as she examined and re-examined the day, she could think of few examples of people other than the Tylers, really hugging. No one else, unless she counted the way Rob and Debra sat or stood with an arm around each other, did any of that sort of thing. Although Mr. and Mrs. Eldridge did shoot each other secret looks when they thought no one else was looking. Even with Tucker and Heather there had only been a single gesture of affection. *After all,* she concluded, *I have been pretty protected and insulated by my family and so far I have only lived in Santa Barbara.*

What Dawn didn't know was that her openness, lack of artifice and straight-forward manner had charmed most of the company. Only Heather, who saw her as a definite threat to her plans for Tucker and felt the need to stay vigilant…and Tucker, due to the angst he refused to examine, did not honestly feel any warmth towards her. The rest of the group had come to genuinely like her. The Tylers were both delighted to have her company and had talked in their cabin about how lonesome the big house would be…and how utterly mystifying they found the behavior of Tucker Jones.

When Charlie returned with the salve, he found her, brow drawn in inward concentration, fiercely jamming orange halves onto the round point of the juicer, one after the other. Balm in hand, he looked at the flat tin and thought a little sadly, *Work only on flesh; does not work as balm for heart.*

She looked up and saw him there and her face cleared instantly. "You know, Charlie, I wanted to tell you that I have never eaten food I like better than that you've fixed since I've been at the Tylers. I wouldn't be surprised if you are the best cook on the whole East Coast, maybe even the whole United States." She laughed expansively and threw out her arms. "Who knows, maybe even the world!"

Charlie nodded, taking the compliment seriously, and without false modesty said, "Maybe so, maybe not. One other damn fine cook on this coast."

Dawn handed him the orange-gold pitcher of pulpy juice and went to wash her hands at the small galley sink before proffering her knee. "Really, Charlie? There's someone else? Do you know this person? Were you in cooking school together or something?"

Charlie bent over the knee, noting with satisfaction, the diminishing redness. He applied the ointment with gentle fingers and then stood, shaking his head. "No meet. Just hear from many respectful voices, this lady love to cook very good food they say. Study great books from many countries, take classes, know many secret things, just like Charlie." He nodded to himself. "We meet one day," he said with serene confidence. His black eyes twinkled. "Missee can bet lady also hear about Charlie plenty much. Maybe want to meet this famous good cook, Charlie, too."

Dawn laughed, totally unaware that Charlie was talking about the mother of the man who at that moment had emerged, carefully groomed, looking healthy, fit and incredibly handsome in fresh white trousers and a navy sweater with just a touch of crisp white collar framing his square chin. She groaned inwardly and her hands flew to her hair as he walked through the salon and towards the galley for his morning cup of coffee. She was trapped. She dropped her hands into her lap and Charlie saw her come to a resolution of some sort.

Dawn took a big breath and relaxed her face into a gentle welcoming smile. "Good morning, Tucker," she said in a carefully neutral voice as he came down the two steps into the cozy galley.

Tucker, his hand still grasping the teak railing, paused only for a fraction of a second, mastering the momentary thought to turn on his heel and bolt. Smoothly, he returned her greeting. "Good morning, Dawn." Brown eyes caught and held just for a moment and in that tiny space of time, Tucker had an odd but comforting sensation. Had he allowed himself to examine it, he might have recognized it for what it was--a genuine feeling of fondness. But he did not. Instead he turned his gaze to the cook who was bringing him coffee. "Good morning, Charlie. Thank you." Then, well under control, he turned back to Dawn. "How is your knee today?"

"I think it feels better," she said, again maintaining the touch of reserve she had promised herself. "Charlie has already doctored it this morning. Thank you again for your kindness."

He smiled the gentle smile that had melted the hearts of so many and gave a slight bow. "Not at all. I had never before had the opportunity to rescue a damsel in distress and I must say, I found it quite rewarding."

Dawn moved the comb and elastic band lying on the seat beside her closer to her thigh and moved right, a clear invitation for Tucker to join her if he chose. But maintaining her reserve, she said nothing, watching as he interpreted her gesture correctly, looked momentarily undecided, but then said, "It's a lovely morning, I believe I'll take my coffee on the deck"…without mention of Dawn's joining him.

She looked after him and when he turned at the top of the galley steps, coffee in hand and said again that he was glad her knee was better, she could only hope she looked totally serene and not as perplexed and forlorn as she felt.

With a sigh, she turned a small, unknowingly sad smile on Charlie and said, "Handsome devil, isn't he?"

Charlie was thinking many other thoughts about Tucker, but none of them had to do with looks. "Some time," he said gently, "things not as they seem. Charlie sees things others do not see. Tucker Jones has built wall against you. He is much afraid."

Dawn gasped. *How could this man so easily read her mind? What did he mean that he could see things others could not see? Obviously, he noticed that Tucker had kept the length of the boat between us most of the time yesterday.*

Unfortunately, there was no time to ask. Emory, looking especially lovely, her blonde-streaked hair tied back neatly in a ribbon of green that matched her eyes, tailored cream-colored slacks, green linen blouse and a navy jacket thrown over her shoulders, was approaching.

Dawn did not feel she knew the woman very well and she was surprised when Emory turned to her after taking a healthy sip from her mug of coffee and asked with warmth in her voice, "Dawn, dear, would you allow me to braid your hair?"

"Gosh, Mrs. Eldridge, do you know how? I'd love it! I can usually do it myself...except my shoulder is still a little too stiff, so I've been sitting here feeling really, really frumpy, waiting for Midge."

Emory laughed. "You might have to wait a bit for Midge. She and James are often the last to rise on Sunday morning." She didn't say it, but something about the way she smiled and winked made Dawn immediately think of the sumptuous master suite with its capriciously pillowed bed and heavy curtains." She grinned and they sat in Charlie's galley feeling like naughty conspirators.

Finally, Emory patted Dawn's hand and said, "Of course I know how to French braid. With three daughters, all of whom had horses, a mother learns such things! In addition to braiding their hair, plaiting the manes and tails of their show horses is one of my claims to fame. Come out on the deck. I'm looking forward to seeing if I still have the touch. By the way," she turned her glorious green eyes on Dawn, "please feel free to call me Emory. It makes me feel younger." She laughed again and took Dawn's hand. "Dear," she said, scanning Dawn's face, taking in the clearness of her eyes, the fresh scrubbed look of her skin and the elegant stem of her slender neck all framed by the tousled gold of her hair, "you have absolutely no idea how 'un-frumpy' you really look."

Emory placed Dawn on a chair well within Tucker's view but after giving him a well-modulated, Good morning, Tucker, dear," turned her back on him and began lifting the golden strands of hair and weaving them, slice by slice, into a tidy braid of plaited sunshine.

When she finished and stepped back to admire the smoothness and symmetry of her handiwork, she had a sudden thought. "Dawn, could you braid as long as you didn't have to lift your arms too high?"

Dawn, reaching up with her good arm and feeling the tight smoothness of the heavy braid, grinned up at the elegant lady. "Absolutely! Are you considering letting me do one for you?"

"You read my mind!" laughed Emory. "Let me go and fetch an elastic and some pins from my cosmetic bag. I don't believe this ribbon would hold it tight enough."

By the time Emory returned, Althea and Robert had emerged from their tiny state room, and Clifton, blinking in the strengthening sun, followed his wife across the deck. "Good for you, Dawn," he said. "I've always loved Em's hair that way."

Tucker came from his spot on the rail to join the group as they stood around chatting comfortably, sipping coffee or tea and watching Dawn's skillful fingers part and plait the tawny streaks of hair. But something about watching the braiding made him feel vaguely uncomfortable.

Once she finished the braiding, Dawn looped the tail of the braid back up under the hair, pinning it securely at the nape of the neck. It gave Emory just the right look. The style was less casual than Dawn's and just right for a woman out for a day's sail. Emory, even without a mirror to check, was pleased. She could see the admiring look in her husband's eyes. Dawn reached over her shoulder and gave her a peck on the cheek, realizing as soon as she did it, that she had already broken her resolve to be more reserved.

When the Tylers opened the door to their state room, they found the entire group, with the exception of Heather, chatting happily. Emory and Dawn, in matching braids, were sitting side by side on the chaise.

Smiling fondly at each other as they left the shelter of their suite, the Tylers walked toward the group, each thinking similar thoughts. There was something about making leisurely love on a very gently rocking boat that was very special. And the fact that their guests were all getting along so splendidly made them feel less guilty about their slowness to take back over the duties of host and hostess.

Charlie met them with a smile and a slight bow, handing them their coffee. "Breakfast ready soon. Mam give word." Midge looked around the group noting Heather's absence. "Well, Charlie, I don't think we're in a big hurry this morning. Why don't you just serve the champagne and orange juice and we will wait for Heather."

Robert and Clifton jokingly informed Whip that what they really had wanted was a short sail before breakfast and only their consideration and good manners kept them from knocking on his door. Then Robert, with a twinkle in his voice, suggested that they flip for the master suite on the next sail and the guilty couple had the grace to catch each other's eye and blush.

By the time Heather joined the group, looking cool and perfect in a divided skirt of white cotton and a navy sweater with a perky white collar, the group was ready for breakfast. Emory found herself wondering, as she noted how similarly Heather and Tucker had dressed, if the young woman had peeked out to see what Tucker was wearing so she could match him. Then she scolded herself for being shrewish. They really did look wonderful standing there together, she had to admit. Then her glance drifted to Dawn and then back to Tucker. *The man truly may be a fool!* she thought and wondered if Midge would be calling her to get her perceptions.

The sail home was uneventful. The breakfast, the champagne and the freshness of the sunny sea breeze had relaxed them all. And Emory knew, even before tasting her drink, that the thoughtful and all-knowing Charlie had remembered her dislike of champagne. She was not at all surprised that he had turned her mimosa into a screwdriver.

Once back at the house, everyone paused to give Dawn a pat or a hug and to wish her a safe journey home. They also wished her success in her application to Tufts.

Tucker had been one of the first to leave, but he did come and find Dawn after he had loaded his bags in the boot of the Aston. He took her hand in both of his, and looked directly at her for a long moment. He said simply, "It is a pleasure to have met you, Dawn. I wish you well in your chosen course of study."

Thinking about it later, on the long plane trip home, Dawn felt he really was looking at her and seeing her for the first time since he had last carried her down the stairs. She found his comments strange choices. *Why had he put the comment about meeting her in the past tense? When he'd wished her well in her course of study, why did it sound as though she were starting out to do something illegal or immoral?* Finally, she sighed and forced herself to concentrate on her homecoming and the reunion with her family...a much happier and more worthwhile train of thought.

Chapter Seventeen

As Tucker settled himself into the smooth leather bucket seat of the Aston, he admitted to himself that he could not remember being so glad to be away from a group of people in his life. He felt numb with exhaustion in both body and mind. He found his jaw clenched to the point of pain as he waved casually to the other guests grouped in the shade of the porte-cochere waving goodbye. It was only by forcing himself that he could drive slowly away.

He entered the parkway, heading back toward New Haven and the safety of his parents' home on Prospect Hill, where he knew all the rules. A huge sigh escaped from somewhere deep inside and he began to do a mental check on the correctness of his behavior over the weekend. By the end of his self-developed checklist for correct social behavior, he was sure the Tylers would be unable to fault him. He had talked golf with Clifton and Mr. Tyler, and asked Robert, the Lieutenant Governor, what his boss had in mind for the state of Connecticut in terms of business incentives to attract new companies, knowing that his father would enjoy talking about the topic at Sunday dinner. Robert had a canny mind and he not only knew the answers to Tucker's questions, he enjoyed telling the young man who seemed to listen and understand both what was said and what was left unsaid. When they had finished such a conversation, Robert felt he had provided important and welcome information to a very bright, politically astute young man, which was just how Tucker intended him to feel.

As Tucker shifted gears, he reflected that he talked sports with Rob, teased Deborah, complemented Emory and had been attentive towards Heather...w*hich she seemed to enjoy very much,* he thought with a detached interest. He did not examine his behavior towards Dawn, or even think to ask himself if he had done anything for his own relaxation and enjoyment. Instead, he began to concentrate on his driving; knowing even though a piece of him felt wired, sleep deprivation was a serious issue in reaction time.

He looked at his watch as he pulled the Aston around to the side of his parents' house. He could count on the fact that his father had instructed the current chauffeur/groundskeeper to "wash and wax my son's car if he arrives with remaining daylight." He could also count on the fact that on such a day, his parents, at 5:00 o'clock, would be in the west garden, taking in the sunset, his mother bonneted in some floppy, summer straw hat, his father in a flat-brimmed Panama.

He made his way along a cobbled path and then through a very old and cleverly concealed wrought-iron gate. He thought of Kathryn McCall and stood for a moment listening to the hum of late working bees gathering nectar from the honeysuckle vine that arched over the gate. *I must remember to share this with her.* His eyes drifted over the huge white oak trees, the tall hedges, the shade loving hostas, impatiens and begonias. Farther on into the garden there was even a bank of China asters, like the one she had just planted and other flowers like hers as well. However, in his state of exhaustion, he could not bring their names to mind.

He continued on his way, looking forward to seeing his parents, to bask in the pride that lay unconcealed in their eyes, whenever they looked up to see him approaching. Those eyes also brightened when he made a point to which his father agreed, or better, when he gave his father something new to think about.

As he rounded the corner of the house he could tell that, as usual, his parents had been waiting for him. "Tucker, darling," his mother called as he approached, delight evident in her voice, "how prompt you are and how marvelously healthy you look." She reached up a slender hand, which he took in both his own and held gently as he reached over and brushed her proffered cheek with his lips. They smiled at each other and then Tucker dropped her hand and turned to shake his father's. His father had stood from the table at his approach and his grasp, when they shook, was firm without being hearty. It was a proper, manly, gentleman's shake; one Tucker had learned to emulate at an early age. It had always served him well.

Already, Margaret Jones was tinkling the silver bell that would bring cocktails. She turned again to Tucker who was folding his lanky frame into the cushion of the wicker patio chair beside her. True to form, she did not allow herself to see the tired lines around his mouth or the sadness in his weary eyes.

"It must have been a proper weekend for sailing. Your father and I have been so looking forward to hearing about it," she laughed her well-modulated laugh, "armchair adventurers that we are."

They smiled at each other, and like a well-oiled timepiece, the conversation ticked on in its predictable manner. When Tucker ran down the list of guests, his father said, "Aha!" Knowing then that he would soon be hearing accurate, secondhand details about the good governor's latest plan for economic reform. Margaret immediately picked up on the fact that there were two unattached young females aboard the boat and wondered about it silently to herself, though she wouldn't dream of prying.

However, Tucker himself gave her the opportunity to ask a question about the Tyler's guest from the West Coast when he made a comment that the young woman was a "typical California girl."

"Tucker, dear," she interrupted brightly, "forgive my ignorance, but what does the term 'California girl,' mean?"

Tucker felt a sudden pang, quickly squashed, as he remembered a similar conversation held on the steps under the Tyler's porte-cochere, and was able to say, after the slightest of pauses, "Actually, I believe it's more of a cliché than a definition. It seems to define a set of physical characteristics and a mental attitude towards life that is marketed, especially in California, to sell products." He stopped, hoping this portion of the conversation was at an end, but it was not to be. His father's interest had been piqued at the notion of marketing.

"What an interesting concept, son. Do explain yourself."

Tucker looked at them both. His father was leaning forward in his chair and his mother's face had become animated with anticipation. He sighed inwardly and decided he had no choice but to continue. "Well," he said slowly, choosing his words with care, trying hard not to picture the golden girl stretched out on the blue chaise lounge in her green bikini and failing. "The physical characteristics have to do with being very tan, having long blonde hair, straight white teeth, and...ah! I believe the woman must carry an aura of being physically fit. As far as an attitude, I would say there is a casualness and self-confidence that borders on brashness in these women. It would seem to imply..." He searched for words and could only come up with a cliché. "that the world is their oyster."

"Extraordinary!" exclaimed Evan Jones. "I believe I can see exactly what you mean. All of those billboard ads that show long-legged, athletic women selling lotions, potions, cigarettes, cars and liquor almost all fit your description." He was quiet for a moment, his well-disciplined mind examining and enjoying this revolutionary concept. "Extraordinary!" He said again. "Madison Avenue at work! And I do believe it may have been a concept that started in California. But, now that I think of it, many of our East Coast news programs are featuring women with a similar countenance." He smiled with satisfaction, knowing that he had a topic that would set the old boys at the club on their ears.

"But, Tucker, did the Tyler's houseguest fit this stereotype?" Margaret asked, despite her intention not to pry.

Tucker found himself smiling patiently at his mother, ignoring his urge to either leave or start shouting. "Exactly!" He reached over and picked up his mother's pale slender arm then held his own beside it. "Her arm looks more like mine than yours. Her skin is quite dark and even at rest you can see the definition of muscles."

Tucker did not mention the fact that he had carried her up and down the Tyler's wide curving staircase, never giving a thought to his back. Nor did he tell them that in spite of her athlete's body, she had felt extremely soft and feminine in his arms. He fought the urge to shut his eyes and bang a fist to his forehead.

"Oh, my!" Margaret said, feeling quite intrigued. To her it felt as though they were discussing a specimen from another culture. Her curiosity again got the better of her.

213

"Darling, you don't suppose you could bring her by so your father and I could meet her, do you?"

Tucker looked at his parents with surprise. Seldom had he seen them so animated. He leaned back with satisfaction and said with finality, thankful to be able to finally leave the topic. "Sorry, she leaves for the West Coast tomorrow."

He got up and walked to the cart at the edge of the flagstone steps. The newest housekeeper had just brought out both a pitcher of lemonade and one of iced tea. Unlike the Tylers, his parents seldom indulged in alcohol before dinner. What they called cocktails ranged from mineral water to iced tea, lemonade or other juices. "Mother? Father?" He lifted a glass in the age-old gesture that meant, "May I fix one for you?"

Both nodded, pleased with his good manners in asking.

A sudden thought, as he handed them each a glass of lemonade, made him ask, "Father, what is the name of our latest groundskeeper? I seem to keep forgetting."

"Thomas. Thomas and Beth Lively are the new couple. They seem like good people. Young though. What makes you ask, son?"

"Actually," said Tucker, the thought formulating clearly in his mind, "I thought, with your permission of course, of asking him to dig a pot or two of the silver hostas on the north side of the house."

Tucker, clearly visualizing Kathryn's garden, could see just the right place for the lovely broadleaf tropical looking plants at the foot of her smoke tree. *It's certainly a suitable way to repay her hospitality,* he thought.

"Certainly. By all means. I wouldn't be surprised if Thomas is finishing the car about now." He nodded his head in a dignified way, giving Tucker unspoken permission to go and find the man. Tucker smiled as he took his departure. In this household, the Jaguar was called the Jag, the Lincoln Mark V was called the Lincoln and the Aston Martin was simply referred to as, "The Car."

Sure enough, as he retraced his steps, he found Thomas lovingly polishing the last of the wax from the gleaming, gray rear quarter panel. He looked up at Tucker's approach and smiled, waiting for Tucker to speak first.

Tucker introduced himself without flair. "Hello, you must be Thomas, I'm Tucker Jones. Welcome to the household and thank you so much for cleaning the car." He sounded grateful and welcoming without being condescending.

Thomas, who indeed seemed very young, shook his hand gravely. "Hey, don't thank me. It's a pleasure to run my hands over James Bond's car."

With difficulty, Tucker kept from clenching his jaw; this time, not from irritation, but from that sudden pang that hit him as he remembered a similar conversation with the limping woman who had sticks in her hair and blood on her knee. He paused for a moment, keeping his face carefully composed. "Well," he said, "I'm afraid I have another request of you this afternoon. There are several clumps of silver hostas over on the north side of the grounds. I'd appreciate it very much if you would dig them, pot them and put them in the boot here."

Thomas put down his polishing rag and put his hands on his hips. He grinned. "I'll have to admit, I know a lot more about cars than I do about plants...but I'm learning," he said quickly, less Tucker mistake his words. "If you wouldn't mind taking the time to show me which ones you would like, sir, I'll dig them right up."

"Of course," Tucker said smoothly, "I'll show you now and then you can dig them up at your leisure. I'll be here through dinner."

Leaving Thomas to his task and retracing his steps toward the west patio, he suddenly realized that the lack of sleep was really catching up with him. His eyes felt heavy and full of grit. He looked at his watch and nodded with satisfaction. His mother would now be in the kitchen preparing whatever it was she had planned for them this evening and his father would be watching CNN's 6:00 o'clock news. Usually, he watched with his father, but tonight the chaise lounge, still bathed in a dappled sunlight, looked irresistible. He sank wearily into the soft cushions, leaned back, closed his eyes and was immediately asleep.

That's where his mother found him and went to call her husband away from his newscast. Together, they stood and watched him. So peaceful and untroubled was his sleep that they found it difficult to interrupt. Finally, when the seconds had stretched into minutes and they had watched their fill, each deeply stirred by unshared memories; Mrs. Jones reached out a gentle hand and touched her son shoulder.

He came awake slowly at the feel of her gentle touch. *It's a good picture to wake to,* he thought, seeing them standing so close together, his father's hand upon the elbow of his mother. He smiled up at them, stretched, and said without a trace of sleep in his voice, "Dinner must be ready." As his mother nodded affirmation he said cheerfully, "Good thing. I'm really hungry."

Tucker had learned to live his life on catnaps; to take sleep wherever it would come. The hour's rest had done him a world of good. As he walked to the Aston after a dinner deliciously and entirely created by his mother, several new gourmet offerings under his arm, a clean car with its gift of hosta plants in the boot, he found that he was thinking about the Monday appointment with Kathryn McCall. Perhaps he would let her massage his head after all.

Driving home, he smiled, thinking how quickly his demure mother broke character when she started grilling him about Charlie's cooking. It was a good thing he had spent part of his sleepless night remembering details of the "boat food" served with such grace and style by the smiling, bobbing little man.

"Mother," he finally said, "you should meet the man. Not to learn how to cook," he added quickly, before she could take offense. "I don't believe either of you could improve much. It's just that Charlie presents his food with a kowtow, hands folded, toes together, you know, proper Asian style."

His father caught the teasing tone immediately, but as usual, his mother looked from one to the other, her brow drawn, trying to decide whether she had missed something or if there was a joke involved. Predictably, her hand went to the jewelry at her neck. This evening it was a lovely amethyst in a heavy Baroque setting, an unusual piece that went unexpectedly well with the dark lavender summer silk she was wearing. "Kowtow, dear? I don't understand. Do you mean it makes the food taste better?" She looked from her husband to her son and then back again, noticing their

216

smiles and the twinkle in their eyes. "Oh, you two!" Fondness crept into her tone. "After all this time, you'd think I'd catch onto your banter." Then she said in a serious tone, "I do think you are mistaken, Tucker. I think there is more to Charlie's cooking than kowtowing. I suspect his talent matches, if not exceeds my own."

Downshifting for a traffic light, Tucker reflected on his mother's familiar use of Charlie's name. It was as if she knew him; that they were somehow old friends. *How unlike mother, he thought.* But then again, he decided, *I've served as their go-between for a long time; perhaps they do feel that they know each other.*

Neither his mother nor Charlie had ever indicated a desire to meet, but he wondered, with sudden insight, if it might be a secret wish for both of them. He decided to ask Midge about it when he called to thank her for the wonderful weekend.

As he drove the Aston into the safety of his underground parking, he thought honestly to himself that the weekend WAS wonderful--HE had been the problem. Usually, he enjoyed sailing, enjoyed the Tylers and their friends, and enjoyed Charlie's cooking. Since no fault could be found with the sailing party, it had to be him. Why had he felt so tense and miserable the entire time?

He pulled his bags from the boot and decided that the carefully potted and boxed hostas would be fine in the coolness of the garage for a day. Wearily, he push the elevator button and decided what he really wanted was a long shower. Then he decided, he might try booting up his computer and doing some self-exploration into what had made such a shambles of his weekend. He stepped into the elevator carefully balancing his dinners under one arm and his bags in the other hand, very much looking forward, as he always did, to stepping through his own front door and hearing the solid click as the lock caught behind him.

It would have surprised Tucker to know that he was the focus of attention in the minds or in the conversation of more than a few people with whom he had shared the weekend.

Charlie had retired for the evening, tired after the work and excitement of the sail. He had been the one to steer the graceful motorsailer back to her mooring spot and his skill had been roundly applauded by the whole group. It had been a perfect weekend he thought...except for whatever misfortune had fallen on the friendship of Dawn and Tucker. He shook his head to clear his mind of the unhappiness as he knelt respectfully before the small Shinto shrine and lit a joss stick, thus combining the Japanese culture of his father and the Chinese culture of his mother, before he began to pray.

The Tylers too had retired--Midge practically pulling her husband up the stairs after getting assurances from Dawn that she would be right up after giving a goodbye hug to Clarice. Once in their bedroom, with the door tightly closed, the couple confessed their confusion over the events of the weekend. "But I can't understand what could've happened between the time he carried her down the stairs and the time she came into the kitchen. You should have seen her face," Midge said with frustration. "She covered it quickly, but when I first looked up, I thought she might be going to cry. I'll tell you it wrenched my heart. I think Charlie and Clarice saw it too. You can bet I'm going to ask them."

James looked at his mite of a wife as she flung the throw pillows from their bed, some of them disappearing into the corner behind the couch, others bouncing off and falling on the floor, only a few landing on the seat where they belonged. He walked to her and folded her into his arms. This time it was he who offered the words of wisdom. "Let's not count our golden girl out so quickly. Heather can't, in the long run, hold a candle to her. You and I both saw Tucker more relaxed than we've ever seen him on Friday. But then, something scared the shit out of him and I think it may have been Dawn."

His wife leaned back in his arms and looked up, a glimmer of hope in her eyes. "Really, dear? Do you think so? Oh, I do hope you are at least partly right, for I find I have, for some inexplicable reason, taken a sudden dislike to Heather Anderson! Charlie and I are going to have to change almost everything we've written about her in the magic book. Do you realize she ate all that spicy garlicky food without blinking?"

Dawn was saying her goodbye to Clarice who wouldn't be at work before Dawn left to catch the plane. It turned out to be a lengthy parting. Little by little, Clarice, who was good at such things, was worming from Dawn, the details of the weekend. She had seen her sweet girl sitting like a whipped pup in a corner of the breakfast room, saw the look on her face as Tucker and Heather strode through the door and had pretty much figured things out for herself. It was well past her leaving time and she'd have to go pretty soon if she wanted to catch the last bus. But for now, she wanted to get some firsthand details straight.

"Dawn, honey, you told me everything I wanted to know about this weekend, but I notice ol' Tucker Jones' name never came up even once. Why would that be, child? Seemed to me, from the talk I heard right here in this kitchen, that you and he had gotten to be real good friends in a short time."

Dawn looked up from where she had been tracing a pattern on the tablecloth with her teaspoon and found herself caught inescapably by two magnetic brown eyes flecked with a strange gold highlight. She gave a small smile, imagining how this woman's six children must have been caught in the same snare of the powerful gaze and how the truth must've come tumbling out. Then she shrugged and said in her usual honest fashion, glad to finally share her jumbled thoughts.

"I have to say, Clarice, it's very confusing to me. I'm afraid I may have offended him. I didn't know that he had a girlfriend, honestly. I really didn't know much about him. I mean, I don't remember the Tylers talking about him before I left for my trip, though it's obvious they know each other very well. Then he rescued me, you know, and carried me up and down the stairs and he really seemed to like doing it. Once, I think I even caught him sniffing my perfume, but I'm not sure." The pent-up words tumbled out and Dawn's face was a study of confused sadness.

"Then," she said, "I think I said something, or did something he misinterpreted... Or maybe he thought I was..." she swallowed, "like maybe coming on to him or something and he needed to make it clear he wasn't

219

interested and put me in my place." Then she laughed, a miserable little sound, and looked directly at Clarice.

"Truth is, I was thinking about coming on to him, just a little, all morning. But really, all I can remember doing was standing a little closer to him than would be proper. And then later, when I understood about Heather and tried to just be friends, there was some huge barrier he'd built between us. I really don't know why. Heather isn't the jealous type, so that's not it. She even invited me to go hiking with Tucker and herself in the Maine woods..."

Clarice reached over and held Dawn's hand on the table as the flow of words stopped—two brown hands clasped in friendship and caring, one a rich mahogany, the other a deep gold. "Dawn, honey, you got feelings for this boy?" She asked gently, already knowing the answer, but wanting Dawn to be able to recognize them so she could get her thinking straight.

"No! I mean, yes...or maybe I mean maybe. I really don't know, Clarice. I mean, I hardly know the guy and from what I do know of him he seems like a real tight ass. I mean, I have never--and I mean, never ever--been attracted to stuffed shirts."

At Dawn's profanity, Clarice had covered her mouth with her hand to hide her smile, shaking her head in wonder. The girl never ceased to surprise her. 'Look like an angel, talk like the devil,' was what her own Southern Baptist mother used to say when her children swore. But, "tight ass," had been Clarice's secret term for Tucker since she first had known him. The first time she met him, she went home and said to her husband, "That boy got some sort of cob up his butt." Her husband had known exactly what she meant. But, over time she had halfway changed her mind. "Something bad troublin' that boy," she was lately more inclined to say.

Dawn turned a miserable face towards the housekeeper. "You know, looking at me, you'd think by now I'd have fallen in love at least a dozen times. But I haven't. So, I don't know for sure what it's supposed to feel like. I can tell you one thing, from my training in psychology, for some dumb reason, as we'd say in the profession, 'my emotions are engaged.' Not that it's doing me a bit a good!" She added sourly, as an afterthought.

Dawn looked at their still joined hands and then up at the kindly face. "There you have it. Thanks for listening and helping me admit what I needed to. But you know," she paused thinking hard. "There's something, some little missing piece in all this and I can't quite figure it out. I'm really pretty good at reading people; it's partly me and partly my training. But I really misread Tucker for some reason...unless he was giving me mixed signals..." Her voice trailed off, the thought finished, but not forgotten.

Clarice nodded. "That's it honey. That's the important piece. You hang onto that for a while." And then she told Dawn something that gave her additional food for thought on the long plane ride to Santa Barbara.

"I been knowin' that boy for more than three years. He practically lives here weekends. The Tylers treat him like a son. Missus Tyler is always managin' to find him some pretty girl to spend time with. But the boy just ain't been even a little bit interested. When he walked in with that girl all lovey-dovey on his arm, you could have knocked this ol' woman over with the feather of a banty hen."

Clarice disengaged her hand from Dawn's, gave it a final pat and moved her bulk from the table. "I gotta catch the bus, honey. But you mind what I say. Two and two ain't even close to makin' four in this case."

She went to get her shopping bag and sweater. Dawn got up and followed her to the door. They stood facing each other, two women of the same height though much different in bulk. It seemed natural for them to wrap their arms around each other. Dawn put her head on the older woman's shoulder feeling immeasurably comforted and Clarice rocked her gently for long seconds. "You remember what I say, girl. You ain't no whipped pup. You fine." She chuckled. "You can bet I'll be wormin' some things outta Charlie come tomorrow evenin'. That gentleman see a lot. And Missus Tyler...she'll be a working on the both of us, trying to figure things out. She's a fool about romance, that one."

Clarice opened the door and then turned to look at Dawn. "I got one last question in my head. Why was that boy showin' interest in one of Missus Tyler's pretty girls for the very first time just when you was there? Now that seems like a coincidence too big to ignore." With those words she turned on her heel and hurried down the driveway.

"Thanks so much, Clarice. I'll tell my mom what a wonderful mother substitute you were," Dawn called to her retreating back. She watched the older woman disappear down the lamp-lit drive. It was quite a walk to the bus stop. It was not bad on such a night, but Dawn wondered as she locked the door and began turning off the lights, what she did when it rained.

As she headed up the staircase, Dawn found that no matter how hard she tried, she could not shut out the images of the morning she'd been carried down the same steps, laughing, her ear lying close to a strongly beating heart.

Chapter Eighteen

The next morning, Midge looked at her husband flabbergasted, when he announced, in the middle of shaving, that he too was going with Dawn to the airport. Granted, it was an early flight, but she couldn't remember ever before such an occurrence, and said as much.

James grinned and looked sheepish. "Yes, well," he said, wiping his chin, "ordinarily I wouldn't be able to...but the South America project is on hold while the team checks some references and gathers some necessary data that Tucker found missing. There's not a damn thing else cooking that Clifton can't handle. I already mentioned to him on the boat that I was thinking of coming in late and he acted just like you're acting!" He beetled his bushy brows trying hard to look offended. "I'm president of the damned place. Can't I take my nose from the grindstone long enough to take our guest to the plane without everyone having a conniption?"

Midge laughed, "Of course you can, dear. I assume that I am to be included in this adventure?"

James looked at his wife in surprise. "Hell yes! I want both of us to see her safely handed over to a porter and then I'll bring you home and go on to the office."

Midge waved her hand. "I love it! I can't wait to see Hank's face when you get in the car with us. Did you already cancel your car?"

James nodded. "First thing this morning when you were in the shower."

"Well," Midge said with satisfaction, "you seem to have taken care of all the details. I love it!" She said again. "I can now totally relax and enjoy our remaining time with that lovely young woman."

As they descended the stairs, Midge turned and whispered fiercely to her husband, "We will not mention the name of Tucker Jones around here this morning!"

223

James smiled at the top of her once carefully combed, but already tousled head. He knew she was really talking to herself. As much as she wanted to question their guest, she would not bring potential sadness to their last morning together.

Dawn found them in the breakfast room, sipping coffee, waiting somewhat impatiently for her to arrive. She was dressed for travel in a simple cotton skirt and blouse. There was the moisture from early morning dew on her flats and a glow on her face.

"I just took a quick goodbye tour of the grounds. It is so lovely and peaceful. Charlie has already taken the Rover down to retrieve some things from Faith. I told him to thank her for the lovely sail." She said the last quite seriously and both older people nodded their heads with equal seriousness, knowing just how she felt.

Midge leaned up for a hug and said, "Dawn, darling, James just announced the nicest surprise through his shaving cream this morning. He's decided to come to the airport to see you off as well."

James, who had risen from his chair at Dawn's entry to the room, looked down fondly at the two women embracing. He smiled a little self-consciously, but felt exceedingly pleased with himself. He felt even more so when Dawn gave a little gasp of surprise and fixed serious brown eyes on him. To her credit, she did not protest or question his decision, though he could see she was very touched. She walked very close to him, took his hand and held it to her cheek. "Thank you," she said humbly. "It makes a perfect end to a visit so lovely I don't even know how to thank you properly."

He cleared his throat and gave a left-handed pat to the two brown hands clasping his one and said, "No thanks are necessary. In fact, Midge and I were just saying last night how empty this house is going to seem without its ray of sunshine."

He paused and looked down to where her mid-calf skirt covered the skinned knee. "Now, I saw that your limp seems less pronounced this morning. Can we assume that Charlie's ointment is continuing to do you some good?"

"As a matter of fact, I was telling Charlie that it is still a little stiff, but the soreness is mostly gone. I think I'll be

224

back on the running trail in just a couple of days." Dawn smiled and lifted the hem of her skirt. They could see a healing scab had formed and that the skin surrounding the abrasion was nearly normal in color.

"So then," said James with satisfaction, "if I know you, you're already packed. Just help yourself to a cup of coffee and relax with us. Hank should be here in about 15 minutes. I thought we'd go and have a bite at the club before heading to the airport."

When Hank arrived, Dawn asked him to take a picture of the three of them with her camera. She took more pictures at the club while enjoying what turned out to be a breakfast that was overly leisurely, causing Hank to push the speed limit in order to turn Dawn over to the porter on time.

Since Dawn had made it clear that she did not want them to feel obligated to wait until her departure time, there was a sudden flurry of sidewalk goodbyes. James thrust a $20 bill at the porter, saying, "Take extra good care of this one, she's got a bum leg."

It did not seem like a proper transition, leaving her on the sidewalk instead of at the gate. It made the visit seems somehow unfinished and it made the Tylers feel a little unsettled. They were mostly quiet on the short drive back home, talking about the details of their week, trying to change gears and get back into their respective routines.

James did mention that he needed to read the preliminary outline draft Tucker had done on Friday and that he was sure the boy would be holed up in his condo, working on the South America project, doing a more detailed summary. "He gave me a quick outline on Friday and then had to rush off somewhere. Peggy said he left the office at a clip."

"Really, dear?" mused Midge, "Now that's not very much like our Tucker, is it?" Silently, she wondered if his destination had anything to do with Heather and then sighed. *I am absolutely not going to allow myself to ruminate on the subject of Tucker Jones' love life and spoil this beautiful day!*

She turned to her husband. "You know he will be calling to thank us for the weekend. He always does. But

I've made up my mind that I will not ask a single question about his private life." *Even if it kills me,* she added silently to herself.

Little did she know, as she kissed her husband on the cheek, the course of events that her late morning conversation with Tucker were going to set in motion.

Tucker awoke with a start. Then he groaned, remembering. He had turned off his computer at 4:00 A.M., had lain, trying for a blank mind until 5:00 A.M. Now it was 7:00 A.M. He shut off the alarm before it could ring, deciding with resignation, that two hours of uninterrupted sleep were much better than none. For some reason, as he began his morning stretching, he felt inordinately pleased with the two solid hours of sleep.

At the door of his bedroom he paused, momentarily bewildered by the wads of paper snowballs littering his living room. Then he frowned, remembering how he'd finally shut down the system, eyes gritty with exhaustion and had thrown himself into bed…only to lie there, thoughts refusing to still in his mind.

But evidently he HAD gone to sleep and…he thought with wonder, had not needed to blank his mind to do it. *Why was I able to do that? This is a mystery.* He ran his hands through his hair. He couldn't even begin to call his self-imposed session with his "feelings journal" all that successful, though for the first hour he thought he'd really gotten the hang of it. However, when he printed out a hard copy so he could really concentrate on what he'd written, he'd discovered with dismay and a horrible insight, that almost every sentence was again a reflection of how he thought others were feeling about him. In a fit of late-night frustration, he'd wadded and tossed the offending papers about the living room. Finally, he had settled himself down and called up his very first effort at examining his feelings and the words of his last sentence struck in his mind. I am good at knowing other people's feelings. This journal is supposed to be about my feelings.

He grabbed one of the crumpled missiles and read what he had written. After he'd read a few sentences, he re-wadded it in disgust. *I started it out okay*, he decided. He'd written: This weekend should have been really enjoyable, but it wasn't. I need to sit here and figure out why. **Then, the next words he'd typed were very revealing and showed him reverting to type.** It wasn't that I behaved badly, in fact, Mr. and Mrs. Tyler seemed quite glad to have me along.

It was then he had looked at the clock. It was just past midnight. With a wavering sigh he sat himself back down and hunched over the computer, remembering the silly trick that seem to loosen his mind before and decided to address his remarks to his ceiling.

Listen, Ceiling, I have just come off one of the worst weekends of my life and I can't feel a thing. In fact, I spent the entire time not allowing myself to feel. Why, Ceiling???

He paused, eyes clenched, picturing the events that had transpired and suddenly his face cleared. What I wrote is not quite true, Ceiling. On Friday I rescued a beautiful damsel in distress and I felt... **He paused and drummed his fingers on the smooth enamel of the desk, allowing himself to clearly recall the gentle evening.** MANLY! **He typed with conviction and in capital letters and then added:** PROTECTIVE! **But, instead of continuing the line of thought and attaching Dawn to those feelings, he changed course and wrote,** I made Mr. Tyler laugh. **Then, looking at what he'd written, he deleted it and wrote,** I felt like I was being funny. **That sentence caused him to sigh and again close his eyes in deep concentration. It was not uncommon that he made others laugh. He was often complimented on his wit and gentle teasing humor.** *What made Friday night feel so different?* **He knew it was important, perhaps critical, to uncover the difference, but after long minutes as it continued to elude him, he decided to skip it and continue. But it seemed as though his fingers knew something his mind did not. They typed:** I was, for some reason, feeling quite relaxed that night and I wasn't trying to be funny to please my boss. I was enjoying my own humor. I was pleasing myself. **He chewed on the thought for long moments, recognizing it to**

227

be true. Then he put his fingers back on the keys and continued. Then, on the boat I felt sad, but I don't know why. Again he paused, thinking hard, recognizing that the logical mind he had come to depend upon did not work very well when it came to uncovering his feelings. Shrugging, he continued. I also felt anxious, very anxious, most of the time. I think I was afraid I was going to embarrass myself or let someone down.

Unfortunately, since the computer was not programed to psychoanalyze or ask probing questions, Tucker was able to skip from Friday evening to Saturday on the boat, ignoring his feelings during the morning conversation with Dawn under the porte-cochere. He totally blocked the strong feeling of attraction. Also blocked was the onset of angst and anger when she told him she was a psychology major. The closest he could get to his feelings about Dawn and the only time her name appeared, other than the oblique reference to rescuing a damsel in distress, in any of these attempts, was a single line that said: I found myself especially anxious around the Tyler's house guest, Dawn Simpson.

About Heather, he wrote more freely and at greater length. I feel quite comfortable around Heather Anderson. I seem to know the rules. It is easy to make her happy. She is a beautiful woman and I think she would like to see more of me. He looked at what he had written was satisfaction, not realizing he was again dealing with the emotions of others rather than his own. He smiled, thinking of her cool elegant composure and as an afterthought added, I am going to kiss her after the concert Friday night.

Somehow, that statement did not make him feel as happy as he would have liked it to. That was when he decided he would shut the computer down and think about it while lying in bed.

Tucker finally turned away from looking at his living room mess and went to turn on his shower. A glance into his bathroom startled him. There was a pile of clothing and his wet bath towel still on the floor. Remembering the condition of his living room, he frowned and shook his head, unable to recall another incident of having gone to bed with his quarters so unkempt. Vaguely, as he hung the towel and hampered the dirty clothing, he realized he wasn't as upset as he might have been.

He looked at his bedside clock and realized it was past time for him to be at the computer, especially since he planned to have the entire meeting summary fleshed out so he could take it to review in Kathryn's garden before his massage.

True to form, he hurried through his shower, his breakfast and then picked up his littered living room before kicking the machine to life. Also true to form, he worked with complete concentration until the document was finished. Just as he pushed the button that would activate the transmission on the modem, he remembered that he had not yet called Mrs. Tyler to thank her for the weekend.

He sent the document and hastily pushed her number on the phone. He knew what he was going to say was going to sound dreadfully insincere unless he was careful to concentrate.

When Midge picked up the receiver, he said, trying to sound cheerful, though in no mood for chitchat, "Hello, Mrs. T, this is Tucker. Sorry to be so late in calling to thank you for the weekend, I was on the computer until late and somehow allowed myself to oversleep."

"Oh, hello, Tucker, dear," Midge said cheerfully, picking up on his tone but ignoring it. "James and I just got back from taking Dawn to the airport and I was walking to the phone to call her mother to tell her that her daughter was safely on her way, so your timing is perfect as usual."

Midge felt a small twinge of satisfaction at the silence on the other end of the line as Tucker digested what she had said. *Clearly,* she thought, *he didn't miss the fact that James took time from work to see Dawn off on the plane.*

However, Tucker's thoughts were far from how his boss was spending his time. He was dealing instead with the sudden clear picture of Dawn sitting, clasping a cup of coffee, hair tousled, fresh from sleep, in Charlie's galley. She'd moved over a bit so he could join her. Instead, he

229

declined somewhat abruptly and had gone to drink his own coffee on the deck. He turned at the top of the stairs for a moment to say one last thing to soften his action and had caught her looking after him with a look of puzzled sadness. The picture was vivid. Now, he felt a quick stab of loss in finding her actually gone. He also felt a strong and sudden desire to know more about what her look had meant. But now it was too late.

Finally, Midge said, "Tucker, are you there?"

Smoothly he said, "Sorry about that pause, Mrs. T, I had forgotten Dawn was to leave so early and was wondering if I had said a proper goodbye to her yesterday."

Midge, thinking of all the things she wanted to better understand about what had happened between Dawn and Tucker, remembered, just in time, her promise to her husband and held herself from asking. Instead, she said soothingly, "Oh, I'm sure you did, Tucker. It just wouldn't have been like you to have done otherwise. Anyway, we're hoping she'll be back in the fall. James and I have already been complaining how big and empty this place seems without her. Charlie is absolutely moping about this morning and I suppose Clarice, when she arrives, will be out of sorts as well. It is truly amazing how attached to her the four of us got."

Midge laughed, "As James said, 'She's like having our own personal ray of sunshine.' She is truly a remarkable young person, don't you think?"

Midge rushed on, not waiting for Tucker's reply. (It was only later that she realized what she was really doing was getting her licks in on Tucker for virtually ignoring Dawn on the boat.) "We're sure she'll have no trouble with her admission to Tufts. There just aren't that many young people with her obvious talent willing to work with handicapped children these days."

Suddenly, Tucker felt he couldn't tolerate talking about Dawn another second. The fact that she planned to work with handicapped children, something he hadn't known, went unremarked upon, and in fact, was successfully blocked from his mind as the image of her sadness again washed over him.

Grasping for another line of conversation, he remembered his thoughts about his mother wanting to meet

230

Charlie. When Midge paused, Tucker quickly interjected, "By the way, I had an interesting conversation last evening at my parents. I believe my mother has a secret desire to meet Charlie."

It was Midge's turn for silence, her mind quickly digesting the ramifications of setting up such a meeting. Finally she said, "Really dear? That IS an odd thought! But, I know you well enough to know there is probably something to it."

Tucker chuckled. "Oh, I don't really know for sure, but over the years I have noticed that Mother has shown more than a passing interest in the meals he prepares. Lately, when I call to tell her I'm spending the weekend with you, she invariably says, 'be sure and pay close attention to what their cook comes up with this time.' Then, I suddenly noticed at dinner last night, my unfailingly polite and gracious mother was actually grilling me for weekend menu details."

Midge laughed aloud. "You know, Tucker, I wouldn't be surprised if Charlie would like to meet her as well. Of course, you know Charlie. He'd never let on for a second if he did."

Tucker, remembering how often he and Charlie had talked of his mother's recipes and how carefully Charlie had listened when he described the similarities of the kitchens, chuckled knowingly and said simply, "I wouldn't be a bit surprised."

When Tucker hung up after again thanking his hostess for the wonderful hospitality and making a comment on the congeniality of the assembled group, he was still smiling. *That,* he thought was satisfaction, *will give the lady something new to think about.* Little did he know where that thinking would lead!

Midge sat quietly for a moment, digesting this new startling piece of information. *Really, it does make sense,* she decided and tucked the thought away to think about later and went to find the telephone number of her college roommate.

When Dawn's mother answered the phone, she was not at all surprised when the familiar, cheerful, slightly impish voice began with their age-old salutation. "Hello, beautiful Barbara from Santa Barbara, this is the midget,

Midge, who misses you." It was a special greeting that Midge had invented when they had become newly graduated, newly married and living with a continent between them.

Barbara, the pleasure evident in her voice, perched herself on a barstool in her sunny kitchen and said, "Well, Midget, I'm assuming this call is to tell me that Dawn is safely winging her way west."

"Yes, unfortunately for James and me, she is. Listen, Barbara, you and Charles should win some sort of award for raising that girl. She is an absolute delight! Thank you so much for sharing her with us," Midge said sincerely.

Barbara laughed comfortably, but was deeply touched by her old friend's words. The strands of their friendship had withstood the test of time. They still shared their deepest hurts and their most special joys. When Scotty had died, it was Barbara to whom Midge turned. It was Barbara who held her for the hours she wept, inconsolable. It was Barbara who insisted she share her tears with her husband, thus forcing him to weep deep wracking sobs that he might otherwise have buried. And it was Barbara who kept the household running with some semblance of normalcy as Clarice and Charlie too dealt with the loss of Scotty.

But that was in the long past, part of the shared memories that bound them. Today, they settled back for a chat about Dawn. By the time they were done, Barbara had heard about the fall, the rescue, the seeming rise then extinction of electricity between Tucker and Dawn, James' unheard-of taking time off from work to escort her to the airport and how impressed they both were with her ability to handle Faith.

Barbara, in the course of conversation, mentioned the fact that she was glad Dawn was on her way home because she was up to her ears in their club's annual fundraiser for high school scholarships--a barbecue cook-off.

Midge's ears perked up and in a single brilliant flash, she could see how such an event could be used, not only to raise money for S.O.S. and give Charlie and Margaret Jones the opportunity to meet each other...but for James and her to meet Tucker's parents.

"Barbara, it just so happens that I'm, by default, the somewhat permanent chair of our S.O.S. fundraising. I've been having a miserable time trying to come up with a fresh idea and your barbecue has given me food for thought," Midge quipped and then waited. It always took a moment for Barbara to catch her play on words. It always had. This time was no exception.

"Well," said Barbara, as the words sank in, "it sounds as though you're cooking now." They laughed, taken back 40 years in time. Charles and James had started the silly wordplay banter one night at a football game that was too lopsided to be entertaining.

Now, it was Midge's turn to continue. "I WAS starting to stew about it," she said.

Thinking quickly, Barbara finished, "But now you don't have to stew about it anymore, do you? You can always count me in to help you out of a jam."

Midge smiled into the receiver, knowing the smile was being returned from the other end. "Thanks for the game. It's nice to know we've still got the talent. And, thank you so much for the idea. I have a fund raising meeting scheduled for Wednesday, but two of my good friends are also semi-permanent members on it and I'm going to give them a ring as soon as I'm done picking your brain. I'll see if we can't flesh out some ideas to present to the full committee. Now, tell me how your cook-off works."

But the time they were finished, Midge realized with mounting excitement that she had developed the germ of a fantastic fundraising idea. Not a barbecue cook-off though, something more suited to the East Coast, thanks to both Tucker and Barbara.

Chapter Nineteen

An observer, even a careful one, would have been willing to bet that the well-dressed, tousled-headed older lady was on the verge of napping after she gently replaced the phone receiver, leaned back and snuggled deep into the cushions of her chair, cradling a throw pillow in her arms. They would have lost the bet. The quiet body with lowered lids was a deception. It was also very unlike Midge. Usually, thinking caused her to begin the idle plumping of pillows, stacking of papers, room-straightening sorts of things. This was different. She felt suspended from her physical body, her mind a popcorn popper of ideas; each one colliding with the next. Problems presented and solved themselves.

This, she decided, *has the potential to be the most successful fundraiser ever attempted for S.O.S.* She knew she should be scratching some of her thinking on a piece of paper, but she didn't think she needed to. What she really needed to do on Wednesday was to see if the fundraising committee was as enamored with the fledgling idea as she was.

With a huge sigh, Midge pulled herself from the depths of the cushions. Althea and Emory were the two she needed to talk to first. There was no way she was going to give her wonderful idea to the full committee until she knew exactly how it would work and that the key players would cooperate. Right now, she needed her two best friends for collaboration. Althea was a genius for detail and a good organizer, and Emory's infallible sense of timing and her ability to understand the nuances that might be involved in developing this plan could be critical in its success.

Midge got determinedly to her feet and headed for the garage. Before she called either woman, there was one detail that must be handled. Flicking the garage door open, she hopped in one of the waiting golf carts and headed for Faith. First and foremost, Charlie must be consulted.

234

Down in the motorsailer, Charlie was standing back, quietly admiring the gleam he had just finished putting on his again spotless stainless-steel cooktop. He heard the hum of the electric motor and turned to hasten up the galley steps. That Mam should come down to Faith this time of day was most unusual. *Perhaps it has something to do with Dawn.* His brow furrowed with worry as he trotted to the teak rail. But even from the distance, he could see his boss was not upset. Midge parked the cart with a flourish, waved and trotted toward Faith.

They looked at each other--the patience of Charlie's demeanor belied by the question marks snapping in his dark eyes, Midge more than a little breathless from hurry and excitement.

"Oh, Charlie, I have just had the most fantastic idea! At least I think it is. But, if you don't think so, then it isn't!" And with that mysterious comment, she hurried up the docking platform and onto the deck. Standing squarely in front of her cook, she hit him directly with the question she most wanted to know. "Charlie, would you be willing to be involved in a cooking contest?"

With no little pleasure, Midge noted that for once the Asian gentleman could not conceal his emotion. The look of shock registered in waves on his face. *Of all the things that come out of Mam's mouth, this is most...unexpected.* She waited quietly, wanting him to digest the idea, feeling just a twinge of guilt at the abruptness, not to mention vagueness of her question.

Finally, with a calm face and a voice of dignity, he replied simply. "This person had not thought he ever wanted to contest cooking skills. Would Mam please enlighten further, most surprising question."

"Yes, I will, Charlie. It is a brand-new idea so I haven't worked out the details. If you agree to participate, then I'll get together with Althea and Emory to do just that. Anyway..." Midge fairly bounced in place as she warmed to her own idea. "...anyway," she said again, "here's the skeleton. As a fundraiser for Save Our Spaces, we will hold a $1000 a plate dinner. The recipes for the selected dishes will be provided by participating chefs from up and down the East Coast. Everyone who sends a recipe will receive a cookbook, but only seven finalists will actually provide the dishes for the dinner. S.O.S. will purchase the ingredients. Of course, it will be participation by invitation only, with cash prizes for the seven winners." Midge was making up part of the plan as she went along. "I'm so sorry to have to exclude you, Charlie, but you'd probably win and then people might wonder, since it is my idea, if the contest were rigged. So, when I said, 'Be involved,' I was thinking more of asking you to co-chair the recipe selection committee with Margaret Jones."

Charlie, following Midge's rapid-fire conversation with great intensity, jumped as though he'd been stuck with a pin, so great was the impact of Margaret Jones' name. Slowly, as he understood Midge's intent and his role in this fundraiser, a delighted smile started to build and only with great effort was he able to keep it from covering his face. He gave a small hop of pure joy, clapped his hands and then bowed from the waist. *This is better than timing the stock market; even better than picking the winning dog,* he thought as he continued to bow. The thought of not only getting to meet his idol, but to be able to work side-by-side with her as an equal, was almost more than he could fathom. But a sudden thought stopped him cold. He stood erect. "But, Mam," he said in a low but clear voice, "what if the honorable Mrs. Jones does not choose to participate?"

"Well," said Midge matter-of-factly, "she might decline. We won't know until we ask. But, you can see why I had to ask you first. I don't want to tackle something like this without you."

Charlie nodded solemnly. Her words softened the fear holding tight in his stomach like a fist. She had honored him. He would do what he could to make her idea a success. If Tucker's mother would agree to participate, it would be auspicious. If she did not, it was not meant to be. He opened his mouth and took a deep, long breath of air, then exhaled strongly to allow the fist of fear to take flight. With clear eyes and a peaceful smile, he said his thoughts aloud. "You do me great honor with the responsibility you give me. I will do my best."

They looked at each other for a long moment, Midge, for the first time, fully realizing just how right Tucker had been about Charlie's wanting to meet his mother. She could only pray it was a reciprocal feeling. *If it's not,* she thought a bit grimly to herself, *I'll just have to convince her or get Tucker involved.*

Aloud she said, "Don't worry about this yet, Charlie. I'm going to go and call Althea and Emory and invite them to breakfast tomorrow morning. And, if they'll agree to help, we'll do some serious planning over your berry scones and coffee in the kitchen garden. I want to have my thinking very organized before I approach Mrs. Jones or the committee."

Althea, after thanking her profusely for the wonderful weekend, agreed to come and promised to do some thinking in the meantime. The idea of asking Margaret Jones to participate delighted her. "Really, Midge, this might be your best idea yet. We're all so tired of auctions, black-tie dinners and gala events. I do think there are a fair number of you gals who think each other's chefs can't hold a candle to your own. This might be the event of the year!"

Midge laughed, catching Althea's gentle barb. She did think Charlie would win, had he been able to enter; in fact, she would've bet money on it.

"Oh, dear, Althea, I believe you are absolutely correct. In fact, you've just given me another splendid idea. I'd better run it by James tonight, and if he likes it, I'll tell you about it in the morning," she said mysteriously. "But now, I have to ring Emory. It's going to take the three of us to do this right."

Emory was not at home. It didn't matter, Midge knew from weekends past that the woman would soon be calling to rave about the weekend and, if Midge came right out and asked, might share a few of her weekend observations. Otherwise, Midge also knew from past experience, observant, intuitive Emory generally kept her thoughts to herself.

So it was very unexpected when the return call came and the familiar, throaty voice first thanked her warmly for the weekend and then without preamble and before Midge could invite her to breakfast or breach her glorious idea, went on talking without pausing for breath. She declared Dawn a "splendid young woman," then admitted candidly that she "felt the strange vibrations" floating between Tucker and Dawn, and "couldn't figure them out."

Midge, fundraising for the moment totally forgotten, interrupted. "Oh, Emory, thank you for bringing it up. Neither James nor I can figure it out either. Like I said in the salon on Friday night, we were both convinced that they were very attracted to each other. You really wouldn't have believed how relaxed and spontaneous Tucker was. And Dawn, despite the dramatic fall and very sore knee, seemed to be glowing. Then, for some reason, that light went out Saturday morning. Heather Anderson showed up and you saw the rest," she said sorrowfully, recapping the sequence.

There was a pause on the other end of the line and then a soft laugh. "Of course," Emory said thoughtfully, "that helps explain some of what I felt."

"What do you mean, Emory?" Midge said more sharply than she intended, fearing that the woman would keep her insights private and leave Midge dangling without a clue as to what she was talking about.

Fortunately, Emory did not easily take offense, and she was not one to pull a punch. "Well, I'm not sure, but I think what I was feeling between them was thwarted sexual energy. Tucker, for some reason, seemed to be desperately blocking it. Did you notice how he kept putting actual distance between them? He would have liked a deck twice as long. It seemed like he was either angry or... maybe afraid. In fact, it seemed to me that he was using Heather as a shield. I mean, that would explain some things, wouldn't it?"

Midge, on the other end of the line was nodding "yes" so vigorously that her curls were bouncing. "Yes. Oh, yes! What you say does make sense. In fact, James said something along the same line last night. He remarked, and I must quote, 'Something scared the shit out of Tucker.'"

Midge felt great relief at being able to share her confusion with someone as astute and perceptive in human behavior as Emory. She'd planned to tackle Charlie in the afternoon, though she dreaded it, because he was usually even more obscure than Emory at her worst. This was better. This was straight talk, and as far as she was concerned, Emory at her best.

"Well," said Emory neutrally, "it appeared to me that Heather was a more than willing buffer. I'd say she has set her sights on your boy. And I don't mean just a fling. I think the young woman has decided it's time to be married."

Midge groaned inwardly. Emory had just sliced through to the heart of a fear she wasn't really quite willing to face. But, Emory had been open with her, she could be no less. "Yes, I'm terribly afraid I agree. I feel I have allowed that young woman to totally manipulate me for the purpose of snaring Tucker." She knew she could not reveal the magic book, but she did add, "And I have found some inconsistencies in her behavior that makes me wonder about her character."

Emory absorbed the information and then said, letting Midge know she had stepped back into the privacy of her true nature, "Well, what will be, will be. She's a safe choice for Tucker, don't you think?"

Midge certainly did not think, but she knew it would be useless to continue. With great regret, she let the subject drop and thanked Emory sincerely for her perceptions. Then she laughed and said, "Oh, my word! I almost forgot. When I tried ringing you earlier, it was with a favor to ask. You see, I have had this marvelous idea for a fundraiser for S.O.S. and wondered if you could come for breakfast in the morning? I already have Althea's promise to come, but we need you to beef up the brainstorm team. I know it is short notice, but are you free?"

After Midge briefly outlined her idea, Emory said, "Of course I'll come. In fact, this one even sounds fun! I have mixed feelings about Charlie not participating in the actual contest. He'll do a good job judging, but you and I both know he'd come up with something tremendous for the yacht. However, your point about conflict of interest is well taken, I suppose."

Midge made a mental note to tell Charlie about Emory's compliment. They discussed briefly the politics of bringing on board the other S.O.S. fundraiser committee members. Emory thought that the idea should first be on paper, but only in outline form. Midge agreed, knowing the importance of everyone feeling a part of the project.

Once she and Emory had finished their conversation and said good bye, Midge found the popcorn popper in her brain was still busy popping ideas.

Idly, she pulled a pad of paper from her desk drawer and almost unwillingly, her hand began to fill the first of several pages. By the time she was done, there was a theme: yacht food; a location: the yacht club; and an organizational chart, blank except for herself as chairperson.

She tapped her pen, thinking hard. The idea she wanted to run by her husband was whether or not he thought people would be willing to place bets on whose cook would be the winner and in what category. One thing was for certain, the committee would have to be convened quickly. The event should take place no later than September. After that, too many people turned from yachting to watching football, snow skiing and other cold-weather sports. *Can we put the affair together and pull it off in three months?* That would be the first question she would put to Althea and Emory in the morning.

Looking at the pages of her own neat script, Midge felt a twinge of guilt. *All this detail worked out, right after I wholeheartedly agreed with Emory that it wasn't the thing to do.* Then she shrugged. *Any ideas the women don't like can be tossed.*

Reluctantly, Midge put the papers in a desk drawer and for the first time realized how absorbed she had been. Nearly two hours had passed. *This was supposed to have been my time to get organized.* With determination, she put the cooking contest out of her mind and pulled her engagement calendar from the drawer. *It's a booked week* she noted and with a frown saw her Thursday golf date with Elaine Anderson. Her frown deepened. *Have I been manipulated by Heather? How in the world did I come to invite her on the boat? It was my own initiative, wasn't it?* She wished she could remember the details of the telephone conversation. One thing was for certain, she would pay sharp attention to Tucker's new love interest at lunch on Thursday. Emory didn't share her intuitions easily. Some strong feelings must have caused her to break character.

With that thought completed, Midge got to her feet and went to see if Charlie had time for a cup of tea and whether he had made the necessary changes regarding Heather's food preferences in the magic book. She really was finding it difficult to stop thinking about the fundraiser and decided she would call Tucker after the lunch hour and see if he would be willing, as he had done so many times before, to be her computer expert.

However, when she called Tucker, he was neither at the office nor at home. *He's probably off with Heather on this lovely afternoon,* she thought glumly, the frown coming back, as she left him a pleasant message request and hung up the phone.

Tucker had, in fact, only just left his condo, computer printout under his arm. He was dressed in a jersey and chinos and was whistling softly. A back pack holding tuna sandwiches, a thermos of lemonade and two plastic cups was slung over his shoulder. His mind was on the hostas in the boot of his car. *I wonder how Kathryn is going to feel about receiving them from a relative stranger? No,* he corrected himself, *I'm not a stranger, I'm a client.* He nodded to himself. *Besides, I'm just going to set the plants under the tree in their box and tell her about them…unless she has time to sit and drink lemonade after the appointment.*

He was still whistling as he pulled the Aston into a parking place on her street and retrieved the hostas from the boot. They looked perfectly fresh and he found himself feeling quite satisfied with himself as he carried them into her garden and put them under the tree.

The garden was as warm and welcoming as he remembered. Hastily, he returned to his car for his printout and backpack. It was going to be splendid to have more than an hour perusing his work, sipping lemonade, enjoying the quiet, broken only by occasional street traffic or other neighborhood sounds. However, such quiet was not to be.

Tucker had just settled himself at the table, taken his fill of looking at the garden and was pulling the printout towards himself when he heard the hinges on the gate that led to the front lawn squeak. There was a moment of silence and then he heard the soft bang of the gate closing

241

itself. Slowly, he turned in his chair and looked over his shoulder, prepared to see Kathryn returning from changing a sprinkler. Instead, he saw a very disgusted, bonnet-clad cat, dangling from the arms of a small girl dressed all in pink. Cat for the moment forgotten, she looked him over carefully. He waited patiently for the scrutiny to end. Finally, she smiled a welcoming smile.

"Hello." She said in a bright but comfortable tone, "You must be the man my mom said might be using the garden from time to time."

"Hello," he said softly as if afraid the cotton candy vision might disappear. "Yes, I'm Tucker Jones and you must be Allison."

She nodded vigorously, and he noticed that although her hair ribbons trembled, the round, brown tufts of hair gathered up in hot pink bows on either side of her head stayed perfectly still. He wondered briefly if they would feel soft or wiry to the touch.

"And this is Jon Bon," she announced, advancing towards the table. "We were going to come in here and play house. He was going to play my baby."

"Yes," said Tucker somewhat wryly, stifling the urge to grin. "I can see that. Actually, Jon Bon and I have met before. However, he didn't tell me that he liked to play house."

Allison's eyes widened. Keeping a tight hold on the cat's neck, she plopped him on a chair. Her mom and she often pretended Jon Bon talked to them, so Tucker's comment didn't surprise her. What did surprise her was that it came from him. Her mom had said he was very stiff and a little sad, but that the garden made him feel better. *Well, he doesn't look particularly sad and he doesn't seem stiff to me. In fact, he has a very nice smile.* She grinned, showing her missing teeth. "Oh," she said, affecting a motherly tone that he thought might sound a great deal like Kathryn might sound when dealing with this bundle of energy, "and just what did this naughty boy tell you?"

"Well," said Tucker, feeling a sudden great admiration for the patience and forbearing of the obviously distressed Jon Bon. "He said he really loved living with you and your mom, especially when someone would share tuna with him."

242

Her eyes widened again and she favored him with another gaping smile. *I like this game*, she thought. "Yes, pray do continue." She commanded.

This time, her voice had the ring of cultured authority that somehow reminded him of Emory Eldridge when things weren't going just right. Hard as he tried, his grin wouldn't stifle as he wondered how he could rescue Jon Bon from the hat.

"Well, he told me quite a lot and I'll be glad to tell you, but first, you'll have to decide if you want to sit here and share a bit of lemonade and a bite of tuna sandwich from my backpack or go ahead and play house with Jon Bon."

"Oh," she said using her own voice, "so that's what's in the backpack. I was wondering." She reached up and untied the ribbon under the cat's chin. "I can't turn him loose with it on," she said seriously. "He tries to claw it off, if I let him, and that would get me in trouble with mom because it was mine when I was a baby... and she likes to look at it."

Smiling a soft smile that did a funny thing to Tucker's heart, she continued. "She says she likes to remember when I was that tiny."

Jon Bon, sensing freedom, launched himself from the chair just as Allison grabbed the hat. They watched him for a second and then nodded to each other with complete understanding. A deal had been struck. Tucker reached for his backpack and Allison seated herself across from him saying, matter-of-factly, "I just got home from school and since this is the last week, things are pretty hectic."

"Are they?" asked Tucker, pouring glasses of lemonade and pushing a tuna sandwich towards her, "How so?"

Thirty minutes later, with very little prompting from Tucker, Allison was still talking. Tucker knew all about her star chart at school and the one missing library book that kept it from being perfect; her wonderful teacher, Miss Roseblat; her friends in the Brownie troop; and going to visit her dad in Texas.

Jon Bon, after regaining his dignity by completely inspecting the box containing the hostas, was back sitting on his chair, lured by the odor of tuna. Since Allison had long since devoured hers, Tucker felt obliged to share his and was rewarded by a deep rumbling purr as the handsome cat polished off a generous bite and looked hopefully for more.

"Sorry, old boy, that's all for today, but I want you to know I brought tuna today because I knew it was your favorite."

"You did?" Allison was delighted and said happily, "No wonder he talks to you." She found she was enjoying her conversation with this tall, gentle man very much.

Suddenly, she had a brilliant idea. She had been having a terrible time trying to decide which of her friends to ask to go to the zoo on Saturday, knowing no matter whom she asked, those not asked were bound to have their feelings hurt. Perhaps, the solution was to ask none of them. Her mind raced. *Did Mom say I had to invite a school friend?* She was sure she had not. It never even occurred to her to wonder whether Tucker might want this wonderful invitation she was about to bestow on him.

Suddenly, she jumped from her chair and went to stand by him, hugging herself, eyes shining. She was about to do something wonderful and generous. She felt just like a fairy princess granting a wish. "Mr. Jones," she said, grinning with satisfaction at her own cleverness, "my mom said I could invite one person to go to the zoo with us on Saturday. It's going to be a wonderful day. We even get to go on the train!" Suddenly, she stopped, not knowing quite how to go about bestowing the honor.

Tucker had turned in his chair to face her and she was standing right at his knees leaning forward. As he looked into her face, he was touched by how much a simple train ride and visit to the zoo meant to her, but he had absolutely no clue as to what her next words were going to be and found himself speechless when she finally decided just what she wanted to say and how she wanted to say it.

Affecting, once again, her regal voice, she said dramatically, "And I have selected YOU to accompany us!"

With that announcement, she put her hands on his knees, leaned forward to look into his eyes, so as not to miss one minute detail of his reaction, and said, breathlessly, in a voice of pure joy, "Isn't that wonderful!"

It wasn't a question. It was a declaration. For long seconds they stared at each other, faces only inches apart. Allison was waiting for an expression of joy to light up Tucker's face. Tucker, glib of tongue, never at a loss for words, was fighting and failing to force sounds from his vocal cords. Finally, he could at least clear his throat, and just barely in time. Allison's look of joy was fading. Her merry brown eyes, so confident and trusting, were beginning to shadow.

"Allison," he croaked, "give me a minute here." The next words were absolutely critical and he knew it. Without conscious thought, he reached out and captured her small hand, making a connection and allowing her to feel the fact that his own big hand was trembling very slightly. He closed his eyes and drew a long wavering breath. And in that moment, he understood the power of his own reaction. Here, in this garden, he could allow the memory of Ethan, Mary and himself at the zoo to surface. He opened his eyes and smiled at the small confused face peering worriedly, but patiently into his own. She had given him his minute.

"I haven't been to a zoo in a very long time. In fact, I was probably only a little older than you are now. But I do remember having a wonderful time. I assume were talking about the Bronx Zoo?"

She nodded, more cautious, but hopeful that this was going to turn out all right after all.

Well," he said, a slow smile lighting his mouth and then extending to his eyes, making them soft and wonderfully warm, "I absolutely can't think of anything I would rather do next Saturday then go with you to the zoo. But, I suspect your mom was expecting you to ask a school friend, so you'd better clear this with her--don't you think?"

Allison found she had been holding her breath. At his words she gave a long wavering sigh and took his hand in both of hers, making a handshake motion. "Okay! I will...but I don't have to. She said I could invite the person of my choice and my mom means what she says."

She said the words with such confidence that Tucker got the impression that meaning what one said was the party line in this household.

Allison stood back and picked up her glass, long since empty of lemonade. "This calls for a toast!" She declared, looking meaningfully at the thermos bottle.

Tucker took the hint and poured the small amount of remaining lemonade into both their glasses while the "princess" looked at him and said seriously, "You know, Mr. Jones, you sure do take a long time to think things over."

He grinned, wondering briefly what Kathryn's reaction was going to be, and then raised his glass. "Only on things as important and wonderful as being invited to the zoo by Jon Bon's mother," he said.

It was then they heard the bells signaling the fact that Kathryn's current client was leaving. Tucker looked at his watch for confirmation and said hurriedly, "I meant it when I asked you to check this brainstorm of yours with your mother. It's almost her last day with you for a while and she might not want to share it..." he chose his next words carefully..."with a friend so new."

In his mind's eye, Tucker pictured Allison bringing the subject tactfully up that night at dinner. He had not been around children often enough to know that was not how their minds worked. Before he had really finished his sentence, Allison was off her chair and skipping through the garden entry and towards the office door calling, "M-O-M-M-M!"

To Kathryn's credit, thought Tucker, she didn't bat an eye. She came through the gateway being towed by a small determined tugboat of a daughter, who was spewing words instead of smoke. In fact, the woman was laughing. "You what? Mr. Jones? You've invited Mr. Jones? How do you know HIM?"

She looked up to see Tucker, slouched back, hands behind his head, long legs extending comfortably across her bricks. He looked very relaxed and quite pleased with himself.

"Hello, Mr. Jones. I see you've met my daughter," she said, her lilt quite evident. Then she stopped suddenly, her eyes flying past Tucker and lighting on the hostas. What on earth...?" She said, mostly to herself and then hurried forward to lean down in front of them.

Tucker uncrossed his legs and sat up straight. This was it. She would either tell him he was being too forward, that she didn't accept gifts from clients, or she would accept the gift and they could be friends.

He didn't have long to wait. "Oh, how beautiful!" She exclaimed. As she turned to thank him, the pleasure of knowing they were for her was evident by eyes and smile. "Remind me to feed you again sometime!" She said, intending to sound glib but failing.

"I shall," he said quickly. Rising to his feet, he went to stand beside her, leaving Allison still standing by the table. The politician of the second grade recognized something important was going on between the adults and was trying to be patient, but her mother had not yet answered the question about Tucker's coming with them on Saturday. She opened her mouth to interrupt the two who were now discussing where and how to plant the silver hostas, when the front doorbell rang and she heard the piping voice of her friend, Jenny, call, "Allison, I found your book!" And as she rushed from the garden to see if it was true, her mother called after her conversationally, "Of course Mr. Jones can come with us, if he wants to."

"Yay!" She yelled over her shoulder without slowing her pace. "He wants to Mom. He told me so!"

The garden seemed very quiet although the excited voices of two little girls could be clearly heard. Kathryn turned to look up at Tucker. "Did you?" She asked sounding somewhat perplexed.

He nodded. "Yes, I'm afraid I did. But I certainly made it clear to her that you had veto power."

"Oh, no! I don't want veto power. You're more than welcome to come with us, if you think you're up to it. It's just that..." She paused for a moment and then continued as if thinking aloud, "I never know what she is going to come up with next. She IS the most amazing child!"

"Well, after the first shock of it, I was surprised to find myself quite touched by her offer," Tucker said quite humbly. "I really don't know any children very well, and I'm beginning to realize I might be missing something."

Kathryn looked at him sharply. "Yes," she said with conviction. "I think you might be, but now, time for a massage." So saying, she began to stride briskly across the garden towards her office door.

"Right," said Tucker, falling in behind her. "And today you are also doing my head." It was with inordinate pleasure that he noted her obvious surprise. He laughed as her head snapped around. "You assumed you'd have to talk me into it, didn't you?"

She grinned and nodded. "I had my speech all prepared. Would you like to hear it anyway?"

Chapter Twenty

When Tucker arrived at his condo it was nearing 6:00 P.M. and his telephone light was flashing its warning that more than one person wanted his attention. He sighed. He really did not feel like talking to anyone. After submitting himself to Kathryn's ministrations, including a neck, head and facial massage that actually left him feeling very relaxed, he had stayed to help her plant the hostas. What he really had done, at her insistence, was drink apple juice and supervise. She had wanted to do the work herself. She had changed from her uniform to jeans and a sweatshirt and, after trying several different spots, decided Tucker was right in his assessment of placement. Flanking the smoke tree was going to be perfect. However, the plants were much bigger than Tucker had realized and Kathryn ended up needing to transplant several of her existing, shade-loving flowers.

"You just sit there!" She admonished when he got up to assist. "I'm not going to have you undo all my good work. Besides, this is my therapy, remember?"

Allison returned, ecstatic that Jenny had returned the missing school library book and was content to sit with Tucker and watch her mother work. With her penchant for organizing, she soon had the details of Saturday pinned down. Tucker said he would be privileged to drive them to the station, and might they allow him to treat them to a bite of breakfast on the way there?

Kathryn, her back to them, listening, on the verge of saying no just on general principle, bit her tongue. The man seemed to be enjoying himself. She had wanted to make the day really special for her daughter and breakfast in a little café was certainly going to set the stage. However, she was not going to allow him to assume the expenses for the entire day. She would make that clear to him when he came for his next massage. She listened to them laughing and teasing like old friends. Perhaps there is magic in my garden she thought, or perhaps it's the garden AND my daughter.

Whatever its cause, Tucker was indeed very relaxed and curiously happy to sip apple juice, chat with Allison and watch Kathryn lovingly prepare the ground for the hostas. He knew he should be on his way. The computer printout, now out of sight in his backpack, was nevertheless accusing him of negligence. However, he made no move to leave until Kathryn tamped carefully around the transplants and stepped back to admire the effect.

"Yes, indeed, just perfect!" She declared. "What a wonderful gift. Thank you, Mr. Jones."

Tucker had accepted her thanks with a nod of his head and then had taken his leave, wondering if it would violate her professional sensibilities to call him Tucker. After all, she had asked him to call her by her first name. He decided not to ask. It had been a perfect day and she had accepted the hostas straightforwardly and with obvious pleasure. He had expected the usual gift giving games he'd seen played his entire life. They started with words like, "Oh, I couldn't possibly accept..." And generally ended with, "Well thank you, but you really shouldn't have..." which left one feeling that perhaps some gift giving code had been violated and that the receiver was simply being polite in accepting the offering. *That certainly was not the case with Kathryn,* he thought, as he stood staring at the blinking light. *As unassuming as she seems to be, she knows how to accept a gift.*

Without warning and catching him completely unawares, the image of Dawn floated into his mind. She too, seemed to be an unassuming woman. Beautiful...he thought with sudden candor, but still, unassuming. Dropping his head in shame, he thought again about the hurt expression in her eyes and wished desperately he could replay the scene on the steps and in the galley. *What devil made me behave so badly?* He searched his mind, unable to recall any words, just his feelings of anger under the porte-cochere and the desire to keep his distance in the galley.

Backpack still in his hand, his mind flipped back to the garden where he had already been nearly sabotaged by his emotions earlier today. It was a little different, he

250

realized. This time, a bouncing girl invited him to the zoo. And only because her joyful face was inches away from his own, had he forced himself to deal with whatever was making him feel the need to escape or explode, hands trembling and his stomach clenching. That was the exact reaction he had on the steps with Dawn. Thankfully, today in the garden, he was able to associate the feelings with the memory of Ethan and Mary, just in the nick of time. He felt their loving presence in the garden and had eventually been able to quite comfortably except Allison's generous offer. *Could my reaction to Dawn's statement about being a psychologist have anything to do with Ethan and Mary?* He shook his head sadly. If there was a connection, he couldn't see it.

He moved on into the living room, but for the first time, it did not feel welcoming. He looked around wonderingly. It was exactly the same tastefully done, high tech condo he had left this afternoon. *Why, four hours later, does it look sterile and feel lonely?*

He sighed and reached a hand to the base of his skull. Only an hour ago he was sitting, completely relaxed, in a magic garden, enjoying the pleasant company of people he felt quite comfortable with. His neck had felt more mobile than he could ever remember. But now, he felt agitated, as though he'd opened Pandora's Box and couldn't find a way to lower the lid.

He changed his focus to the telephone's blinking red light and stifled a second sigh. There was no sense putting it off; he'd always prided himself on promptly returning calls. *Just because I'm feeling out of sorts doesn't mean I have to lower my standards,* he thought sourly.

The first message was from Midge. Her cheerful voice asking for his help on her next S.O.S. fundraiser seemed like a lifeline. He looked at his watch. *It's too late to return her call today.* By tacit agreement their calls to each other were during her husband's working hours. He knew that during the week, the Tyler's evenings were private times, reserved as often as possible for each other.

The next call was from Heather Anderson. Her finishing school voice told him she had very much enjoyed the boating weekend and had called Midge to express thanks for both of them. She also said that her parents had invited them for cocktails before the concert; she would be glad to pick him up since they lived in his vicinity… And did he want to go out to dinner after?

He put the machine on pause. *Heather called to thank Midge for both of us? That seems a little odd.* He shrugged, remembering that he told her he had a busy week coming up. Perhaps, not knowing how often Midge and he talked and how promptly he always thanked her either with a note or by phone, or even occasionally sending flowers, Heather probably thought she was saving him time. Having cocktails with her parents also seemed a bit odd, but dinner after the concert seemed logical. And, if she wanted to drive, that would be fine with him. That way, he could fill the Aston with gasoline and have it ready for Saturday's outing with the McCalls.

The last three calls were from Mr. Tyler's secretary asking him to call at the first opportunity. *Oops!* He thought, feeling suddenly very irresponsible. *Wonder what happened at Zitec during my afternoon of playing hooky?*

He walked over and booted his computer, knowing there would be something significant from Mr. Tyler in his electronic mail file. He suddenly felt very settled and anxious to tackle whatever presented itself. This was territory he knew and flawlessly controlled. He had confidence that by tomorrow's 10:00 o'clock meeting with Mr. Tyler anything needing to be uncovered, addressed and researched would be waiting at his boss's terminal.

Midge was waiting under the porte-cochere when Hank drove up and deposited her husband at the doorstep. James smiled at her, knowing the signs. She had been sitting on some information and was very tired of waiting for him to come home so she could finally share it. *Funny creatures, women!* He thought as he opened his door, thanking Hank as he exited.

"Oh, James," she called, "you've only just missed Dawn's call. She's safely back in California's sunshine and said to thank you especially for helping her plan her trip to Boston and for letting her handle Faith. She said she misses us, but I could tell she was absolutely delighted to be reunited with her family."

James smiled down at his wife. It was amazing, after all these years, how he could feel the cares of his business day dissolve into the back of his mind with the force of Midge's enthusiasm for life. Now, she slipped an arm around his waist and gave it a delighted squeeze. "And guess what, darling? Dawn asked me for Tucker's address!" The satisfaction, as she made the announcement, was quite evident. James suspected there was going to be more to the story; these tidbits were just teasers. She was very pleased and very excited about something; he could tell by the way she was hurrying him through the front door.

"By the way," James grumbled, "have you talked with Tucker today? I tried to have Peggy reach him all afternoon, and finally left him an email, thinking he was immersed in the South America project and ignoring the phone, but he didn't respond to that either."

Midge raised her hand in a dismissive gesture. "He called this morning and thanked me for the weekend. He tried to sound sincere, bless his heart, but he didn't. Although, James, he did tell me an amazing thing."

The big man smiled as he listened to his wife. There was another teaser, he thought, and in spite of himself, he found his curiosity piqued.

She stopped with him at the foot of the stairs, knowing he would want to go up to change, freshen up and glance at the mail before they settled down for their "talktails." "But, to finish answering your question, I tried to call Tucker at the office and when he wasn't there, I called his home and got his machine. He didn't call me back, so I assumed he was out for the day, perhaps with Heather, frolicking in the sunshine.... But then I got an odd call from Heather.... And now, I don't think so."

James laughed aloud. "Just let me get changed and look at the mail. Then you can put all these pieces together for me. I can tell you've had a busy day."

"Yes," she said happily, "I will. And I need your advice, so do hurry a bit."

When James finally settled himself, scotch in hand, Midge found it difficult to know where to begin. She finally decided to simply tell about the events in her day, inserting her thoughts as asides. James was an excellent listener, but he did like a story with a semblance of order.

She started with the phone call to Barbara and the off-hand remark about the barbecue for raising scholarship money and how, with Althea's and Emory's help, she had worked the idea into a cooking competition featuring "yacht food," the purpose being a fundraiser for S.O.S.

"But, James, I haven't told you that I would like Charlie and Margaret Jones to serve as co-chair of recipe selection."

Midge paused, looking carefully at her husband's face. She knew this might be one of the details she would have to let go. "I did ask Charlie if he would do it, and he said he would. But I didn't want to ask Mrs. Jones until I spoke with you."

She then explained the comments Tucker had made about his mother and Charlie having a secret desire to meet each other, admitted her own growing curiosity regarding the Jones and finished with, "Then there is also the fact that we would be stepping over the line we drew about not getting to know the Jones because Tucker works for Zitec."

It was fortuitous that James had honed his listening and organizational skills working with Tucker. He was able, though just barely, to follow her breathless patter. He understood the concept of the cook-off, thought the theme of yacht food was an excellent, fresh idea and that the yacht club setting could be easily arranged. He did not quite understand how Margaret Jones got into the picture.

"Margaret Jones? I can understand Charlie as a judge; he has had a lot of experience preparing menus to take on Faith. But, not even considering the Tucker connection, how is it that Mrs. Jones qualifies as a judge of boating food?"

Midge waved her hand in her characteristically dismissive gesture. "Oh, James, that doesn't really matter. You're being too logical. She's evidently a splendid chef which means she will recognize quality. Remember, Althea told me that story of her evaluation of a past employee's cooking and it sounded as though Margaret enjoyed the whole sampling process. What is important here is that I think Charlie wants to meet her and I want to meet both

Margaret and Evan. I think I'm going to understand Tucker a lot better when," she paused, thought a moment and continued, "I mean IF, we do."

James grinned, "I thought the important thing was to raise money to save and rehab more land."

Midge had the grace to blush slightly. In truth, when thinking about the project during the day, the fact that the whole thing was to raise money for S.O.S. had slipped to the back of her mind. "Oh, darling, thank you for reminding me. I wanted to ask you whether you thought the families would be willing to wager money that their chef would win?"

James thought for a moment and then nodded. "Sure," he said. "Especially since Charlie isn't in the competition."

Midge laughed "Althea says most people with a good chef feel just as we do. She said she was positive that if the Bartelsons' chef, were selected for the competition, Sue would be convinced she would win. That's what gave me the idea of giving people the opportunity to place wagers."

It wasn't until after Charlie had announced dinner and they were walking towards the dining room that Midge remembered Heather's call. She stopped mid-stride, causing James, who was holding her arm in the crook of his elbow, to turn and look at her.

"I meant to tell you that I had the strangest call from Heather Anderson. She thanked us for the weekend on behalf of herself AND Tucker. It sounded very much like her mother sounds when she calls to thank us on behalf of Herb and herself. She sounded quite..." Midge paused and looked up at her husband, looking for just the right word to convey the ownership she heard in the young woman's voice. "It sounded..." Again, she searched for the right word. It was more than possessive. There was an assurance there, a ring of confidence that bespoke of the comfort of a long-term relationship. Finally, she threw up her hands and spluttered, "MARRIED!"

"Good heavens!" James said, sounding properly shocked. "When did all this happen?"

"But that's just it," Midge declared, "I don't think it actually has. I found myself mainly curious rather than upset after her call. You see, if she and Tucker had agreed

255

that it was her responsibility to thank us, he wouldn't have called me this morning."

"Ah!" said James. "That explains your curious comments that Tucker was not out frolicking with Heather after all. But then, where is he? I really needed to talk with him today and couldn't reach him. That's a first--other than that episode with his back--since we've been working together."

Midge smiled as he seated her at the table. "I haven't the foggiest idea, but I imagine he didn't get home until after 6:00 o'clock or he would have returned my call."

"Well," grumbled James, "he'd better be in my office at 10:00 o'clock sharp. We've got work to do!" Then he smiled and his face softened as Charlie served him a lovely porcelain bowl of consommé. "Now tell me about Dawn."

Midge glanced quickly at Charlie's retreating back. She had indeed, as subtly and skillfully as possible, tried to probe the thoughts of her cook as well as her housekeeper. Charlie had been his usual obscure self, his comments woven with ancient Chinese philosophy. Actually, if she had understood him correctly, he told her only fools try to predict the outcome of affairs of the heart. But then, when she had tried her technique of trading information with him and told him what Emory had said about Tucker keeping a distance between Dawn and himself by using Heather, she could tell he agreed and that it worried him. "Sometime what seem safest course of action, instead most dangerous." He said, and then turned on his slipperier feet to busy himself at the sink.

She sighed. It was such a worry. It was possible, even probable, that Emory was quite correct; Heather was weaving a silken web around Tucker and that he, in avoiding the feelings Dawn seemed to awaken, would willingly become the prey.

Clarice, when consulted as to her opinions had been very clear. "That girl don't belong in California. She belongs here. She's got feelings for that boy and she better come back here and figure 'em out before that fancy girl gets those long pretty nails into him. That boy's liable to not to know what hit him, and he sure is ripe for pickin', is what I say."

Charlie came to take their empty bowls and Midge suddenly realized she had let her mind wander and that her husband was waiting patiently for her to fill him in on Dawn. "Well, other than being a little jetlagged, she's fine. She said she misses us very much and that she had her mother stop so she could drop her film off to be developed on the way home from the airport. She also thanked all of us again, very profusely, and said she would let us know the minute she got word one way or the other from Tufts."

"Oh, and she said to tell you, Charlie, that she now has developed a taste for Chinese beer and can hardly wait to take a six-pack down to the beach and introduce it to her friends...." Her voice trailed away and she looked at the two men. "It really seems that she's been gone for more than a day, doesn't it?"

They both nodded solemnly, each lost in their own personal memories of their time with Dawn. Charlie left with their bowls and returned to the kitchen to bring forth the next course. The Tylers sat in companionable silence, continuing to ponder the events that had taken place in the last two weeks.

After Charlie brought in two elegantly presented plates of grilled halibut with a jasmine rice and green beans in a lemon-butter sauce, James was the first to break the silence and his words were a continuation of the very thought that Midge had been having. It surprised neither of them very much, as twin thoughts were not uncommon, especially when they were discussing the lives of their friends.

"Funny how things go along pretty smoothly for a long stretch and then something happens that causes other things to happen and our lives change, isn't it?" He said.

She nodded and replied, "It's just what I was thinking. However, in this case, I am not sure what the catalyst is or what the change will be, are you?"

James grinned ruefully and shook his head. "Charlie would probably call it fate. But isn't it interesting that Tucker was so different after his back went out and we had our talk? Or maybe it wasn't our conversation; maybe it was the circumstances of meeting Dawn." He threw up his hands. "Who knows? But you've been trying to fix him up with young women for the last three years and now, he seems interested in one and frightened by the second. Maybe we should be satisfied that the lad is genuinely feeling something."

Midge looked at her husband with a glint of steel in her blue eyes. "I don't think we even know a tiny part of what makes our Tucker tick. We didn't even know he had that gentle, playful side he showed us after he rescued Dawn. I think she brought that out in him and I don't for one minute believe Heather has that capacity."

James put down his wine glass and looked up in alarm. He recognized the tone in his wife's voice. It was the same tone she used when taking up a new cause. But, the love-life of Tucker Jones had entertained her for the last three years, so this had to be something different. He was almost afraid to ask and said as much.

"Darling, I recognize the look in your eye and the tone of your voice. It sounds as though you are about to go on the warpath against injustice again. You aren't seriously thinking of interfering in Tucker's love-life are you? I know you've had fun introducing him to a variety of lovely young ladies these past years, but you aren't planning anything more serious than that, are you?"

Midge looked startled for a moment, then gave a heartfelt sigh and looked sadly at her husband, "Probably not," she said, shoulders slumping, "but I certainly would like to! You and Emory both think Tucker was frightened by his feelings for Dawn and I think you are right. I also think you were right in your assessment that Tucker doesn't really trust people. Don't you wonder why that is? Actually, James, that's the real reason I want to meet the Jones. I feel like I've got to get this puzzle sorted out before Heather snags that boy!"

Suddenly she stopped her tirade, realizing that she was leaning forward and waving her fork about in a most unseemly fashion. "Gracious! Look at me! I am wrought up over this, aren't I? What do you suppose has gotten into me? I do apologize, darling."

James looked fondly at the chagrined bundle of energy sitting across from him and had a sudden insight as to exactly what had gotten into his wife. "I suspect," he said somberly, "I suspect for some reason you're holding yourself responsible"

After a moment she nodded in agreement. "I suspect, as usual, you are correct. I am going to have to think about this, aren't I? Gracious, James, I'm a little ashamed of myself."

Midge took a deep breath to steady herself, took a sip of wine and then looked at him over the edge of her glass, a look in her eyes that he couldn't fathom. "But," she said, "With your permission of course, I would like to call Margaret in the morning and invite her to participate in the recipe judging."

He laughed softly. "Do as you like, my dear. As I think about it, I cannot see how her acceptance or rejection of the honor is likely to affect my working relationship with her son, wherever the hell he is," he finished grumpily, remembering the missing Tucker.

Tucker was, as Mr. Tyler spoke, reading his electronic mail most of which was from his boss. He buried his head in his hands and had a serious talk with himself. It seemed to him that his job performance, since his back went out, had been marginal. He grimaced as he thought of all the times he had put off work to do other things, including spending time in Kathryn's garden. He admitted sadly to himself that he was using his computer as much to talk to his ceiling as he was doing work for Zitec. The message from Mr. Tyler had been simple: "Tucker, where are you? Will you be prepared for tomorrow's meeting? Here are some additional data that came in from Washington, D. C. today. Does it mean anything to you?"

Tucker scanned the data and grimaced again. The figures in front of him were import and export quotas newly developed for trading with South America by the U.S. Department of Commerce.

The earlier feeling of being settled and in control faded and reality set in. If he was to be ready for Mr. Tyler in the morning, he would need to spend most of the night at the computer. Mr. Tyler wouldn't have sent him the figures unless he had decided to pursue the next step. Tucker bent over the glowing screen; a corner of his mind recognizing with relief that he was glad to have a single-minded task on which to concentrate.

Chapter Twenty-one

Midge's morning routine, after seeing her husband off to work, was to get a second cup of coffee and read the "New York Times." But this morning, she found herself on "pins and needles," as her mother used to say; unable to concentrate or even sit still. Waiting impatiently for Althea and Emory to arrive, she spent time thinking about whether to spill her concerns about the Tucker-Heather-Dawn triangle to her friends and decided against it.

The agenda for this morning was to brainstorm about the cooking contest and she did not want energy diverted from that purpose. She had already called to remind her board of their usual Wednesday meeting and had dropped mysterious hints about the exciting purpose, the need for a tight timeline and the importance of participation in the meeting.

She gave herself a mental shake and sighed. Really, there was nothing to be gained by bringing up Tucker Jones. She still didn't understand what had upset her so. Besides, Heather had called to confirm their luncheon date, which she found herself looking forward to on a number of different levels. It was time to re-examine her perceptions. In the light of day she had to admit to herself that other than the seeming inconsistency of what she liked to eat, the young woman had been a very considerate guest. She really had extended herself to make Dawn feel welcome, mingled nicely with the guests, set the pace for the swimming excursion and showed good humor and spirit the whole weekend. With resolution, Midge turned back to the paper and gave it a shake as if commanding it to help her concentrate. It was of little use. Ordinarily, when she was in such a mood, she would either go and find Charlie or grab her gardening tool carrier and head outside. But, Charlie was off today, though he had made their breakfast scones and even chicken sandwiches for lunch before he left. She frowned. There was not enough time to really get anything done outside, as the ladies were due any moment.

With a sigh, she closed the paper and went to retrieve her working notes about the meeting from her desk in the morning room where all was in readiness for their breakfast meeting. As she forced herself to review the pages one more time, the magnitude of the project gradually drew her in and she found herself once more captured by the intricate details to be resolved. Bending over her notes, she was amazed and pleased by how well the outline flowed, both the general idea and the details of the timeline. She decided it would be handy if both ladies had her notes in front of them; that way they could all make the changes and fill in the details. She hurried up the stairs to make the copies on her husband's copy machine and just as she finished, she heard the heavy chime of the front doorbell.

"Thank heavens!" she exclaimed and rushed towards the stairs, copies in hand, curls bouncing, just as Clarice was showing the two women towards the morning room. They turned at her call of welcome.

"Thank goodness you've finally come! I feel as though I am about to explode; my head is so chock full of ideas and questions...." The words tapered off and died in her throat at the look on Althea's face. Emory's look was more subtle, but again, quoting her mother, "They both looked like the cat that ate the cream."

Midge laughed her tinkling laugh and finished descending the stairs. "My, but you two ladies look pleased with yourselves this morning. What do you know that I don't?"

"Well, dear," Althea admitted, "we do know something, but we don't know if it really means anything and we won't know--until we can determine just how successful this fundraising idea of yours is likely to be." The calmness of her words belayed the sparkle in her eyes. Emory simply nodded in agreement and Midge could tell from her manner that the story, whatever it was, belonged to Althea.

"Well, do come in and sit down. I can see that Althea is going to try my scattered patience and make a

261

story out of this news. So, it might as well be over scones and coffee," said Midge in resignation.

Emory laughed at Midge's understanding of Althea's nature and Althea nodded in agreement. "Yes, it is a story-- but not a long one; it's more of an accidental one, actually," she said as she seated herself on one of the plump floral cushions and took the cup of coffee handed to her by Clarice.

"This is tricky because the only reason I know what I know is that Robert was talking on the phone in his study and forgot to close the door. I didn't ask, but I think we can safely assume that what I heard is not for public consumption."

She paused only long enough to look slightly conscious stricken. "But, I thought it might be important for just the three of us to know as it has to do with land acquisition. Land we never in our wildest dreams thought would become available."

Midge's hand flew to cover her mouth. She knew better than to interrupt Althea as she was building the drama into her story, and the gesture was an unconscious act to prevent impatient questions.

Emory sat silently, sipping her coffee. She had already been through this scenario and had felt her own impatience and growing excitement.

"Robert's conversation was about a line item in the budget that the governor was going to go to the mat for. I can't tell you why, but I can tell you it has to do with state-subsidized housing in the warehouse district. The governor has been putting the quiet squeeze on the man who owns the huge tenement on Front Street, but it hasn't worked because, as bad as that place is, the people who live there defend this slumlord saying, 'It is awful, but it's better than being on the street.' So, the new tack is for the state to acquire the brickyard that HAS already been condemned, put up a housing project about two blocks from this guy's property and match rents. Now, of course this was all said in "government speak," but I do think I got the gist of it."

Midge nodded. "I'm certain you did, but what does it have to do with S.O.S. acquiring land?"

"Well, this may be simplistic, and I know you two accuse me of sometimes being too straightforward in my thinking, but when I put myself in this guy's shoes, here's what I see: First of all, he's been getting bad press for a number of years. Secondly, it would take too much money to do anything with that tenement but tear it down. Thirdly, because it is on the waterfront and there are now so many issues regarding public access, environmental concerns and building restrictions, it will be hard to find a buyer. Finally, if the man decides to sell, it will be to anyone BUT the government. So, if we play our cards right and can get him some positive press for a change, he just might be willing to deal with S.O.S..

Suddenly, the picture of what Althea was talking about fell into place. An opportunity to buy waterfront property and turn it into a greenspace two blocks from government-subsidized housing. Midge drew in her breath and looked from one woman to the other while Althea calmly pulled a map from her purse.

"But," she gasped, "this is far beyond the scope of what S.O.S. funds were ever intended to acquire." She scrutinized the map carefully, nearly bumping heads with Emory who was doing the same.

"Emory, for heaven sake, you've been on the acquisition committee for years, don't you think they'd assume you'd lost your mind if you asked them to consider such a thing?"

Emory raised her liquid green eyes to Midge's troubled face. "Perhaps..." she said in her sphinx like way, "...perhaps not. Really, Midge, don't get so upset. Right now, all of this is smoke and mirrors--based on a single overheard, confidential I might add, conversation." Here she paused and looked at both of her friends. "Let me rephrase what I just said. "It is premature to be so upset." She chuckled so deeply in her throat that it sounded like a purr. "Later on, if there is substance to this idea, I'm quite certain there will be plenty of opportunities to get really upset."

Althea nodded solemnly. "Emory and I had plenty of opportunity to discuss this in the car before we got here. It's more of a dream than an idea at this point. But, you can see its potential and it does give one a certain charged-up feeling, doesn't it? It's just the right kind of feeling to carry us through this project of yours with a fervor we might not otherwise have had."

Midge was not so easily pulled back to earth. She had already felt strongly that the fundraising project was going to be successful and pulled Althea's map towards her, tracing around the blue line drawn to mark the property boundaries with a fingernail. To have that money go to such a worthwhile acquisition seemed to guarantee its success. In her mind, she could already see play fields, baseball diamonds, swings, benches, picnic tables, an area for a community garden and, last but not least, a wetlands bordering the river; all of that where the squalor of a tenement once stood.

Her friends watched her with quiet fondness, munching their scones and sipping their coffee, knowing that it would take a bit of time for her to change gears, but when she did, they would be expected to be at their critical thinking best. When Midge said she wanted her ideas "torn apart," she meant exactly that.

"Well," Midge finally sighed, carefully refolding the map. "it's an idea!" Then she ordered, "Here, take these notes and let's get started on making this happen." She stopped and grinned impishly at her friends, "But, I'd love to have time for us all to go and look at that property after we're done here."

Emory looked up sharply. "I don't think so, Midge. It is not a place where we would be particularly welcome or safe at this point. I guess it's one reason Governor O'Neill has his eye on the place. The crime rate is higher on that block than anywhere else in the city."

Clarice, who had been unobtrusively refilling coffee cups, gave a deep sigh of relief. She had just been painting a picture of the three women cruising Front Street in Althea's big Jaguar, like babes in the woods, intent on doing good and giving no thought to their personal danger.

Midge's eyes flew up to Clarice's face when she heard the sigh. Mentally, she catalogued the fact that she intended to pick the black woman's brain about the tenement and the surrounding area. That Clarice was absolutely trustworthy was an accepted fact by all three women who were quite aware that Althea's overheard

264

conversation would be political dynamite in the wrong hands.

"Emory," Midge finally said, "thank you for that humbling reminder. Now, I really am back to earth and ready to put the tenement on the back burner and get to work. I'll give you a few minutes to read my notes."

Three hours later, Midge began looking satisfied, knowing that she could field any question the board threw at her on Wednesday. Her challenge, she realized, was not to close her mind to the changes they might suggest. Althea said as much to her as they pushed back their chairs at the end of the meeting and headed for the kitchen to find the sandwiches left by Charlie.

Midge waved her hand in a 'not to worry' gesture. "Listen, the truth is, I am much more nervous about calling Margaret Jones than I am about talking the board into this. For some reason, I suddenly have my heart set on meeting that woman."

"Really, Midge?" asked Althea, as usual taking her friend's words at face value. "I am so glad. She's very shy and hard to draw out at times, but I think you'll like her."

Emory digested Midge's remark and wondered what had really triggered her desire to meet the mother of Tucker Jones. She recognized in her friend, the ability to be a master manipulator. Just as the board was likely to go away from their Wednesday meeting feeling, that as a group, they had come up with the hottest idea of the year, she had the feeling Midge was considering some manipulation regarding the emotional lives of Tucker and Dawn. *Life is certainly never boring if one watches and listens carefully,* she thought and then laughed to herself as she admitted to stirring the pot with yesterday's phone chat with Midge. *It's so unlike me to share my private observations like that, but there is something about that Anderson girl that I simply don't trust.*

As the ladies sat on the patio munching the chicken sandwiches made from the chicken breasts baked for, but un-eaten by, Heather Anderson and looking over the rolling green lawn towards Long Island Sound, Dawn, on the West Coast, was having a late breakfast of raisin bagels, cream cheese and deliciously ripe cantaloupe with her mother.

265

They sat on a deck under a patio umbrella, overlooking the rolling rhythm of the Pacific Ocean at a fairly low tide. Whitecaps sparkled and danced in the morning sun and a cool breeze ruffled the edges of the umbrella.

Last night at the dinner table, Dawn had sketched out her trip in a travelogue fashion for the whole family. She described the Tyler's home, her drive up to Massachusetts, the horrors of driving in Boston and the beauty and venerability of the Tufts campus. Last, but not least, she described, in glorious detail, the wonders of Faith.

This morning, the conversation with her mother had taken a very different turn. What Barbara wanted to know had to do with how her old friends were really doing, how Dawn felt about being so far away from home, and, if Dawn so chose to share, her feelings about the young man Midge had mentioned on the phone. She had the feeling, with a little gentle probing, the whole thing would come spilling out. It usually did with this daughter who had always worn her feelings on her sleeve.

Dawn first responded by recounting her discovery of Scotty's name carved into the window sill of her room. "It was hard to wake up in the morning, look out over the empty stables and not think of how it must have been for Mr. and Mrs. Tyler. How'd they manage to get over it?" Dawn asked.

Barbara covered her daughter's hand. "I really don't know more than I told you, honey." She shook her head. "I'm pretty certain they aren't really over it. They have, however, learned to live with it and move forward…which takes great courage."

Her daughter smiled sadly. "I remember how you hugged us all when you got back and told us how much you loved us. We all sorta brushed you off, didn't we? I was thinking about that in Scotty's room and I'm really sorry."

Barbara was very touched that her daughter had remembered so clearly that painful moment in time. "Dawn," her mother smiled, "you really are a very special person." And then she sat for a moment, reflecting, before she continued.

"I think other people's tragedies make one especially aware of how fragile one's own happiness is and how closely our happiness is connected to those we love. I

266

think that's what I was feeling back then, and it made me feel much better to be able to say it to you three at the time. It does amaze me that you have remembered the incident so clearly all these years."

"I know, Mom. I do remember things. I think maybe I'm a little weird because I still feel happiest when I'm here at home with all my memories. I read all that stuff about individuation and how teenagers are supposed to rebel to find their own identity. I've honestly never felt that way."

Dawn paused, looking inward. "I thought a lot about this when I was driving back to the Tylers after visiting Tufts. Leaving home is going to be very hard for me; maybe the hardest thing I've ever done. But thank goodness you introduced me to the Tylers." Dawn's head had been lowered and she had been idly pushing a piece of cantaloupe around her plate with one finger, but she squared her shoulders, raised her head and said with the ghost of a smile. "At first, I thought it would be wrong of me to use them for surrogate parents, but now I think of them as my crutch to lean on while I adjust to standing alone."

Barbara found she was fighting tears. "Darling, what you don't really understand is that you will be giving back to the Tylers even more than they will give you. I don't think it was an accident that you were given Scotty's room." She mused, "Maybe it was subconscious, but it was not an accident. If I remember correctly, they have about four or five separate guest rooms available."

Dawn's eyes widened as she thought. "Gosh, mom, you're right! I never thought about it. There were plenty of other rooms they could have put me in."

She was silent for a long moment, thoughts turned inward. Then she drew a deep wavering breath. "The thing that gives even more weight to your words is the fact that the Tylers have another friend, about my age, who stays with them quite often. But he said he's never seen my room before. I didn't tell him about Scotty, but I did wonder to myself if the reason they put him somewhere else was because they didn't want another young man in Scotty's room."

Well, Barbara thought, *now's the time. Either you do a little probing, or you don't…what's a mother to do?* She

267

poured them both another half cup of coffee from the carafe on the table while she gave into her curiosity.

"This must be the young man Midge mentioned on the phone when we talked yesterday after you were safely on the plane. I believe she said his name was Tucker and that she was quite fond of him. She said he quite gallantly rescued you after your fall."

She didn't add the part that Midge had told her about the chemistry and how it had suddenly appeared and then mysteriously disappeared. Instead she asked, "What was he like?"

Dawn didn't answer directly; instead she began her idle pushing of the uneaten piece of cantaloupe once more. Then she asked, "Mom, Midge said that after you and dad met, you didn't have eyes for anyone but each other. She said she and James used to tease you about how oblivious you were to anything but to each other."

Barbara laughed a clear ringing laugh. "True enough!" she said. "The funny thing about it was, just before I met him, I wondered if I was ever going to fall in love. Most of my friends fell in and out of love so easily; I thought maybe something was wrong with me, that I wasn't capable."

She noted that her daughter was listening with fierce intensity, cantaloupe prodding forgotten. "But you were capable," Dawn said softly. And then, in a low voice that carried the inexplicable tone of disgust, she said, "Lucky for you, Dad loved you back."

"Yes," said Barbara, for the first time getting an inkling of where the conversation was going and trying to choose her words honestly and with care. "I don't know what I would've done, had he not. I remember in those days, even thinking about the possibility made me almost sick with worry."

They sat quietly in the strengthening morning sun, needing to change the direction of the umbrella, but neither noticing. A yellowjacket came to search their plates. That too went unnoticed.

Finally, Barbara leaned over and wrapped her arms around her daughter, wishing she could absorb some of the sadness she could feel emanating from the slender frame. Deciding to take the bull by the horns, she asked softly,

"Honey, do you want to share what's making you so blue this morning? Why are you asking the questions about Dad and me? Are you wondering if you are in love with this young friend of the Tylers?"

That did it. Dawn gave a stifled sob. "Oh, Mom, I just don't know. I can't get it figured out. I am so afraid that I am, because I can't seem to get over this deep feeling of sadness. It's like I've lost something very important. I thought maybe it would go away once I got home, but it's not going away, it's getting w-o-r-s-e!" Her words ended in a wail. She jumped up, her face flushed, tears streaming down her cheeks. She fished in her shorts' pocket for a nonexistent tissue, gave up and took the cotton breakfast napkin silently offered by her mother.

Trying to smile through her tears, she said woefully, "Boy, I really needed to come home to you and have this cry. I talked this whole thing over with Clarice, the Tyler's housekeeper, Sunday night and it made me feel a little better, but she wasn't you."

Dawn adjusted the umbrella, blew her nose, and sat back down facing her mother who was sitting quite still, feeling the irrational urge to ring the neck of Tucker Jones. Instead she said calmly, "I think you'd better tell me about this young man. He must be very special to have captured your feelings so quickly. I know many very handsome, personable young men who have tried and failed over the years."

Dawn looked at her mother, the disgust manifested earlier in her voice, clearly evident on her face. "That's just it...you know how good I am at figuring people out. I guess I probably inherited it from you, since you're pretty good at it too. But, this guy is the last person you would think I would be attracted to. He's too much of everything...too handsome, too rich, too polished, too formal, too perfect to be real. And besides that, he's already taken by a very gorgeous woman who is a carbon copy of him. But," she hastened to excuse herself, "I didn't know he had a girlfriend when we first met. In fact, Mom, that first evening, as I told Clarice, I really thought he was interested in me." She went on in a low, sad voice, filling her mother in on all the details of the last weekend, comforted immeasurably by her mother's concerned look and quiet, attentive listening.

269

Barbara was not surprised how closely Dawn's story of the rescue and the magical evening paralleled what Midge had said. She held up her hand when Dawn got to the part of the story where they were standing on the front steps under the porte-cochere, drinking coffee and talking about what Midge meant by a "typical California girl," and asked Dawn to remember, as clearly as she could, the nuances of that part of the conversation.

Dawn looked at her sadly. "I can't, Mom. Whatever I was saying was just idle conversation. We were standing pretty close to each other and I was thinking mostly about how beautiful and gentle his eyes were and how they contrasted with his behavior when he was acting formal. And I was feeling glad he wasn't acting that way with me. She sighed, blew her nose and gave a rueful laugh. "My heart was thumping so loudly I can remember wondering if he could hear it." She leaned her head back on the patio chair and tears started slipping down her cheeks afresh. "It was just as I was having that thought that, BAM! His voice changed and he literally handed me his empty coffee cup and dismissed me. And the rest of the weekend went just like that--like he couldn't keep enough distance between us. Of course, when I understood about his girlfriend, Heather..." Dawn didn't finish the sentence. Instead, she paused in puzzlement. "But there's a little mystery here. Clarice says Midge has been fixing Tucker up with women for years, but he's never been interested. So, the morning of the sail, when he walked onto the east patio with Heather on his arm, it was the first time she had ever seen them together." Here Dawn groaned. "Honestly, I don't think it means that much. I'm just hoping that all is not as it seems. Because it seems that I fell for some other woman's man."

Her mother looked at her. "Perhaps...though, you don't often misperceive another person's intentions. Tell me about the rest of the weekend."

By the time Dawn had finished her story, including Tucker's strangely worded goodbye, the sun was baking the deck and the morning had entirely slipped away. Her mother sighed and asked, as she rose to clear the table, though she suspected she already knew the answer, "Dawn, why did you choose to share your feelings for Tucker with Clarice instead of Midge?"

270

"Oh, Mom, I don't know if you remember Clarice and Charlie very well, but both of them seem to know things about you that you don't even know about yourself. Only, Charlie would never pry. Clarice would, but she didn't have to. When she fixed me with those penetrating eyes, words just came tumbling out. Besides, Mom, I couldn't talk to Midge. Tucker is her friend and so is Heather. She's the one who introduced the two of them in the first place. It would just make her feel sorry for me and sad because there would be nothing she could do about it."

Barbara thought to herself, *Knowing Midge like I know Midge, I wouldn't be so sure there's nothing she can do.* Aloud, she said, "You know me, I'm going to want to spend some time thinking about your story and this whole situation. Why don't you run down to the store and retrieve your photos. I need to get a visual look at all these new friends of yours. Then, I know you are going to want to go to the beach, but I have a whole list of things lined up for us to get going on for the scholarship barbecue, so I'd like a couple hours of your time first.

Chapter Twenty-two

Midge waved goodbye to the departing tailpipe of Althea's Jaguar and hurried to find Clarice. Long ago, James and she had agreed to limit their charity works to causes they really understood. Buying undeveloped land with S.O.S. funds was generally simple and straightforward. However, trying to buy a tenement would not be simple at all, and certainly went beyond the bounds of what the S.O.S. charter intended, not to mention, violated what she and James had agreed upon. Such a purchase was almost certainly going to be bathed in controversy. Perhaps Clarice knew something about the owner or the property that would be helpful. She looked at her watch. 2:00 o'clock. She sighed, feeling pushed. Hopefully, she would have time to get her outline and notes organized enough to fax to James so Peggy could type them. After that, she would call Margaret Jones.

She found Clarice folding bed linens in the laundry room. They smiled at each other and Clarice confessed, "I know what you're here for. Don't much get by you. Let me finish makin' the beds and all, and then find you. Where you gonna be?"

"At my desk, or in James's office. Take your time. I've got a lot to do. Althea and Emory were most helpful in tearing this fundraising idea apart. Then," Midge smiled, "I thought I might call the West Coast. I need to talk out a few more details with Dawn's mother and thought maybe, if Dawn were home, we both might want to talk to her."

Clarice wiped her brow with a broad hand. "I do." She said simply. "This house seems empty today."

"Yes," Midge nodded, "I felt it too. I was quite out of sorts and all wound up this morning and I couldn't quite figure out why. Perhaps I'm just missing...what did you and James call her...our ray of sunshine? Anyway, come find me and fill me in and then maybe we can talk with her."

272

Midge turned to leave and then turned back and said tartly, "Tucker is such a fool!"

Clarice chuckled, nodded her head in complete agreement and as Midge turned again to leave, looked sympathetically at her retreating back. She had been amazed when Midge had requested that she prepare Scotty's room for Dawn. Tucker Jones had never been allowed to set foot in that room, though the Tylers treated him almost like a son. Maybe that was it. Dawn had been nearly an unknown, so it wasn't as though they were replacing Scott's memory; whereas, with Tucker, it might have felt that way. Besides, the room did have its own bath, something a female guest would especially love. She shrugged and thought about her employer, shaking her head in resignation. *This lady be a fool for meddlin': them young folks, the project housing on Front Street; anybody who ain't happy. She wants the whole world to be happy. She ain't going to like what I'm gonna tell her about Front Street. Ain't no live-happily-ever-after down there.* She grunted softly as she lifted a corner of the mattress where Tucker had slept. Deftly, she mitered the corners of the crisp white cotton sheet and thought of him. *That boy sort of like these corners--neat and tight. Need someone or somethin' to fuss him up a little bit.*

Tucker sat in his office feeling particularly "unfussed." He felt wired, keyed-up and powerful; his thinking, crystal-clear. The briefing with Mr. Tyler, the staff meeting and the customary oral debriefing had gone very well. He looked at his watch. At this point, he had been without any significant sleep for a very long time. Certainly, he had not slept well on the Tyler's boat. He had the one catnap on his parents' patio, but Sunday night had been a disaster. Last night, he had spent at his computer. He had checked and rechecked figures; he knew what each of the targeted countries of South America currently exported, imported and what the trade balance was, both historically and currently. More importantly, he finally felt he had a handle on each country's potential. From a list of 400 variables, he had deleted all but the major 10. Those were location, size, natural resources, population density, transportation and communication, current versus potential

273

industrial production, agricultural production, and last on the list, but not least in importance, political stability.

Those 10 variables were really the key to whether the climate in a country would be right for Zitec to be able to assist in helping private ownership create the manufacturing plants necessary to become competitive in world trade. The 10th variable, political stability had given him the most difficulty and was the one he had discussed the longest with his boss. It was the most nebulous. Ironically, it seemed that the countries with the most volatile histories currently had the brightest hopes for successful manufacturing ventures. Raw materials, transportation, stable workforce, available capitalization, local interests…those positive factors could all be wiped away by a single military coup.

Simply because it interested him, he spent several hours creating a data set that eliminated government politics and political boundaries. He showed the graph to Mr. Tyler when they were through with their discussion and about to go to the meeting.

"Look how simple this decision would be if there were no political dictators or political boundaries to consider," he said, whimsy evident in his voice. Mr. Tyler looked carefully at the graph, his brows drawn into a scowl. Then he sighed. "Funny, isn't it? How what would really be best for a people has so little to do with what seems to get done. Actually," he said quietly, almost to himself, as he stood and gathered Tucker's report into a neat pile, "peculiar is the better word."

Tucker remembered the look of sadness in his boss's usually steely eyes. But, the old man had been able to thrust aside his sadness and the meeting had proceeded satisfactorily. Tucker felt he had been able to concentrate as well as always. When he finished summarizing the process with his boss and rose from his chair, he said, "I'm heading home to bed." But he hadn't as yet; he was still sitting at his desk. He couldn't seem to mobilize himself. It was dark and cool in his office with the blinds drawn and the track lights dimmed. It smelled richly of wood that had been recently oiled with something lemon scented.

Lemon. His thoughts took a sudden unbidden turn and for once he let them. In his mind's eye he pictured himself lifting Dawn in his arms drawing in the spicy, citrus scent of her until she had looked up at him with a question in her brown eyes.

He leaned back in his chair, lack of sleep lowering his defenses and allowed himself to picture her fully, to remember every detail of her clothing, every expression...but the one that centered and stayed was the look on her face when she had moved over on the cushion in Charlie's galley, a wordless invitation for him to sit beside her. He'd understood it immediately and couldn't leave fast enough. *Why? And the look on her face! It was a sad and puzzled expression that he had turned his back on.*

Tucker stood and abruptly kicked back his chair. *No sense thinking about it. I was rude. If I ever see her again, I will apologize, that is, I will if she'll even speak to me...which I doubt. My goodbye to her was barely civil.* He shook his head in disgust. *A California psychologist; a rare specimen to take home for his parents to examine...while at the same time, she would be examining the three of us.*

He realized his mind was wandering unproductively and went to turn out the lights, once again shutting Dawn out of his mind. This time he resolved to put Dawn out of his mind for good. There was no way that he could know, on the other coast, Dawn was setting events in motion that would make a shambles of his resolution before very many days had passed.

When Midge heard James call, she was in the kitchen, happily humming to herself and reading a recipe. She looked at her watch with surprise. *Good heavens! I didn't even hear Hank drop him off.* She wiped her hands on her apron and rushed through the swinging kitchen door to find him looking expectantly up the stairs.

"Here I am, darling. How was your day? I was in the kitchen fixing dinner," she said somewhat breathlessly.

He turned at her voice, paused and a slow smile touched his face. "You look pretty good in that apron, Midge, much better than Charlie ever did."

"Oh you," she said flipping her hand. "Go change your clothes and read your mail. Then make us a drink and come talk to me. I've decided to make a casserole out of all that chicken Charlie cooked for Heather to eat. In fact, chicken is what the ladies and I had for lunch today."

James leaned over and kissed the top of her tousled curls. He wondered silently if she would ever forgive Heather for being inconsistent in her food preferences and decided with a twinkle in his eye, *probably not.*

"Be right with you," he said. "I imagine you have a few things to tell me. Peggy handed me your typed outline and a couple of pages of notes just as I was leaving." He tapped his briefcase. "It's here." He stopped at the foot of the stairs. "By the way, did you call Tucker's mother?"

Midge flipped her hand again. "Yes, but I have even more than that to tell you and most of it is good. So hurry." With that, she slipped back through the doors and left him shaking his head at her energy. He was, if he admitted it to himself, feeling a little tired. This stuff with the South America project seemed far more complicated than it should be. It was taking way too much of his time as well as staff time, and he hadn't been able to use Tucker for anything else. But, Lord could that boy unearth the data! Actually, Tucker looked tired and tense today, too. He said he was going to go home and catch up on some sleep. He hoped he would. He didn't like the circles he saw under the young man's eyes. He wondered again where Tucker had been Monday afternoon. He'd said, "I couldn't reach you on Monday afternoon, Tucker." Expecting that Tucker would say "Yes, I know, sir," and then fill him in.

But instead, Tucker had simply said, "Sorry, sir." His response left James feeling as though he had been prying, which he had to admit to himself, was the case. It left him scrambling for words. "Don't be silly. There's nothing to be sorry for. You know your schedule is your own. You did another damn fine job on this report"

James sighed as he sat on the edge of the bed and removed his shoes. Perhaps, he and Clifton could get away to play some golf tomorrow. His second in-command still wasn't real sold on expanding to South America and he thought he knew why. It was exactly what Tucker had demonstrated to him so graphically today; something good for a country might not be good for politics. But Zitec was, by now, used to all that. Of course, Clifton was often the last one to be convinced of an idea, but when he was, you could be confident that it was a good one.

Midge seemed to like the idea, and damn it, he did too. At this stage, Zitec could afford to do a little risk-taking. He just had to be convinced that his company would be able to ship materials into the country if they weren't otherwise available, that they could hire a local, reliable workforce, would not run into bureaucratic red tape and that the proposed capitalization was real. He also needed to know that the Zitec team left behind to assist in the management, training of staff, and maintenance of the equipment and buildings would be both well received and listened to.

With a small start, he realized he was still sitting on the side of the bed and hastened to remove his suit. It felt good to trade it for his ancient cords, cotton sweater and loafers.

Midge was chopping herbs when her husband came through the kitchen door, empty ice bucket in hand. She waved the chopping knife at him. "Casserole's in the oven. Fresh herbs from our garden are going to grace our salad dressing. I just love it! Make our drinks while I shake this up, and then we can go and relax. Dinner is an hour away."

"So," said James, once his wife had plopped herself in one of the easy chairs, curled her feet up under herself and accepted her drink, "tell me about your conversation with Margaret Jones."

Midge shrugged. "There's not much to tell. It did take some courage on my part to finally call her. I explained the whole concept of the contest and told her that she and Charlie were my choices as judges if she would possibly consider it. I made it clear that everything was still in the planning stage and had yet not yet been presented to the full fund raising committee or the Board of Directors. If she was surprised by my call, I couldn't discern it. She asked me several questions, said she would certainly consider my proposal seriously, thanked me quite graciously for thinking of her and said she would give me her decision within a day or two. That was pretty much how the conversation went. Althea says she's shy and perhaps she is, but what she sounded like is Tucker when he's being very proper and very much in control. But," Midge shook her head, puzzled.

277

"she did ask me to convey to Charlie her regards, and that Tucker had been very complementary about his cooking. Don't you find that odd?"

"No, not particularly," said James. "But then I wasn't in on the whole conversation. What made it seem odd?"

"Oh, I don't know." Midge sipped her scotch. "Maybe because I expected her to say, 'give my regards to your husband. Tucker speaks so highly of him.'"

James gave a bark of laughter. His wife was right. Most people they socialized with would put giving regards to the head of the household ahead of giving regards to the cook. "I think I like this woman," he said. "She's letting you know something about her priorities. But, I am surprised she didn't say, 'yes.' My guess is that she wants to talk it over with her husband and Tucker first. Perhaps, they have concerns about fraternizing with us, just as we have with them."

"Yes, that is what I had decided too. But, it did leave me feeling a little flat. Then, after that, I called Santa Barbara. Clarice and I were feeling a bit lonesome for Dawn and besides, I wanted to talk to Barbara about some more cook-off details. Regretfully, Dawn was at the beach but she already had her pictures developed and Barbara said she had double prints made so she'd have some to send to all of us. She's going to send Tucker the one she took of Heather and him. She already got his address from me, you know."

Then Midge un-curled her legs, sat up and leaned forward. "And I'll tell you something else that Clarice and Charlie evidently already know. Dawn thinks she is in love with Tucker, but for some reason he isn't even willing to be friends!"

James looked at her with enough surprise registering in his face to make his wife happy. She leaned back and re-tucked her feet. He tried not to smile at her obvious satisfaction at having this bit of information to fit into her puzzle. "Just how do you know that?" he asked.

"From Barbara, of course! Evidently, Dawn spilled her heart out this morning. Barbara says she told Dawn she needed to think about the whole situation and if Dawn wanted, she would then share her thoughts. I think they must have an exceptional mother-daughter relationship," she said quietly, her eyes unfathomable.

James nodded and waited, realizing the last comment was simply an aside. There was more to the story.

"Clarice listened to my end of the whole conversation and is standing by her original statement that if Dawn wants him, she'd better get back here and fight for him."

James smiled at his wife. "Well, we'd certainly like that--having her again--wouldn't we?"

Midge nodded solemnly. "You know, James, it was a good decision to put her in Scott's room. I went in there today and for the first time, I didn't feel that awful clutch of sadness. I found myself thinking of Dawn instead."

The big man looked at the diminutive form curled up in the chair and the tired lines around his mouth seemed to deepen, but he said simply. "It is time, my dear."

Then he sat deeper in his chair, took a long pull at his drink as if weighing carefully and painfully his next words. Finally he said slowly, "It is also time to let go of your image of Tucker. I am afraid he is the consummate actor. His skill is such that he is believable. We all believe him to be laid-back, affable, polite, genuine, because it's the illusion he creates with his acting skill. I go back to my unseemly scotch-slopping tirade just after he landed in the hospital; the man is a shell."

Midge gasped. "But, James, it sounds as though you have just written him off entirely. What about the Tucker Jones we were seeing on Friday night after Dawn's fall? Don't you think we were seeing the real Tucker then?"

James shook his head sadly. "I have not written him off. I'm trying to accept him for what he is, a troubled but very bright young man who is a great asset to our company and a pleasant houseguest. I don't know what Friday night was about. Probably he was making a stab at being real with us. But you saw how long that effort lasted."

Midge looked closely at her husband, realizing what the words were costing him. He was not one to give up on people easily. She suddenly saw the tired gauntness of his face and heard the flatness of his tones. She leaned forward, fixing her eyes on his, waiting for him to continue.

"I guess what I'm really trying to point out is the fact that he is not attracted to our Dawn is perhaps a blessing in disguise. She seems a genuinely warm and wonderful person. Why would you want her in love with someone who wouldn't know a genuine feeling if it hit him over the head?"

Rising, still in her stocking feet, Midge went over and removed the forgotten drink from her husband's hand. Then she slipped onto his lap and put her arms around him. Her first inclination had been to tell him that his tiredness was making him overly pessimistic. Just in time, she realized the core of what had driven his words. It was Dawn. He was trying to protect her from a hurtful experience.

Snuggling deeper under his chin and feeling comforted as his long arms wrapped around her, she also realized that her tactful husband was telling her to back off-- to let well enough alone. There were five people living who knew her tremendous power to manipulate events and people to do her bidding: Charlie, Clarice, Barbara, Emory and her husband. She leaned back, brushed back his silvery forelock with a gentle hand, stood up and then leaned over and kissed him on the lips. "I heard you," she said glumly. "I don't like what you said, but I did hear you and I will think about it. But right now, I am going to serve you a simple but delicious dinner and then you are going to put your feet up and watch TV or read or do whatever you would like. We are not going to solve the world's problems or even have a serious conversation for the rest of this evening, I promise."

James pulled her back into his lap. "In a minute," he said. "This feels awfully good, just the two of us. Then, when you go and get things ready, I believe I'll light the fire. I noticed when I got out of the car tonight the clouds were building over the bay and that the temperature has dropped. A fire, some news and then early to bed sounds just right, doesn't it?" He said, giving her a final hug and releasing her.

She slipped from his lap, looked down and nodded ruefully. *Now that I think of it, I'm feeling pretty worn down too. One of these days we are going to have to face the fact that age is creeping up on us.*

280

Chapter Twenty-three

Dawn lay drowsing, listening to the gentle sound of the surf and the idle conversation of her friends. The heat of the day was moderated by a cooling ocean breeze. It was wonderful to be home were things were comfortably the same. She wiggled her toes deeper into the sun-warmed sand of the Carpenteria beach as if to convince herself.

The core group had really, for the most part, fallen away over the years, lost to the workforce, the service and marriage. Those that remained were mostly home from college for the summer, working in temporary, or tourist-related jobs, many of which were odd or night shifts. But, though the numbers had lessened, the tone of the group and the activities stayed pretty much the same. Any minute now someone was going to start another game of volleyball or try to talk her into throwing a Frisbee, both of which she could legitimately decline because of her knee. There was also the chance that someone else would join the group and ask her about her trip east. Then, as much as she didn't want to, she would recount the story one more time, forcing enthusiasm into her voice, describing in detail the Tyler's estate and the beautiful motorsailer. It wasn't that she didn't like telling them; it was that afterwards the hollow feeling would be there and once again she would find herself ruminating over the puzzle of her feelings for Tucker Jones.

Her mother had taken her sister, Lisa Ann, to the dentist and then to do some shopping, so they had not yet had their talk. However, her mother had looked carefully at her pictures, pausing long over the picture of Tucker and Heather but saying little except that she could see why Dawn might have been attracted to his good looks. She also looked at the picture of Deborah and Rob wrapped comfortably in each other's arms and the close-up Dawn had taken of Deborah showing off her ring. "I like the looks of that girl. There something so nice and genuine about that cheery little face. Once you get established at Tufts, perhaps you can get to know each other better."

Dawn noted that there was absolutely no doubt in her mother's mind that Tufts University would jump at the chance to enroll her eldest daughter. She laughed and said, "They have to accept me first, Mom. But you are right about keeping up the friendships I've made. Both Deborah and Heather talked about doing things together once I got back there." Then she said, much too brightly, her mother thought, "Heather even invited me to go hiking in Maine with Tucker and her."

Dawn noticed that her mother looked carefully at all the pictures but that the ones that really drew her attention and put a look in her eye that Dawn couldn't read, were those many pictures she had taken of the Tylers: The two of them together, Midge in her garden; James leaning against the red Mustang and at the helm of Faith; and a wonderful picture of the three of them standing in front of the yacht club, snapped by Hank, just before he hurried them into the car and to the airport.

Dawn sighed and opened her eyes. She found her friend, Amy, watching her speculatively and Dawn knew why. Usually, it was she who was the last to succumb to the sun's relaxing rays. It was she who borrowed Pete, their friend, Tom's dog, to play Frisbee when no one else would play; wanted to go to the Rincon and surf when the waves were really too flat; or wanted to solve, if not her friends' problems, then the problems of the world.

She sat up, reached into her bag to check her watch for the time and found herself somewhat relieved that it was nearly time to go. Grinning, she said, "Sorry to be so quiet, guess I've got jet leg or something."

Amy, who had known Dawn since kindergarten, snorted, gave her a sharp look and said, "The 'or something' would be my guess."

"Maybe so," Dawn said mysteriously, adjusting her sun visor to protect her face, "but it was unkind if you to notice, Amy, especially since I am just about to introduce you all to my newest find." So saying, she slid the top back on her cooler and displayed four large bottles of beer poking brown necks out of their ice cube bath. "Tsingtao beer introduced to me by a genuine Asian gentleman and philosopher," she announced with a touch of the old Dawn in her voice.

A chorus of: "Hey! Awesome! Nice job, Dawn!" told her that her timing had been perfect. Amy was distracted and the moment of tension had passed.

Since the drinking of alcoholic beverages was really illegal on the beach, it took a few moments for the group to gather around accepting their draughts in empty pop cans, plastic Slurpee containers or water bottles. A token amount went into the bowl of the Frisbee for Pete, who had a known taste for "suds."

Dawn had been unable to find the same brand served by Charlie, but the man at the Chinese market had assured her that "this one fine beer, too."

His dialect had made her think fondly of Charlie. Now, she gave a small sigh, remembering. *I wonder what he and the rest of the Tyler household are up to now that their lives are returning to normal.*

Dawn took a sip and nodded with satisfaction as the golden, slightly malty-tasting liquid filled her mouth and slid coolly down her throat. It was almost the same.

The six in the group sat silently around her, sipping quietly, considering. Since most of them had been drinking beer since their preteen years, they were quite sophisticated in their taste. Not that they spent their money on expensive beer, but they did enjoy drinking it when the opportunity arose.

"Not bad, Dawn, old girl." It was Larch, laconic, witty and the only male in the group who was truly not attracted to her looks.

Amy nodded in agreement. "Decent, truly decent beer, I vote you bring it again tomorrow."

Tom laughed. As usual he was sitting with an arm around his dog, positioning himself back just far enough from the group so he could swing a look at women in their bikinis any time he wanted to, without being obvious. "Pete agrees with Amy, he likes the beer but he thinks Amy is the one who should cough up the coins to bring it tomorrow."

Smiling, Dawn rose and brushed herself off while the conversation continued to flow in its well-worn circles about her feet. She slipped into her shorts and flip-flops. "Glad you liked it. It's nice to provide a little culture to this group occasionally. See you later. I've got to go help my mom, so help yourself to the rest of it."

Fondly, she looked at the group as they hastened to empty the bottles, trying to ignore the distance she felt and had been feeling all day. She had been away for two weeks and should have been dying to see everyone and find out what it happened in their lives since she left. The fact was, she had felt like a fake all afternoon.

Tucker, on the other hand, was feeling, more like himself than he had for a long time. He had come home from the office, fixed himself a decent late lunch, sitting down properly and giving his meal the attention it deserved. Then he turned on his music and took a good long nap. After that, his mother called to tell him that Midge Tyler intended to present the idea of a fund-raising cooking contest to the Save Our Spaces board and had invited her and Charlie to possibly co-judge the recipes, if the board approved the project. She wanted to know what he thought of her participation.

Is that excitement I hear in her voice? Tucker couldn't be sure. "Well, mother, this is quite a surprise. What does father think of the idea?"

He could almost see her standing at the phone, worrying the necklace at her throat with distracted fingers. "Well, he was quite startled at first. I don't believe a Jones has ever been asked to do anything quite like this before. It is for a very good cause, we understand. Your father called one of his friends to find out about the organization. The group seems to be doing a remarkable job of purchasing land to be used for..." Margaret stopped and searched hard for an elusive word..."people." She finally said quite firmly.

Tucker understood perfectly well what she meant; she was talking about "the common people." A part of him was detached, admiring the speed with which Midge had been able to put together a plan for having Charlie and his mother meet. "Yes," said Tucker smoothly, "It is, in fact, one of the charities I support."

"Is it really, dear? I don't believe your father and I knew that. Well, I must say, that as I have thought about it, I do feel I am qualified and am quite sure I would enjoy the collaboration with Charlie."

Tucker noted that she said Charlie's name with a very familiar tone. He smiled, his suspicions confirmed. It was excitement in her voice. "Charlie would seem a very good choice, and knowing the two of you, I suspect you would work quite well together, that is, if you both agree to do it." He said this in a businesslike tone, giving no hint of his participation in setting the events in motion.

There was a long pause. "Well, yes, I hadn't thought of that." Tucker was certain there was a hint of disappointment in her tone. "Truthfully, dear," she said, confirming exactly what Tucker had related to Midge, "I'm not sure I would want to try something so...so...public...unless Charlie were to do it too."

There was that familiar tone again. He was fairly sure that in his mother's mind, Charlie was a friend, a respected colleague or both. His reputed culinary skill had transcended all other factors including station in life. He smiled into the receiver. "Well, mother, call Midge tomorrow, if that is what you and father decide. Tell her you will accept on the condition that Charlie accepts."

"Really? Oh thank you, dear. I could say that, couldn't I?" This time, the note of excitement actually bubbled through her reserve.

"And, Mother," said Tucker, "don't pay too much attention to the fact that Midge said she had to clear it with her board of directors. I don't believe she will receive other than a very enthusiastic response." He did not add that Midge Tyler was the driving, organizing and energizing force behind S.O.S. and that she had hand-picked her own board.

He'd hung up the phone smiling broadly. He could picture what the afternoon had been like at his parents' house with his father strategizing how to determine if the cooking contest would be suitable for his wife to be associated with. He could imagine his mother's rising excitement as the ramifications of the offer became more real and then calling--really asking his permission because of his affiliation with the Tylers--to proceed.

Well, he thought to himself, as he rose to go put on his running clothes, *I'd better give Mrs. T a call in the morning and reassure her that my trusty computer is again at the ready.*

285

As Tucker stepped out onto the street, he realized that the day had deteriorated. Looking east he could see dark clouds billowing, and as he began to run he felt the first sharp gusts of a wind-driven rain.

He bowed his head, liking the feeling of overcoming the elements, having the streets and park to himself and already looking forward to the hot shower afterwards. He was also looking forward to tomorrow. He shot a glance skyward, realizing for the first time that the weather might preclude sitting in the garden. But he would still get to see Kathryn and have his massage. Or would he? A sudden conviction stopped him in his tracks. *My Wednesday appointment! Did I make one?* He remembered telling Mavis, Dr. Beemers' nurse, that he planned to make permanent appointments, but he could not recall saying any such thing to Kathryn after Monday's session. His head had been filled with thoughts of Allison and their trip to the zoo. He looked at his watch. Almost 7 o'clock.

His inclination was to turn immediately and head back to his condo to check his computer. But he knew it would be a useless exercise. There would be no reminder on his calendar. He forced himself into motion, hoping to quell his growing sense of agitation, which seemed a living thing and beyond his control. His head began to fill with the familiar senseless dread and he unknowingly picked up his pace as though to outrun the cause. By the time he reached the bark chip trail he was nearly sprinting, long legs flashing under the lights, arms pumping, breath coming in irregular gasps. Only a small part of his mind was in touch with his foolishness, one small part actually felt the beginnings of pain; the rest of it was intent on outrunning the clutch of panic that robbed his mind of control.

Finally, his body could run no more. His legs had turned to rubbery useless things and the searing pain in his chest had grown strong enough to assert itself. He leaned over and grabbed his knees, gasping, trying to draw in great draughts of the moisture laden air.

After minutes, he straightened his body, shaken to his core, but feeling amazingly calm. He tried to recall the root of his earlier angst and could barely connect it to the fact that he had forgotten to make an appointment with Kathryn McCall. The whole thing seemed so absolutely illogical...crazy. *Yes, it was crazy! There is a good chance that I am crazy,* he thought coolly.

He wondered idly if he had done damage to his back, but was not overly concerned. It didn't seem to matter. Nothing really mattered...*except that I face myself and get some things straightened out.* For the first time, Tucker Jones was able to admit he might need some professional help to do so.

He raised his head to see where he was just as the rain began to fall harder, and was surprised to see he was only a few hundred feet from where he'd entered the path. He must have covered the whole trail in a blind panic. Slowly, he drew in several deep breaths and began to walk back to his condo, lost in glum recognition of his own vulnerability.

Like a robot he walked, placing one foot in front of the other, until he stood, rain soaked, at his door and fumbled with the key. He let himself in and stood inside the door waiting for the feeling of safety and control that he usually felt to come over him. He waited in vain. Instead, he found himself really looking at his condo furnishings. He knew he needed to keep moving, to cool down slowly, to get in the shower and to keep his back warm. Instead he walked to the Chickering and gently eased back the lid. Ignoring what the sweat of his body might do to the ebony bench, he sat down, closed his eyes and began to play. He played as he had run, mindlessly, out of control. For a long time there was little for a listener to glean from his notes. There was no beauty, note order, very little cadence--only the sense of unleashed agony. But gradually, the mathematical order of music reasserted itself and snatches of List, Mozart, Beethoven and Salieri began to take on order and create a wonderful medley of Tucker's boyhood memories. He began to play with wild abandon. What he could not remember in his chaotic mood, he improvised--playing with fierce concentration until his fingers slowed and stopped. He looked at his resting hands benevolently and sighed, "I may be crazy, he whispered to the now silent instrument, but I can still play the piano!"

Gently, he unstuck himself from the bench, got to his feet, walked to his phone and dialed Kathryn's number. "Kathryn, this is Tucker Jones," he said, surprised at the

287

steadiness of his own voice. "I wouldn't bother you so late, except I'm quite sure your machine is taking your calls. I'm very afraid I neglected to make my Wednesday's appointment. I would appreciate a slot if you have one, if not, Thursday afternoon will do. Friday would work as well. And so this doesn't happen again, could we schedule permanently for those 3:20 times on Monday, Wednesday and Friday?" Thank you very much."

When Tucker put down the receiver he turned and looked one more time at his condo; for the first time seeing the sterile, impersonal environment he called home. He shook his head and walked slowly towards the shower, suddenly too weary for words, but resolved in spirit. He was going to make some changes, face some things, and one of those "things" was a small cardboard box buried in the back of his closet on Prospect Hill.

There must have been a reason I kept that carton all these years, he thought doggedly, allowing the pain to wash over him and resisting with all his might the urge to blank his mind.

Chapter Twenty-four

Several times during the night, true to his initial resolve, Tucker did not block the thoughts that came into his mind. He found it unexpectedly difficult--found the nameless agitation threatening to return--until he remembered the wisdom of Dr. van Castle. "You need to be able to pull the memories of Ethan and Mary up to comfort you."

And so, in the stillness of the night he tried. It, too, proved exceptionally difficult. *I seem to need Kathryn's garden to help me remember,* he thought, feeling suddenly frightened that he had suppressed the O'Sheas for too many years to clearly recall them. He changed his tack and instead began to think of his parents; to contrast their way of loving him to the way the Irish couple had loved him. He began to remember little things like how, during his freshman year in high school, his mother had his room redecorated to reflect his latest sport. Never anything so tacky as basketball players on his walls, but certainly the framed Neiman oil painting of Wilt Chamberlain and redecorating in green and white, the colors of his favorite team, the Boston Celtics, showed her effort. He smiled, feeling comforted, as he again drifted off.

Waking a third time, he got out of bed, turned on lights and fixed himself a cup of tea. He drank it, wandering around, something he had never done before. He found himself thinking of Kathryn, seeing each of his rooms through her eyes. He suspected she would see them as he now saw them, absolutely without warmth or character. He wondered what her house looked like, begin idly to picture it in his mind and then stopped with a start. He wasn't picturing Kathryn's house at all. It was the O'Sheas' cottage in fine detail. He nodded to himself with sudden understanding and again feeling somewhat comforted, headed back to bed.

The next morning he awoke ravenous and decided to do something else he had never done before. A check of his back reassured him that he had not done himself harm the night before and he slowly uncoiled himself from his tousled bed, did a few stretching exercises, wrapped himself in his robe and padded into the kitchen. *Breakfast before shower,* he thought to himself. *Now tell me that isn't a major change!*

Tucker ground a few coffee beans, set a kettle on to boil and poured a huge glass of orange juice. It was a ham and egg morning. He grabbed his Calphalon skillet and got the ham, (97 percent fat free), started. Pausing every now and then to sip his juice, he set up the timing so everything would be done at the same time and wished for once that he had a daily paper. Instead, he turned on the television and watched it throughout his breakfast.

As he did the dishes, he admitted to himself that like his first massage, this order of doing business "hadn't killed him." In fact, he had rather liked watching the news, though the weather report confirmed his fear that the cloudy, rainy weather was likely to be with them for several more days.

Just as well, he thought serenely, as he headed for the bedroom, *I can delay my garden sitting; however it would be so nice if Saturday were clear. It won't be as much fun doing the zoo in the rain with the animals in their houses and not out for viewing.*

Tucker wanted to be out of the shower before 8 o'clock. His assumption was that Kathryn would be most likely to return his call about that time and he was correct. The phone began ringing just as he finished dressing.

Kathryn sounded her usual professional self, although he did note that she called him Tucker instead of Mr. Jones and found himself inordinately pleased by the small familiarity.

"Your back give you a bit of a twinge, Tucker?"

"No," he admitted, "not really, although it deserves to. I didn't treat it very well yesterday. This is still Dr. Beemers' preventative medicine. I go in to see him on Friday and I want him to be impressed with my mobility so he will allow me to continue my running."

"Well, I'm sorry to say I've given away your 3:20 time slot today. You can come in first thing Thursday morning if you'd like."

Tucker shook his head though she could see it, thinking, *It wouldn't do to miss my meeting with Mr. Tyler for a massage.* "Sorry, that won't work. What about Friday?"

"Your 3:20 time slot is open if you'd like and perhaps by then the garden will be fit again for sittin'."

Again, Tucker felt pleasure when she referred to the time slots as, 'your time slot.' "Yes I would like the 3:20 time very much. Perhaps Allison will be available and we can pin down a few more details of our zoo trip."

Kathryn laughed. "She's been wantin' to call you at home, but I've been putting her off. I'm not sure that is something you would want started."

"Why, no, I wouldn't mind at all," he said, the pleasure in his voice unmistakable, heightened by the fact that her accent was very definite. The familiar Irish cadence and lilt struck him like an old tune newly recalled. "Really, feel free to give her my number. And, Kathryn, please do put me into your Monday, Wednesday, Friday afternoon schedule next week," Tucker said rather quickly, suddenly remembering that the woman probably had a client waiting and didn't have time for socializing.

"Yes," she said, "'tis done. See you Friday then. Goodbye, Tucker."

Midge Tyler had been having a serious talk with herself all morning, replaying her husband's words about Tucker over in her mind. The somberness of her mood was punctuated by the grayness of the rainy day. In the morning light, gloomy as it was, she decided that he was absolutely right. Dawn didn't need Tucker Jones in her life. She was too loving and spontaneous. He was too controlled. But, she admitted to herself once again, she really liked Tucker, perhaps because she knew little things about him that others didn't--like his anonymous giving to her causes and the way he called her Mrs. T--though only in private or on the phone. She always felt better after talking to him. It certainly felt like something genuine passed between them.

She had just completed the thought when the phone rang. It was the cool cultured voice of Margaret Jones asking very politely if it would be an imposition for her to speak to Charlie. After just a small pause of startled surprise, Midge managed to say, "Not at all; just one moment, Margaret."

If Midge was surprised, Charlie was flabbergasted to hear that he had received a call on the Tyler's personal line from Tucker Jones' mother. She watched his face as he dried nervous hands, swallowed vigorously several times, took the phone and then paused to compose his face and mind before answering.

Oh, Tucker was so right! She thought as she eavesdropped shamelessly, heard the obvious accolades passing back and forth and saw the unflappable cook begin bowing as if the lady on the other end of the line were at that moment gracing his kitchen.

All at once, Charlie smiled hugely, turned and handed the receiver back to Midge saying, "Most honorable Mrs. Jones wish to speak to Mam."

Did Margaret Jones sound a little less cool and collected? Midge couldn't be sure. It flashed through her mind that this woman and Tucker had a lot in common that way and then she concentrated on the words.

"Mrs. Tyler, I do apologize for the unconventionality of my call. However, I realize that being in your employee, Charlie might have felt under some pressure to accept the position of judging with me and I felt I wanted to clarify his position before making my final decision. Happily, I felt he was quite sincere in his desire to share the responsibility. So I, of course, accept."

The joyful enthusiasm in Midge's voice contrasted sharply with the cool, calm voice on the other end of the line. "Wonderful! I simply can't thank you enough. But please call me Midge. Really, I can't thank you enough!" Midge's voice bubbled on. "I will be back in touch with you as soon as the board has met and made a decision."

When she hung up the phone, she turned and said, "Well, Charlie, this calls for a celebratory cup of tea. I have time before my meeting. Please put the kettle on while I go hang up the other phone."

Thinking of her earlier musings about Tucker, she remembered it was he who had suggested the connection between Charlie and his mother. *Now, why would he have done that?* Shaking her head and smiling at the events that one telephone conversation had put into motion, she wondered if she should ask Charlie what the Tao had to say about interfering, manipulative old ladies.

After talking with Kathryn, Tucker called his mother, partly to find out if she had decided to accept Midge's proposal. He suspected that she had, but he wanted to hear it from her and to find out what time she intended to call Midge to let her know. He shook his head and admitted to himself that he was enjoying his own part of this intrigue. He couldn't wait to hear what Mrs. T had to say.

The professional, crisp voice of the Jones's newest housekeeper answered the phone, the one whose name he could never remember. His mother and father were quite strict about the telephone protocol and anyone who answered the phone did it properly, including Tucker.

"Hello," this is Tucker, the son of Mrs. Jones. Would she possibly be available?"

After a short wait, he heard the familiar, beautifully modulated voice say, "Tucker, darling, how unusual of you to call at this time of morning."

"Hello, Mother. Yes, it is and everything is perfectly fine, but I was thinking about you and wondered if I had ever properly thanked you for doing my room in the green and white Celtic colors when I was in high school." He was surprised at the words. *Whoa! That is not at all what I intended to say!*

There was a long pause. "Why, Tucker, how dear of you to remember! It is odd how certain memories come back to us from time to time, isn't it?"

And that, my dear lady, is an understatement, thought Tucker to himself. Aloud he said, "Yes, it certainly is. By the way, I am very interested in your decision regarding the cooking contest."

Now, that, he thought, unconsciously running a hand through his carefully combed hair, *is what I meant to say!*

"Well, as a matter of fact, your father and I decided that I should pursue further details. So I called Charlie not more than ten minutes ago."

Tucker couldn't believe his ears. He finally really understood the term "speechless with surprise." She went on. "You see, since he is an employee of the Tylers, I didn't want to put him under any undue pressure if he didn't want to do it."

"But, Mother, Mrs. Tyler generally answers her own phone. How did you get around that?"

"Oh, she did, dear. But I just identified myself and asked if it were possible to speak to Charlie."

Tucker quickly covered the receiver to muffle the strangled sound of his stifled laugh. He was picturing the look on Mrs. T's face. It took a lot to surprise her, but it could be accomplished, and he was sure his mother had just done so.

"She readily agreed and put him right on...and Tucker, do you know what he said? He said that it would be an honor to assist me in judging. Then I assured him that it was my equal honor to assist him. And that was that!"

Tucker found his state of near speechlessness continuing. He had never, that he could remember, heard quite this tone in his mother's voice. The only word he could think that would describe her was "ruffled." Not flustered, he could never picture her as that, but definitely ruffled in a happy sort of way. Suddenly, he felt very proud and protective.

"Good for you, Mother. I am sure father and I are both very pleased for you. Did you let Mrs. Tyler in on your decision?"

Margaret laughed, in what for her, was rather an immodest manner. "Don't be silly, Tucker. Of course I did. As soon as Charlie and I finished talking, I asked to speak again to her and I explained my strange behavior. She seemed to understand perfectly and appeared quite pleased with my decision."

Quite sincerely, Tucker said, his voice warm, "And so she should be. Remember, I alone have been well exposed to splendid recipes from both you and Charlie. Now, I believe I will call the lady and reconfirm that my computer and I are willing participants in this noble venture."

Then Tucker, trying to sound casual, got to the second reason for his call. "Oh, and Mother, I almost forgot to mention that I will be driving out today. There are some things in the closet of my room that I want to retrieve."

"Why, Tucker, what an unexpected surprise!" She gave a small, pleased laugh. "What an exciting day this is turning out to be. I must go and tell your father. He was planning on lunching downtown today and I'm certain, if he knew you were coming, that he would want to change his plans. Do you suppose you could stay for lunch?"

Tucker looked at his watch. "Of course I can. Who wouldn't want to dine at the table of the woman just selected to judge one of the most prestigious cooking events ever to be held on the East Coast."

Margaret's voice sounded pleased. "Oh, darling, I'm sure you exaggerate. But I do confess the newness of this decision and its ramifications has me feeling a bit breathless."

Midge and Charlie had just finished their cup of tea when Tucker called. She took it in the study. "Hello, Mrs. T," the familiar gently teasing voice said. "Word has it that you're about to need a computer expert's assistance."

"Oh, Tucker, bless you! You must have talked with your mother. Isn't it wonderful? You are right you know, about them wanting to meet. I wish you could've seen Charlie's face when I announced who was calling him on the telephone."

He chuckled. "You should've seen my face when Mother told me what she had done. I don't believe we would find that course of action in an etiquette book."

"No," said Midge, her voice turning suddenly serious. "I don't suppose we would. It may not have been a proper thing to do, but it certainly was the moral thing to do. I think you should be quite proud of your mother, Tucker."

"Yes," said Tucker, "I see what you mean. Actually, that rather smacks of my father. He would be the one to point out Charlie's position." He paused, thinking. "But mother is the one who agreed and acted on her convictions and when I go for lunch today, I will be sure and tell her so."

"Good for you, Tucker! I'm sure it will please her," Midge said, while at the same time thinking, *James isn't quite right. He's much more than a shell, but he isn't what he seems. He's exactly what I had decided before, a puzzle, and events are now in motion that will perhaps help me better understand him.*

As he hung up the phone, Tucker looked at his computer, felt the strong desire to boot it up and lose himself within its amazing capabilities, but instead he walked over and ran his hand over the piano keys, remembering last evening. He looked at the bench and saw where the salty moisture from his rain and sweat-drenched running shorts had left a definite light-colored outline, marring the perfect finish and resisted the urge to go and get furniture polish to rub it out. *It doesn't have to be perfect,* he thought resolutely to himself. *In fact, I must be certain to inform the cleaning service that I want the marks left there.*

With that odd thought, he went to get his jacket. There was a serious mission to accomplish this day.

Driving through the pillared entrance of his parents' estate, Tucker took a deep breath. The grounds were well kept. Thomas said he had a lot to learn about the gardening end of things. Obviously, he was putting some effort into it. It would be one of today's self-assigned tasks to visit the caretakers' cottage and tell him so. But first, he would go and say hello to his parents and then go retrieve the things he wanted from his room before he lost his courage.

If his parents realized that Tucker was not quite himself at lunch, they never let on, never so much as mentioned his mysteriously quick trip to his room or his disappearance just before lunch was served. They were obviously delighted to see him. Talking about the cooking contest was the order of the day and he was glad for the focus.

Going to his room--the first time he'd done so since leaving home more than three years ago, had been a moving experience. It was clear that his parents had made the decision to keep it exactly the same. His trophies still graced his bookshelf and bureau. Certificates, starting to show their age, were still on his bulletin board. Though the room was no longer green and white, the Neiman painting was there on the wall. Everything was perfectly dusted, the nap in the thick, toffee-colored, plush carpet vacuumed to perfection. The windows, with their carefully raised blinds, were rain-spotted but clean. He breathed deeply. In his imagination the place still seemed to smell of his college aftershave. *Take it easy, Tucker,* he cautioned himself as he stepped into the room making foot prints in the deep carpet. He headed for his closet and opened the door where more reminders from his past awaited him: his letterman sweater, two basketballs, and an old tennis racket. These he pushed aside to reach for the small cardboard box, sealed and deposited at the very back of his closet so many years ago. Gingerly, he picked it up and backed out.

Just holding this Pandora's Box created a kaleidoscope of sensations. He had assumed when he tossed the *Robinson Crusoe* book from Dr. van Castle into the box and refolded the edges that he would never have to touch it again. He felt his resolve waiver, the nameless dread threatening. Turning quickly, he rushed from the room, thinking, *the sooner I get this into the boot of the car, the better.*

Going down the stairs and crossing the polished marble entry he felt as though his body and his thoughts were in slow motion, but working solidly together to help him accomplish this simple but most difficult of tasks. He felt hyperaware, could hear his footsteps on the wet paving stones, though the soft- soled loafers made little sound. It seemed that he not only felt, but actually heard his heart beating. The trunk lid shutting the box into darkness sounded as though he had slammed it with superhuman force, though he knew he had closed it gently.

Tucker stood there then, in the drizzle of rain, looking absently at the car's smooth grayness, taking an odd measure of comfort just in looking at the sculptured lines. He had accomplished another step of the mission, and reminded himself, actually silently mouthing the words as he had the previous evening, "I didn't throw it away. There must've been a reason I didn't throw it away."

With resolute step, he turned and headed quickly for the caretakers' cottage.

Chapter Twenty-five

On Thursday morning, Midge awoke, stretched luxuriously and then looked over at her still sleeping husband. For two nights they had consciously planned quiet time and had retired early. *Good sleep and the fact that James had taken the afternoon to play a very soggy game of golf with Clifton should erase some of the tired pallor from his face,* she thought.

Golf! She suddenly remembered that this was her day to play with Elaine Anderson. She sat up and looked out the French doors, wondering about the weather. It looked very gray, as if more rain were threatening, though at the moment, it wasn't actually falling. Sighing, she turned back the covers and slipped from the bed. A part of her would have been very happy to cancel the whole luncheon date; she was tired of thinking about the mystery and love life of Tucker Jones!

Thinking of Tucker made her remember her conversation with Mrs. Jones and then the Wednesday S.O.S. meeting. She smiled, remembering her presentation to the group. They were, as she had suspected, enthusiastic about the idea from the first and wild about it by the time she had finished outlining the plan. She asked them to tear it apart and they tried, but Althea, Emory and Charlie's effort at planning had been there before them, and the cohesiveness of the outline struck them all. They did, however, as she suspected, balk at the date she had chosen. Since there was no way she could tell them about the Front Street property, even to hint about it, without betraying Althea, she had hedged, something so unlike her, it caused her normal eloquence to fade and be replaced by a tone of petulant waspishness that startled everyone. "Listen," she said peevishly, "this first cook-off is a trial run. It isn't supposed to be perfect. The date really isn't open for discussion, just the idea."

What on earth possessed me to make the comment about the cook-off not being perfect the first time through? She knew it sounded phony even as she spoke, especially since each member, sitting with the document she had so carefully crafted right in front of them, could see for themselves how much effort had already gone into making sure the fundraiser was as perfect as good planning could make it. She sighed again, more than a little disgusted with herself, but seeing no way to retreat from her position.

Fortunately, in some ways, her friends had been so shocked by her attitude they let the date stand, probably wondering what was ailing her.

Thinking back on the meeting, Midge recognized again the tremendous number of details to be worked out just in setting the contest rules. *It would be helpful to call Barbara to see if a set of rules for their barbecue has been developed, but that would have to wait,* she decided. It was 4 o'clock in the morning in Santa Barbara and she would be on her way to her golf date long before it would be a decent time to call the West Coast.

Uncharacteristically, James slept on. She wondered what his Thursday calendar held that had allowed him the luxury of neglecting to set his alarm. As she padded towards the kitchen to get his coffee, she could hear Charlie banging pots and pans. *Good heavens,* she mused, *my household is going topsy turvey. My husband sleeps in and my cook is having a temper tantrum.*

She slipped through the swinging kitchen door and watched silently. The man was definitely agitated; his brow furrowed in concentration; his usually spotless kitchen in disarray. Charlie appeared to be "cleaning house." Deciding the best course of action would be to pretend everything seemed perfectly normal, she discreetly cleared her throat and said, "Good morning, Charlie. Is there coffee?"

Charlie, facing the range, his back to the door, jumped as if shot. He whirled. One could see at a glance that his usually placid face and composure were gone. She held her concern inside and stood waiting, knowing how important it was for him to present to her his best possible face.

"Oh, Mam," he declared without preamble, "Charlie in one big fat pickle, but coffee ready." He hurried to set two mugs on a tray as though he had read her mind about taking a cup up to her husband. He did not elucidate further, so she took the steaming mugs and beat a silent retreat.

What was the man doing? It looked as though he was rearranging every pot, pan and dish in the entire place. As far as she knew, his kitchen was always perfectly organized and spotless. *What on earth has motivated him to engage in such frenzied behavior? I hope it wasn't something I've said or done.*

Putting the tray on James's nightstand, she leaned down to kiss him awake and noticed again that his skin color seemed slightly gray beneath his tan. She frowned and put her hand to his forehead as he mumbled a good morning and opened his eyes.

"James, I do believe you've caught something, perhaps a cold from playing golf in the rain. Are you feeling ill?" She said softly, concern written in every line of her face. This man was generally impervious to ailments. She couldn't remember the last time he'd had the flu or even a serious cold.

He sat up slowly and she propped pillows behind his back while he came awake enough to consider.

"Maybe." He said. "I sure don't feel like jumping out of bed. It's been so long since I've been sick, I don't know how it's supposed to feel."

His attempt at humor touched her and she put her hand again to his forehead, brushing back his forelock and laying a cool palm firmly against his skin. "I believe I'll go find a thermometer, darling, you might have a fever."

When she returned, James was sitting just as she had left him, coffee untouched. *Just as well*, she thought, as she slipped the cool glass stick under his tongue, suddenly remembering the many times she had done exactly the same for Scotty. As if on rehearsed queue, the words rolled smoothly from her, soothing in the age-old way of mothers. "Keep it under your tongue, don't try to talk, this will only take a few minutes."

Meekly, James did as instructed. Midge pulled it from his mouth minutes later and fiddled with the slender column until she could read the scale. She looked at him and surprise. "It's not a bit elevated. You are entirely normal. It must be that you are still overdoing it at work. Perhaps you should consider staying tucked in bed today."

He propped himself up straighter on the pillows, reached for his coffee and took a swallow. "No, I probably won't do that. But I'd appreciate it if you'd call Peggy and tell her I'll be in by 10:00 o'clock. And have her let Hank know, please. No sense in him cooling his heels in the driveway. Really," he smiled reassuringly at Midge's worried face. "I don't think I feel all that badly, still just a little tired. Thanks for the coffee. Just the jolt I needed.

She sat on the couch, one leg tucked under, one satin slipper dangling, sipping her coffee speculatively. He didn't seem all that ill, and his temperature was normal. "All right," she said, finally coming to decisions of her own. "I guess you're a big boy and can decide whether or not to go to work. I just hope you're not contagious, darling, I hate to think of you giving your bug to the rest of the company."

James frowned, considering, and then shook his head. "I really don't think I have a bug. The coffee is helping and I really do need to make a decision on that South America project. For some reason, it has been absorbing tremendous energy. Tucker has done his usual remarkable job of researching every variable under the sun. You know, he is careful never to give an opinion, just points out the patterns, does projections, and double checks the staff's conclusions from the research by using his computer databases. And now, when it seems most staff would favor offering our services to Venezuela or Brazil, for some reason, I find myself favoring Chile." He shook his head. "As usual, I can't figure out if Tucker shaped my thinking or not. However, after I have my 10:00 o'clock meeting with him, I have the feeling I'm going to walk into the management meeting and have them try to convince me why Chile isn't the best choice...if we decide to expand at all."

He looked speculatively into his empty cup, then up at his wife. "Remind me what you have scheduled for today?"

"I'm having lunch with Heather and Elaine and then playing nine holes, if the weather holds."

James noted her unenthusiastic tone. "Well, after the S.O.S. meeting yesterday, at least you have a topic of conversation."

Midge nodded and smiled. "You know, I felt almost over prepared for it because I knew they were all going to say we should wait until spring, that we needed more time to prepare. Even Charlie says that. But, you see, I have a special reason for wanting to get it done now." Her look was quite mysterious and James raised an eyebrow and waited.

"Midge finally laughed and waved her hand. "Oh dear, it's only that there might be some property coming onto the market and I want to see what the potential revenues from our cook-off might be. I want to see if it's even feasible to think about negotiating a deal. It's all quite pie-in-the-sky, not worth talking about yet," she said merrily.

Midge glanced out the window and indeed the sky did seem to be clearing. "I almost wish it wouldn't be suitable for golfing for some reason," she sighed.

James swung his legs out of bed. "You know how you are when you tackle a project, darling. You get single-minded. And it sounds to me that the cooking competition is complicated and you have good reason to get focused. If Charlie has doubts about the viability of your schedule, you'd best pay attention."

Midge frowned. "Perhaps. Perhaps it's the combination of that, your health…and my unfounded reluctance to have lunch with Heather."

She rose from the couch and put her arms around his pajama-clad trunk. "Please do take it easy today and come home early. No plans for this weekend, no matter how good the weather is…and no matter who asks. I mean it, James. You really do need to take care of yourself."

James leaned down and kissed the top of her tousled head. He was feeling better now that he was standing and the urge to crawl back into their huge, comfortable bed was passing. Instead of answering, he gave Midge a hard squeeze, enjoying as always, the softness of her breasts just below his sternum and the feel of her head nestled on his chest. *She feels both fragile and resilient at the same time,* he thought, pleased with his perception. But to her he said, "Actually I'm starting to feel pretty good. The coffee helped and the shower will make a new man out of me. You've got plenty to worry about today. Scratch me off the list."

Midge stepped out of their embrace and looked up at him. She knew from their many years together that it would be useless to press her point. Instead she said demurely, "Yes, dear. I'll go and start your shower."

At the doorway, she turned and smiled. "I just thought of something. If you don't mind, Hank can drop me off at the clubhouse after he drops you at work. I was thinking about driving myself today, but if Hank is free, that would be wonderful. He could wait for me at the club and then we could pick you up at the office and come home."

James thought for a moment and then a light dawned. *Damn! This is one clever, manipulative woman. If she picks me up after her golf game, it means I'd be leaving the office about 4 o'clock; just what she wants.*

He nodded his head and chuckled in acquiescence. "I'll start the shower. You call Peggy and see what can be arranged, my dear but conniving wife."

Midge smiled sweetly as she brushed past him, not at all chagrined about being caught. *It's for a very good cause,* she told herself as she picked up the phone.

After Hank and Midge dropped a still somewhat subdued James Whipple Tyler III off in front of Zitec, Midge's day began to pick up pace and didn't slacken until Hank open the rear door of the Mercedes and she slipped wearily in, allowing him to deposit her bag and clubs in the trunk. She leaned back and closed her eyes. "What a day!" She said aloud entirely to herself, as Hank was closing the trunk and could not possibly hear her.

She sighed, sank deeper into the cushions, and rubbed her hand across her forehead wondering why she felt so depleted. *It can't be the time with the Andersons; that turned out to be quite pleasant.*

She had been very anxious about seeing Heather and yet, Heather seemed very glad to see her and was still expressing appreciation of having been invited to the weekend party on Faith.

"Rescued from a weekend of total boredom!" Heather had declared, reaching over to cover Midge's hand with her own. "And just ask Mother how I absolutely despise being bored."

They had all laughed and lunch progressed amicably, Tucker's name came up only once in passing and that was not until Midge and Elaine had finished their nine holes and went to find Heather, still on the courts, playing flawless tennis. She looked graceful and fit in her simple white, traditional tennis dress. Her opponent was an ageless, supple man of tremendous energy. Hair white, skin turned to leather by years in the sun, he returned stroke for stroke, volley for volley, lob for lob. Midge found herself fascinated by the intensity of the play. *It's almost sensual,* she thought.

"Elaine," she finally whispered, "I had no idea Heather could play so well. And who is that man?"

Elaine smiled proudly at Midge's quietly murmured appreciation of her daughter's skill and then shrugged. "I don't know who he is, probably just someone who signed up to play an advanced game. He might even be a reciprocal."

"Well," Midge declared, "they are simply tremendous together."

Finally, one of the man's net-skimming, cross-court drives touched the net, popped up, faltered and fell across to the court. Heather was there and with posed control, feathered the ball back to his side, dropping it softly, just over the net. He could only stand in the backcourt, defeated but seemingly elated by the quality of the play. He hastened to the net, a smile stretching on his face to shake her hand while the two women watched.

"Really, Elaine, I am so impressed. Heather is a beautifully accomplished player!" Midge said sincerely, awe evident in her voice.

"Yes," with just a touch of materialism in her voice, Elaine said, "we've been told she could be quite successful playing competitively. She has both the talent and the drive." There was a slight pause as if Elaine had gotten lost in a thought, before she continued. "But of course, it wouldn't do, would it? All that publicity, the invasion of one's private life, the attendant commercialism," she grimaced unconsciously and said grimly, "No, it simply wouldn't do."

Midge looked at her golfing partner sharply. She definitely could see Elaine's point. Why did she think there was much left unsaid? *Good heavens,* she chided herself, *stop looking for mysteries about Heather!* Then she looked up just in time to notice the fact that at the end of the congratulatory handshake, the opponents seemed reluctant to end it and let each other's fingers drift lightly, touching from palm to fingertip. She shook herself, irritated by her own over-active imagination.

Heather, turned away, spotted them and strode to the fence, perspiration tracking from her headband, down her temples, dripping from her chin. Her makeup however, including her lipstick, was perfect. *How DOES she do that?* Midge wondered to herself, even as her voice rose in admiration. "Heather, now I know why you only had a small salad for lunch. That was simply splendid play!"

Heather leaned her racket against the fence, the hard light of competition still gleaming in her eyes, the smile on her face almost feral. "Thank you," she said softly and both the tone and the words were at odds with her face. Her ragged breathing calmed and her face lost the look of conquest. "So," she said, "are you two on your way home?" At their affirmative nods, she smiled. "I'm going to play this gentleman one more set, if he's up to it." Then she turned sincere eyes on Midge and said, "Thank you for coming. Perhaps we can do this again."

Midge waved her hand. "No, dear, don't thank me. It was delightful. I enjoy playing with your mother, even though she always beats me. And I enjoy the opportunity to play this course. Thank you for arranging it."

It was then, as the two older ladies walked away from the fence that Heather called, "Remember, Mother, I'm using the Friday concert tickets. Tucker is going to pick me up about 5:45, we'll do the concert and then we'll have a late dinner at Le Montrechet."

Did Elaine look momentarily surprised? Midge thought so, but couldn't be positive. What Elaine said was, "Thank you for reminding me, darling. Perhaps when you to come for the tickets, you two could stay long enough to have a cocktail with your father and me."

Heather laughed lightly and said smoothly, "Yes, of course, I've already planned it that way."

Slowly Midge brought herself back to the present and chided herself for being such a suspicious busybody though her last thought to herself was, *However, I'm certain Heather told me she was having a lesson and that man may be teaching her something, but it's not tennis!* Then she began to think about her husband. She reached for the car phone to call and let him know they were on their way. She hadn't thought much about James' health all day and felt a sudden clutch as she remembered.

But, James declared himself fine as he sank into the leather cushions of the Mercedes. Still Midge wondered. She noticed he seemed quite content to leave work early and hoped it was a sign that he planned to take sensible care of himself. She told him about her day, as he lay, head canted back, eyes closed, resting against the smooth, coolness of the cushions, trying to ignore the fact that his tiredness persisted.

He opened his eyes and looked at Midge. "By God, but Tucker and I pinned things down today. I talked to the U.S. Ambassador in Chile as well as the Chilean Ambassador living in D.C. As you'd expect, the U.S. Ambassador was quite guarded. If we do this, he's going to have to take some licks from other private U.S. investment interests that want to go down there. They aren't going to like the idea of us coming in to help local business at all. They'll see it as cutting into their private profits playground." A spark showed briefly in his eyes. "The ambassador from Chile is flying down from Washington tomorrow to meet with me privately, one-on-one, no intermediaries. He's excited." James chuckled and let his head fall back against the cushion again. "You can bet he's got his organization doing a check on us that will turn up every wart and wrinkle in the company," he said comfortably. "I didn't promise him anything. I just explained how our organization worked and told him we were thinking of expanding from Europe and Asia to South America." He laughed again. "So, darling, I am going to work tomorrow, before you even ask, but I will promise to take the afternoon off. And I will retire early tonight. How's that?"

Patting his knee, Midge admitted, "Probably the best deal I can get you to cut. Besides, I can see why you find this stuff with Chile fascinating. One's image gets skewed by the bungling of Allende, Pinochet's brutality and pictures of military strongmen with blood on their hands."

He smiled and gave her hand a squeeze. It always surprised him to find out how much Midge knew about a variety of things: philosophy, history, religion, international politics, psychology. It wasn't a deep scholarly knowledge, but it was a functional, working knowledge and it made her an excellent conversationalist.

"Well, as a matter of fact," according to Tucker's research, it was Pinochet, along with a little behind the scenes U.S. policymaking, who encouraged free-market capitalism and also scheduled a fairly-run, open election. He smiled and for the first time there was a hint of energy in his voice. "Not something an authoritarian dictator normally does, especially since he was on the ballot and lost."

"Fascinating, isn't it?" "Don't you wonder what the ambassador will be like?" She asked innocently.

Chapter Twenty-six

Dawn sat at her desk pondering how much better she felt since she and her mother had talked. Her mother's degree had been in home economics, not psychology, but her wisdom and her knowledge of human nature made her a natural born counselor.

She sighed deeply; it was neat to be feeling more herself. If she reached for it, she could still feel that confused, empty spot, but mostly she felt ready to take control, to get on with things, to stop moping and take action.

"The thing is, Dawn," her mother said, "you may never understand what happened. It may have just been in your head and it may not have. What seems clear, from what you say, is that you feel you have been the object of a mysterious injustice."

Her mother didn't use the word victim, but Dawn filled that word in for herself and then things started falling into place. She had been feeling just like an unfortunate victim, like everything was beyond her control and she had to take what life dished out.

Thoughts turned inward, she remembered in her practicums, all the clients she had worked with who had just that same attitude. She looked at her mother and said, "Yuck!"

Then she had turned to her mom, eyes shining. "Mom, you don't have to say another word. I know exactly where you're heading. You might not use the jargon, but you are going to say exactly what I would say to a client." She kissed her mother soundly and jumped up. "I'm off to make a plan," she called over her shoulder.

Already she had finished writing to Deborah, a short newsy letter, thanking her for the shared time, asking that regards be given to her parents and to Rob. She had looked at the pictures as she enclosed them and sealed the envelope. *That's exactly how they should look if they are in love,* she decided.

Then she pulled out the pictures set aside to send to Tucker and studied them, trying to be objective, and sighed. *Objectivity sucks! He and Heather look perfect together! But,* she thought, *if Tucker Jones had his arm around me, I'd hope the look on my face would be more like Deb's. Heather looks like she owns him.* Resolutely, she turned the photo upside down and pulled a fresh sheet of stationary towards her.

Last night she had spent long sleepless hours deciding what she would write. It had to be simple and it had to be the truth.

Dear Tucker, she wrote, in her clear script,

> *I decided you might enjoy having this*
> *picture of Heather and yourself and the*
> *one of Heather in her new suit. I thought*
> *they turned out well.*

She stopped and looked at the picture again. These next lines were important ones.

> *Tucker, I want to thank you one more*
> *time for stopping to help me. I will be forever*
> *sorry that I called you James Bond.*
> *I confess that I very much liked being*
> *carried up and down the stairs…*

She started to finish the sentence there, but instead, remembering her goal of absolute clarity, added:

> *… in your arms. I can see, especially once I*
> *knew about Heather, why you felt the need*
> *to keep a distance from me.*
> *Evidently, you are more perceptive than I*
> *thought a person could be. But Tucker, if it*
> *would be at all possible, I would still like to*
> *be friends. On your terms is fine.*

Dawn reread what she had written. *I guess that's what I wanted to say, she thought glumly.* Then she added:

> *Please give Heather my regards and tell*
> *her I still think it is she who does the bathing*
> *suit the honor.*
>
> *Dawn*

Sealing the flap on the envelope, Dawn decided she felt better. Now she could write a cheerful, long-winded letter to the Tyler household. She looked at the pictures she was sending them, the ones that had caused her mother's unreadable look.

She had finally asked her mother about it. Barbara laughed and shook her head as if to shake off the thought. "It was just that I keep remembering James and Midge as they were in college. In your pictures I am forced to see them, and thus myself, as we really are...old! And it made me a little sad that time was passing so quickly and that we'd been able to share so little of it. She looked at her daughter and smiled. "Midge Tyler has the capacity to be the most manipulative person I know...though always for a good cause or reason as far as I know. I think it's because she wants the whole world to live happily ever after, and in that, she reminds me of you."

Tucker drove homeward through the heavy traffic, trying to unwind. The meeting and Mr. Tyler's focus on Chile had been stimulating. The mission to get the box from his parents' house had been draining. He tried to keep his concentration on his driving although every so often his thoughts would skip ahead to what the rest of the day held in store for him. He needed to make himself sit at the computer. *Odd,* he thought, *I can't recall ever being reluctant to use my computer. It is one of the things I enjoy most. Research is the thing I do best, besides being an accurate objective listener,* he thought wryly.

Then, when he was certain he was ready for his next meeting with Mr. Tyler, he was going to have another, calmer he hoped, run. After which, he would eat a good dinner and spend time going through the box. He gripped the wheel, remembering the willpower it took to keep his feet on the path towards the caretakers' cottage. He also remembered the wash of relief he had felt when no one had answered his knock.

As he stood waiting for the door to be answered, he realized that the loud rock music he had been hearing was coming from the "recovery room" where Ethan and he had carefully trimmed dead blossoms and put the spent plants in the soil for a rest. He'd gritted his teeth. He hated the music, but somehow it made it easier to turn from the door that he'd so often burst through and go in search of Thomas.

Thomas looked up as the draft of cold air entered the room with Tucker's entry. He jumped to quell the music, looking extremely uncomfortable and very guilty about something.

Tucker shut the door carefully against the offending draft of cold air and smiled a reassuring smile as he advanced down the row. "Hello, Thomas," he said extending his hand. "I've been looking for you."

"For me, sir?" His face had grown even redder.
"Yes," said Tucker. "I wanted to tell you in person how nicely you're keeping the grounds." He leaned back against the potting table and made himself look casually around the long room, waiting for Thomas to relax a little and then realized the source of the man's guilt and discomfort. He had been reading. Tucker couldn't tell what. From the thickness of it, it could've been a textbook.

"Um, thank you, sir. It was good of you to notice."

Tucker could see the younger man was struggling to think of something further to say and failing.

"Well, I know you expressed concern about your lack of knowledge of horticulture and so I just wanted to be sure and tell you that I think the place looks fine." He spread his hands. "I don't mean to intrude."

"Intrude? Oh, no, sir, I don't think you're intruding." Thomas looked at him earnestly, shrugged his shoulders and decided to fess up. "You surprised me, that's all…caught me reading. I'm enrolled in the summer term, trying to pass chemistry."

Tucker nodded, his suspicion had been correct. "It gets a little slow on a rainy day," he said mildly, "especially if you've been keeping up the greenhouse, as I noticed you

311

have. I've spent a lot of time in here and working on these grounds, so it means something to me to see them in good repair."

Thomas looked at him directly for the first time, interest in his eyes. "Did you, sir?"

Tucker nodded. "Most of my time as a boy." Then he straightened up and said, "Well, thank you again for the care you have been taking. Some sunnier day perhaps we could walk the grounds together and you can show me what's new."

"Sure thing. I'd like that. Thank you, sir," said Thomas and for a moment Tucker thought he was going to salute.

He smiled, walked to the door and then turned and said, "If I remember correctly, the cottage with a fire going is a much cozier place for reading on such a day. I'd try it if I were you...and, Thomas, please try calling me Tucker. Every time you call me sir, I feel a bald spot coming on."

This time Thomas did raise three fingers in salute. "Right! Okay! Will do! Thanks again, Tucker."

Actually, thought Tucker as he drove, *visiting the 'recovery room" wasn't so bad. I think it was easier because I ended up focusing on Thomas's discomfort instead of my own. It was certainly much easier than digging into that box is going to be,* he thought grimly to himself as he turned onto his street and pushed the entry button for underground parking.

As usual, when Tucker entered his condo, carrying the box as if it were full of something either deadly or very valuable, the red light signaling telephone messages was blinking. He set down the box and went to listen. When he heard Heather's voice wondering politely if he had gotten her message regarding dinner after the concert, he slapped himself on the side of the head. *How did my well organized mind forget that detail?* he wondered, chagrined that he had allowed such a breach of manners. Clearly, a sincere apology was in order. He dialed her number, and was relieved to hear her cool voice answer.

"Heather, this is Tucker," he said in a rush. "I sincerely apologize for not returning your call sooner. I thought your plan was an excellent one. Please allow me to make amends by picking YOU up and taking YOU to dinner at Le Montrechet before the concert."

There was a pause at the other end of the line while Heather decided what tone to take. That Tucker had neglected to return her call and admitted that he had actually forgotten was, in her opinion, an almost unforgivable breach in etiquette. *A simple white lie would have been far more complimentary. Perhaps this man wasn't quite the catch I thought.*

Then she remembered the effort she had already put into their forthcoming date, the fact that she had made public that they were going out Friday night and decided to steer a middle course.

"Well, Tucker, it certainly was not very flattering of you to forget. However, if you are extremely charming and attentive on Friday, I may forgive you, especially since you have chosen one of my favorite restaurants in which to make your amends." She kept her voice low, throaty, but withheld real warmth.

Tucker got her message and felt his embarrassment increase. Suddenly he could think of nothing more to say. The picture of Thomas filled his mind. He thought he knew just how the man had been feeling. She continued, not noticing his silence. "It might be nice to dine after the concert. Why don't you make reservations for 9:00 o'clock?"

Thomas still strong in his mind, Tucker found himself saying, "Right. Okay. Will do." And was somewhat shocked to find himself raising a three-finger salute in the silent air of his living room. He tried for levity. "Rest assured that I will not forget to make the reservations."

"Fine," she said simply. She'd made the point. Now she could allow her voice to soften, "and Tucker...I am looking forward to seeing you, though in the interest of time, it would be best if we met at my parents. I know they would enjoy meeting you." She allowed her voice to warm one more notch. "Perhaps you might schedule in time for cocktails. Father loves to have guests in for cocktails."

Tucker agreed meekly, confirmed directions to the Anderson estate, said, "Wonderful, Heather. See you there about 5:45. Have a good evening." For some reason, he couldn't wait to end the conversation.

313

Tucker replaced the receiver feeling guilty and out of sorts, which made him most unprepared for the next message. "Hello, Tucker. This is Allison McCall and today is Wednesday. My mom said I could call you, but that if you couldn't call back before 8:30, you couldn't call at all, because she says it's a school night and I have to be in bed by then. I hope you get home because I want to talk about our trip to the zoo."

Tucker played her message again and chuckled. *Was I ever filled with that much youthful optimism?* He wondered. He played the message a third time. It was a voice full of innocence, confidence and sunshine, he decided as he pushed the buttons that would connect him.

Belatedly, he looked at his watch, knowing it was fairly early but wondering if he was about to disturb the McCall's dinner. Evidently not, Allison answered after the first ring.

"Oh, Tucker," she exclaimed happily when she heard his voice. "I have been sitting here right by the phone. I just knew you'd call back. Mom said I shouldn't get my hopes up but that if you did call, I should remember to ask you if it would be an inconvenience to talk."

He could clearly picture the small energy bundle talking earnestly into the receiver, pom-poms rigidly at attention, everything else mobile. He smiled and hastened to assure her that he did have time to talk and that he especially wanted to talk with her.

"Well," she said with evident satisfaction, "that's what I thought! Now Tucker, don't be worried by this rain. Mom and I watch the 5:00 o'clock news to get the weather forecast. The weather woman said that the weekend would be much nicer." She stopped suddenly, evidently temporarily out of words.

"Actually, Allison," Tucker said sincerely, "I was worrying about it a bit this morning. Not that I mind going to the zoo in the rain, but so often the animals I particularly like are not out and about on a rainy day. Thank you for the report."

With a big sigh of relief at having delivered him from worry, she said, in what he was sure she considered her grand voice, "You are entirely welcome." Then after a tiny pause, she said in her normal voice, "What did you want to talk to me about?"

"Oh, mostly about details; you know…times, train schedules, whether you had a favorite place near the train station to eat. I am completely at your disposal, madam," he said trying his best for his own grand voice. Playacting with a child was a new experience and made him glad only Allison could hear him.

She admitted candidly that she would need to check with her mother about the time and the train schedules and it was on the tip of his tongue to volunteer to use his computer to solicit the train information and decided just in time the Kathryn might want her daughter to be responsible for those details. Instead he said, "Well, if I can do anything to help, just let me know. I will be coming for my Friday massage tomorrow, perhaps I will see you then and you'll have the details down pat. In the meantime, rest assured that my carriage will be full of gas and awaiting your disposal on Saturday morning. And, if you do not have a particular breakfast spot in mind, perhaps you would allow me to surprise you."

"Oh, Tucker, I do so love surprises! Yes, you certainly may!" It was the grand voice again. He wondered with sudden embarrassment if Kathryn was listening to all of this.

They said awkward but merry goodbyes and Tucker hung up and looked at his phone speculatively. It was hard not to contrast the phone calls of the "two women in his life."

He stretched and felt suddenly light of heart. The box still sat squatly significant on his counter. But, he could legitimately block it from his mind. It was in his plan for the evening, but first he needed do a couple of hours work on the computer, take a run and eat. All in all, he admitted, the day had gone far better and had been less painful than he had any right to expect. Unfortunately, the man of splendid memory and total recall had forgotten his promise to call Le Montrechet.

Chapter Twenty-seven

Friday morning, when Tucker arrived at Dr. Beemer's office, Mavis noted how tired he looked. His appearance was as neat as ever, his hair carefully combed, but his lovely brown eyes looked like burned out cinders and there were dark circles under them. She chose not to make comment, simply greeted him in her usual cheerful, breezy manner, found his chart, put him in one of the examination rooms and went to find the doctor.

The doctor was in the process of writing a prescription for a boy with a nasty bruise on his forehead and a terrible scrape along the entire left side of his jaw. He was saying in a gentle voice, as much to the mother as to the boy, "Sometimes when we try new things they backfire, don't they? But, usually, if you learn something, and no one gets seriously hurt, it's worth it."

After they left, he looked at Mavis and said, shaking his burly head, "He's lucky. Don't kids do the damnedest things? Whenever I think I've seen everything, Johnny Wright shows up after trying to hook his Shetland to his wagon and making a cart horse out of him."

He closed his eyes for a moment, picturing how the event must've transpired. "What's next?" He murmured more to himself than to Mavis.

"Actually, Tucker Jones is next, and he looks like he hasn't slept for a while," she said softly in response.

The doctor sighed and took the chart. "Tucker Jones! Wonder how he's getting along with our Kathryn?" He smiled at Mavis. "It was your idea, you know. You said, 'If it was a son of mine I'd make him take a long soak and then I'd give him a rub...' or something like that, remember?"

She nodded. "I do." She turned to precede the doctor from the room and threw over her shoulder, "How could I forget when I can still count on one hand the times you've actually taken my good advice! No wonder you're

316

such a confirmed, grouchy bachelor!" She smiled with satisfaction when she heard him snort.

When Tucker saw Dr. Beemers, he smiled his usual engaging grin. "Hello doctor. Here I am."

The doctor took one look at Tucker, feared the worst and barked, "Obviously, you haven't followed through on the massages, you look like hell."

Tucker's grin broadened. "Sorry, doctor, you're wrong. I've had a total of four massages; have one scheduled for this afternoon and three scheduled for next week. Besides that, I've been asked by Kathryn's daughter to accompany them to the zoo on Saturday. You could say I've become a family friend."

Beemers digested the news first with poorly concealed surprise and then in a pleased silence, giving a throaty "Harrumph!" to cover his emotion.

"Well then," he said gruffly, "get on the table and lie face down so I can stick my finger into your ribs. Then we'll do an x-ray and some tests of flexibility. You been running?"

Tucker nodded and did as he was told. Silently the doctor prodded and measured, took the x-rays and put Tucker through a series of bending and stretching maneuvers, saying little. When he was done, he sighed with satisfaction but said, matter-of-factly, "Well, we won't know until the x-rays are developed, but on the whole, if you aren't experiencing any pain, I'd say you are doing relatively well. Certainly, you are more flexible." He was quiet for a moment then continued. "I must admit, I'm surprised. You really don't look so hot."

Tucker nodded. "I know. I was up most of the night, but it was by choice." He hastened to add. Suddenly, he had the overpowering urge to tell this giant anchor of his childhood of his resolution to go through the box. Without preamble he said, "You see, I have this cardboard box that I put things into when they made me sad as a child, mostly stuff from Ethan and Mary."

He looked the older man straight in the eye. "As you know, I am not big on dealing with emotional pain. But on Wednesday I visited my parents and retrieved the box from the closet of my bedroom. I spent last night forcing myself to go through it." He turned his eyes on the doctor showing

317

him two undisguised pools of pain. "I decided to try and make some changes. I really don't know what they are, but I figured I might find some answers in that box."

Dr. Beemers found he had been holding his breath. He let it out with a whoosh. Never before had Tucker voluntarily allowed him to see that shuttered anguish. "Did you? Did you find answers?"

Tucker smiled sadly. "No, there weren't any answers, because I don't know the questions. I looked in the Yellow Pages for Dr. van Castle's number, but it wasn't there. I figured he might be the person who would be best at helping identify the questions."

Tucker gave a small shrug and a rueful smile ghosted in his eyes. "For a while I tried using my computer as my therapist, but that didn't really work very well. In fact, it made me feel pretty crazy." His words that had first tumbled over themselves, slowed, softened and finally halted in a whisper.

Son-of-a-bitch! Son-of-a-bitch! The words rang with silent vehemence inside Dr. Beemers' mind as he quickly absorbed the disclosure. *How much pain can one human being absorb and continue to carry?* He wondered to himself. But to Tucker he said, "Dr. van Castle is still in the area. In fact, we still see each other on a regular basis. It's just that he's no longer seeing clients in private practice. He's now teaching at Yale."

They sat looking at one another quietly, the naked vulnerability on Tucker's face made the doctor suddenly realize that if ever Tucker were to get the help he needed, now would be the time. Coming to a sudden decision he stood and said, "Excuse me for just a few minutes, Tucker. Get your clothes on. I need to make a phone call."

Tobin van Castle's secretary was reluctant to put the call through as he was holding office hours and didn't like to be disturbed when meeting with students. However, Dr. Beemers identified himself and convinced her that it was an emergency.

When the psychiatrist's crisp, still boyish voice came on the line; the doctor bowed his gray head in relief. Quickly, he apologized and then stated his concerns about Tucker. "You know how you are forever talking about seizing the 'therapeutic moment'? Well, I think Tucker is having one and I don't know what to do. He said he'd tried to look up your number in the Yellow Pages so I think he's willing to talk to someone."

On the other end of the line the psychiatrist was sitting very still, listening intently. When his friend paused, he said, "Excuse me for a moment, Jeff." Then he turned to the graduate student sitting by his desk. "Marshall, would you mind waiting outside for just a moment. I'll apologize profusely when you return," he said. The young man nodded and began gathering his papers, preparing to leave, saying, "Aw, it's okay, Dr. van Castle, I only had a couple minutes left and I already know what I've got to do."

Returning his attention to the phone, Tobin paused a long moment and then said, "Jeff, you have no idea, because I'm so well-trained to keep my voice from showing emotion, what I'm feeling right now. Tucker Jones haunts my dreams. If that kid sued me for malpractice, I wouldn't even contest it. I'd like to talk to him if it's possible."

Beemers sighed in relief. "Hell, yes, it's possible. I'll go get him. Whatever you say is going to be better than what I probably would've said. Kids having pony wrecks is much more my specialty."

"Don't underrate yourself, my friend." Dr. van Castle ran a hand through his blonde tangle of curls. "You are the man who probably kept Tucker from suicide, remember? I'm the one who let him down and I'm going to tell him so. Then I'm going to ask him if we can meet on a regular basis, no charge, as much for me as it is for him," Tobin said gravely. "And I mean that."

Jeff Beemers felt a sense of well-being wash through him. "Yes, you've mentioned similar feelings before. It's one reason I felt free to call you. Hang on, I'll go and fetch Tucker."

He seated Tucker behind the big cherry wood desk, ignoring his puzzled look and put the receiver in his hand. "Dr. van Castle." He said gruffly, beetling his brows as if daring Tucker to refuse the call. He needn't have worried. The young man grasped the receiver in both hands, as though it were a life preserver and raised it to his ear. As Beemers made for the doorway and pulled the door shut behind him he could hear Tucker say, in a voice filled with an unknown quality, "Hello, Dr. van Castle. This is Tucker Jones."

"Hello, Tucker." said the familiar, unpretentious voice. "It's good to hear from you, although for a moment I must confess I was a bit startled to hear a man's voice. I guess I forgot what the years do." Tobin went on without pause. "Listen, Tucker, I want to thank you for being willing to talk with me. My guess is that you were pretty mad at me for a very long time...and I think I deserve your anger."

Tucker was silent. He had started to deny the psychiatrist's words and then with an honest candor he didn't know he had within him said, "I don't know for sure, Dr. van Castle. If I was angry, I don't think I allowed myself to know it. I can't remember feeling angry. But I did take the book you gave me and put it in the back of my closet and never looked at it again until last night. So, it seems like I might've been. But I really can't say for sure."

On the other end of the line, Tobin was trying to imagine what the youth, grown to manhood, looked like. He heard the struggle for truth. *The voice sounds exhausted,* he thought.

"Listen, Tucker," he said, hoping the sincerity in his voice carried across the line, "I'd really like to see you. I've carried your memory like an abscess on my conscience, always wondering, but never knowing, if I had let you down. In all my years, I have never met anyone as strong-minded as you. I suspect I let you dupe me. I think you were testing our friendship and that I failed the test. In retrospect, I was not proud of most of the work we did together; although at the time I remember feeling quite smug."

Dr. van Castle, sitting alone in his cluttered office put his hand over his eyes as if blocking a glaring sun. "I guess what I'm saying, Tucker, is that I know you, know some of your issues and now that I'm older and wiser, might be of some help. I'd like the chance."

Tucker took a deep breath. The doctor's word shocked him. He saw the man as invincible, incapable of making a mistake. What was he saying? He heard the words, but what was the message? His tired mind couldn't seem to comprehend. Dr. Beemers said Dr. van Castle no longer took clients, yet this man seemed to be saying just the opposite.

Finally, he said tiredly, "Sorry, Dr. van Castle, I'm a little confused. I thought Dr. Beemers said you no longer saw clients."

"Actually, I don't Tucker. I'm at the University, teaching now. But you are an exception. I'm doing this as much for me as for you and if I could have my way, we'd meet several times a week until you were really ready to call it quits. Jeff said you are ready to try some new things. It might be good to have someone like me in your corner." He laughed ruefully. "I do understand quite a lot about human behavior you know."

There was silence which Dr. van Castle honored even as it lengthened. He could only imagine the thoughts tumbling through Tucker's head. He had no way of knowing that Tucker was sitting rigidly in the comfortable overstuffed chair, remembering snatches of conversations he'd had with the man who made everyone on the psychiatric ward feel just a little better by his mere presence. That the man had been worrying about him all these years didn't seem possible. But he had said it, so it must be true

"Dr. van Castle," Tucker found he had to clear his throat to find a speaking passage around the lump of pain caused by the fear he was about to share. "I don't want to do this...talk to you, I mean. I'm afraid you'll find that I'm either crazy or else that there is a part of me missing and unrecoverable."

Dr. van Castle digested and interpreted Tucker's words carefully and when he spoke, it was to the point. "Tucker, if you are afraid the missing part is your heart, you're dead wrong. Your trouble is a heart that is so big you felt you had to build a wall around it to protect it. Now, for some reason, you seem to be finding the courage to at least think about dismantling that wall. We can do that together if you'd like--one block at a time."

Tucker sighed in exhausted resignation. "Yes, I guess that is what I'd like. I know for sure I don't want to go on the way I am, and my boss told me the same thing you did. He said I needed to learn to trust people."

Van Castle closed his eyes. Then he quickly checked his appointment book and looked at his watch. "Are you free for lunch, Tucker? We could grab deli sandwiches, sit in the University Park enjoying the sunshine, catch up a bit and perhaps make a plan. I'm big on making plans, if you'll remember."

For the first time he heard Tucker's soft chuckle. "Yes, I remember and yes, I'll come. I think if you are in the clinical psychology building, I can find you. Just give me a time."

Tucker could hear the phone starting to ring as he put the key in the lock to his door and he hurried to answer it before the machine picked it up, noting with surprise that there were four other calls already on the machine.

It was Midge Tyler. Tucker raised his eyebrows at the note of anxiety mixed with frustration evident in her voice. "Oh, Tucker, I'm so glad you're finally home. I've been calling you frantically all morning. You can probably ignore most of those other calls recorded on your machine. They are probably all from me."

"Mrs. T," Tucker said, alarmed by her tone, "is everything all right? You sound upset."

"I am upset, Tucker, and it is all James's fault!" She rushed on. "I suppose you noticed that he was not feeling well on Thursday. I tried to get him to stay home from work today, but of course he wouldn't. He said he was fine, but he really isn't. His energy is low and he has very little appetite. But he said he had to meet the ambassador from Chile and then would come home. Then he called two hours ago to say he was feeling much better, which I seriously doubt, and that I should plan on having houseguests for the weekend--the ambassador and some people from an organization called SOFA, whatever in the world that is. I know he told me, but I was too upset by then to remember."

As she rattled on, Tucker thought, *SOFA? What organization would that be?* Then a light went on and he whistled silently through his teeth. SOFOFA, Chile's powerful industrial association! *How had Mr. Tyler put that together so quickly?* He wondered.

Midge drew breath but didn't pause, "I couldn't believe what he was saying to me and I'm afraid I got quite sharp with him. But you know James, when he makes up his mind; he just digs in his heels. He said the South America project was far more important than some little bug

322

and that it would be a quiet weekend and that I worry too much. But Tucker, I know you know more about the project than anyone..."

Tucker, with a sinking heart knew exactly what she was going to ask of him. His plans to spend the day with the sunshine smile and pom-pom hairdo flitted quickly through his mind.

"...and I know you have a date with Heather for the concert and dinner at Le Montrechet tonight, but could you possibly drive out on Saturday morning?"

When Tucker heard the words Le Montrechet, his tired brain froze. He had completely forgotten his promise to Heather to make the reservation. He looked at his watch. There was no way in the world he was going to get a reservation at this late date, not on a Friday night after a concert. He dragged his mind back to what Midge was saying. "Excuse me, Mrs. T," he said without apology, "you'll have to repeat your last few lines, I'm afraid I wasn't listening."

His words stopped Midge in midsentence. *Tucker, the consummate listener, not listening?* That was most unusual. "Tucker, dear, are you coming down with something too?"

"No, I'm fine. You just reminded me that I neglected to make that reservation at Le Montrechet and I got distracted. So, you'll have to repeat your last few lines," he said again, with still no hint of apology or humor to soften the bluntness of the faux pas.

"Forgot to make a reservation? Good heavens, Tucker!" Midge exclaimed, temporarily distracted from her own problems. "That is not at all like you, dear! Are you certain you are not ill?" Her concern wrapped around him like a down comforter.

"Yes, I'm certain. I am a bit tired, but I feel fine. Now help me out with what you were saying," he said striving to concentrate.

"Well, I guess I was asking you to drive out on Saturday morning to spend the weekend and help James and me entertain our guests." She laughed self-consciously. "Actually, I think I was babbling somewhat incoherently. I find myself somewhat distressed and a bit undone."

Tucker drew a deep breath, rocking back and forth on the balls of his feet, wiping imaginary dust from the spotless countertop and suddenly Dr. van Castle's earnest, boyish face presented itself, one eyebrow cocked. "Here you go, Tucker. Your opportunity to make the decision to do something you want to do over something someone else wants you to do. Can you do it?"

It's not that simple! Tucker groaned silently to the image. *But here goes.* He cleared his throat. "Truthfully, Mrs. T, I already have plans for Saturday, but if it would help, I would come out when I'm done, say late afternoon and stay until I leave for my parents' house on Sunday."

Midge was surprised at Tucker's tone. It was more than just tiredness. Something was different. For one thing, he had always been available when she'd invited him out on a Saturday. She wondered if Heather was the difference but decided not to pry. *Besides, I really don't even want to know. I've got too much on my mind to even think of things like that!* She thought with something close to panic.

"Oh, Tucker, if you would. I'll take any piece of you I can get. At this point, I'm not sure when they are due to arrive. Now that I've talked to you and am calmer, I'll call James back for details." She sighed, "Besides, I need you to talk to Charlie. He's not himself. I've not gone near the kitchen all day. Clarice, as she left today, declared he had been swearing in Chinese. I dread going in to tell him we're about to have a houseful of SOFAS." She laughed her old tinkling laugh and Tucker could tell she was rising to the occasion.

"Now, Mrs. T, you'd better not call them that even in jest. Right now, I'm not sure what the acronym SOFOFA stands for, but they are the group from whom I gleaned a great deal of my information for your husband. They have tremendous databanks and track the climate for successful investing as well as any conditions that affect the economics of Chile." He paused, thinking. *This is going to be a very interesting weekend!* He found himself wondering just exactly what Mr. Tyler had in mind. The cart seemed a little before the horse. Almost as an afterthought he asked, "Has Clifton been invited?"

"Why, I don't know dear. I'll ask James when I call. I do want to sound calm and organized when I talk to

Charlie. He puts up with this last-minute stuff all the time you know. Maybe that's why he seems so upset."

Tucker could tell from her tone that she was really worried. "I'll tell you what, Mrs. T--a man I respect very much would tell you the thing to do is ask. Ask before you worry yourself to death."

"Yes, dear, you are right as usual." Midge sighed and could feel herself actually growing calmer. "Tucker, you feel like my life raft for some reason. I think just hearing your voice steadied me. Bless you, dear."

"Well, sorry I can't be there the whole time, Mrs. T. And I thank you for reminding me about that reservation. I think Heather Anderson isn't going to take very kindly to the news, since she had to remind me once already."

It passed through Midge's mind to let Heather be furious with Tucker. *Perhaps it would cause her to lose interest.* But she pushed the thought away and said comfortingly, "Darling, don't worry. I can take care of your little oversight. What time would you like the reservation?"

As Tucker hung up the phone, he realized he had not even asked Midge how she could pull such strings. He hadn't the energy. *I'll remember to thank her profusely the next time we talk,* he thought as he walked woodenly towards the bedroom, loosening his tie as he went.

Vaguely, even in his state of near exhaustion, something pricked at his mind, something that made him feel those stabs of fear that signaled the nameless dread... Was it something Mrs. T had said? Firmly, as he slipped off his loafers and lay back, he blanked his mind. That Midge Tyler had started the phone conversation with concerns about the health of her husband was shoved with finality into the oblivion of his subconscious. With a final effort he set his wrist alarm and closed his eyes.

325

Chapter Twenty-eight

Tucker's alarm woke him from his catnap at 11:00 o'clock. He laid on the bed, fighting the urge to turn it off and return to that too brief, but blissful state of dreamless, sound slumber. Only with effort was he able to force himself to recall what had made him remember to set it in the first place. His recollection brought him quickly to full wakefulness. Dr. van Castle...Yale University. He was having lunch at University Park with Tobin van Castle. He swung his legs over the side of the bed and looked with distaste at his rumpled clothing. He hadn't even removed his tie or shoes and he felt smelly and unkempt. Quickly, he removed his clothes and headed for the shower. There was no way he was going to see the good doctor without a clear head and clean clothing, the meeting was too important.

As the water blasted him to full consciousness, he shook his head is if shaking off heavy chains. What a day this had already been and was going to continue to be...Dr. Beemers, Dr. van Castle, massage, Allison...a pleasant evening listening to good music and having dinner at Le Montrechet with Heather, thanks to Mrs. Tyler. *It would be nice to have had a longer nap*, he thought ruefully. The last thing he needed to do was look sleepy or inattentive in the company of Heather Anderson.

At 12:45 Tucker eased the Aston into the visitor parking lot and spent a moment looking at the formidable brick building that housed the clinical psychology department. He read his directions from Dr. van Castle yet another time and with a sigh of resolution climbed from the car. *In some ways,* he reflected, as he walked slowly towards the glass-fronted entry, *this is harder than retrieving the box.* This part of his past was not something he could thumb quickly past when the part got difficult. There was no way to close the cover and walk away to get control. This part of his past was a human being, in fact the human being that knew more about him than anyone. This person was likely to give him feedback, tell him things he didn't want to hear. *On the other hand,* the logical part of Tucker's brain thought, *you are a bit curious about meeting this man and you have decided to make some changes. Seeing him once, if that is what you choose, shouldn't be that traumatic should it?*

That logic got him through the door but sheer courage kept him there, made him give his name and make his request to see Dr. van Castle pleasantly to the very young receptionist and to take the hard vinyl bench, looking relaxed to the point of nonchalance.

Dr. van Castle found him there several minutes later, nose buried in a magazine. Tucker looked up quickly as the man rounded the corner and his first feeling was one of disbelief. He remembered a giant of a man, as big as Dr. Beemers, if not bigger. But he knew, when he stood, that he was going to be looking down at the top of the doctor's slightly thinning blonde curls. His second feeling was one of relief. The eager stride, the kind twinkle in the eyes and the welcoming, benevolent smile were all the same.

Somehow, he got to his feet and put out his hand in time to meet the other man's. They looked at each other wordlessly. Powerful emotions rocked them both. Tucker felt his throat close beyond any hope of squeezing out a greeting. He had the absurbed feeling that he was going to reach out and hug the man. And as if his mind had been read, Tobin van Castle did just that. It was brief and hard, and when he stepped back, Tucker noted with surprise that Dr. van Castle too felt the need to clear his throat several times before he could speak.

"Tucker, ah-hem, Tucker, ah-hem, I... Well..." Finally, he threw up his hands in a gesture Tucker remembered clearly. It meant the doctor's mind was working faster than his vocal cords.

Finally, at the same time the men found their voices and social graces. "Good to see you," was Tucker's contribution.

"You're looking well," was Tobin van Castle's.
Then, they'd just smiled and looked at each other for a long moment and as they looked some of the tension flowed away.

The doctor was the first to break the silence. He spoke not to Tucker, but to the riveted receptionist who was making no attempt to do other than watch the two men. "Sarah, this is my good friend, Tucker Jones, whom I have not seen for far too long. We're going for a late lunch and I may be a bit late for my 2:00 o'clock. But I promise, just a little late. Okay?"

Sarah felt her heart actually flutter as the tall and very handsome man leaned over the reception counter and offered his hand. "Very nice to meet you, Sarah. Thank you for lending me the good doctor for an hour." As they walked through the glass doors, Tobin chuckled. "Do you always have that effect on women?" He asked.

Tucker glanced at him and said, apparently with great sincerity, "What effect do you mean?"

The older man looked up at him. He noted the slight look of puzzlement on Tucker's face and decided to play the line straight. "I mean the effect of having them to wish for a mirror to check their lipstick, hair and necklines while conjuring romantic notions."

"Oh that effect. Yes, I suppose that's mostly true. Anyway, I'm asked to attend quite a few functions and ladies call me from time to time. My bosses' wife says she owes her status as famous hostess to me, but I think she's kidding."

Tucker's tone spoke volumes to the doctor. It seemed totally detached and quite analytic. Also, there was a touch of something akin to humbleness. *He's grown into a nerd who looks like Adonis,* was Tobin's quick analysis. Later that day he was to reflect just how simplistic first impressions could be.

It was a day of high clouds rushing in banks through the sky as though in close order drill. The passing of one formation left long moments of glorious warm sunshine before the next unit was called up to march. It was perfect weather, despite the light wind and sporadic cloud-induced coolness, for sitting at the little wood tables in the park and talking, talking, talking.

It seemed to Tucker, as he reflected on their time together, that he couldn't seem to stop talking. He didn't feel out of control, rather simply eloquent and that he had a lot to say to a very good listener. From time to time, the doctor would prompt a bit, but only with an "and then?" Or the old familiar command, "Tell me a little more about that." There was no notepad, no tape recorder, only two men at a picnic table, one munching slowly, listening, the other animated, sandwich still wrapped and totally ignored on the table in front of him.

"So," Tucker was saying, "that was behavior too crazy for me to ignore. I mean, I was literally out of control. I could tell there was just a very small piece of my mind hanging onto reality. I FELT crazy. I would've LOOKED crazy to anyone seeing me run that way."

The doctor listened quietly while Tucker went on to explain about the retrieval of the box, the circumstance of its having been buried in the closet, his sadness when the answers he hoped would come from the box didn't, and thus his decision to get some help. He sighed deeply and for the first time, paused and looked at the doctor, allowing him to see the inner anguish. "I told Dr. Beemers the reason I didn't find any answers in the box was that I didn't know the questions." He continued in a voice that died in almost a whisper.

When the doctor finally spoke, there was a dreamlike quality to his voice. It was a voice of fond remembering. "When you were a boy, I could generally tell when we were getting close to something you weren't ready to tackle, or perhaps had no intention of sharing. You'd say, in a most engaging, lighthearted way, 'Aw, Doc...' It was your very polite way of telling me to buzz off. You haven't said it even once today. But for old time sakes, let's keep that as your signal. But this time around, I want our relationship to be different. I don't want to be your therapist." He paused thinking exactly how to clarify his own intentions--saw the startled look in Tucker's eyes and rushed on.

"What I mean to say is, I'd rather be your mentor and I'll explain what I mean if you will relax and eat your sandwich while I talk, rather quickly, I might add. We've used up all my time."

The doctor smiled. "Here's the thought that struck me. You do have some of the symptoms of a person with poor mental health. Chronic insomnia for one thing and those feelings of an unknown dread sound like panic attacks to me. You are a man who makes a splendid living with your mind, have a wealth of information available on your computer. You have databases full of information on any aspect of psychology you'd care to name, reams of information on both a technical and practical level. But..." Here the doctor paused. "...but did you ever once try to do some self-help sort of stuff. I mean, of course, besides trying to talk to your ceiling via the computer?"

The younger man, listening intently, shook his head silently.

"Don't you find that interesting? What it says to me is that you didn't really want to solve the problems until now. Now, for whatever reason, you do. And, like I said on the phone, I know quite a bit about human behavior and I'd like to try to help you. But, I prefer my role to be...if not of mentor, then of informed friend. That way YOU are in control. My role would be to help you find out what you are ready to know. What do you think about that as a proposition?"

To his surprise, Tucker looked down and found he'd eaten every crumb of his corned beef sandwich. His throat felt dry, but he had also drunk his coffee. He simply nodded, unfolded his long legs from the bench and taking his empty cup, walked over to the drinking fountain. Once he'd had a long drink, he filled his cup and walked back to the quietly waiting doctor.

"Dry throat." He said smilingly, standing, looking down at the questioning blue eyes and what was indeed a small bald spot peeking through the fair curls. "I think I must have been holding my breath."

He drank deeply from his cup. When he lowered it, the doctor knew his reply before the younger man nodded his head. He could see a flicker of hope mixed in with a good dose of uncertainty.

"I think," said Tucker, "that I understand the proposition. If I do, it sounds really good. Although I would insist on paying you just as I would pay registration fees to any college class," he said, showing that he had indeed understood the concept.

"No! And don't try to change my mind on this, Tucker. Mentors don't charge for their services. In fact, this

330

is something I really would appreciate being able to do for…or should I say…WITH you."

Tucker looked steadily at the doctor and finally said, "Okay, professor. So tell me, how does it work? Do you give me assignments?"

The doctor nodded and they started strolling back towards the psychology building. "In a way, that will be true, but also true is that you will ask me if you need help in understanding a concept or perhaps a connection in your life and I will help you either with my own personal knowledge or perhaps help you identify the proper descriptors so you can access information on your own computer."

Tobin van Castle was talking in language Tucker readily understood. "Great. That's great. Tell me what to do first."

"Well, first, if you agree, I'll need to review my notes on your case and the next time we meet let's see if we can agree on a synthesis of those earlier years, your developmental years so to speak."

By then they had reached the front of the psychology department and, in fact, Tucker was just in the process of opening the inner door as Dr. van Castle was still holding open the outer door for some incoming students. Tucker was glad for the brief interlude. He felt awash with emotion, flooded and drained at the same time. Fear was followed closely by elation, elation by dread. How could the doctor be so matter-of-fact? He was talking about Tucker's life at a time so emotionally traumatic that it had caused him to consider suicide. *Do I really want to…have the strength to…dig through those memories?*

He felt a strong hand on his arm and looked down to see the doctor's right hand outstretched and waiting. He grasped it like a lifeline and felt connected as if by a cord.

"Think about it, Tucker. Don't decide now. This is not an easy journey I've suggested we take. It's liable to feel as though we are dragging out your insides."

"Yes," said Tucker honestly, "I was just thinking that. It's as if you've been reading my mind. I can remember when I was a boy, wondering seriously if you could really do that, you know."

331

Dr. van Castle smiled and looked at his watch sadly. "I'll tell you one thing I remember. I remember looking at my watch like this, at the end of our sessions and wishing I had just another few minutes...and that's just what I'm wishing now." He held out his hand again. "But I don't. Goodbye, Tucker, think on it."

Tucker smiled a smile that for the first time fully reached his eyes. "No need to think on it, doctor. This is a rare opportunity and I recognize it as such. I don't suppose we could have lunch again on Monday?"

Tobin van Castle, after a moment of feeling suspended in time, felt his professionally genial grin turn into one that stretched across his entire face. "Sounds good to me, Tucker. Let's do it at the same time," was all he said as he flipped a final wave and disappeared around the corner.

Tucker stood in the foyer with the doctor's final words ringing in his ears. "Sounds good to me, Tucker." That meant they were having lunch. That meant he'd committed himself. But he couldn't tell whether he felt better or worse. *Actually,* he thought, *I feel neither.*

He stood thinking, remembering when he talked to his ceiling via the computer about feelings and tried to identify them. He mused on; unaware that Sarah was covertly watching him with a dreamy expression on her face. Suddenly, he turned to her and said, "Determined, Sarah, that's how I feel."

And Sarah embarrassed herself and her dreams for the rest of her life by responding, "Yes, sir." The only word she had managed so far to utter in his presence...to his retreating back.

By the time Tucker shut down his computer and prepared to go to his massage he had learned to manipulate both the psychology abstract database and another related database known as Dialog. He hadn't had time to read the abstracts on insomnia or panic attacks, but had printed some of the more relevant articles in full so he could read them at his leisure. He was fascinated by the descriptors that accompanied the abstracts and couldn't wait to share the information with Dr. van Castle. Leaning back, he frowned, knowing he probably should have spent the last hour resting, if not sleeping. He had a feeling that he had better be at the top of his game with Heather.

Thank goodness for Mrs. T, he thought. He didn't even like to think what the evening would have been like had he, after making a bit of small talk, said to her in his casual way, "By the way, Heather, I hope you don't mind, I've taken the liberty of booking us at... (His mind couldn't think of another suitable place in the area that wouldn't have been booked on a concert Friday.) ...instead of Le Montrechet."

"Whew!" He said aloud as he rose to check and see if the weather was still improving. He really did want to sit in the garden and read some of his new articles, or perhaps visit with Allison.

Thinking of Allison made him remember her enjoyment of sharing his juice and he ambled toward the kitchen with a smile on his face to get some apple juice and plastic glasses. He knew just where they would breakfast-- in the old trolley diner--just as he had with Ethan and Mary on their many trips to the zoo.

With a sudden pang of anxiety, he realized it had been a long time ago. Perhaps the diner was defunct. He grabbed the Yellow Pages, trying to remember the name. He needn't have worried. There it was, easily spotted with its trolley car advertisement. "Jake's Diner" he read. "That's right!" he said softly to himself.

It came back to him then. Jake was also Irish, with an accent even broader than either Ethan or Mary's. Jake said things like "begorra" and called both Tucker and Ethan "me bucko" or "boyo." Tucker smiled at the memory as the picture in his mind grew stronger. On a whim he dialed the number.

It was a crisp, male voice that answered. Tucker knew, since Jake was much older than Ethan, it couldn't be him. "Hello," he said feeling just a trifle awkward for some reason. "I used to come to your trolley for breakfast when I was a boy and I'd like to know if I would need reservations for a Saturday breakfast."

There was a chuckle on the other end of the line. "Which Saturday would you be speaking about? I can help you if it several weeks from tomorrow."

Tucker paused, allowing himself to feel the disappointment. "No, I'm afraid it was to be this Saturday. I'm taking a little girl to the zoo. Sorry, I didn't think to call sooner. I would've liked to experience vicariously what it's like to be a child walking into the diner for the first time. Of course, a lot of that memory had to do with Jake and I suppose he's long since retired."

There was a snort at the other end. "My dad retire? Naw. He thinks the place would fall to ruin without him. He's just gotten more crotchety. Want to talk to him?"

"Well," said Tucker, taken aback, "my name is Tucker. I don't suppose he would remember me, but he might remember Ethan and Mary."

There was a long pause. "Ethan and Mary? Do you mean Ethan and Mary O'Shea?"

"Yes," said Tucker, the catch in his throat strangling the word.

"Just a minute!" Tucker listened in amazement as he could hear through the muffled receiver, "Hey, Pop, you won't believe this, but Tucker, Ethan and Mary's boy, is on the phone. He wants to come for breakfast Saturday."

Within seconds he could hear Jake's voice growing louder as he imagined the son holding out the receiver to him.

By the time Jake grabbed the receiver, he was shouting. Tucker winced and held the phone a little further from his ear. "Lord Jesus and me sainted Mother Mary. 'Tis you is it, me bucko? I used to say a nightly prayer that I'd get a small sign that you are all right. The Lord sartinly took his own sweet time in answerin'."

The familiar voice wound down and Tucker, relishing the rounded tones and flood of memories said "Hello, Jake. You sound wonderful. I can't believe you even remember me after all these years."

"Not remember you? Not remember you--with Mary's family being neighbor to me cousin in the old country?" Jake's voice grew even louder with the pretended indignation. "Of course, I remember you! But as a boy…and now you're a fine strapping man for sure. Me boy tells me you had thought to bring your family in for a Saturday breakfast just like you used to do with Ethan and Mary."

"Well," said Tucker, "it's not my family--friends though. But I know you're booked so will make it another time."

"Don't be daft, me bucko!" The old man was bellowing now. "Not have room for Ethan and Mary's boy? When his call is the answer from a prayer to the good Lord in heaven? I'd pitch me own mother, God rest her soul, into the street to make room. What time would you like the table?"

Tucker was mildly shocked at the blasphemy, but he began to vaguely remember Jake always brought his dead mother into his conversations in times of stress.

As he hung up the phone, Tucker patted it gently, eyes closed, remembering. *Odd that I wasn't able to remember the name of the diner.* Now he could picture it perfectly in his mind, see the sign, the crisp red and white checked curtains, and the red and white vinyl booths...about the color of his childhood backpack if he wasn't mistaken. He hoped it would be the same.

Tucker hadn't been in the garden for more than a few minutes when Allison burst through the gate, friend in tow. "There!" She said with obvious satisfaction, pointing to Tucker. "There he is. I am not making things up! So say sorry, Sunny, and perhaps I'll introduce you."

"Whew!" thought Tucker. He recognized the grand voice in its most imperious tone when he heard it. He felt secretly glad it was directed at the stubby girl with old-fashioned, round, wire-rimmed glasses sliding down her button nose. Her eyes, round with surprise behind the lenses, were a startling aqua.

Tucker had just taken a seat and had begun his perusal of the recently rain-soaked garden when the children appeared. He leaned forward and extended his hand. "Hello," he said gently, "allow me to introduce myself. I'm Tucker Jones."

To his complete and utter amazement, the as yet, nameless girl dipped her head and dropped him a perfect curtsy. With her head still bowed she said, using what he recognized immediately as her own grand voice, "Very pleased to meet you, Prince Tucker. My name is Nicole Angelica Barton, but you may call me Nicki."

He, with superhuman effort, choked back the laughter he felt might consume him and shot a quick glance at Allison. But she was simply looking at her friend with a smile that clearly said, "See? I told you so."

Tucker pulled in his still extended hand and cleared his throat, willing his years of properly executed social graces to come to his rescue, and said without so much as a hint of a smile, "Very nice to meet you, Nicki. I don't believe I've ever seen a curtsy so grand."

That did it! Both little girls looked at each other. Nicki ended her curtsy with a little bunny hop with both girls, clutching each other and doing a little dance of joy while they broke into a fit of squealing giggles. Then, they separated still holding hands and looked at Tucker as if to see what he was going to do next. He could tell there was an expected script and suddenly he somehow knew just what it was.

"Please," he said, keeping his voice as matter-of-fact as possible, "won't you join me for a bit of juice?" He was tempted to get up and help them into the chairs, knowing what a hit it would make, but was afraid it would start another round of the giggles which he had somehow found alarming.

He saw Allison nod with satisfaction. Simultaneously they said, again grandly, "Don't mind if I do." which of course set them off on a second round of giggles.

A light dawned for Tucker. "Ah!" he said. "I can see you have been practicing court manners. Very well done!"

The little girls looked at him earnestly. "Well, yes," said Allison. "We've been pretending you are a prince, only Nicki didn't believe you were real. So now she has to skip around me three times and say, "Sorry, Lady Allison Amanda McCall, I have judged thee most unfairly."

Without any trace of animosity they grinned across the table at each other and then fixed their eyes expectantly on Tucker's backpack. He took the hint and quickly poured two glasses of the apple juice.

Nicki was looking at Tucker closely. "It's true then…that you and Sunny are going to breakfast and to the zoo."

He nodded at her and returned her careful look, noting with some surprise that her eyes were exactly the color of Jon Bon's. "Yes, as a matter-of-fact, she has invited me, with her mother's permission, to be her companion at the zoo."

"Oh," she said. Again, as the silence lengthened, Tucker had the vague feeling that he was somehow finally blowing the lines of this secret, prewritten script. Finally, Allison gave him a little prompt.

"My mother didn't say for absolutely sure that I could only take one friend," she said in a rather subdued voice. Tucker immediately caught the unspoken drift. *Ah ha! Allison can't really feel free to invite another friend because I'm providing both the transportation and the pre-zoo feast.* He thought fast, but he had no experience with the finesse of two little girls out to manipulate the adults around them. His logical mind was simply seeking a reason that another little girl would be a problem at the zoo. He said, "Well, if neither of your parents objects, perhaps we could make tomorrow a foursome."

He watched them sit back and shoot each other conspiratorial looks of satisfaction before turning beaming smiles on him. "Oh, thank you so much, Tucker," said Allison sincerely. "I'll be at my dad's all summer and I really, really miss Nicki when I'm gone. We'll tell our moms that YOU asked her."

With that, they drained their juice quickly, got up from their chairs and as if on cue, push them carefully in. Allison came around the table and patted his arm paternally, as if telling him he had done well. Nicki, somewhat impulsively hugged what she could reach of his shoulder. Then, after giving him their best final curtsy, they were both gone with a giggling rush, through the gate, out of sight, but not out of hearing.

As the front gate slammed behind them, he could clearly hear their shouts of glee and could picture them jumping up and down hugging each other. When their cheers quieted he eavesdropped in amazement as they begin to strategize the rest of their plan as they walked out of earshot.

"No. We've got to ask your mother first. She'll probably just say it's okay with her if it's okay with Mom. But, if she does say no, then I won't even ask Mom. It's going to be tricky anyway." Allison's voice was adamant but faint as the distance lengthened.

Tucker didn't get to hear what was going to be so tricky about getting permission from Kathryn. He smiled and shrugged, letting the garden again claim his attention. *Everything looks just as I remember it,* he thought with satisfaction, *only better.* Obviously, the rain had done it some good. Bees hummed busily around the blossoms and a small black and yellow butterfly lit daintily on one of the fountain rocks as if resting in the shade before continuing its never-ending task of seeking nectar. Its wings fluttered slowly while it rested.

Tucker thought about the articles in his backpack and decided he would rather think about this amazing day. There was so much to think about, Mrs. T's near melt down, Dr. van Castle, the talk with Jake, the zoo trip.

Jake had made Tucker sound like he WAS Ethan and Mary's son. *In a very real way,* he decided with a pang, *it is true.* He closed his eyes and breathed deeply the way the physical therapist at the hospital had taught him. Suddenly, a fanciful picture of Ethan and Mary standing in a corner of the garden, watching the antics of the two little girls as they cheerfully and skillfully manipulated him came to Tucker's mind. He noted with joy how sharp and clear their features were. He felt they understood what had been going on and were absolutely entertained by it, by them, by him. He felt incredibly peaceful and content as the image faded, aided somewhat by the fast pounding of little feet.

"Oh, Tucker, thank heavens you're still here. Nicki's mom said yes, she could go, but then just in time I remembered that we forgot to talk about the... um..." She searched her mind for the words Tucker had used. "...details," she finally finished. There was a train schedule clutched in her hand.

"Well," he smiled, "I did do my part. I think you'll really enjoy where we're having breakfast. Do you want me to tell you, or would you like to be surprised?"

The two little girls looked at each other, eyes round and sparkling, wiggling like happy puppies in their pleasure. This was almost too much excitement. How could they ever decide such a thing on the spot? He could almost see the telepathic communication flowing between them. To be surprised or to know and to be able to talk about what it might be like all afternoon and perhaps all night if they got their way and Nicki was allowed to spend the night.

Suddenly, Allison grabbed Nicki's hand and said soberly, "Tucker, we're not a hundred percent for sure Nicki gets to go. When I said that about Mom not saying for sure if I could invite two people...I meant she didn't say no OR yes. If you know what I mean." She looked pleadingly at him and he understood her immediately. If Nicki wasn't going to be allowed to go, then it would be better for her not to hear the plan; the disappointment would be much greater.

He looked at his watch. "Right. Well, I would guess someone is going to walk out that side door in about two minutes with your mother right behind them. It seems like it would be a good idea to sew things up before we talk further, doesn't it?"

The girls nodded gravely. "Tucker," Allison almost whispered, "do you think it would be true if I said to my mother that you asked Nicki?"

Tucker raised an eyebrow. *Ah, the wee one has a conscience;* he thought and immediately wondered what Mary's response would have been. "I don't know," said Tucker, letting the puzzlement show in his voice. "I did suggest making it a foursome, but now that I think of it, you perhaps set me up to say it."

They looked levelly at one another. A boundary had just been tested and set. Allison sighed and looked miserably at her friend. "It's okay, Nicki, even if I had said Tucker asked you, my mom would probably ask me if I had put him up to it. You know how she is."

"Well," said Tucker, "don't count the foursome out yet. Not until you ask. In the meantime, let's look at that train schedule and pin down some times. We do have a confirmed breakfast reservation and I have an evening engagement, but other than that, the day is ours."

After Kathryn appeared at the office door and waved goodbye to her client she turned to them, putting her hands on her hips. "Well, well, what have we here? A party?" She smiled a welcome at Tucker and then turned her attention to the two anxious faces.

339

Yes, he thought to himself, *Allison knows her mother very well.* It took Kathryn only moments to get the entire truth of the conspiracy from the stricken girls. Then she looked at Tucker, shrugged her shoulders and grinned. "I can stand it if you can. Besides, if they get too unruly, we can just feed them to the big alligator, I'm thinking."

The two adults walked toward the office door with a chorus of gleeful thanks following them. Then, just as they were about to disappear through the door, Tucker heard Allison's frantic call. "Where, Tucker? Where are we going to eat breakfast? Oh, please, please tell us!"

He grinned. "Jake's Diner. A place I used to go. It's in an old trolley car," he called over his shoulder and stepped over the threshold, accompanied by a cacophony of excited squeals.

From a deep and dreamless sleep, Tucker swam sluggishly toward consciousness, aided by the nagging sound of a buzzer. For a moment he lay listening, orienting, unable to identify the hard surface below him. Then his eyes snapped open. The first thing he saw was the egg timer which had just finished buzzing and a note that read:

Tucker,

I'm sorry to only give you an hour, but fear you might have something planned this evening and I know how tightly you are sometimes scheduled. You fell asleep almost as soon as I put my hands on you. I want you to know that it seems a great compliment.

See you at 8:30 in the morning. I hope you know what you are doing, taking two giggling little girls on a day's outing.

I hope I know what I'm doing allowing them to spend the night together.

She had signed the note with her first initial. He looked at it and grinned, remembering. He swung his legs over the edge of the table and stood. He decided he felt great. Then he glanced at his wristwatch as he picked it up

340

and put it on. It was nearly 4:30. He groaned softly. In less than an hour he had to be in a suit and out the door for a 6:45 drink with the Anderson's. Hurrying into his clothes, he wondered why it was, when he hated hurrying with such a passion, that he was a person always in a hurry.

When Tucker opened his door, he saw his answering machine light was blinking frantically but he ignored it and headed for the shower; traffic had been terrible. It was nearly 6:00 o'clock. Luckily, he could call for his phone messages from the car.

By 6:30 he had rocketed through the shower, cut his chin shaving, thrown on the first suit he came to in his closet, ran a brush through his hair and bolted for his car. He would be late, but not by much. It would be easy to call Heather from his car phone and tell her he was stuck in traffic, but he really was not inclined to do so. He'd never been an excuse maker and didn't want to start now.

But traffic had been heavy and he was nearly ten minutes late. The butler showed him immediately into the garden where the Andersons', including Heather, were having a cocktail. She rose, looking quite lovely in a shimmering dress with just enough blue in it to keep it from being called emerald green. It set off her eyes, hair and slim athlete's figure perfectly. He whistled softly from pure appreciation when he saw her. It was the right thing to do. She smiled and extended her hands.

"You're late, Tucker, darling. We were beginning to worry." Then she laughed a small tinkling sound. "But we did start without you, hope you don't mind." He caught the mild reprimand immediately

"Not at all," Tucker took both her hands and leaned forward to kiss her cheek. She was wearing something subtle and musky and for some reason a clear picture of Dawn Simpson flashed through his mind and the contrast between Heather's musk and Dawn's spicy, lemony scented perfume seemed to clash in his nostrils and still his tongue. Heather looked at him sharply. He recovered. "Sorry," he found himself saying softly, "I think I got distracted by your perfume." Again, she was pleased. He found himself relaxing a little as he moved forward to greet the senior Andersons. He'd met them once before at one of

341

the Tyler's functions and remembered them as gracious, but aloof, people.

Tucker knew that Herb Anderson was the chief executive officer of a large and well-managed mutual fund. Elaine Anderson, if he remembered correctly, had been extremely wealthy in her own right, but had worked as a market analyst for some years under her husband's nose before he noticed, courted and married her. Now, she played golf and served on boards. They stood and greeted him graciously and he was mildly surprised by the unexpected warmth and familiarity of the greeting.

The small talk flowed easily. Elaine Anderson talked of the golf game with Midge Tyler. It made Tucker smile. One of the messages had been from her. "Tucker, dear, when you give your name at Le Montrechet, you will be shown to one of the better tables."

She had also reassured him that things were under control, but in her next breath, she entreated him to come as soon as was possible on Saturday. "James is so pleased...no, I think it's more than pleased. He's also quite relieved that you have agreed to come."

She had also discovered what was bothering Charlie, but said she would wait to tell him in person.

Luckily, Tucker was not single-minded. As he was finishing his replay of Mrs. T's call in his mind, Herb Anderson asked him a question about the situation occurring at Tiananmen Square in China, and he was able to respond flawlessly, saying, "If one side doesn't back down, and I don't believe that they will, my guess is that there will be bloodshed." No one in the room would ever have known that his thoughts had been elsewhere.

"Well," said Heather brightly, as if they hadn't been talking about people dying, "rush your scotch a bit, Tucker. We don't want to be late for the concert."

Again, Tucker caught the gentle barb and saw that Mrs. Anderson had also noted it as her face flushed ever so slightly and she lowered her eyes.

For some reason, it made him feel slightly protective of the older, beautifully groomed woman. "Right!" He said just a shade louder than necessary, tossed back the last of his scotch and rose quickly to his feet. His alacrity caught the butler slightly off guard and sent him scrambling for their coats. As Tucker deftly helped Heather into her coat, he looked at Mrs. Anderson, and with a twinkle in his eye, slightly lowered one lid. To his surprise she seemed to know immediately what the wink implied and startled them both by returning the gesture.

The music was quite wonderful and Heather, a most agreeable companion. The waspishness seemed almost imagined by the time they had finished their coffees and brandy at Le Montrechet. The nap at Kathryn's had cost him time, but he wondered if he'd have survived the evening without it.

Luckily, Heather was a good conversationalist. Although, when he tried to tell her about the manipulative antics of Allison and Nicki, he could tell she was immediately bored. She thought going to a masseuse was an excellent idea but couldn't understand why he didn't simply take advantage of someone at the club. He found he had absolutely no desire to try to explain it to her.

As the evening progressed, she grew even friendlier towards him, once apparently absentmindedly drifting her carefully polished nails up and down the length of his arm as if mesmerized by the softness of the silk in his suit coat. And when he let her into the Aston and walked around to get in, he noted that she was sitting as near to him as the shift lever and bucket seats would allow. He began to fret slightly about whether after ten years, he still knew how to kiss. He needn't have worried. Halfway to her home he felt an electric sort of a jolt as Heather gently put her left hand on his thigh. Quickly, though later he was not sure why, he covered her hand with his own, removing it only when he needed to shift. He decided that as usual, he acted out of fear. Fear that he might not be ready for where that hand would travel next. It made him feel disgusted with himself.

He parked the Aston smoothly in front of the Andersons' lovely granite entry and tried not to hurry as he went to assist Heather from the car. Somehow, as he leaned down and she stood up, their bodies swayed together and she put her arms around his neck. It seemed very natural to put his arms around her back and pull her into an embrace. She was soft and pliant in the circle of his arms. Slowly, gently, their lips touched. He felt, or at least imagined, he could feel the softness of her breasts against his chest. Her lips began softly moving over his and sometime in the process he felt her tongue slip searchingly into his mouth and a fine tremor seemed to run through his entire frame. His breath caught. He felt suddenly engulfed, but fought the feeling. *In a way, this is like therapy. I'm finding out some things about myself, that's for sure.* He did not release her, but finally lifted his head and took a deep ragged breath. Then he smiled down at her and could see that she was very pleased with her effect on him, could feel that he was becoming aroused, and liked it.

As Tucker started to lower his head again, she gently disengaged. This was all a part of her carefully crafted plan. She slipped from his arms and smiled. "Mmm. Nice. Walk me to the door now please, Tucker."

At the door, she gently avoided his embrace and gave him a light peck on the cheek. "Thank you so much for the lovely evening, Tucker. Next time, you think of something for us to do."

He stood, smiling inscrutably. There was something in his face she couldn't quite read and it made her nervous. Perhaps she'd overplayed the hand. But no, he finally smiled warmly and said, "Yes, next time I will. Good night, Heather. I'm glad you enjoyed yourself."

Driving home, Tucker again reflected on his day, thinking that it was perhaps a turning point in his life. Meeting with Dr. van Castle; finding Jake and renewing a real connection with Ethan and Mary's memory were significant. But, being so relaxed during his massage that he had fallen asleep was something he still found hard to believe. Added to that, was getting everything organized for what was likely going to be a wonderful day with three people he genuinely liked and last but not least, finding out for absolutely sure that his sex drive was probably normal. He laughed and saluted the beautiful image of Heather Anderson. "Thank you, Heather," he said softly and sincerely in the quiet car interior and then began humming quietly to himself, tapping a melody on the leather of the steering wheel as if playing an imaginary piano.

344

Chapter Twenty-nine

Tucker pulled the Aston to a stop in front of the small white house. Looking at it, one would never guess that behind the fenced, gated side-yard was a special garden. There simply wasn't any clue. It looked just like all the other trimly kept, modest, white, beige, and gray-toned houses that stretched down the street. In some way, its anonymity made the garden even more magical. He smiled to himself and stepped from the car.

Immediately, the front door burst open and two bundles of energy came charging across the porch, down the steps to meet him. He found himself being escorted...no, towed by two child tugboats who had turned his arms into towlines, and were pulling him towards the front door while walking backwards and assailing his ears with a patter of chatter he couldn't, even with his superb listening skills, begin to keep up with. The gist of it, however, was that Nicki had spilled hot chocolate on her blouse and had to run home and change. She'd only just gotten back. But, they'd only had hot chocolate and it would not spoil their breakfast at the diner one bit. Allison hadn't been able to find her tennis shoes until the very last minute and Kathryn had packed them a picnic lunch so that they could relax in the zoo's park. And did he have a car blanket, because if not, they had a perfectly lovely picnic quilt ready to take if he'd prefer. They also told him that they thought they wouldn't be able to sleep a wink but that Kathryn had had to wake them both this morning.

Tucker kept looking down at the upturned faces, amazed at how comfortable he actually felt. "Whoa." He finally said, surprised both at how warmly, but firmly the word had come out. He was also pleased at its magical effect on the girls. It was as though he'd put the lid down on a jack-in-the-box. They both stopped mid-stride and dropped his hands like they were sizzling hot.

Without saying a word, he took them by the shoulders and lined them up side-by-side. Still without a word he carefully and expressionlessly looked them over from head to foot. *It's amazing,* he thought. *They look almost like caricatures of schoolgirls with shiny faces and carefully combed hair.* Allison's curls were in her normal pom-poms and Nicki's hair had been carefully braided, a blue headband added to make certain everything stayed in place. They wore shirts and shorts with hair ribbons that matched. Nicki even had a bright blue Band-Aid with white stars covering a knee that had obviously been recently scraped.

They stood perfectly still, anxious eyes riveted to his face. What was it that Tucker wanted? Were they in trouble? Kathryn had warned them not to be rambunctious, a warning definitely ignored. They certainly had been showing off, partly for each other, no doubt about that.

Finally, Tucker nodded seriously. "Yes, perhaps you'll do after all." Taking Kathryn's lead from the day before he said, "For a moment I was thinking I was either going to have to leave you in the parrot cage or the monkey house. But, I can see I was mistaken, you are well-behaved little girls who just got a bit carried away with excitement. Now, one at a time, who wants to tell me something?"

Again, the boundary had been set. This man was no pushover. He required a certain amount of respect. They looked at each other. "Sorry, Tucker," Allison said contritely and reached immediately for his hand.

"Me too, Tucker." Nicki's voice came out in a whisper, her cat eyes grave. He held out his hand to her and smiled at them both. "Apologies accepted. Now let's go and find the missing party."

"I'm right here." Kathryn appeared at the screen door, a canvas bag in one hand, a cooler in the other, pushing the disgusted Jon Bon with her foot. "Out, out now. That's a good boy."

She smiled at Tucker. "Did the girls remember to ask you about a blanket?"

He smiled back, taking note of how young and carefree she looked out of her office attire and reached for the cooler, while she fished for the front door key.

346

"Yes, they remembered. There's a car robe in the boot. It should serve nicely."

Kathryn's hair was no longer bound into its unruly braid. Today, though the sides were pinned back with two large combs, it was otherwise free of confinement. Even in the shade of the porch it seemed full of coppery, curly sunshine. She was wearing a shade of yellow that was nearly gold, a color not one woman in a dozen could have been able to have near them, but it suited her perfectly.

Tucker couldn't decide whether it would be appropriate to compliment her or not, so he chose the safer course. "Ladies, it is indeed going to be a pleasure to introduce the three of you to my old friend, Jake. His Irish heart will turn green with envy at my good fortune. You are all looking splendid."

It was the perfect segue. As they settled in the Aston, Kathryn said, "This is a lovely car, Tucker. Now tell us, what's this about an old Irish friend?" And so Tucker told them about Ethan and Mary taking him to the zoo and how they would always stop and visit with Jake and have breakfast on the way.

"I haven't seen him for many years, but he certainly sounded the same on the phone. He's the sort of person that raises his voice a lot when he's pleased about something...when he's annoyed...when he gets sentimental and when he gets excited. As I remember, it can be deafening."

He could hear the little girls giggling softly in the jump seat and it struck him again how real this all felt and decided it was because, although he was with other people, he was doing this for himself, because he wanted to. It was hard not to reflect on the previous evening with Heather where he felt more like a pawn in a chess game.

"Tucker, do you think Jake likes little girls?" came hesitantly from the rear.

"I really don't know," Tucker said thoughtfully. "I know he liked little boys because he always said..." Using his best Irish brogue imitation he quoted Jake. "'Now, me young boyo, will ye be havin' just one more scoop of strawberries and a dab more whippin' cream on those pancakes?'"

347

He heard gasps of pleasure from the back and glanced in his rearview mirror just in time to see them look at each other, throw a hand over their mouth as if to control an outburst of sound and grab each other's hands in a joyful gesture. He glanced at Kathryn and found she was looking at him, interested in the story, relaxed and smiling.

They found they had a lot to talk about: The garden, how he fell asleep during the massage, what she'd pack for a picnic. They were still talking as Tucker eased the car into the diner's parking lot where it was well posted as to what would happen if you parked but didn't eat.

Tucker turned off the key and said quietly. "Now before we go in, I need to tell you that I haven't been here since my friends, Ethan and Mary, passed away. I don't know what it is going to feel like when I see Jake. I don't know what it is going to feel like when he sees me. I just thought you ought to know."

Kathryn noted the death grip of his hands on the leather steering wheel, the cords standing out in his neck, both contradicting the calmness of his speech and suspected immediately how difficult the words had been to say. Again, she thought to herself, *this man is certainly full of surprises.* Aloud she said, "Thank you for letting us know." Then she turned to look at Allison. "We're pretty used to excitable old Irish men aren't we, sweetie?" Allison nodded and grinned.

"She means Grandpa McCall. He's always kissing me and telling me stories about friends and dogs and things. Then he has to blow his nose a lot to keep from crying."

Kathryn nodded. "You know that old cliché about the sentimentality of the Irish?" When Tucker nodded she said, "I'm afraid it's true."

It was good that they had taken a moment to prepare themselves. It did not matter that every stool and every booth, except for the one reserved for Tucker, were filled with people. It did not matter that waiters and waitresses were hustling hot plates of food and coffee down the narrow aisle. The moment the bell on the door tinkled, from out of the kitchen rushed a gaunt, raw-boned, medium-tall man, with a shock of dark brown hair that had only turned silver at the temples. It gave his lined face the

348

distinguished look of some famous character actor. He was, as Tucker had warned them, beginning to bellow.

"There ye be! There ye be! Saints be praised! I'd recognize you anywhere, lad. Come in! Come in!"

Tucker shot a quick look at his trio. Their mouths, including Kathryn's, were slack-jawed with surprise. And it was no wonder. Throughout the diner all activity had stopped. People with forkfuls halfway to their mouth, waitresses in the act of pouring coffee, the busboy clearing the table; all ceased activity. They looked for the world like a tableau of Middle America or a Norman Rockwell painting.

It could have mattered less to Jake. "Everyone," he shouted, including every patron in his announcement, "This is me good friend, Tucker Jones, now grown to manhood and isn't he a fine specimen at that?" He beamed, encompassing them all in his joy and goodwill. As if on cue there was a smattering of clapping, a few calls of, "Hi, Tucker" and a bit of self-conscious laughter as people identified with what it would feel like to be so heartily and publicly introduced to a diner full of strangers.

Tucker smiled, strangely not at all embarrassed to be the center of so much attention. Jake had to be in his 60s now, but except for the silver in his hair, did not seem much changed, and that felt wonderful.

"Hello, Jake," he said. "It's very good to see you. I'd like to introduce you to three of my friends."

Jake, who had been pumping his arm up and down wildly, noticed for the first time, the two wide-eyed girls who had attached themselves to the khaki legs of Tucker's trousers. Then his eyes shot to Kathryn with her auburn hair, fair skin and sprinkle of freckles. It stopped him cold.

"Begorra, lassie, sure as I'm Jake O'Connor, you're as Irish as a shamrock."

Kathryn's laugh floated gently through the still silent air of the diner. This was high drama and the diners, many of whom had been coming in for Saturday breakfast for years, would rather eat stone cold eggs than miss a moment. She held out her hand and broadened her lilt into a fine accent. "Kathryn McCall, sir. Aye, Irish, though t'would be a fair stretch to call me a lass with me own

349

daughter, Allison, and her friend, Nicki, standing by me side."

Some of the diners who hadn't, from their particular booths, been able to see that there were two children included in the entertainment, actually raised up for a view. Jake, on the other hand, squatted down to eye level. "Well," he said in what was a whisper for him, but still carried from end to end of the diner, "'tis indeed a pleasure to meet such fine children. But, here I am blathering on with wee colleens starvin' in me own doorway." He held out his hands. "Come, me darlin's, I've saved ye the best table in the house."

Typically, both little girls exchanged their special look, daring each other to be brave, and then gave their well-rehearsed curtsies. "'Tis nice to meet you, I'm sure, Mr. O'Connor," Allison said clearly with just a touch of her grand voice called in to assist her newly found brogue.

Tucker and Kathryn shot quick grins at each other and tried not to laugh. *What will she think of next?* Kathryn wondered. *Especially when she has an entire captive audience to charm?* It was a very short wait to find out.

When their curtsies had ended, they each placed a trusting hand in Jake's and allowed him to escort them to their table. "Hello... Hello, so nice to meet you." smiled Allison at each booth. Nicki took the cue. She hadn't a proper brogue, but she did her best grand voice imitation and the performance between them gave Kathryn the giggles. A man in the booth nearest the door, himself the father of four little girls, saw her give way, heard her giggle, and he too started laughing. Suddenly the entire eatery was awash with laughter, Tucker included. It was impossible not to. Watching the two grand princesses being escorted to their booth by a man whose chest was puffed out so that one would have assumed that royalty did indeed trail beside him was an amazingly funny sight. Still grinning, Tucker took Kathryn's elbow and followed.

Kathryn whispered over her shoulder to Tucker, "You see why I miss her so much when she goes? It's always like this. I can never even anticipate what she's going to come up with next."

When they were at last all seated and Jake had gone off to fill their order-- his famous strawberry pancakes all around--the diner resumed its normal drone and clatter.

350

Then, Tucker could look about and fill his eyes with the past. He felt very grateful that Jake had chosen to preserve the diner he remembered in his mind. Of course, the appliances were modern, and the interior had obviously been redone as was necessary to prevent its getting shabby, but the essence was still there. The checkered curtains were a different material and a little different style, but they were still red and white. The booths were exactly the same and the individual jukeboxes still graced every table.

Finally, when the plates had been cleared down to Kathryn and Tucker's last cup of coffee, Jake rejoined them squeezing in beside the girls. He was calmer by then, but the place was still packed and since he was the head cook, he couldn't visit long. But surely, he insisted, they would come back. Tucker assured him that if he could persuade the ladies, they would. Kathryn reached across to touch Jake's arm and said she never could resist an Irish gentleman.

Tucker filled Jake in on what he had been doing with his life and could tell that Jake was proud of him. By some unspoken agreement, there was only one reference to Ethan and Mary. Tucker found himself nodding in agreement and feeling quite at peace with his memories when Jake said, "Ah, God rest their blessed souls lad, don't ye know that at this very moment they're both lookin' down from heaven above an' sayin' to each other what a fine lad ye've grown to be." Jake took a corner of his cook's apron and wiped at the suspicious moisture threatening at the corner of each eye.

Kathryn took one look at Tucker--green eyes probing brown ones and found a kaleidoscope of information. *This is really new for him,* she thought, *but very important. I'd wager it's not like him to put himself in a position where he might lose control of his feelings.* And with consummate skill, she gently turned the conversation back to Ireland. Tucker shot her a grateful look.

Then they were off in a flurry of goodbyes into the Aston and off to the train station. Jake stood at the door of the diner and waved until they disappeared. He shook his head at the wonder of it all. "A fine lookin' family," he muttered to himself.

The Bronx zoo, other than being smaller than Tucker remembered, was the same, only better. Now, the big cats were no longer in cages. They roamed an interpreted natural environment of grassy veldts with trees to flop under in the heat of the day. There were also caves to disappear into for privacy or against the chill of a winter's night. He knew it was an illusion, but it was a good one and he made himself a mental note to check into their funding sources. Perhaps they were in need of a little extra funding for some program or another.

The little girls wore themselves down very quickly, running from exhibit to exhibit, insisting on reading every sign, begging for snow cones, standing in arm-clasped wonder before a sign that said:

Ursus horribilis
Grizzly Bear

The huge beast at the very edge of the moat that separated him from the freedom to roam, gracefully rose to an incredible height, balancing carefully on huge, long-clawed pads, front paws curved in toward his chest. He looked wild and formidable as he dropped to all fours, stretched his short neck and swung his massive head from side to side. En masse, the crowd watching drew a collective breath and many mothers unconsciously reached down to check the nearness of their children.

Kathryn looked at Tucker. "It's hard not to wish that he was somewhere roaming wild and free." She paused, looked at the bear again, looked at the spellbound little girls and then smiled. "Somewhere way out west of course...way, way out west."

The girls' constant scamper had turned into a slow walk and then the request for piggyback rides began. They returned to the car for their picnic things and Tucker saw his overnight bag in the trunk. He remembered that his day was far from being over. There was the evening at the Tylers yet to come. He sighed feeling somehow intruded upon and then quickly shut the thought from his mind.

352

They chose a spot for the picnic near enough to playground equipment that the adults could keep an eye on the girls, but far enough away to feel peaceful. Every now and then a look of sadness came to Kathryn's eyes when she looked at her penny-bright daughter. She sighed. "I hate this time of year. Once she's really gone, I adjust after a bit, but already I feel lonesome, mad at her father and very sorry for myself, if I allow it."

Tucker didn't quite know what to say. He had been watching her, thinking again that she reminded him of a daisy, sturdy, cheerful, able to withstand the up and down of life's weather. Finally he said, "Does she have to go?" Not wanting to pry, but very much wanting to know.

"Lord yes, she has to go. She loves her dad and he's crazy about her. They spend the entire month with his folks on their ranch in Texas. Allison has a pool, a pony, and adoring grandparents." A look of resigned pain came into her eyes and she sighed again, and went on as if answering Tucker's unspoken question, which indeed she was. "It's just that he is a miserable, useless man unless he's in some remote area of the world trying to uncover the mysteries of history with an archaeologist pick and brush. And I'm a miserable woman if I have to try to raise a child in a Third World country. I was meant to have roots I fear and I married a fine man, but a rambler. So I told him it would be better if we just didn't see each other and he said he had a better idea. Allison should go and live with his parents and I should come with him."

She threw herself onto her stomach, fists and eyes clenched tightly. Tucker noted two things simultaneously: that only with superhuman resolve was he able to keep himself from jumping up and leaving to avoid the emotional pain that seemed to emanate from Kathryn and flow like a charge of electricity into him; and, that never in his life, even with Dr. van Castle, had he let another human being look so clearly inside him as she had just allowed him to look inside her.

He literally clutched his car robe with both hands to steady himself as he allowed her sadness to wash through him, mingle with his own, and tried with all his might to examine how he felt, to put some word to it that would help him think about it later. But, all he felt was numb, cold, like a slab of granite and so he was quite unprepared for what happened next.

Unbidden and without preamble something broke free in Tucker's mind. He took a deep shuddering breath and it felt as if new blood were rushing through his body. He felt lighter, cleansed and full of something he could not name. But it felt very good.

"How did that feel?" He asked softly, in a warm and caring voice that sounded more like Dr. van Castle's than his own.

But if his voice sounded strange, Kathryn, eyes still clenched as if to prevent the tears on the inside from ever reaching the outside, didn't seem to notice. After a moment she mumbled, "Selfish lout! Asking me to choose between my child and him, asking me, as usual, to make all the concessions, to go with him to God knows where, to live out of a suitcase and let my girl grow up without me."

"Did you ask him to make some concessions?"

At Tucker's soft query, Kathryn's eyes flew open. She sat up and looked at him strangely. He sat calmly looking back at her, still feeling the strange sensation of blood rushing through his body and suddenly he knew just how he was feeling. *Interested! I'm not just pretending, not just being polite--not just listening carefully so I can remember to make the right response.* He was not only interested; it would be fair to say he cared. He felt his heart beating with a steady, strong rhythm.

Finally, she drew a little breath and said, with just a hint of the lilt returning to her voice. "Concessions? No, no, I'm afraid I didn't," she said. "Instead I lost my temper and threw him out, shouting and swearing. I made him send a cab for Allison the next day. It was terrible and wonderful at the same time. I think I still love him very much; probably I always will. But I was also very, very angry with him and it felt good, at the time anyway, to blow some of it his way."

They sat in quiet reflection for long moments, she thinking, and he unwilling to break the spell. With a sigh, she turned clear green eyes on him. "You know, Tucker, when we first met, I couldn't get any sort of emotional feeling from you. 'Twas stiff-necked you seem to be and far too polite and smooth to be real. But now, I find I have just finished telling you things I haven't even told my own mother. How could that be?"

Tucker closed his eyes lightly, as if lost in thought and after a moment he stood up and stretched, gracefully, like one of the big cats they had watched that morning. Then he put down his hands to help her up. "I don't know," he said humbly. "I do know, though I just learned recently, in your garden in fact, that I haven't been very happy with parts of my life. I don't, or at least I haven't, allowed people to get too close to me. But, just now, when we were talking, I could feel your pain and I wanted to jump up and run away, but I didn't. Suddenly, I found myself really caring. And this morning at Jake's, when he was talking about Ethan and Mary, you changed the subject. I could tell you cared about me, and it felt actually good instead of scary."

She looked at him, considering. The words just didn't fit the polished, obviously privileged, package before her and she wondered if he was putting her on. But she could see the furrow in his forehead, could read the confusion and the intensity in his eyes and hear the wonder in his voice. Finally, she made a decision and held out her hand. "Friends?" She asked.

He looked startled for just a second and then he grinned at her, looked her right in the eye so she could see inside him if she wanted to. he shook her hand. "Absolutely! Thank you very much."

On the way home in the car, with both girls sleeping soundly in the backseat, he had told her about the importance of Dr. Beemers in his life and she told him that it was Beemers who had made her realize that she was acting like a spoiled child and feeling sorry for herself after her husband left. He was the one who had encouraged her to take some training, and do something useful with her life. Being a massage therapist seemed the perfect thing. She could do it out of her home and it was something she knew she would be good at.

"Evidently, Dr. Beemers thinks so too," Tucker said.

They glanced at each other, mutually remembering Tucker's first visit and smiled. "One of these days, Tucker Jones, you are going to submit to a full body massage and then you'll feel downright foolish that you resisted it for so long." Kathryn said with a trace of seriousness in her voice.

"Perhaps," was for his reply. But, she noted with hope that he hadn't refused, and let the subject drop.

Chapter Thirty

As Tucker drove up the Tyler's winding drive, he realized in some panic, that he hadn't switched mental gears. His mind was still jumbling with the amazing events that had filled his day. It had, he reflected, been one of the happiest days in his adult life. *And the worst day? What was the worst day?* He groaned aloud in the deep silence of the Aston. *That's easy to remember. It was the day I spent avoiding Dawn on the Tyler's boat.* He sighed deeply as he pulled the Aston around to his usual slot by the garage, noting the black embassy limousine parked under the porte-cochere.

In all honesty, he supposed he would also have to admit that the evening he had rescued Dawn would also have to be catalogued on the happy side. In fact, he felt that night, much the way he felt today: energized, interested, and something more. But, as he swung his bags from the boot, he realized he was out of time for thinking about himself. He was now on duty. With an effort, he pulled himself into the moment.

The first thing he found himself wondering, as he walked toward the front door, was what Mrs. T had discovered about Charlie's bad mood and then shook his head. He was about to be meeting some very important men. That was what he needed to think about! He rushed up the steps to ring the bell.

To his surprise, the retired butler sometimes hired by the Tylers on very formal occasions, answered the door. He was wearing his usual black butler's suit, brought out of mothballs for just the occasion. Tucker groaned. He was sure Midge had said "a quiet informal weekend." The butler's presence meant just the opposite and he had brought nothing suitable to wear.

He managed a small smile. "Hello, Jason, you're looking well. I believe I'm expected."

"Indeed you are, sir. Mrs. Tyler said to tell you that they were taking their guests for a short motor trip on Faith. It's not any sort of a sail, just sightseeing around St. Helena. They plan to return in time for cocktails. She said she hoped you had gotten the message about dinner that she'd left on your machine."

Tucker sighed. "Unfortunately, I did not. The best I can do is a sports jacket and slacks. By the way, just how many guests have they invited?"

"Seven, sir; eight including yourself and the Eldridges. Mrs. Tyler said that when you arrived, I was to take your bags up and put them in Master Scotty's old room. She thought you might prefer the privacy."

Tucker relinquished his bag and hang-up mutely. *Five other overnight guests? Whew!* He calculated beds. *There are plenty. I believe there are five bedrooms in the west wing, two in the main part of the house: the master suite and Dawn's, no, I mean, Scott's room. That she's putting me there is surely is a first!*

Things were a little crazy feeling. No wonder Mrs. T had been so upset. And why had he chosen this day of all days, not to call his phone machine from his car to retrieve his messages? Nodding to himself, he realized the answer to his question was the simple fact that he was still reliving his time with Kathryn and the girls until he drove up the Tyler's drive.

He decided to pop into the kitchen and see how Charlie was faring before going up to have a shower and change. That he didn't have a tuxedo didn't upset him very much he decided, although this was the very first time in the history of his adult life that he wouldn't be socially correct. Somehow, the thought made him smile.

In the kitchen he found both Charlie and Clarice. They seemed to be in their stride and greeted him warmly. "'Bout time you got here, Tucker Jones. Miss Tyler's been worryin' all day. Said yo' voice don't sound right on the phone and then she couldn't get a hold of you. She even called yo' folks. I told her to never mind. A man your age deserved time to his self, you'd be here when you said you would." Clarice smiled hugely, but Tucker could read the unspoken question in her eyes.

He laughed and said, "You are absolutely right. I was taking time for myself and I quite enjoyed it." And then he changed the subject and saw Charlie hide a smile at Clarice's startled look.

"I need to go up and shower and change. Unfortunately, I didn't call in for my messages, so I didn't know this was a formal affair. Rather spur of the moment, isn't it?"

They nodded simultaneously. Charlie smiled serenely, deftly turning the heat down under one kettle and up under another. It seemed to Tucker that the odors in the kitchen were tickling a memory, but he couldn't place them.

Charlie laughed. "This one big whoop-tee-do. No problem. Charlie tell Mam--have tea, cut flowers. I call your honorable mother for one quick consultation. Everything fine."

It took a moment for what Charlie said to sink in. He had already turned to leave the kitchen, but he stopped and turned in his tracks. "My mother? You called my mother?"

Again Charlie smiled serenely and nodded. "Need to consult on quick dish for South American gentlemen. You say many time, honorable mother cook with international flair." He nodded to himself. "Most helpful."

Tucker's laugh filled the kitchen. "And just what did you two decide would be suitable for one South American diplomat and four South American analysts?"

"Beef piccadillo. No problem. Honorable Mrs. Jones provide recipe. Charlie go to store. All in pots. Everything okay." Charlie's slippered feet had continued to move about the kitchen, stirring this, tasting that.

Tucker laughed again. "I thought I recognized those odors, but I was trying to place them among your repertoire of recipes, not my mother's! Good for you, Charlie! I'm certain she felt your call was a great honor, and I'm sure I will hear all about it tomorrow night."

At those words Charlie's serene face broke into a wrinkled smile and he nodded his head. "Yes. Honorable mother asked that you bring this humble cook, too."

Taking the stairs two at a time, Tucker found that he was still smiling. Not only was Charlie invited for Sunday dinner with his parents, Mrs. T had arranged for Hank to

359

come and pick him up and bring him back to the Tyler's afterwards. And more surprising still, his mother had been invited to the Tyler's for lunch the following Tuesday. According to Charlie, they were to discuss their role in the forthcoming cooking contest. But Tucker suspected a second reason. His mother and Charlie were dying to satisfy their mutual curiosity about each other's kitchens.

As he entered his assigned bedroom, thoughts of Dawn flooded his mind. He could almost see her sitting, skinned knee carefully flexed, looking absolutely breathtaking in pale blue, her hair held from her face by a matching ribbon. Drawing a deep breath, he was disappointed to find no hint of her perfume remained. He looked at the carefully made bed and got a curious knot in his stomach to think that in several hours he would be sleeping, or at least trying to sleep, where she had slept. That Midge Tyler had put him in this room, hoping he would have just those exact thoughts and feelings, did not enter his mind.

Once in the shower, Tucker switched gears, began reviewing his Spanish. Language had, of course, come very easily to him and his ability to remember what he heard so perfectly, fortunately extended even to his accent. He wished he'd been in contact with his boss. What WAS the purpose of this weekend? How HAD he been able to assemble key members of SOFOFA so quickly? He wished he'd had time to review bios of the people he would soon be meeting. He shook his head and again reflected that he had been far from the perfect employee lately. No doubt about it. Before his back went out, he'd have spent the entire Friday evening on his computer, would have come out to their house on Saturday morning, been there in time to help greet the guests and put them at their ease, his Spanish flawless, his tuxedo in his hang-up bag.

Despite the warmth of the shower, Tucker felt stiff, could feel his anxiety mounting. *Maybe Mr. Tyler really is ill. Maybe I've really let him down. There might be something in my electronic mailbox from Mr. Tyler--something critical-- something to do with this business weekend and I wouldn't even know it because I've been so busy doing other things that I didn't bother to check.*

360

The shower was beginning to make him feel claustrophobic. He couldn't seem to breathe properly and grabbed the shower door. Then, stopping himself firmly, he allowed his hand to drop, and stood there, facing the still closed door, panting. With great resolve, Tucker cleared his mind, as he had so many times before. Only, this time it was for a different purpose. Concentrating on keeping his mind blank, he turned off the water, stepped out, toweled down and stood in front of the bathroom mirror drawing great, deep, measured breaths until he had counted to 50. Then and only then did he allow an image to filter into the white, peaceful void of his mind. The twinkling, blue eyes were quizzical but the face had its usual gentle smile. *Whew! Dr. van Castle to the rescue,* thought Tucker with relief.

Suddenly, he realized that somehow, subconsciously almost, he had done just what the article he had pulled off his computer had said to do to prevent oneself from being consumed by a panic attack: keep still, breathe deeply, focus on something calming. *Well, if something calming could include a person; that is just what I did. I'll remember to tell him on Monday that visualizing his presence was calming.*

As Tucker hurried to unzip his hang-up bag, he decided he had better put in a quick call to his parents. There was no way of knowing otherwise, if Midge, in her search for him, had alarmed them. And besides, his mother would need some assurance that her decision to invite Charlie to their Sunday dinner was a good one. He paused, as he finished knotting his tie. Doing unconventional things was not her strong suit. If she happened to ask him about his day, which she sometimes did, he thought, *for the first time I will be able to say I spent it with new friends.* And that simple truth made him smile. It had been a very good day.

Conversely, at that very moment Midge, sitting in Faith's salon, was feeling just the opposite about her day. It had not been a good day. It was only thanks to the steadiness of Clarice and Charlie that it hadn't been a disaster. As soon as she told them about the guests they had turned to. By the time the long black car with the flags on its fenders had pulled up her driveway, Jason was in place. The house was spotless. She had huge bouquets from her garden everywhere. Charlie had the menu completely under control and was making some strange little South American sausage things for hors d'oeuvres. But, her worry about her husband had turned into a nagging fear. She kept trying not to watch him like a hawk. He seemed fine, showing one of the gentlemen from Santiago how to handle the helm as they moved in a wide circle around St. Helena Island. For the first time, she recognized just how much she had come to depend on Tucker and was disgusted with her own reaction when he said he couldn't come until this evening. She was still feeling extremely put out with him and then, with chagrin, realized how unfair her thinking was. *It is just that for three years he's always been available. And now, when I really need him, he has other things to do. Well,* she admitted, *that isn't quite true. He wasn't going to break his plans for me, but he was coming as soon as he was free.*

She frowned, remembering how, after she had calmed down and had called James for details, she found that he wanted a formal dinner on Saturday night. He told her that Clifton already knew about it and was at that moment, phoning Emory to have her break a previous engagement. He also told her that he absolutely wanted Tucker to attend.

When they had finished talking, her resolve to remain calm had vanished. She needed to talk to Tucker! But when she called, he hadn't been home. So, she had left him messages that he hadn't bothered to return. Finally, in desperation, she had been forced to call and leave all the details on his phone machine.

Just as she was working herself up into what Clarice would have called a "tizzy," she remembered with self-castigation that not very long ago her husband had told her to cut Tucker out of their social life and she had meekly agreed, would have done so, had he not relented. She sighed. "Sauce for the goose, sauce for the gander," she muttered and looked around her realizing how lost she had been in her thoughts.

She could hear the comfortable conversation of the men on the flying bridge and wondered if she should join them. But, she decided, if I can get this sorted out in my mind, perhaps I can relax and enjoy the rest of the weekend.

It had been a measure of her agitation that she had called Margaret Jones to see if Tucker was perhaps there. He wasn't, but in the course of their conversation, straight out of the blue, the cool, cultured voice asked her if she would mind terribly if Charlie were invited to their Sunday dinner with Tucker.

Only years of training and the fact that she was talking to Margaret Jones prevented her from gasping in surprise. "What a wonderful gesture." She was able to say smoothly. "I'm sure he would be delighted." What she didn't say was that her cook had been working up his courage to issue Margaret a similar invitation. Only, Charlie wanted to invite her to lunch and, with Midge's permission, to the Tuesday S.O.S. meeting with Althea and Emory. He had, in fact, worked himself into quite a kitchen-organizing and cleaning marathon over the idea before even broaching it to her.

"Good chance. Five of us talk, talk, talk. Get contest one step closer to fine organization. Very good to meet. Charlie maybe make humble Chinese lunch for ladies."

When he had very diplomatically made clear his wishes, she had managed not to laugh, glad to finally know what the early morning pot banging had been about. It was one worry she could cross off her mind.

Midge wasn't really surprised that Tucker wasn't with his parents. A piece of her had already decided that he was spending the day with Heather. It was then that she decided Tucker would be put in the room last used by Dawn. Her own perversity made her smile with secret embarrassment, but somehow it calmed her down and helped her organize her thinking.

She stretched her legs, frowned and remembered how, on Friday afternoon, after saying a very cool goodbye to her husband who was being much too bossy on the phone, she'd headed for the kitchen thinking, *poor Clarice! Six overnight guests to look after. Poor Charlie! Another last-minute do. What was my husband thinking? I'll never be able to get Jason on such short notice! What will I do then? Thank goodness Emory is coming to dinner. She can easily handle five Latin men.* Her thoughts flew on as she headed towards the kitchen to tell her staff and start her list making.

Charlie and Clarice had both been in the kitchen, Clarice scrubbing the pantry floor, Charlie sitting on his high round stool at the counter, making notes in the magic book. They both looked up sharply at the sound of her steps, long ago having distinguished the staccato sound of Midge on a mission. Her face confirmed it as she stopped just inside the doorway and looked at them for a moment.

"Oh dear! You're both here!" Which, she was sure they recognized immediately, was a very unusual thing for her to say. Then she paused so long that Clarice got to her feet in time to see her agitated mistress throw up her hands and say with a laugh that sounded not at all mirthful, "No, that's not what I meant. It's good that you're both here." Then she had stopped and sighed. "What I am trying to say," she finally said firmly, "is that I just talked to James...my husband...the man who faithfully promised that we would have a quiet weekend...has just invited five guests from South America...Chile to be precise...to spend the weekend. Dinner is to be a formal affair. He would like the food to suit ethnic tastes..." Midge's voice trailed off as if she felt the puzzled silence filling the kitchen. *And rightfully so!* She thought abruptly. Certainly this was not the first time Midge had told them about last minute plans, many far more elaborate than this. She was the mistress of impromptu get-togethers and both Charlie and Clarice took pride in that fact. But, this was the first time they had ever seen her upset about it and she could tell she had them both worried.

Clarice had been the first to find her voice. "Missus Tyler, you is plumb worried about yo' husband's health, ain't you?"

The sympathetic tone had almost made Midge break down. She had no idea that either of them knew of her concern. She tried to change her tactics and the tenor of the conversation and had to clasp her hands to keep from ringing them. There was no sense in alarming Clarice and Charlie. Aloud she said, "Well, yes. I guess I am. But I suspect I'm overreacting. I took his temperature and it was normal. He's just been a little tired, that's all. But, taking it easy hasn't seemed to have fixed his problem, so..." She paused and shrugged with resignation. "Let's face it, when I say it out loud to you, it sounds as though I'm making a great deal out of very little."

They had seemed to brighten at that and Charlie, as was typical, said, "Mam not worry. Everything okay. Plenty time to make list. Plenty time to shop for food. No guests tonight?" He made a question out of the statement and Midge shook her head. "No, no guests tonight. No guests until tomorrow after lunch. Then Tucker will be arriving tomorrow afternoon or early evening and the Eldridges will also join us for dinner. Which reminds me, I must call and see if I can persuade Jason to come out of retirement and help us one more time." She looked at them and smiled a bit too brightly. "Having a butler will simplify things, will it not?" Then she turned to escape their scrutiny and to get herself together.

By the time a calmer Midge returned with the news that Jason was available and would be delighted to lend his services, Charlie, brow furrowed, was sitting with several cookbooks in front of him but with his eyes closed and Midge knew exactly what he was doing. He was visualizing Chile: Chile the country; Chile, the people; and finally, Chile's food. He felt it helped him to do justice to what he prepared. It was his way of honoring the country, getting the feel of it, she supposed. Anyway, she always respected it as a private moment and didn't interrupt. Instead, she reached for the waiting piece of paper and began to quietly construct her list. She was feeling just a bit contrite for her earlier outburst and planned to tell Charlie so when he finished his internal concentration. But instead, the kitchen phone had rung and it had been Margaret Jones asking to speak to Charlie. By the time he hung up, Charlie was so pleased with things that his mood had affected her mood. The fact that he had actually asked Tucker's mother for a recipe and that Margaret Jones had been so delighted to have been consulted, was no less than astonishing. Even now, the thought made her smile.

And then...and then on Saturday, just before the guests arrived, had come the mail. In it were the wonderful pictures from Dawn. They were accompanied by a long, newsy letter. Midge called everyone together and read it aloud while the pictures were passed around and around. Dawn admitted that she was a little bored with the beach scene, said she missed them all, knew she was counting on admission to Tuft's fall term too much and that it didn't help one bit to have such overly confident parents. She had written letters to Deb and Tucker and had sent them pictures too. Midge raised an eyebrow in surprise and sneaked a peek at Clarice who was smiling and nodding serenely. James, however, had snorted at the news. Besides the pictures and the letter, Barbara had included the budget, the committee structure and the barbecue scholarship organization's mission statement, goals and policies. Midge was delighted on all counts.

The timing of the packet had been perfect she reflected. When their guests arrived, she and James had still been discussing the letter and she was able to meet the men with the merry ring to her voice that made the welcome seem especially sincere. *Funny how things work out,* she thought. *As Charlie says, 'It has much to do with timing.'*

On the heels of that thought came another--one that made her stop reminiscing, stand up and square her shoulders. Monday morning she was going to call and make a doctor's appointment for her husband. Sunday evening, after everyone had gone, she would sit on his lap and tell him, not ask him--put her foot down and tell him--and her timing would be perfect.

Suddenly, she felt immeasurably cheered. These were indeed pleasant guests she decided. So polite and for the most part, their English was perfectly understandable, in some cases it was impeccable. Although she noted they really appreciated it when she tried out her college Spanish. *What will they think of Tucker?* She wondered as she went to join them and to remind her jovial husband that the Eldridges and Tucker would be showing up soon for cocktails. They would need to move smartly to be changed and ready.

The evening seemed to flow smoothly. Clearly, the purpose of the dinner had to do with business, but until the ladies excused themselves and left the men with their brandy, the conversation had been quite stimulating.

366

Emory, generally the listener in mixed groups, had risen beautifully to the occasion and put herself out to make everyone feel comfortable. Unused to American women, especially ones this tall, blonde and elegant, looking taller still with her tawny hair piled high on her head, the Chileans fought their jet leg and tried not to make fools of themselves when she turned her darkly-fringed green eyes upon them and asked them serious, thoughtful questions about their country.

Had the setting been different, their culture would have permitted them to flirt outrageously. But they were well-versed in proper protocol and instead, they sincerely complemented Clifton on his choice of a wife, which for some reason greatly amused the portly ambassador who had watched the interplay with delight.

Tucker, too, was at his best. He slipped from Spanish to English and back to Spanish easily. Midge was sure that all the men were secretly convinced he had learned the language in their country, so well was he able to model their accents. Knowing how important correct social behavior and dress were to him, Midge tried to apologize to him publically for the late change of plans but he had been very gracious. If it bothered him to be the only man present not wearing a tuxedo, he hid it splendidly.

Early in the evening, everyone agreed that out of respect for the men who had just deplaned at the East Haven Airport after an 18 hour flight that included stops in Texas and Pennsylvania and had then been driven straight to the Tyler's, it would not be a late evening. But it was. Midge and Emory, quite content to sit and visit could hear the voices rise in excitement from time to time and then drone on without any real pauses.

Finally, when the Eldridges had driven away, and the guests, still talking softly to each other, mostly in their native Spanish, ascended the stairs to the west wing, Midge looked slowly from her husband to Tucker. It was easy to see that they were both excited. Not a trace of the earlier pallor or tiredness showed on James' face as he grinned at Tucker and asked, "Do you think Clifton is finally convinced?"

She felt her heart lighten. It was his old voice. Full of energy and drive and she found herself joining in with the

367

laughter when Tucker said seriously, "I think so, but you'll have to give him a couple of days to admit it."

Later, just as James was reaching up to shut off the light, he remembered to tell her that plans for tomorrow had changed. After breakfast, the men were interested in seeing the home plant and the corporate office. Then, he thought he'd take them to the club for nine holes of golf, a late lunch and off to catch their plane home.

She gasped in surprise as the light went out and lay for long moments feeling claws of anxiety tearing at her. She tried to remain objective. *He does seem much better. I'm overreacting. That's what comes from having a husband who is always healthy.* Finally, when she knew her voice was calm, she said, "Well, that's good in a way. Because if you get things wrapped up tomorrow, you can easily go to the doctor's on Monday afternoon if I can get you an appointment."

The words rang in the silence of the room and she heard him snort. *So much for timing,* she thought with a cross between disgust and sadness as she turned over and waited for sleep to come.

Chapter Thirty-one

Tucker lay in, what he continued to think of as "Dawn's bed," also waiting for sleep to come. His mind was sorting through the week's events and recognizing the magnitude and importance of the things he was allowing himself to experience: playing the piano; calling the diner; dating Heather; meeting with Dr. van Castle; not canceling the zoo trip when Mrs. T beckoned. He sighed deeply and then realized with sudden insight that he had nearly blocked the most important thing--opening the box.

After putting it off for a day, Tucker had grabbed the box and up-ended it, spilling its contents onto the sleek beige and glass coffee table. Once out of the box, the jumbled pile looked naked and somehow less significant. But, it was not. Carefully, he plucked out his journal and *Robinson Crusoe* and set them aside. Then he gingerly picked out of the pile a stack of photos that at one time had been carefully taken from Mary's refrigerator door and wrapped with a piece of Ethan's green, flower-staking string.

For many minutes it was all he could do--hold the precious pile of childhood memories, knowing once he untied the string there would be no turning back, he would have to force himself to look at every detail in the photos so lovingly taken. He could feel his resolve wavering, so he untied the knot, realizing that failure was not a choice. *I really cannot afford to fail. If I do, it might mean that I really am crazy.* The sudden truth alarmed him, but it also steadied his fumbling fingers, made his pain take a backseat to purpose and strengthened his determination.

For long moments he sat gently holding the neat stack, trying to breathe deeply. Then something caught his eye and he leaned forward again to look at the pile on the table. Amid the mostly paper jumble, the back side of a picture frame had caught his eye. He put the stack of photos down and with great care, reached out, retrieved it from the pile and turned it over. *Their wedding picture! Ethan and Mary's wedding picture, the one they kept on the mantel along with my school pictures and pictures of their Irish relatives.*

He looked at the picture closely and recognized how young they both looked. They were not really like the people he had known and cherished. In this picture, they were kids. They looked to be about 17 or 18 with clear, unlined faces and smiles of unbounded optimism. With a shock, he realized he was now about ten years older than they were when the picture was taken. Somehow, that made it easier; realizing all the years they had lived before they came into his own young life. He set the picture up firmly on the coffee table as if to give himself courage but found instead it gave him hope. He reached again for the stack of photos and began to study them, one by one.

Hours later, Tucker had turned the last picture, read the last of the papers which were mostly his school papers that Mary had first put on the refrigerator so, "everyone could see just how smart was me darlin' boy." She had evidently saved every single one.

He had also read their personal letters and had a new understanding of the family left in Ireland and how hard it must've been to leave them. The letters, especially the ones from Mary's mother, were full of pride and love for her children. Tucker understood then that Mary raised him as she had been raised. And, even as emotionally drained as he was at the moment, it was, he knew, an important understanding and one to hang onto.

This going through the box was a very different sorting than when he had quickly dipped in, grabbed a few loose photos so that he could show them to Dr. van Castle, which he remembered as exceedingly painful. This time he had dealt with the old pain and had allowed the goodness of the memories to remain. He not only carefully considered each item, but then began a slow, almost unconscious sorting, and by morning had arranged a chronology which for want of an album he put in file folders carefully labeled: Mary and Ethan before Tucker, Tucker as a baby, Tucker goes to school, and so on. The wedding picture he left sitting on the coffee table along with the book, *Robinson*

Crusoe--the parting gift of Dr. van Castle. The last thing he had done was to reread his journal.

Now, as he lay in the dark and waited for sleep at the Tyler's, he thought honestly to himself that if the day with Kathryn and the girls at the zoo had been the happiest day in his adult life, the day on the boat with Dawn the most unhappy, then that night when he'd finally forced himself to confront the box, was probably the most important one. He thought that Dr. van Castle would agree.

Tucker turned in his bed, sleep still elusive. But, he recognized that it felt different from other sleepless nights; those many nights when his whole energy had been directed at keeping intrusive thoughts at bay. His mind rambled on. *Things are going well so far with the gentleman from Chile.* Certainly, Mr. Tyler seemed pleased with what he'd heard from the ambassador and the gentleman from SOFOA. Unless Tucker missed his guess, a team from Zitec would be dispatched within the week for Chile. Who knew what their report would contain, but at least it seemed the next step would be taken. He found himself wondering idly how well the golf game would go tomorrow. He wished he could play with his own clubs, but luckily, he always carried an extra pair of golf shoes in the boot of the Aston...

Those were his last thoughts until he awoke several hours later thinking about Dawn. It seemed harder not to think about her, lying in her bed. He remembered that Midge had said, in passing, that they had received a long letter and pictures from Dawn. But at the time, Tucker couldn't think how to respond and had merely said, "Oh?" hoping she would elaborate. Instead, she looked at him oddly for a moment and changed the subject. *So, I guess she knows how badly I treated her houseguest.* He wished he'd had the opportunity to tell Midge... *Tell her what? I guess I would have to tell her that whatever caused me to behave like such an absolute idiot towards Dawn seems so illogical now that I can't even be certain of the cause.*

In the darkness of the room, he felt an old familiar feeling wash over him. He felt slightly nauseated as he pictured Mrs. Tyler's slight frown as she reassessed him, decided he wasn't the person she had come to trust and turned away in disgust. *No, I'm certainly not ready to cause that reaction.* With practiced ease, he emptied his mind.

For Midge, the sunshine streaming through the French doors of their bedroom the next morning came as a total surprise. She was certain she hadn't slept a wink and yet here it was morning. She sat up quickly and looked at her husband. He was snoring softly making soft puffing sounds. *Well, that's normal,* she thought with relief and then leaned over him checking for the pallor that had caused her concern. *Yes,* she decided. *It's still there. But then, he had quite a day yesterday. In fact, we both had quite a day!* Midge sighed. *Really, if I allowed myself to look closely in the mirror, I too, might be pale.* With that comforting thought she kissed him softly on the ear, knowing he'd want to be up before his guests. On the other hand, Tucker was an early riser and would be quite comfortable in the role of surrogate host. Clarice and Charlie certainly had things under control, perhaps she'd let him sleep longer. But it was too late. The familiar kiss caused his eyes to flutter open and then focus sleepily on her.

"Good morning, my love," he said softly with the burr of sleep still in his voice. He raised his arms and happily Midge snuggled against his chest. They lay quietly for long minutes. When he next spoke, his voice was clear. "By God but that was a productive day yesterday! Tucker may have come late, but he sure made up for it, didn't he?" He was silent for a moment and then he chuckled. "And did you notice how pleased our guests were when Jason served the piccadillo? It was a rare stroke and I must remember to compliment Charlie. He may have trouble pronouncing it, but he sure as hell could cook it!"

Midge smiled. "Charlie will of course give all the credit to Tucker's mother. I can't believe the mutual admiration society that is developing between the two of them. Tucker must've been right when he said he thought they had been curious about each other for a long time."

Her husband gave her a hard squeeze which, over the years, she had come to know meant the hugging was over; it was on with the day. She got up to start the shower for him, somehow relieved that he hadn't said anything about her final salvo before sleep concerning the doctor's appointment.

Actually, she thought as she went to get his coffee, *this has the potential to be a lovely day and I'm glad everyone is going away. I can concentrate on the material from Barbara and be ready for Monday's phone calls and Wednesday's fundraising committee meeting.*

She would also have time to call Emory and thank her sincerely for her wonderful participation during the evening. *But,* and she smiled at the thought, *perhaps the first thing I will do is sit in the quiet of the morning room after everyone leaves and write a long letter to Barbara and Dawn.* She began to feel her usual cheerful, energetic self.

Kathryn's alarm went off at 6:30 and she immediately came awake remembering: *My last day with Allison and we've so much to do.* It was a good thing, she decided, because if she allowed herself to sit around she would get maudlin. She lay for a moment, picturing the two little girls sashaying and curtsying down the aisle of the diner behind Jake and grinned to dispel the tightness of her throat. *What will that girl come up with next?* She threw back her quilt and went to wake her daughter before going to make coffee.

She paused a moment before the bedroom door, stealing herself to be cheerful, reminding herself how important it was not to let on how lonesome she would be, how important it was not to admit how her heart caught in her throat when she thought about sending Allison down the long causeway to the jet by herself... She gave herself a mental shake. *I am going to have to do better,* she chided herself as she opened the door and Jon Bon made his usual graceful, unhurried exit.

Crossing to the bed, she purposefully did not linger over the form of her sleeping daughter but instead shook her lightly saying, "Wake up, darlin'. Remember, it's 8:00 o'clock mass for us today, and since we played all day yesterday, we've got a fair amount left to get organized."

She didn't wait to see Allison rise, instead quickly retreated, practically running down the stairs to let out the cat. *I really am going to have to do better than this,* she thought in disgust.

Allison unknowingly helped. She came bouncing down the stairs, her brown hair a kinky cloud around her face. Already she was recalling yesterday's events, organizing today's tasks, getting excited about her first airplane ride without a parent and trying to talk her mother out of going to mass. There was so much on her mind she didn't know what to say first, which made her start to giggle.

Kathryn, who hadn't heard her barefooted entry, turned with surprise. This was her Sunday morning slug-a-bed. She had expected to have to give two or three more wake-up calls. It distracted her enough to take the edge off her sorrow and allow her voice just the right amount of its usual lilt.

"Hello, darlin', you certainly found your sense of humor earlier than usual. Did you put it under your pillow to keep it handy?"

They smiled at each other. It was an old saw. Allison said, with the laughter still in her voice, "I was just thinking so many things at once it seemed like my mind got jammed and I didn't know what to say first; and if I said something it would come out like a foreign language."

Kathryn laughed. "Well, me darling', if one of those thoughts was to talk me out of going to mass this morning, that's one you can set aside."

Allison gave a theatrical sigh and walked across the cool linoleum floor for her hug. *How does my mother do that?* She once again wondered fondly. Aloud she said, "Well, maybe I did think that just a little, but mostly I was thinking about yesterday. Wasn't that fun, Mom? Nicki said it was the most fun in the world! Do you think Tucker will really take us to Jake's again? Wasn't he simply wonderful?"

Kathryn wasn't quite sure who her daughter was referring to as 'wonderful', Tucker or Jake. But, on reflection, it didn't matter. They had both been quite lovely. She laughed and gave her daughter a pat. "I'll be the first to admit that I had my reservations when you chose Tucker as your friend to go to the zoo. But I'll also admit that it did turn out quite well. It was a perfect day and I was very proud of your manners when you thanked him. I hope he noticed that you 'curtsied' him out of sight. It was a nice touch."

Allison looked at her, soaking in the compliment, and then she said, "I believe I'll have Trix for breakfast," before turning to scoot back up the stairs, leaving her mother standing, shaking her head while she finished making the coffee.

While she waited for it, she thought about Tucker. *How different he seems. Throughout the day he would get all stiff and proper but each time, he seemed to consciously shake it off. He was certainly wonderful with the girls. And didn't he have a natural way of setting limits while indulging them just the same?* She smiled to herself. He had been a comfortable companion, easy-going and even easier to talk to most of the time. She still couldn't quite believe she had told him the sordid details about Allison's father.

She stopped her thoughts. "PETE!" She said aloud in the empty kitchen. *The man has a name,* she thought with a bit of self-disgust. *Why do I insist on referring to him as 'Allison's father?'* The old familiar pain washed over her. *Will I never get over missing the man?* She wondered sadly if ever a day would go by that she wouldn't have to fight the image of his face bending over hers and the feel of his arms. With a grimace she realized she had her own arms wrapped around her body as if giving herself a hug. *It's your own fault,* she thought with vicious honesty. *He'd be here this very minute. We'd all be going to mass together... and then on Monday I'd put them on a plane and spend the entire summer recovering.* The old anger reasserted itself. *Damn! Damn his selfish, globe-trotting soul to hell!* She clenched her fists as the anger swept over her and then with a frown she realized that there was to be no blessed communion for her today, not without confession first. With a sigh, she went to rob coffee from the pot.

She heard Allison turn the shower off. *Maybe I should try to fall in love with Tucker Jones,* she thought as she mounted the stairs, coffee in hand. And then she sighed. She'd been over this route many times before. Pure sexual need had made her bed with a man or two, but her conscience had smote her dreadful blows, both because of her strong religious convictions and because she knew she was simply using someone. Tucker Jones seemed troubled enough already. What he needed was a friend--and she could use one too.

375

Tucker found that he was having a very good day on the golf course despite the strange clubs. Mr. Tyler had split their group and the two foursomes were playing a great game of best ball, which worked out perfectly as it took the edge off his bosses' famous competitiveness and allowed those in the group who hadn't played much to relax and have fun. It also moved the game along faster, which was important because the visit to Zitec had taken longer than either Mr. Tyler or he had anticipated. Each man seemed to have an area of expertise, and by the time the men had finished asking questions, it was clear they had touched on all areas considered relevant, including economics, engineering, research and development, and human resources. Tucker was sure one of the men, Julio, had leanings towards environmentalism. There had been questions on that front as well. *One thing's for sure, these guys are more than just accountants. I wish my father could've watched the team operate.*

Thinking of his father made him remember that Charlie was driving to New Haven with him for the evening. He had seen Charlie only briefly in the morning and he seemed as serene as usual, but Tucker wondered if it was a façade. His mother, when he'd called to check in, had certainly admitted that she was feeling a bit nervous about having such an accomplished chef at her table. He shook his head. *This is going to be an interesting evening. It's funny how the lines in my life that had run so predictably straight are now getting intertwined.* He surprised himself that the jumble seemed perfectly acceptable.

For Charlie, the day had not seemed to have found a pace. First it rushed. Then it shuffled on slow feet and now it was rushing again, just when he least wanted it to. There was something on his mind. He had been thinking about a gift for Mrs. Jones. He had rejected flowers. Tucker said she had gardens full of flowers and besides the flowers really belonged to the Tylers. He wanted the gift to be something from him. Candy was too common and too Western. He wanted the gift to reflect the Asian culture. Food, in this case, was out of the question. Any delicacy he might make she would compliment and that would take the edge off of her gift of allowing him to sit as a guest at her table. Any small trinket would be presumptuous and besides, he did not know her tastes. Sighing deeply, he kneeled, with back straight, on a small cushion in front of a low table. There was only one thing he could give her--a piece of himself. He looked at the carefully assembled items, picked up a slender rice brush, dipped it carefully in the small pot of black ink and composed in his mind:

Life,
a fragile
heartbeat and wings
lights, safe for a moment,
in the gentle hand of a friend.

He worked quickly. The real work had already been done. This was simply a transfer to paper what had been carefully pictured in his mind. The brush dipped again and around the triangle of calligraphy grew a simple spidery spray of purple iris. He did not add the butterfly that was in his mind, confident that if the gift was well received, Tucker's mother would see it there.

He waited patiently until he was sure the ink had dried, rolled the small piece of rice paper carefully and tied it with a slender thread of purple ribbon. Then satisfied, he rose to begin preparations for dressing. The matter of his dress had also been given careful consideration. Generally, when working, he wore the comfortable trousers and loose over-blouse of his mother's countrymen. However, when he visited his stockbroker or visited the track, he dressed as others dressed. It would seem most appropriate to dress as the Tylers dressed when going out to dinner.

Clarice, who secretly thought the whole idea of his going to dinner at Tucker's home was probably a big mistake, had nevertheless held her tongue and agreed that she would stay and serve the Tylers the dinner he had prepared. She was sitting at the table sipping coffee, resting her tired legs on a second chair, when Charlie walked through the doorway from his quarters. From the startled look on her face, he suspected that for one brief moment, she didn't recognize him. If so, it was a very satisfactory response.

377

He stood before her silently, waiting with carefully composed face while she looked her fill, trying to reconcile the fact that her friend of many years and this very dapper man dressed in a dark camel jacket of cashmere, conservative in a white shirt, burgundy tie and gray slacks, were one and the same.

"My!" She said at last, "my, but don't you look fine. You is lucky I had dese ol' legs of mine propped, elsewise I'd cracked yo' haid wif de nearest kettle fo' I knew it was you."

Charlie bowed low, but not before she saw the pleased smile on his face. Then she looked down at his feet and saw the dark tasseled loafers peeking below the sharply creased slacks. It was almost too much. Suddenly, she felt almost shy. "I don' know 'bout dis. Seems like you a stranger. I cain't call a man yo' age wearin' them tasseled shoes, Charlie. Be like callin' Mr. Tyler, 'Jimmy'."

There was so much sincerity in her voice that Charlie felt at a loss to respond. He searched his mind frantically for the right words and like a small gift they came to him. "Okay," he said, "okay, when I dress like this you call me Mr. Wong. I call you Mrs. Johnson. We drink coffee do nice talk about world." So saying, he casually poured himself a cup, unbuttoned his jacket and sat down across from her. "All the same, we know same fine people inside." He wished he'd written her a poem too.

Chapter Thirty-two

Tucker felt pleasantly tired when he unlocked the door to his condo. It had been an evening full of surprises, starting with when he went to find Charlie and instead found a dapper, well-dressed man sitting at the table with his back to the door, chatting with Clarice.

He had said apologetically, "Oh, excuse me, Clarice. I was looking for Charlie." And then Charlie turned around, with a smile so glowing that it made his whole face into a prism of shining creases.

Later, driving to New Haven, Tucker had tried to somehow prepare Charlie for the fact that the dinner table conversation was generally relegated to his mother's latest recipes and that generally, she did the serving herself. Only, that wasn't how the dinner had gone at all. His mother was very nervous at first, but Charlie, whom his father had called Mr. Wong, was clearly at ease. In fact, he seemed to be enjoying the evening immensely. Over cocktails on the patio, the talk had been of international finance, the world economy and the stock market. Only now and again over dinner, did his mother's recipes come up and that was when the conversation was initiated by Charlie or himself. Thomas's wife, Beth, whose name Tucker could finally remember, did a competent job of serving and clearing.

After dinner, Charlie and his mother excused themselves and disappeared into the kitchen for about 20 minutes while Tucker told his father about the possibility of Zitec expanding to Chile and how impressed he'd been with the thoroughness of SOFOFA's data collection. Then Hank had come. Charlie had handed his mother a small round cylinder pulled from the inner pocket of his jacket, thanked them both sincerely, complimented his mother's cooking once again, shook hands all around and departed.

At his condo, Tucker flipped on a light and the first thing he saw was the wedding picture. His mind froze for only a moment and then he smiled. *Somehow, with them in it, the room does not look quite so sterile. Tomorrow,* he decided, *I will ask Kathryn what she knows about houseplants.*

He looked at his phone and its blinking light and sighed in resignation. At least some of the calls would be from Mrs. T. At least one of them was telling him to bring his tuxedo. *At this point, Friday seems a long time ago.* He sighed again, pushed the button and listened with surprise at the note of stress in Midge Tyler's voice. He mulled the cause as she had seemed fine over the weekend and decided he would call her in the morning and do some gentle probing.

Then, into the quiet of the condo came the clear confident voice of Allison...*Sunny*. Sometime, during the zoo visit he had followed Nicki's lead and had begun calling her that. Let Kathryn continue to call her Allison. He would call her Sunny. It suited her.

"Hello, Tucker. This is Allison Amanda McCall. I'm calling to thank you for taking us all to breakfast at Jake's and then to the zoo. Nicki said to tell you thank you, too. She also said to tell you her father saw your car and was very impressed. My mom said, 'If you didn't mind, she would give me your address so that I could write to you from Texas. Remember, I leave tomorrow morning, on an airplane, all by myself."

Tucker smiled at the evident pride in her voice. Then he could hear her turn from the receiver and say, "Mom, do you want to talk?" He could hear Kathryn's distant voice say, "No, I'll thank him in person tomorrow." It gave him a good feeling.

He had known that Allison was leaving on Monday, but for some reason, on Saturday, it seemed far off. He wished he'd called her to say goodbye. He would miss her he realized with a pang. *And if I'm already missing her, what is Kathryn feeling?* He thought he knew and again, the feeling of caring washed over him. *It's funny how life works. If anyone deserves a happy home and a loving, sensible husband, it is Kathryn McCall.* He remembered once wondering how it would feel to kiss her. Now it felt more like he wanted to hug her and pat her on the back.

Tucker picked up his bags and headed towards the bedroom, leaving the unopened mail in a clutter on his counter. There was seldom anything in his mailbox that couldn't wait another day; important things came by computer. What he wanted now was a long steamy shower and sleep. He decided not to set his alarm.

As he slipped between cool sheets, it passed through his mind that he felt truly sleepy, which was his last thought for several hours. By morning, after having slept soundly for most of the night, Tucker awoke to the jarring ring of his telephone.

"Tucker, this is Tobin van Castle. Listen, sorry to call you so early, but is there any chance we could meet for a little longer today? The two graduate students I see on Monday at 1:00 o'clock are doing a co-presentation at a mental health conference. Friday really did feel rushed to me."

Tucker sat up and cradled the receiver to his chest, trying to get oriented. Finally, when he realized the pause was growing too long, he said. "Give me a second, Dr. van Castle, I'm right in the middle of a miracle." Then he laughed. "First of all, for the first time since I can remember, I slept through most of the night and now I wake to find YOU asking ME for more time. If that's not a miracle, then I'm still dreaming."

He heard the familiar boyish laugh. "Great. I can't wait to hear. Got to rush now. I'm late for my eight o'clock class. See you at noon, same place, same drooling receptionist." There was a click and Tucker looked at his clock. The good doctor WAS late. The clock read 8:05.

Tucker lay back and thought of Allison. *By now she and her mother are headed for the airport.* He wished again that he'd thought to call. Perhaps instead, he would get her address in Texas from Kathryn and write to her there; provide her personally with his address so she could write to him if she wanted to do so.

He stretched luxuriously and swung gently out of bed, fully awake, to begin his limbering exercises. He felt supple, full of energy...and hungry. He put on his robe and headed for the kitchen, grabbing the remote control on the television as he went. A little news; a little coffee; a great day.

He flipped casually through the mail, saw the envelope, looked in disbelief at the return address and felt the world turned to glue. He saw his hands reach out, felt himself back away from the counter, hook the leg of one of the chrome and leather kitchen chairs, pull it towards himself and sit down, all in slow motion. He put the letter flat on the table in front of him and stared at it. Then he closed his eyes and felt himself return to regular time.

His fingers drummed the table beside the letter. His heart was lurching in his chest. His stomach was in a knot. *What does this overreaction to a piece of mail mean?* It was a letter from Dawn, the woman he was sure would never speak to him again, the only woman to whom he had been unspeakably rude.

Suddenly, what it meant came to him. *She's writing to tell me what a jerk I was and how she hoped he would absent himself if ever she was again visiting the Tyler's. Yes,* he thought grimly, *that would be logical.*

Tucker rose from the table and put the kettle on the stove, prepared the filter, and ground the beans. *A man needs a little coffee in his system before he reads a letter like that--even when he deserves it,* he thought glumly to himself. Then, irresistibly, the letter pulled him back to the table. He picked it up, smelled it, hoping for a hint of perfume and walked to his desk for his letter opener. He slit the top precisely and withdrew the folded note paper. Two pictures fell out. He looked at them absently...one of Heather and another of Heather and himself on the Tyler's boat. Peering into the empty envelope, he felt vaguely disappointed that Dawn had not included a picture of herself.

He looked down at the round script and read--then he paused and read again, and again. He didn't understand. *Once she knew about Heather...know WHAT about Heather? What had Heather to do with his keeping a distance?* But he ignored that thought for a moment. Two sentences were ringing like bells in his mind. *She liked being in my arms. That's what the letter said. "In your arms."* The other bell ringer was that she hoped "they could be friends."

The whistle on the kettle was shrieking. He hurried to the stove and turned off the gas. In his excitement he slopped hot water on the stove and on the counter as he tried to make his coffee and control his mind. He laughed aloud. The old Tucker would've gotten a towel and carefully mopped up the mess. The new Tucker didn't care; he was just thankful he hadn't burned himself.

Hunger forgotten, he took his coffee and the letter into the living room. This time he read it through slowly, savoring each word. Then he looked long and hard at the picture of Ethan and Mary. "Whew!" He said to the silent, smiling couple. "I'm glad you two are the only ones who can see me acting so crazy."

Then he grinned and sipped his coffee. It wasn't a very long letter he decided. He turned it over looking for words on the back. There were none. *What did she mean...that he was more perceptive than she thought possible? About what?*

He rose and drifted over to the piano, lost in thought. Absently, he pulled his robe tighter, sat at the bench and raised the lid. He began to play softly, lost in thought. But gradually the music took over and he played the keys as if he were caressing them. The music was light and full of air. He knew this music. It was from his childhood. He even remembered the name of the book, *Classics of Springtime.* He thought of his old teacher, Mr. Hermann and knew he would be delighted to know that Tucker remembered the music.

Getting up from the bench, he retrieved his cup from the coffee table. That it was nearly cold didn't faze him. Walking to his desk, he pulled out a piece of his stationary and sat down at the table.

> *Dear Dawn,*
> *I Just read your letter. Thank you for sending the pictures. I will see that Heather gets them as requested. I also will give her your regards.*

Tucker read what he'd written. It sounded stiff and pompous. He wadded up the paper. *Maybe if I eat something I can do better.*

During breakfast he pondered what to say. After breakfast, he addressed the envelope and then decided that he should shower and dress before he tried to write. During his shower he realized that he had not yet summarized his impressions of the weekend and if he didn't get them out before he left for the university, Mr. Tyler was going to be wondering where they were. He dressed in a hurry and sat down at the computer. He sent the summary to Mr. Tyler at 11:15 and then looked at his watch. He needed to leave in five minutes. He groaned. *No time to write a letter now!*

Tucker walked into the psychology building in a state of high agitation. His face when he asked for Dr. van Castle destroyed the well-rehearsed, casual conversation Sarah had been rehearsing and planning for since the preceding Friday. One couldn't carry on a casual conversation with a man who was striding about the foyer, hands jammed in his pockets, frowning like thunder. "Yes, sir. I'll ring him immediately," she said in what she hoped was a very professional voice, but he seemed not to have even heard her. She sighed. He was definitely what her Grandma Collins would call a "dreamboat."

When Dr. van Castle rounded the corner and saw Tucker's level of agitation, he feared the worst. The man seemed very distressed. The doctor had spent the weekend worrying about the number of changes Tucker had been making in such a very short time. He planned to alert him to the fact that too many changes too fast could cause him to feel out of control and susceptible to depression. Letting go of old ways and replacing them with new ways of thinking and doing needed to be done slowly and with careful thought.

Tucker looked up from his pacing to see the doctor bearing down on him, the look of worry altering his normally cheerful face.

Tucker managed a weak smile. "Hello, doctor. Am I ever glad to see you!"

Van Castle took a deep breath and let it out slowly while looking Tucker carefully over. He was shaven, neatly dressed and his eyes, though worried, were clear. Perhaps then, he wasn't in such bad shape after all.

384

"We could go into my office if you'd like," he said simply. To which Tucker smiled a genuine smile and said, "Fine!"

When Tucker finally unraveled the story about Dawn, if anything, he exaggerated the magnitude of his rude behavior. He gave himself no quarter, though he stumbled a bit trying to explain the rescue and his reaction to carrying her up and down the stairs. But Dr. van Castle, having himself been often very physically attracted to women, caught and interpreted correctly what Tucker was telling him and barely managed to hide his smile.

"Would you describe this woman to me?" He said mildly and then sat back, eyes twinkling, while Tucker recalled every lovely detail, surprisingly, starting with the odor of her perfume. Then he stopped talking and frowned, "But, then the next morning, we were standing together on the porch. We were laughing and talking...and I...I guess I had one of those attacks. But I think I changed my fear to anger. I handed her the coffee cup I was holding, literally turned on my heel and stalked off. For some reason I was furious...and I stayed furious. The whole weekend I was absolutely miserable and I kept as much distance between us as possible."

The twinkle left the doctor's eyes and he leaned forward in his chair. "Can you remember what you two were talking about when you first felt anxious?"

Tucker shook his head. "No. Not really. Something about what people meant when they described her as a 'California girl'...and..." Tucker stopped and looked puzzled, "and something else..." Then he shook his head.

The doctor was still leaning forward. "Don't you find it interesting, Tucker--that you can remember the conversations of an entire board meeting, but that you can't remember the contents of a conversation with the woman to whom you are obviously attracted?"

He was pleased to see that Tucker looked shocked. They sat for a moment in silence, looking at each other and then the doctor continued, speaking very softly. "This is important stuff we're doing, my friend. For the first time we are talking about something deep and painful for you and you haven't given me your, 'Aw, Doc, routine.' It's a significant change. Let's stick with this. Let's think about it

385

together. My guess is one of you said something that triggered what you kept suppressed for these many years."

Tucker seemed to be thinking hard, but then he shook his head. After a moment, the doctor leaned back and took a deep breath. "Let's try something else. But first," he laughed ruefully, "we both need to try to relax."

He was impressed when Tucker nodded obediently, closed his eyes and began taking measured, deep breaths. After a second of reflection, the doctor followed suit.

After a long minute Tobin said, "Okay. Now let's assume, although it might not be true, that your anxiety was triggered by Dawn or some circumstance surrounding her. Perhaps she reminded you of something?"

Tucker shook his head.

"Does she remind you of anyone?"

Again Tucker shook his head, but this time he grinned. "Other than that she looks like a Madison Avenue promotion for selling holiday packages to Southern California beaches."

The doctor chuckled but was not deterred. "Why was she at the Tylers?"

The smile suddenly left Tucker's face and was replaced by a puzzled frown. "Her mother and father are old friends of the Tylers. Dawn is thinking about going to Tufts." He stopped and his frown deepened. "I thought it was a Master's degree in psychology, but I can now remember clearly Midge telling me that she planned to work with disabled children...no, I think she is a psychologist and does what you do...analyzes people I mean." He laughed nervously. "I don't know why I think that."

The doctor sat quietly as Tucker's voice dribbled to a stop and he raised his eyes to the doctor's. With satisfaction, the older man could see that the eye contact was really an almost subconscious touching of bases. Tucker was still wrestling with the truth.

"Physically handicapped kids, like kids who have been in an accident or who have birth defects...that's very different than what you do, isn't it?"

Tobin nodded and found himself holding his breath. Inside his whole being was a one-man cheering section rooting for the psyche of Tucker Jones. "Yes, it's very different from what I do. Although some of the upper division, undergraduate courses would be the same: psychology, sociology, philosophy." *There,* he thought hopefully, *that's a tiny clue to help Tucker attach his wonderful mind to the real issue.*

Tucker continued as if the doctor had not spoken. "What YOU do has to do with helping a person on the inside...with their feelings. What Dawn does has to do more with the person's, in this case, a child's outsides. But why was I so sure..." He stopped and corrected his thought and as he did his face cleared. "I was AFRAID she was going to try to analyze me...and THAT was what caused me to behave like such an ASS!" The silence in the little office was complete.

Say it Tucker. SAY IT! Keep on. You are almost there!" Internally, the psychiatrist was imploring. Externally, his face was bland but attentive, his body relaxed. If only Tucker could get through the next bit, then he could admit to him his piece of what had been profoundly troubling him about his work with Tucker these many years.

Tucker exceeded his expectations. "It's amazing actually. Now that I've said that, I can remember our conversation very clearly. She simply said she had a degree in psychology...and I came apart because I was S-O-O-O afraid this woman I was S-O-O-O attracted to would see inside me, see what a mess I am!"

Tobin van Castle took a deep breath. "WAS!" he said with such heartfelt gratitude in his voice that it startled them both. Then he made a sound in his throat that passed for a laugh. "It sounds to me that you, at the time of the conversation, WERE a mess. Today, at this moment, sitting in this office, I would say unequivocally that you have made great progress. I was going to give you a lecture today about making too many changes too quickly, but you are an unusual man."

They looked at each other for a long moment and then the doctor spread his hands and took a deep breath, anxious to purge himself. "I did go over your records this weekend." He grinned wryly. "You should have seen my own avoidance techniques. Every time I'd start to reach for those old notebooks, I'd find myself heading to the kitchen for a snack instead. But once I got into those chart notes, I found myself clinically detached and quite fascinated. First of all, I would like to candidly admit that you were too clever for me. Evidently my own boyhood stuff was in my way, so that I couldn't see you clearly." He smiled sadly. "I even gave you a book I'd bought at about age 12 or 13--just your age." A trace of self-anger came into his voice. "It was so clear when I reviewed the notebooks..." He shook his head as if returning to the present and smiled at Tucker. "Would you be interested in my current thinking?"

Tucker nodded mutely, feeling elated and drained simultaneously, but immensely curious about what the doctor would say. He listened with rapt attention and nodded in agreement at some of the perceptions, looked surprised at others, but did not break the silence.

"So, until the time Ethan and Mary left for Ireland, the developmental needs of your childhood were being met. I give your parents absolute credit for setting that up. But afterwards, being so extremely introverted, they may have recognized your grief, but were unable to reach out and comfort you either in words or actions. Actually, they may have even blocked knowledge of the depth of your grief because they were having difficulty handling their own; or perhaps they just loved you too much to admit to each other that you could love Ethan and Mary so much that their loss would make you ill. Whatever the reason, you might want to recognize the role you played in this. According to Jeff Beemers, you acted out a tremendous part. You stuffed those feelings of guilt: (If you'd pleaded with them perhaps they would not have gone to Ireland.) Anger: (How could they leave me like this?) Fear: (Who can/will take care of me now?) And of course, the tremendous sadness: (Who will kiss and hug me now?)" Tobin looked somberly at Tucker. "Who was going to fill that terrible void in your life?"

As he ticked off the repressed emotions, van Castle sounded much as though he were giving a lecture to students. Then he paused and his voice changed. "Jeff Beemers broke down that wall and I, well, it's more complicated than this, but it's like I've said before, instead of seizing the therapeutic moment when your defenses were down, I gave you books to read...because you see, I had somehow allowed what Freud would call countertransference to occur. The doctor, namely me, who should have been there to help you deal with your pain couldn't stand it either. I was your accomplice in rebuilding the wall, brick by brick, finer and more carefully engineered than ever before."

With horror, Tucker recognized that tears were sliding down the doctor's ruddy cheeks and then realized with a shock that they were also sliding down his own.

"I don't know what made the wall start to crumble, Tucker. I don't know what allowed you to begin feeling again. But I have the strong sense that whatever the circumstances, you have come through the worst and I can't even express how glad I am to be able to be any part you'll permit."

The youthful, older man and the gentle-eyed younger man sat looking at each other, flooded by emotion, unable to think of a meaningful way to break the silence.

Finally, the doctor opened his deep side drawer, pulled forth a large box of tissue and set it on the desk between them. "Now," he said, blowing his nose, "now, you see why I cannot be your therapist when we're sitting here 'therapizing' together? And besides, I feel certain that the anger you felt with Dawn when she had a degree in psychology had actually more to do with repressed anger at me than anything else." He blew his nose again, harder this time. "Jesus, but it feels good to get this off my chest. Until I started talking, I didn't know how much it has been weighing..." He looked sharply at Tucker. "Will you accept my apology, delayed though it is?"

Tucker was still mopping his own eyes, trying to take comfort in how comfortable the doctor seemed to feel with his own tears. He nodded, swallowed a few times to open his throat, blew his nose and with his gentle humor reasserting itself said, "Well, I'm not sure yet. Tell me first what you meant about it being your fault that I was angry with Dawn."

Dr. van Castle smiled sadly and said, "My guess is that the words psychiatry and psychology carry about the same meaning for you. Well, once you trusted somebody, namely me, a specialist, respected expert in understanding the psyche of adolescents, you let me get very close. And then I terminated you. I don't think you were willing to be terminated again. It hurt too damned much! Better for you to do the terminating."

"Oh," said Tucker, his voice unreadable. "I guess I'll have to think about that for a while. But in the meantime, I'll forgive you, even buy your lunch, if you'll tell me what to do about reconnecting with Dawn.

The doctor paused, allowing what felt like a benediction from Tucker to sink in. "It seems pretty simple actually. After you've decided how you really feel about her, write and tell her-- don't mince words. Just tell her the truth."

Chapter Thirty-three

Kathryn was crying and talking softly to herself when Tucker walked into what he thought would be a deserted garden. She was kneeling in front of the fountain with her back to him, the sound of the gate evidently masked by the gurgle of the water. He looked at his watch, surprised that she was not with a client and wondered with sudden insight if she was having a private moment. *After all*, he reflected, *only that morning she had put Sunny on the plane, sending her off to the man she evidently still loved but chose not to see.*

"Hello," he said gently to the bent back, "would you like company or would you prefer to be alone?"

Her head jerked around and he could then see the tracks of tears on her face. She rose, brushing off her knees and giving a quick wipe to her eyes with her sleeve. "Ah, Tucker, I'm just takin' some stray leaves from the fountain and feelin' a bit sorry for myself. It takes me a day or so to adjust to her being gone."

Tucker reached into his pocket for his handkerchief. *Luckily,* he reflected pensively to himself, *since I availed myself to the tissues proffered by Dr. van Castle, it is still clean.*

He nodded, "I can well imagine. I'm sure she is missing you too." He handed her the handkerchief and suddenly she was against his chest, tears flowing anew. "Don't give me sympathy. I'll never be able to stop this blatherin' if you give me sympathy."

Tucker looked down in surprise. Her coppery head was buried on his chest, her hands were clutching his shirt front and she was sobbing softly. There was a queer sensation in his throat. His arms, which had been hanging loosely at his sides, seemed on their own volition, to rise up and fold her in. His body began to sway back and forth, gently rocking in the age-old rhythm of comfort.

Odd, he thought, *how familiar this all feels.* But he couldn't recall ever holding anyone to comfort them. Then he closed his eyes in quiet understanding. *Of course! Of course I know this feeling.* Only this time, instead of Mary holding him to comfort, he was holding a facsimile of Mary. He felt a flood of feeling wash through him.

The garden was again working its magic, connecting him to the unremembered memories and feelings. No wonder he felt so comfortable sharing time with this no nonsense, loving, Irish woman; could tell her about worries and hurts and could tolerate her hands on his back.

Long after her sobbing had ceased, they stood, rocking in the gentle filtered shade of the smoke tree, lost in their own private thoughts. Finally, he stepped back, but still holding her by the arms and said in almost a whisper, "I did some crying of my own today and for the first time I don't deride those who say things about the healing effect of tears."

Kathryn stepped back further and looked up at him in wonder. *Is this the cardboard man of just two weeks ago? Surely not. This man is looking at me with genuine concern on his face and has just shared something very, very private. And just now, when I really needed comfort, I found it against his shirt front.*

It struck her then, that if there was anyone in the world she wanted to see in this time of sad adjustment, it would be either her mother or Tucker Jones.

She put her left hand over the one of his that still held her arm and gave it a pat. "Thank you, Tucker. All the lecturing and chastising I've been doing to myself this day didn't do nearly the good of that hug. Lonesome...and alone I was feeling...and enjoying feeling a bit sorry for myself, I'd wager."

Kathryn smiled and made good use of the snowy cotton handkerchief--one of dozens provided from Brooks Brothers via his mother. She looked at her watch and then she looked at his backpack. "I don't have anyone but you scheduled today. And I only scheduled you in because when you called the other day, you sounded as though you were maybe going to allow me to finally get my hands on the rest of your body." She tried for a bit of humor and was able to manage a small twinkle through the drying tears.

392

He smiled down at her. "Not yet, but soon. The garden is still working its magic you know," he said in a voice tinged with wonder. "What I'd like, if you have the time, is for us to just sit and talk for a moment. I've had quite a day and obviously, so have you."

In Tucker's pack was the latest homework assignment from Dr. van Castle. "Before this is done," the doctor assured him, "you will have an understanding of psychological terms and concepts that would definitely allow you to talk the same language as any brown-eyed, long-legged, blonde psychology major from California."

The assignment had been to read about the function of denial systems and to learn the difference between suppression and repression. He looked around the garden and down at Kathryn again. The assignment could wait. "What do you say?"

She smiled a genuine smile and said, with an Irish accent, "I say you are a fine human being and I thank Jeff Beemers for sending you. Sit yourself and I'll pop in and get us some lemonade."

He used the time to think about his new discovery regarding the qualities of Ethan and Mary that he must have absorbed just by being with them. It felt as though he had been given a gift: The ability to comfort Kathryn when she needed it and to be able to do so without feeling, deep down, that he was a phony.

Returning with the tray, Kathryn said without preamble, "I was thinking again, how you seem to have changed in the short time and I've known you," and noticed his pleased look.

Nodding slowly, he said, "Yes, I think I have...and part of it has to do with your garden."

She looked at him with such disbelief that he grinned. "I'll try to explain, but I must caution you that when said out loud, it may sound unbelievable, but do try."

Kathryn watched the unidentifiable flickers of emotion in his eyes as he searched for words. "Until recently, I prided myself on keeping absolute control. I have a friend who, just today, described what I'd done was to build a wall to protect myself. Well, to do that, one must spend a great deal of energy NOT feeling, NOT trusting,

393

and NOT experiencing. Which means, in my case, my energy was spent on pretending."

Tucker shot Kathryn a quick glance and found her absorbed in his words, her brows knitted with concern and concentration. He sighed again and struggled to continue. "Then my back gave out and Doctor Beemers sent me to you and you sent me to this garden." Here he paused and looked around and she looked too, trying to see it with his eyes.

He continued, "I can't describe how it affected me…it hugged me as I hugged you just now…and it got me back in touch with Ethan and Mary." His eyes closed, remembering both the pain and the joy.

Kathryn sat perfectly still waiting for him to continue. "Ethan and Mary were like my second set of parents, only they died when I was young and it hurt so much to think of them that I made up my mind not to. That was the start of closing down those feelings and other feelings as well."

Tucker looked at her, brown eyes opened and focused so she could clearly see the old sadness of his loss. "I spent much of my childhood in our gardens with Ethan and Mary."

After Tucker had finished talking, they sat quietly, letting the importance of the words lie between them. It was a companionable silence with each feeling grateful for the other's understanding and then simultaneously, each tried to thank the other.

Laughing, Tucker said, "I have been duly warned about making too many changes too fast. My friend, who is also a psychiatrist, says I'm liable to crash. But, it doesn't feel like that at all. I feel hopeful, energized and like I'm seeing things through a different pair of lenses. For example, I have been very satisfied with the looks of my condo. Then, yesterday, I tried to look at it through your eyes. Now, I can see how precise and sterile it looks." He grimaced. "It's actually horrible!"

Kathryn smiled at him. "Maybe it's only because it doesn't suit you anymore. It makes sense that if you are changing, your home will have to change if it is to be a reflection of you."

Tucker looked slowly around the garden. "Yes," he nodded, "that makes sense...as this garden is a reflection of you." He remembered his earlier thought. "I don't suppose you'd like to come to my condo and make some suggestions? I'd fix you dinner in exchange for your advice."

Kathryn laughed, feeling inordinately pleased that Tucker saw the garden as a part of her, but a little embarrassed that Tucker had invited her to his home. She didn't THINK he was romantically interested in her, but still, good Catholic girl that she was, the thought of having dinner with a man, younger to be sure, but eligible and handsome as well... She knew what her mother would say. But then she mentally shrugged. She believed that men and women could be platonic friends. In fact, spending time with Tucker felt just like that. He was just enough younger that she felt safe, a bit sisterly in fact. "Sure. It's kind of you to ask, especially since I'm in my adjustment phase of missing Allison."

They talked on. Kathryn told Tucker that Allison had asked for his address so she could write him a proper thank you letter, something he already knew from the phone call.

Tucker told Kathryn he'd already decided, after getting her goodbye phone call, that with Kathryn's permission, he'd send off a letter immediately and include his return address. She seemed genuinely delighted and insisted that he pull a pen and paper out of his backpack and write it down. "So I won't forget to give it to you. My mind is a bit woolly today, as you've probably noticed." She smiled dolefully and Tucker patted her hand in silent sympathy.

Midge and Charlie were feeling very satisfied with themselves: Midge because, though the doctor couldn't see her husband until Wednesday afternoon, she had made the appointment and when she called James to tell him, he had agreed, without protest, to go.

Charlie was feeling pleased, because Margaret Jones was joining the group for lunch tomorrow. He knew his luck was auspicious because everything had worked out so well. He nodded seriously to himself. *It is important to give credit to Mam. It was her idea, both the cooking contest and inviting Mrs. Jones and my humble self to join the ladies for required planning before she met again with the fund raising committee.* Then he smiled. *Well, perhaps one gentle nudge from this gentleman help Mam make that good decision to include judges in future planning.*

Charlie shot her a quick, fond glance. They were sitting at their regular spot in the kitchen, magic book before them, sipping tea, going over the material that had come along with Dawn's letter. Tomorrow's luncheon menu had already been planned. An agenda for the following day had been developed and now Mam was gently prying from Charlie, details of the preceding night at the Joneses'. Charlie recognize the tiny hint of envy along with the curiosity and so allowed himself to be coaxed into sharing several details, one of which he knew would be of immense interest to his employer.

"Mr. Jones very good at conversation. Very smart. Know many things. Much interested in Madison Avenue. Ask Charlie what he know about marketing phenomenon called 'California girl.'" He kept his face perfectly bland while watching Midge digest what he'd just said.

"California girl? Why, Charlie how odd. What a coincidence…unless…do you suppose Tucker discussed Dawn with them?" He watched her growing conviction that it was indeed the case. She smiled hugely at him. "Was Tucker included in this conversation?"

Charlie nodded. "Mostly he listen to honorable father who knows much about advertising trends like hot market for models. He say tall, athletic women with blonde hair sell products…all products…car, vacation, soap, liquor…even cigars and news."

They looked at each other. "Dawn!" Midge mouthed the words and then smiled as if she had been given into her keeping, a precious secret.

"Of course, Charlie, it could be mere coincidence, couldn't it? I mean, Mr. Jones is reported to be very well-read."

Charlie shook his head. He had been saving the best for last. "Not coincidence, Mam. Mrs. Jones say, 'We want Tucker to bring young lady to visit but no time. She go home to California too soon.'"

Midge's merry eyes sparkled. "I don't know why that information pleases me so very much, Charlie, but it certainly does. In fact, it makes me want to rush outside and do something in the garden." She rose from her chair and then paused and sat back down, her face suddenly growing pensive.

"Different subject, Charlie. This is very confidential." She told him briefly of Althea's story about the potentially available property on Front Street, property that Emory said would be a dangerous place for her to visit simply because of her skin color, even in the daytime...and that Clarice had confirmed it in no uncertain terms.

"She told me some really terrible things, partly I think, to keep me from going there. But there has to be some way I can find out if the owner, I believe his name is Khalif Nubar, would consider selling the property to us if he knew public housing would be coming in to compete. I also had the thought that he might not try to put roadblocks in the way." She stopped, realizing how incredibly naïve she sounded. *What do I want from Charlie anyway? Why am I telling him this story that, sitting in this pleasant kitchen, sounds like the plot to a grade B movie?* He was looking at her, waiting.

She laughed. "I'm trying to remember why I thought it was so important that you know this story. I guess it must be so you understand the reason why I'm being so adamant about holding the fundraiser so quickly. If it IS a success, and the property does become available, we might have a chance." Secretly, Midge knew that she was telling him only part of the truth...and she suspected that he knew it.

Charlie merely nodded, carefully tucking the name, Khalif Nubar, away in his mind. He didn't recognize it; he wasn't familiar with the slumlords of New Haven. However, he certainly had friends at the track who were. He was looking forward to his Saturday at the dog races. It seemed as though it had been a very long time since he'd gotten to go and experience his other self. Perhaps he would ask a few discrete questions.

That evening Tucker sat in front of his computer, after having nearly filled a wastepaper basket with wadded, monogramed stationary in his attempt at writing to Dawn. He'd finally given up and was now pursuing the psychological concepts assigned by Dr. van Castle. He found the reading fascinating and was already looking forward to Thursday when they had scheduled another lunch of deli sandwiches in the park.

He found himself only mildly depressed that he had not been able to find the words to say to Dawn. Dr. van Castle had hinted that until he knew clearly in his own mind, how he really felt and the action he wanted to take, it might be difficult. He had mentioned her to Kathryn today when she had asked him, point blank, if he dated, simply saying that there was a girl who lived in California that he might be interested in dating, now that he was becoming a real person. *It felt good to actually admit it out loud,* he reflected. He could tell she was curious, but she didn't pry.

He looked at his watch: 9:00 o'clock. Then, he called up his calendar and organized his week. The fact that Kathryn had agreed to come and have dinner on Wednesday after his massage made him smile. He looked forward to planning the menu. *Actually,* he thought, *there isn't a thing I have to do. Mr. Tyler has the summary of my impressions of the weekend.* He grinned thinking how he and the managers would carefully NOT exchange looks when their boss bounced cheerfully through the door. *It might be prudent to remember to eat a decent breakfast,* he thought ruefully, *lunch will be very late, unless I miss my guess. Tomorrow's meeting is definitely going to be interesting.*

Tucker leaned back and stretched, feeling uncommonly at peace and was deciding between watching the news or playing the piano when the phone rang. Heather's melodious, cultured voice filled his ear. "Hello, Tucker," she purred. "I realize I said you were to decide what next we would do together, but I find myself in need of a favor."

She went on to explain that she was involved in a doubles tournament and that her partner had hurt his back. "Could you be a dear and fill in? It would only be tomorrow and perhaps Thursday, if we do well. The whole thing will be very low-key and friendly. It's just a club do. And since it's being held at our club, it wouldn't even be out of your way."

Tucker thought quickly, trying to remember how well-seeded Heather was. *Pretty high,* he thought. He remembered the one time she had asked him to play at the club…she had been very good.

"Heather, since you haven't seen me on the courts, you probably know I haven't picked up a tennis racket in two months and as I remember, you had my tongue hanging out the last time we played. I'm afraid I would be a pretty poor choice as a tournament partner for one who plays so well."

She gave a small, pleased chuckle at his compliment. *This is a very charming man, indeed.* The quick thought flashed through her mind: *If only I can capture this man, I'll give him a lovely taste of another of my talents.* She smiled into the phone and made her voice seductive.

"Dear Tucker, I know you're not going to refuse me this small favor. You are too much the gentleman not to rescue me. Besides, this isn't in any way serious play. I'm sure your game will be fine. And, Tucker, I'm also sure we could think of something fun to do afterwards." She was confident that her meaning was clear, but found herself wondering if he chose to pass over it, or responded so subtly that she missed it.

Tucker chuckled and then said gallantly, "You're right, Heather. I would find it difficult to deny you. If this is important to you, I'll be there. Besides, I suppose it is time for me to get back into the swing of things at the club."

He smiled as he walked back to the computer and added: **7:00 p.m. tennis** to his Tuesday and Thursday dates, shut down the computer and turned on the news. His desire to play the piano had evaporated.

Heather sat at her desk wondering. He had said he found it difficult to deny her. That sounded right and he certainly seemed to enjoy the kiss. But, there was something about his tone…she shrugged and pictured how handsome he looked in his tennis togs, how gracefully he moved…they should make a handsome pair on the courts. *Then afterwards, perhaps we will have a bite to eat and a nightcap at his place…perhaps.* Then she sighed with satisfaction thinking of her last tennis partner. She'd had certainly enjoyed playing with Al this last week, always enjoyed it when a reciprocal turned out to match her talent on the courts and in bed. He had been delightful. But in two days, he would be gone and that would be perfect, too. Just thinking about his abilities made her squirm a bit in her chair. *Too bad about his back.*

Chapter Thirty-four

Charlie rose even earlier than usual, taking special care with his grooming, spending a few extra moments kneeling in front of the simple shrine, praying--centering his mind to accommodate the importance of the day. The signs were auspicious. It would go well. He stepped out into the kitchen garden and breathed deeply in the stillness of the dawn.

Only the birds and he were up. He knelt by the herbs breathing in their fragrance. For Margaret Jones, he would prepare a dish his mother had prepared when he was a boy, a simple, traditional Chinese lunch. His small kitchen shears quickly snipped a few scraggly needles from one plant, drooping dime-sized leaves from another. He nodded happily to himself, confident of the meal. Then, he rose to go and make the morning coffee for his employers.

The Tylers were often the subject of Charlie's musings. Their moods, habits and ways of doing things were as familiar as his own. Recently, Midge had come down to take coffee up to their room and had done so every morning since. This was something new and Clarice and he had wondered together if Mr. Tyler's health was the mother of its inception. And Midge's reaction, last Friday, when Clarice had asked her point blank, seem to indicate that it was. He had offered to bring the tray up each morning, but Midge had graciously declined.

"No thank you, Charlie. I want James to continue sleeping on the mornings that he is able, so the times would be too random for you to plan. I'll just pop down and get it."

Clarice arrived, puffing slightly from the walk up the driveway. She was smiling at Charlie, feeling included in his excitement. "Big day ain't gonna to be nothin' but sunshine. I got all good feelin's in my bones."

Charlie bowed and took her shopping bag while she hung her coat in the alcove. Then they stood and looked at

401

the kitchen. Always immaculate, today the kitchen fairly glowed. The wood was newly polished, the floor was freshly waxed, countertops gleamed, cookbooks and spice tins were perfectly aligned. There was not one single piece of copper that showed a trace of tarnish. It was ready for the inspection by Margaret Jones--who would be arriving an hour prior to Emory and Althea. Substantively, the reason for her early arrival was so that Charlie could inform her of the details regarding the role of judges that he and Midge had discussed. But really, just as Charlie had been able to satisfy his curiosity about Margaret's domain, she was to have the opportunity to explore his.

Clarice was the first to speak. "My, it do look fine. But, I been thinkin' this 'ol floor need 'nuther coat of that wax. Don' look quite shiny enough to these eyes."

Charlie looked at her in horror. His day was perfectly planned. Waiting an hour for his floor to dry had not been calculated. Then, just in time, he saw the impish glint in her gold-flecked eyes and saved himself from an unseemly reply. Instead, he folded his hands serenely and said, "Thank you so much for noticing not quite perfect floor. My dim eyes saw only perfection. However, Charlie know Miss Clarice have much to do today. Weekend visitors leave many chores and yesterday your generous spirit said to help Charlie with his miserable kitchen. Your hard work was much appreciated. Charlie very happy. Would not want to delay his friend any longer in her upstairs work."

Clarice threw back her head and laughed. It was an amazing sound that reverberated deep in her chest and exploded joyfully from her throat. She believed it was the longest speech she had ever heard him make. She pretended to cast one final dubious glance at the shining floor, savoring the banter a final moment before giving in by saying, "Well, that is de truth. Dem guest rooms ain't gonna clean themselfs. But we's just gonna hafta be hopin' Missus Jones have her mind on judging and recipes and not on this dirty ol' floor."

They smiled at each other in perfect understanding just as Midge walked through the swinging door and paused to take in the scene. She could see in an instant that their mood matched her own. She was brimming with anticipation of what the day would bring. Smiling broadly, she put her thoughts into words.

"Good morning, dear ones. My, but it is good to walk into a room that radiates such harmony and cheerfulness. It quite matches my mood." She beamed at Charlie, noticing that his freshly scrubbed face seemed even more polished than usual. Instead of his shapeless high collared black blouse, he was wearing a simple, yet elegant, Chinese jacket of dark blue shot with threads of red, under his chef's apron.

"The kitchen is positively glowing and so are you, Charlie. May we assume that it has some small thing to do with the impending visit from Margaret Jones?"

Charlie bobbed his head in acknowledgment. "Very happy day for all, I think," he said as he quickly arranged the coffee tray.

"Yes, it does feel that way. James is certainly excited about his day. He is already in the shower, looking forward to getting one step closer to closing the deal with Chile. It's been a while since he's popped out of bed this way." So saying, Midge picked up the tray, turned to go and then stopped and turned back.

"Oh, Clarice, I was sharing a bit of my dream about the Front Street property with Charlie yesterday. I haven't given up on the idea, but I want you to know that I did hear what you said…and I saw the look in your eye that led me to believe you weren't telling me even a part of what you knew. So, I wanted you to know that I wasn't going to do anything so foolish as to go traipsing down there to interview pimps and muggers." She laughed her small tinkling laugh and disappeared in a swish of silk through the door.

Charlie looked at Clarice. The smiling countenance had given way to a mixture of awe and horror. "Dat be de most meddlesome woman I ever did know," she muttered, stomping heavily across the shining floor to get her own cup of coffee.

"Don't nobody mess wif dat place. Dey be so many hands in pockets down dere it looked like one of your Chinese puzzles. She ain't got no lickin' bit of sense how de real worl' work."

Charlie waited a moment, watching the grace with which, even while stomping, the large woman moved. He caught her eye and nodded. "Yes," he said in his usual oblique manner. "But it is difficult for one not to be hopeful."

She looked at him, eyes wide with surprise. Until he had said the word, she did not consciously realize that the anger she was feeling came from that old fear of having hopes dashed. But, aloud she said, "A fool kin hope themselves to death; ain't no fools on Front Street."

Charlie knew immediately what she was implying: no fools, no hope, only the realism of poverty, drugs and corruption lived in the tenement on Front Street. In that moment, he decided to become informed on the politics of that part of New Haven. He closed his eyes trying to reconcile the Tao belief of accepting what is in front of one without wanting the situation to be other than it is...with the role he planned to assume.

Then he smiled gently and said, "The Tao would teach us the world better only if each person not strive too hard to control others; set own example of virtue. Perhaps Chinese puzzle solve self in time if proper key can be found."

Clarice looked at him uneasily. Sometimes, the words he actually said didn't seem to make sense, but she thought she usually understood his meaning. But this time she wasn't sure. Something was going through his mind. That was for sure. She wondered what her kindly, but busybody boss had said to him and was on the verge of asking, but could see that he had already moved back to the present. He was probably thinking about the impending arrival of Margaret Jones.

Clarice finished her coffee in silence, feeling again that unwanted and unwarranted stirring of hope in her chest. Then, realizing that she might learn a great deal more, since she was taking Charlie's place in the serving of lunch, caused her to smile. She rinsed her cup and went to gather cleaning supplies.

Margaret Jones was in a state of high, barely suppressed excitement as the Lincoln pulled smoothly under the Tyler's porte-cochere and Thomas jumped out to open her door and offer his hand. He noted with surprise that her hand trembled slightly in his own. *She sure doesn't look frightened.* She instead looked regal, composed and faintly reserved. She took his elbow firmly and allowed him to escort her toward the wide steps. "Mrs. Jones, I hope you won't think it overly familiar of me if I tell you how well you look," he said with boyish sincerity.

She stopped, dropped his arm and looked at him for a long moment, searching his face. Then she drew a deep breath and let it out slowly, composing herself. "Thank you, Thomas. I did take extra care with my toilette today." Characteristically, her free hand fingered the antique seed pearl necklace. Its pink cast carefully complimented the dusty rose of her simple linen dress. In her other hand was a small, elegantly wrapped package.

As he reached forward and pulled the handle of the door chime, Thomas tried hard to hide a look of astonishment at her use of the French word. His wife had told him that listening to the Joneses converse was like going back in time or watching one of the classic movies on public television. He really hadn't been around Mrs. Jones all that much, and standing there in his chauffeur's uniform, he felt a sense of unreality steal over him. He felt as though he was lost in a time warp.

The sense evaporated the instant the door open to reveal a small sprite of a woman with tousled hair and merry blue eyes.

Her voice fairly vibrated with delight. "Oh, Margaret, I'm so glad to finally meet you and that you could join us. For the very first time, it seems to me the contest is really going to happen."

Midge reached forward both her tiny hands and captured Margaret's. Thomas wondered if the diminutive woman could feel the tremble and wondered again at the cause.

The two women stood for a long moment, appraising, thinking how best to proceed. Finally, Margaret gave a wispy smile, retrieved her still held hand and said in her soft, carefully modulated voice, "Yes, it is good to meet you too, Midge. Tucker speaks very highly of both you and Mr. Tyler." Thomas noted that there was not even a hint of the tremor in her voice.

Midge stood for a moment, clearly expecting the other woman to say more and Thomas found he was feeling somewhat nervous himself, but felt helpless, in his role of chauffeur, to do anything of significance to ease the situation.

Fortunately, at that moment, the small, apparently Chinese, man, he'd seen at the Joneses' on Sunday evening appeared and the entire situation changed.

His employer's entire demeanor changed. Thomas could see her visibly relax. Her shoulders lost their stiffness, her face lost its strained waxy look and suffused with becoming color. Unknowingly, she took a deep breath and a smile that touched her eyes was on her face. "Hello again, Charlie," she said in a much stronger voice, her hand already outstretched. "I've been so looking forward to seeing your workspace."

The man called Charlie first bowed low and then answered simply, "Charlie much honored by most welcome visit." And then gravely, he took her outstretched hand.

For the first time, Midge seemed to notice Thomas and to his surprise she also stretched out a hand to him. "Hello, I'm Midge Tyler. Thank you for bringing Margaret to us. Please feel free to leave the car parked here in the shade of the porte-cochere. And feel free to peruse the grounds. If you'd like, stop by the kitchen for a cup of coffee or tea. You'll find Clarice there."

Thomas noticed that she really looked at him when she spoke. He'd been less well-treated by the butlers of some of the Joneses' friends. He found himself returning her smile as he returned the firm handshake.

"Very nice to meet you, Mrs. Tyler. I'm Thomas. I will take you up on your offer of a stroll around the grounds. They are lovely and the flowers are magnificent." He touched the brim of his cap.

As Charlie opened the swinging doors to his kitchen and bowed Margaret through it, Midge halted mid-stride. Charlie hadn't said so, but she knew with sudden sensitivity, that this was a time for her to busy herself elsewhere. She caught his eye, flipped her hand and said, "See you in an hour."

Margaret's first and lasting memory of Charlie's kitchen was that it was filled with odors, some of which she could not identify. She stood quietly in front of his soup kettle, drew in a deep breath of the mingled odors and tried to sort them out.

Charlie watched the effort with interest. She stood, the package she carried clasped against her breast forgotten. Her eyes were closed in her effort. When she opened them again, there was a faint smile on her face. "There are six different odors that I detect, but can't identify. Something has an odor similar to parsnip, another rather like almonds. I expect they are secret herbs from China."

Charlie nodded in confirmation. "Yes, exactly six herbs in soup." He held up his fingers and began counting: "Gay Gee. Wai Shan. Nom Haung. Lien Ju. Lo Han Gwoh. Bok Hop." The words flowed musically from his mouth.

Margaret's pleased laughter filled the room. She turned to Charlie and proffered the gift. "I couldn't think what to bring you that would halfway match the lovely poem, so finally I gave up and brought you this instead." The laughter was still in her voice. "When you open it, you will see why I laughed."

With precise movements, Charlie unwrapped the parcel, folding and setting aside both the ribbon and the paper as if they too were to be cherished. Then he studied the small, unprepossessing notebook in his hands. He read the carefully controlled spidery script of its title and his round eyes widened as he realized the magnitude of the honor.

It seemed that Margaret Jones, after carefully quizzing her son, had tried to replicate some of Charlie's recipes. What he held was a record of her attempts. It was all there, a scientist's careful research--doomed to failure because she lacked the ingredients from his herb garden and others that he sent away for.

"I didn't tell even Tucker what I was up too, though I can't really think why I didn't. But on occasion, when I thought I had a recipe right, I would serve it to him on a Sunday evening. And when he would compliment the dish, I would say, very casually of course, "Does Charlie make anything like this?" He would say something like, 'Actually he does. Though your seasonings are a little different.'"

407

She smiled again. "So after a year, I finally came to the conclusion that you had a knowledge of herbs beyond my own and therefore beyond Tucker's ability to identify them. So I gave up. But here is the record of my many attempts."

Charlie was immensely flattered. He looked closely again, impressed as always at Tucker's ability to determine what was in a dish. Except for the Chinese herbs, nearly every ingredient was listed.

"It will be a great honor to now fill in missing ingredients." So saying, he led her through the kitchen, past the carefully rounded bao, rising on baking sheets, each cleverly marked to show what was inside the smooth dough. Clarice had careful instructions as to their last-minute steaming. There were also wedges of melon chilling in the refrigerator. Clarice would take them out when she put the bao in the steamer. Melon needed to be at room temperature in order to appreciate its full flavor, but on such a day, and before a hot soup, coolness on the tongue would be refreshing. As would be the Dragon's Eye Creme dessert sitting in whipped and colorful, fruity splendor next to the melon. He nodded to himself with satisfaction at his simple menu.

Charlie retrieved his scissors, small plastic bags and a marking pen before opening the door to the kitchen garden with its rich tangle of herbs.

For the first time, Margaret became aware of her surroundings. She noticed the charm of the setting. *It really is quite lovely,* she decided, looking at the masses of daisies mirroring the puffy clouds that seemed to hover solidly over the sound despite the breeze. She drew a deep breath and realized she was having quite a good time. Then she bent over the tangled rectangle of vines and bushes. Many of the herbs she recognized; they graced her own garden. But the others, some of which looked half dead or untended, were pretzel-bent, brown, withered, spiky, or feathery and definitely would have looked unappetizing to most. That did not faze Margaret Jones. She was here to learn at the foot of the master. She bent to listen as Charlie snipped carefully at the strange plants, holding each up for her to smell and naming it for her before putting it in a labeled bag.

408

Midge knew the moment she saw the look on Althea's face that something extraordinary had transpired. "It's going to hit the papers tomorrow. Robert talked about it at breakfast this morning. Evidently, what Clarice told you was true and according to the governor's blue ribbon panel, careers are liable to crash if the press takes hold of this the way Robert thinks they will."

Midge listened to the words tumble out. Althea was not doing her usual good job of making a story out of events; in fact, she was doing just the opposite. *Is she talking about the Front Street apartment complex? If so, why doesn't she say so?*

Finally, she held up both hands and said, "Stop, Althea. Take a breath."

Emory, who had been standing behind Althea listening intently, laughed. "Althea wouldn't share a word of this the entire way here. I think sitting on the news has unhinged her a bit. But when she can get herself together, I think she has something to tell us about the Front Street deal."

Midge shot Emory a grateful look and then returned her attention to Althea. "ARE you talking about the apartment complex? I'm really not sure."

Althea nodded mutely. "Wonderful!" said Midge with real excitement. "Do tell us all about it, dear. But please start at the beginning."

Althea was only too happy to comply and did make the effort to be coherent. "I'm sorry, Midge." Althea looked at Emory and smiled. "I'm sorry, Emory. I don't know why I wanted you both to hear this at the same time, but it only seemed fair, since it is so exciting."

She drew a deep breath. "All right--from the top! Here we go! In the paper tomorrow morning there will be a front-page article that is probably being written as we speak. It will announce the purchase, by the state, of the old warehouse...as well as the intention to build a rent-subsidized apartment complex and job training facility that includes some offices for mental health workers and a daycare program."

She was still talking very quickly, but seemed

determined to get her message across succinctly. "It really seems well planned. Furthermore, although it won't be in tomorrow's paper, an investigative reporter has been assigned, with the governor's blessing, to sniff out the kickbacks Mr. Nubar has been giving to the various public servants of this county in order to keep his tenement functioning. Evidently, there is enough evidence to cause heads to roll if the reporter does his job."

Midge was almost afraid to ask the next question. "Are we to hope that the findings and subsequent public outcry will cause the tenement to be condemned and thus possibly available for S.O.S. to buy?"

"Yes! Absolutely! That's the point." Althea smiled hugely and benevolently at her friends. "Evidently the place violates so many codes that the only viable solution is to tear it down."

"Good heavens!" Midge grabbed handfuls of her wiry curls, pressing them tightly to the sides of her head as if to hold in her excitement. "And it will be in the paper tomorrow? Good gracious! I find I am overwhelmed with joy!"

Emory, who had followed Althea's monologue carefully, let Midge enjoy her happiness for long moments before sounding the cautionary note. "Darling, both you and Althea are acting as though this pipedream of ours has become a reality. I must remind you that it has not. It's only that we can soon start to explore the obstacles in our path in a forthright manner."

Her words had an immediate effect. Midge loosened fingers from curls and ran them distractedly through her hair. Althea looked at her friend in sad recognition of the truth.

"Well, yes, that is so," said Althea finally. "I hadn't really thought of it in that way. I was so excited not to have to keep the secret any longer." She gave a huge sigh. "I guess the truth is, we still don't know a single thing about the viability of our idea."

Midge found herself nodding in reluctant agreement. She felt almost defeated by the problems not even yet identified. *Trust Emory to pull us off our magic carpet.*

410

"Well," she said, giving herself a resolute mental shake, "thank you, Emory. As usual, you are right and thank you also for allowing me my moment of unfettered joy. Now, back to today. Margaret Jones is in the kitchen with Charlie. Let me go and retrieve her as I suspect Charlie will want to give Clarice a few last-minute instructions before he joins us."

To Margaret, it seemed she and Charlie had been talking for only a short time when Midge appeared to announce that the other ladies had arrived and ask that she join them in the morning room. Reluctantly, she rose to her feet, feeling anxiety tugging at her once again. But Midge's genuine smile and knowing that one of the ladies was Althea calmed her somewhat. "Yes, of course. Thank you," she said regaining her composure and regal manner as she smiled at Charlie and followed Midge from the kitchen.

The meeting was very successful, made even more so by the fact that they could openly talk about their hopes for raising money for the Front Street property, should it become available. Margaret was a quick study. Within a very short period of time, she seemed to understand the concept, the challenge and the politics involved. Her questions were insightful and to the point. Midge thought more than once how like his mother Tucker was. But, Emory was the one who voiced it over lunch.

"Margaret, I must tell you how like you Tucker is--especially when he seeks to understand something. You both know how to ask those crisp questions that seem to nail the heart of the thing that needs clarifying. It's quite a lovely trait to pass on to an offspring."

By her mounting color, everyone at the table could tell how the words pleased the reserved woman. She smiled shyly and said, "How kind of you to make the observation, Emory. It is quite a compliment, isn't it?"

The group nodded, but she was looking across the table at Charlie for validation and she got it. Midge could almost feel the connection between them grow stronger.

"Tucker one fine man." Charlie said. "Old American saying: 'Apple not fall far from tree.'"

Clarice smiled. *That's my saying!* She found

herself inordinately pleased that Charlie was quoting her to Mrs. Jones.

Throughout the meal, she had served an extraordinary amount of tea to the group in order to be able to hover solicitously while she listened, wanting to hear as many details as possible. Reluctantly, she left to get dessert. *Dragon's Eye Crème! I don't know how that man comes up with some of these fancy names.* She smiled again, this time with satisfaction. She had sampled this desert and knew it was going to draw rave reviews. Still grinning, she disappeared through the swinging doors. *I'm bettin' a week's wages Tucker's mama is gonna be puttin' that very same dish in front of her husband one of these days. That woman is likely gonna have every ingredient figured out before her goblet is half gone.*

Chapter Thirty-five

There wasn't any way the day could have gone any better, Tucker reflected happily as he sat down at his computer, a turkey sandwich in one hand and a glass of milk in the other. He'd stayed at his office desk until he had finished the summary for Mr. Tyler--no simple task either. As he had predicted to himself, the meeting was a charged one. He'd never seen his boss in better form. In both their pre-session and at the general meeting, the man was decisive, informed and ready to take on the group if it opposed his decision to proceed with sending a team to Chile to look at identified undeveloped industrial sites.

He had started the meeting by simply announcing, "Ladies and gentlemen, it was my pleasure to host, for the weekend, Ambassador Baraque and members of Sociedad de Formento Fabrila, or SOFOFA, a Chilean industrial association contingency. I was most impressed by the alacrity with which they responded to our interest in expanding operations to their country, the thoroughness of their research of Zitec and the quality of the individuals involved. So, unless you can convince me otherwise in the next day or so, I plan to send three of you to Santiago before the month is out."

Tucker could tell the group had done its homework. There did not seem to be opposition; at least not overtly. Whether or not they agreed that Chile was a viable choice for expansion did not matter. Their job was to ask the hard questions, make their boss support his decision with solid facts.

Brazil, which at first had seemed the strongest choice, under closer scrutiny had fallen from favor because of huge unexplained government loans secured from Uruguay and now coming to light. It seemed there was corruption from personal gain again rearing its head at the top levels of government. So, while Brazil led in many of the ten criteria, Tucker's criteria, political stability, ultimately

413

made it less desirable than Chile. Besides, Mr. Tyler shared with the group, the SOFOFA'S creative plan to use available technology to provide opportunities for the disbursement of Chile's population, now densely packed into the middle part of the country.

The group was also impressed that the industrialists from Chile saw Zitec's involvement, not as something new, but simply one tool to help them progress in line with a master plan for the country that had been developed in 1939.

So, with the summary of the meeting in Mr. Tyler's hands, Tucker was free to try once again to write a letter to Dawn. He had decided to type it on the computer as his brain seemed to work better that way. Then he would transfer what he had written to his stationary. He finished the last of his milk and put his fingers to the keys.

> *Dear Dawn,*
> *I have been trying to write you a*
> *letter for several days, but am finding it hard*
> *work for some reason. Perhaps part of it is*
> *that I can't really believe you have forgiven*
> *me and want to be friends.*
> *I know I behaved badly and I am very*
> *grateful that you are willing to forgive me*
> *so quickly. Thank you for that.*
> *I am not certain why you think I am*
> *perceptive, but thank you for that too.*
> *I will give Heather the pictures and*
> *your regards.*
> *Again, thank you for the letter and I*
> *look forward to seeing you the next time*
> *you are east.*

He signed the letter: *Your forgiven friend, Tucker Jones.* Then he pushed the 'SAVE' command, printed out a copy, reread it, feeling quite satisfied and copied it carefully onto his stationary. The effort had taken him several hours and a major amount of stressful attention, something he did not realize until he reached for the already addressed envelope and felt the stiffness in his back. He groaned. It would not do to show up for a tennis game with Heather in that sort of condition. He looked at his watch. Perhaps he should do as she suggested and use the masseur at the club for a little therapeutic loosening of the muscles, even have a little swim. There should be plenty of time. After all, she had said this tournament was just a simple informal club-sponsored event.

He called the club to confirm a 30-minute opening with the masseur and went to collect his gear. At the last minute, Tucker decided to walk. It wouldn't take more than ten minutes and he would drop both the letter to Dawn and the one he had written to Sunny in a mailbox on the way. Thinking of Dawn reminded him to put the pictures from her in his athletic bag. He suspected Heather would be pleased with both of them.

On his way to the locker room, he suddenly realized how significant it was that he had actually, of his own volition, scheduled a massage with a stranger and smiled. The first totally spontaneous act of Tucker Jones! It was something to mark on one's calendar--an unplanned adventure. He would go through with it too, but only the back, neck and head. He walked with unfaltering stride to the reception desk and signed the register.

Lola, the woman behind the desk recognized him and called pleasantly, "Hello, Tucker. We've missed you around here." He nodded a greeting and she continued, "You're all signed up with Harold for your massage."

He found himself replying and meaning it, "Hello, Lola. I've certainly missed being here."

She handed him a thick Turkish towel and noticed the racket peeking from his bag. "Ah ha! Having a go at the club tourney, eh? But I don't remember seeing your name on the list."

He grinned. "I'm a last minute stand-in for Heather Anderson's injured partner."

An odd look, quickly veiled, flashed on her face. "Oh really? Have you been playing with Heather long?"

Tucker chuckled easily, but for some reason felt suddenly uncomfortable. There was something about the woman's comment, the way she arched her eyebrow and stressed the word "playing" that suggested a double entendre. He wondered what it was.

"No. In fact, this is our first time to play in a doubles tournament together," he said more sharply than intended and then felt compelled to explain. "I'm simply a last-minute substitute, just to fill the roster. The fact is, I haven't played for months, not since my back went out."

He closed his mouth to halt the flow of words. Lola was looking at him in a knowing, overly-familiar fashion, as if they were sharing a private joke. Again, he wondered what it was.

As he headed on to the locker room, she said, "By the way, you're liable to meet Heather's latest partner in there." Again she smirked. "He too is having back problems and hopes the steam and a massage will help." She grinned and said, with no apparent trace of sympathy, "Poor baby. His back really is sore."

Tucker wrinkled his brow in puzzlement and stopped to look at her. He'd known this woman for the three years he'd been using the club. She was an aging jock, fit and intense, not usually given to small talk. Past conversations, if they occurred at all, had to do with her interest in his training program. Now, she seemed to be almost leering at him, had announced that he might meet Heather's tennis partner and made it sound like a warning. He shrugged his shoulders and let the thought go.

Then she smiled her normal smile. "Harold said this is your first massage from him. He'll want you to do 15 minutes of steam before you get on the table. So go ahead and I'll tell him you've arrived and are in the process."

There were only two other men in the steam room, but Tucker had no trouble picking out the one who must have been Heather's ailing partner. One man was chubby, lobster-red and panting in the heat. The other man was lying face down on the upper wooden bench and even from the distance of the doorway, he looked like an athlete. Though his hair was silver-gray, his body was all sinew and sculpted muscle. He set up gingerly, using both hands as if to ease stressed muscles as Tucker entered and nodded to him.

"Hello," he said. "You can have this bench if you'd like. I've got to get out of here before I go to sleep and miss my massage time."

Tucker returned the man's engaging smile. Just sitting there, vitality flowed from him. "Thank you very much, but I believe I'd better stick to the lower bench. I have a tennis game tonight."

The man was immediately interested. "Do you?" He looked Tucker over. "Yes, you look like you could play a good game. But you must be practicing elsewhere. I've been here as a reciprocal all week and I haven't seen you play."

Shaking his head, Tucker seated himself in a corner. "I haven't been playing regularly, wouldn't be playing tonight..." He paused and grinned, "...if you hadn't hurt your back."

A startled look flashed momentarily in the depths of the dark-hazel eyes and was followed by a deep chuckle. "So you're my replacement, eh? I'm flattered. Heather is quite a woman, isn't she?"

Giving Tucker the same knowing look as had the receptionist, he said, "As much as I travel, it sure too bad other clubs don't have a Heather Anderson to provide the sport a man needs."

Tucker heard the chubby man snort as if choking back a laugh and wondered at the cause. He ignored it and stuck out his hand. "Tucker Jones."

"Al Benbow. Nice to meet you," was the quick reply as the man extended one hand, using the other to keep his towel in place. It was a nice firm grip and a genuinely warm smile. "Perhaps if Heather is unavailable next time I'm in town, you and I could have a game."

"Certainly," said Tucker, meaning it. "I'd like that very much. You can get my number from the receptionist and my phone machine is always on."

There is something very likable about this man; an openness and zest, or perhaps it is his "ready to tackle anything" attitude, Tucker thought, as he watched Al disappear through the steam-swirled doorway. His father would say he was a "man's man."

Harold soon came to collect him bearing a fresh dry towel. He led Tucker to the massage table. *Amazing,* thought Tucker, *I should be nervous, but instead I'm thinking how surprised Kathryn and Dr. Beemers are going*

417

to be when I tell them what I've done. Actually, everything felt very natural.

"Listen, Harold," he said to the wizened little man. "What I'm after is simply having my back, neck and head done." He expected the man to protest as Kathryn was so fond of doing. But instead, he nodded obediently, waited patiently for Tucker to lie down and then proceeded, much as Kathryn had done, to unlock the tension of taut muscles.

The touch was different, but he could tell they both viewed the task in a similar fashion, each muscle group a puzzle to be unraveled. After a few seconds Tucker relaxed and let his mind drift. If he were to describe how he was feeling, he would have to say he was proud of himself. He'd written the letter to Dawn, was of availing himself of this massage, was going to play a friendly set of club doubles with Heather and then they would have a bite to eat. *What had she said? That she would think of something fun to do?* He wondered what she meant by that. He was feeling very relaxed, which was good. In times past, anxiety had sometimes made it difficult for him to concentrate on his game.

Heather, ignoring the drawn curtain that indicated the massage room was occupied, pulled it aside and said, accusation sharp in her voice, "Tucker, what on earth are you doing? We play in less than an hour!"

Harold's back had been to the curtain and he and Tucker were both startled. The soothing motion of Harold's hands came to an abrupt halt and both the jagged, icy tone of Heather's words and the abrupt cessation of motion left Tucker feeling immobilized and flooded with feelings. The first was guilt. The second, as he lay quietly, as if ignoring her presence, was the good, warm feeling of anger.

"TUCKER!" The voice was closer, even sharper. "For God's sake, are you asleep?"

He sat up slowly, noting that Harold was being careful of his modesty by adjusting the Turkish towel to cover his groin. Tucker smiled his thanks at the little man and swung his legs over the side of the table, pulled the towel more snugly around him and only then looked at Heather.

"Hello, Heather," he said, the mildness of his tone belying his inner wrath. "Did I miss hear the time? I thought we played at 7:00.

"We do PLAY at 7:00 Tucker. Right now, we should be warming up. I reserved the practice court for 6:00. Please get dressed and meet me there immediately." She turned on her heel and swirled out.

The two men looked at each other for a long moment, each trying to read the other's thoughts. Harold long trained to keep private thoughts about club members to himself, veiled his eyes, but still felt that the young man had read his thoughts.

"It's okay, Harold. It was a great massage while it lasted. I must not have heard her tell me about the hour's warm-up. Guess I'd better get cracking."

Still, Harold noted with private pleasure, *the man doesn't seem inclined to rush.* Instead, Tucker stretched slowly, languidly, testing his muscles. Then he nodded. "Good job. I feel very supple like a tennis player should. Thank you, Harold."

Tucker walked slowly to the doorway, drew back the curtain and then turned and smiled over his shoulder, giving a conspiratorial wink. "It really wouldn't do to go rushing around and wreck all that good work you did, now would it?"

Harold, despite his best intentions, found himself grinning broadly at the ambling, tall backside of Tucker Jones. *I do believe that bitchy Ms. Anderson has misjudged this one,* he thought. *She may get ahold of his penis, but she won't get ahold of his mind.*

By the time Tucker arrived at the practice courts, Heather was seething, but consciously and with great effort masking her rage. They only had a little more than 30 minutes to warm-up and really, she knew very little about the man's game. It was in her best interest to keep calm. She smiled sweetly and said in her best sensually provocative voice, "Sorry to shorten your massage, darling, but I can do it for you later. You did bring balls, did you not?"

If he caught the sexual innuendo, he ignored it. Instead of answering, he pulled a ball from the pocket of his shorts and with a fluid motion, dropped it to the court and

419

sent it nicely aimed to her forehand. She noted with satisfaction that his position was perfect, the swing smooth, the wrist stiff and the amount of topspin remarkable.

The anger in her eyes was immediately replaced by the hard glint of competition. Planting her front foot firmly, she sent the ball sizzling back, a low, hard, cross-court to his backhand, forcing him to rush madly for position.

This is a warm-up? The thought flashed quickly before he turned his full concentration on the fuzzy sphere once again hurtling back towards him.

Just before 7:00 o'clock, Heather called a halt. She felt exhilarated. All traces of her former anger at Tucker had dissolved. He looked even better on the court then she had imagined AND his game was very good. She rushed around the corner of the net and, ignoring the puzzled look on his face, slipped her arm around his waist.

"Tucker, dear, are you this accomplished at everything you do?" She purred looking up at him.

He smiled and pulled a handkerchief from his pocket to mop the streams of perspiration tracking rivulets down his forehead and into his eyes. "I must say, Heather, that was quite a warm-up," he panted, gently disengaging her arm so he could breathe. "Are you certain we didn't just engage in a fierce competition? It certainly felt that way."

He retrieved a terrycloth head band from his bag at the back of the court, slipped it on and held the court gate for her. He noted her breathing was barely labored.

"Reassure me one last time…" He tried to grin as they walked onto the match court, "…that this is going to be a…how did you put it?…a very low-key and friendly game of doubles."

She laughed and reached up to adjust his headband. "Of course it is, darling. Come, let's go meet our opponents."

It took Tucker only seconds to recognize the tall, blonde couple walking towards them. He shot a quick look at Heather. She did not seem surprised, in fact, did not seem to recognize them, although she waved a hand in greeting.

Stoler and Nelson! They'd played for Yale on the varsity team all four years and were legendary for their teamwork and consistency. They even looked very much the same, the same build with lean, rock-hard muscles and fair hair of exactly the same color. They wore it in the same style then as now. Greta Stoler wore hers short and sculpted; Greg Nelson's was still shoulder length. At Yale it had caused announcers to mix their names. Tucker imagined it still would. At his peak, he could give either one a run for their money in singles. But, that was five years ago, when he played nearly every day. He shrugged, resigned himself and drew a deep breath, glad to feel the knives had left his lungs.

"Tucker!" They said in simultaneous, shy delight. "It is you!" Greg, holding out his hand, said, "We saw your name penciled in on the board and wondered if it could possibly be. But then, we thought probably not, since we never knew you to play competitive doubles."

Tucker smiled and shook hands. He found he was glad to see them. They were both wearing slim, matching, gold wedding bands. "I only play socially, every now and then," he said. "It's good to see you. Obviously, you are still partners, and by the looks of your rings, in more courts than tennis." They laughed and slipped each other affectionate glances. "Yes," said Greta softly, "for two years now we are Nelson and Nelson, not Stoler and Nelson."

Suddenly a feeling of loneliness washed over Tucker. He blocked it and turned to the silently appraising Heather. "Of course you all know each other?"

"No, sorry we haven't met, though I can't understand it, unless you are new to the club?" Heather asked her question graciously while her mind raced. *Why was that Goddamned Al so careless with his back? If I'm any judge, these two are going to be formidable and Tucker is already puffing like a wind-broke racehorse. Where did these people come from? Why didn't someone tell me?*

She had seen the name Nelson on the ladder and hadn't recognized it. *What was Tucker saying? That they had played four years varsity at Yale? WHY DIDN'T SOMEONE WARN ME?*

Greta nodded. "We have waited patiently to afford to join."

The announcer called them to the courts. Tucker took Heather's arm. "I'll do the best I can," he whispered simply. She did not respond.

Thinking about the match, Tucker decided he had not done all that badly. He was no match for the Nelsons, but neither was Heather. She, however, had been inclined to blame him for her own flaws in play. He frowned, remembering Greta's low ball, aimed with incredible accuracy and topspin. It had dropped inches from the net, on his side. Who should have taken the ball? It was on his side, but perhaps Heather was in better position. They had both gone for it and had, of course, interfered with each other's hits. "Sorry," he said as the ball dropped, untouched by either racket.

Heather turned on him then, her amber eyes shooting venom, "You clumsy fool, just try to keep the hell out of my way."

Her voice, thin, tight and venomous, had nevertheless, carried across the court. He sighed and closed his eyes against the remembered embarrassment, not only his, but the Nelsons. Her words had temporarily thrown them off their game.

Then he opened his eyes and congratulated himself for allowing the humiliating memory instead of blocking it and, in so doing, realized he had discovered something important to recognize in Heather Anderson. They had both developed great ability to be extremely agreeable and gracious in social settings while not allowing others access to their real feelings. Perhaps that was what attracted him to Heather, the thought that they were kindred spirits. But they were not. His persona of perfect manners, gentle humor, humility and graciousness had been developed to protect himself, hide the fact that he was an emotional coward. Heather's social graces, on the other hand, seemed to have been developed to disguise her nastiness and to allow her to have her way.

Tucker and Heather had lost all three sets, though each had been hotly contested with good shots on both sides. At the end of the match, Heather had been barely polite, issuing her congratulations to the Nelsons through clenched teeth before stalking off toward the locker room. Tucker had stayed a moment to re-catch his breath and talk with the shy, athletic couple at the edge of the courts.

He found himself asking if he might call them, perhaps ask them to join him at the club for dinner some night to renew acquaintance. Readily, they had agreed and he found himself walking toward the showers with Greg, genuinely pleased by the prospect.

Heather was waiting demurely for him when he emerged from the locker room. She looked at him from under the thickness of her lashes, "Please accept my apology, Tucker. I was a beast and I'll never forgive myself if you won't forgive me. I've already apologized to the Nelsons as they left."

So saying, she slipped her hand, with a childlike gesture, into his. It made him think suddenly of Sunny and he wondered when his letter to her would arrive in Texas.

Looking at Heather, Tucker felt very detached, as if he were watching a badly acted play. Fresh from the shower, dressed in a simple cotton shift, the top cut just low enough to reveal the soft curves of her breasts, the skirt just short enough to reveal a lot of tanned leg without being unseemly, she looked like a slender, spring-freshened willow.

"I'm sorry too," he said obscurely, giving no clue as to what he was sorry about.

It put Heather immediately on her guard. *Oh, oh,* she thought and quickly decided against asking him to explain himself. It would be better if she assumed, mistakenly or not, that he too was apologizing for his behavior. As they walked out into the softly lit parking lot she exclaimed, "Really Tucker, you have nothing to apologize for. In fact, please let me make it up to you by buying your dinner. You must be starving."

She turned towards him, her amber eyes pleading softly to be forgiven, her lower lip quivering prettily, silken fingers from her other hand stroking the inside of his bare arm. She stepped even closer and brought his hand, their fingers still twined, up and casually, as if she really didn't know what she was doing, cupped her breast and then disengaged her hand, leaving only his holding the rounded softness.

Still feeling detached, he realized how easy it would be to slip his hand inside the low neckline; she seemed to be inviting it. Her other hand began roaming down his chest, across the flatness of his stomach and down towards his groin. "Please let me make it up to you, darling," she whispered raising her face to be kissed.

In his state of suspended animation, he thought to himself, *Tucker Jones, you are probably a fool.* Aloud he said, "Sorry, Heather, not tonight I'm afraid, but thank you for the offer." Gently, he un-cupped his hand and stepped back, leaving her hand still outstretched and groping air in the semidarkness. Turning quickly, he strode down the street. Behind him he heard her gasp and then, "You arrogant prick!"

Suddenly, he felt like the pawn in a chess game. "Checkmate," he said just loud enough for her to hear and smiled grimly as he walked towards his condo. *She probably should've added the word 'stupid.' You stupid arrogant prick! And, I must be--passing up such an offer.*

The hand that held her breast, now held his athletic bag and he noted that it still felt as though it was on fire. His whole body felt weak and depleted, with the exception of said prick…which was feeling quite stiff indeed!

Chapter Thirty-six

James Tyler was unused to feeling angry with his wife. He sat behind his big desk drumming his fingers, seeking to sound both patient and penitent on the phone, but feeling neither. "I'm sorry, Midge. You'll just have to reschedule the appointment. Tomorrow or Friday would be fine. No, that won't do. There is no way I can leave right now. In fact, I need to be on the phone to Washington, D.C., within minutes if I am going to catch Ambassador Baraque between meetings. Please, just do as I say, darling, and don't make a fuss. One more day is not going to make a difference. Besides, as I told you this morning, I feel fine."

His voice was gentle and cajoling. *Why is my wife picking this, of all times, to be so totally unreasonable?* A red flush started creeping up from the starched collar of his shirt like the mercury of a thermometer. Finally, just as he felt he might explode, he heard the resignation creep into her voice.

"Yes," she said sadly, "I'll change the appointment, James, but I'm very unhappy and I will expect to talk more about it when you get home."

Was she crying? He couldn't be sure. With a curt, "Fine, dear. See you tonight." He hung up and immediately buzzed Peggy to have her call the ambassador when the first pain hit. Incredulously, he looked down at his left arm to see if something had stabbed him. The pain seemed localized somewhere along his forearm. Then, the second strike hit. This time it was in his upper chest, or perhaps shoulder. He couldn't tell. "What the hell!" The muttered query was silenced with a gasp and he leaned back in the big leather chair fighting for breath, waiting for the pain to subside. Instead, he felt the sudden racing of his heart. It seemed out of control. From inside his body, it seemed as though it had left his chest cavity and moved inside his head to beat loudly in erratic double time, just as though he

425

had finished a marathon. He felt it against his temple, heard it hammering painfully in his ears...for how long? He couldn't tell. Then, as suddenly as the pain and palpitation had come, they left him, leaving only gut wrenching fear. Somehow, Peggy was standing there. He had forgotten that he had buzzed her. She was looking at him curiously. *Can't she see what just happened? Evidently not!* He smiled weakly at her and saw that she was starting to look concerned.

"Are you all right, Mr. Tyler? You're looking a bit pale. Good thing you're on your way to the doctor's office." She smiled tentatively and waited.

He made a sudden decision and looking at his watch, nodded his head. "Yes, I'm fine. Call Hank and get Tucker Jones on the line while I call my wife."

Midge was still sitting by the phone trying to lecture herself into stopping crying so she could call the doctor to cancel her husband's appointment when the phone rang. She let it ring while she blew her nose and wondered whether or not to pick up the receiver. Surely, anyone could tell there were tears in her voice. Then she shrugged and scooped the hand-piece from the cradle. It was her husband.

"Hello, Midge. I'm sorry I was so obstinate. You are absolutely right; it is silly to put one's job before one's health. You were nice enough to make the appointment and unless it's irretrievably canceled, I will go."

James voice was calm, contrite and almost cheerful. His words left her reeling. In more than 30 years of marriage to this complicated man she had never felt more at sea. *What does this mean?* She couldn't grasp it. The silence grew.

Finally, from the other end of the line, James said, "Midge, dear, are you there? Is my appointment still on?"

Somehow she managed, in an even voice, to squeeze out two words, "Yes, James."

"Great! Then I'd better hurry. See you tonight."

She held the now silent receiver in both hands, staring at it as though she could decode the answer to this strangeness, if only she focused hard enough. Then, she came to a sudden decision. The receiver hit the cradle with the slam as Midge hastily tossed it and hurried to get her

426

purse. She and James were just about the same distance from the doctor's office. In fact, if she hurried, she might just be there waiting for him. Cold prickles of fear marched along her spine as she rushed down the stairs.

Waiting in the quiet of his office for the buzz that would let him know it was time to meet Hank, James made a fist of his hand and was surprised to feel very little, if any weakness. He shrugged and rolled first one shoulder, then the other in an exaggerated manner. Still, no pain. Drawing deep breaths with his hand over his heart convinced him that there was not even a residue of pain remaining. He wondered, without alarm, if he just had a mild heart attack. The doctor would probably be able to tell him. He grimaced. *After God knows how many tests?* A sense of frustration engulfed him. *Why now? Why now, when the Chilean project is so close to completion?*

The buzzer signaled time to go. He got up, slowly picked up his briefcase, looked hard around the office and walked to the elevator after telling Peggy he would not be back and that he would call Tucker from his car with instructions to call Ambassador Baraque.

Tucker had just returned from the grocery store, was rechecking his menu to make certain he had all the necessary ingredients and was feeling the first stages of butterflies as he realized he had committed himself to showing his proficiency as a cook for the first time, when Mr. Tyler called.

"Listen Tucker, there is a possibility that I may be calling on you to finish sewing up the contract with SOFOFA." He chuckled and continued, "Actually, other than the actual contract, details have pretty much fallen into place. Clifton can move mountains when he gets gung ho. But, the reason I'm calling you is to tell you that I needed to talk to the ambassador to verify that Clifton, Kelly and Henry are the team we're sending to do the site inspection. He needs to get cracking on their security clearances…but Midge has me buffaloed into a doctor's appointment and I probably won't be done in time to call. So, give him a call about 2:00 o'clock, would you? He's sure do have some other questions that you'll be able to field better than Cliff, or I wouldn't bother you."

427

Tucker nodded into the phone. "Certainly, I'm glad to do it. Anything else?"

There was a long pause. "No, not right now, thank you." Then there was another pause. "You know, Tucker, you have done a magnificent job at every level on this project. If you had to take it over tomorrow, I have every confidence of a positive outcome."

This time the pause was on Tucker's end. The comment seemed out of context and strangely stated. It sounded more like a premonition than a compliment. A lurch of anxiety hit the pit of his stomach. But true to old form, he laughed easily into the mouthpiece, blocking his feeling with practiced ease. "Thank you, sir, but I must admit I'm glad I don't have to."

"Right." Alone in the Mercedes, the older man nodded confirmation to the back of Hank's head. "But it is also nice to know you're there if I need you, Tucker. See you tomorrow, at 10:00 o'clock sharp. Give the ambassador my regards."

"Certainly...and sir..."

Mr. Tyler waited. He could tell by Tucker's tone that the unfinished thought was important to the boy. There was a deeply indrawn breath at the other end of the line. "For some reason I wanted you to know that I have taken your advice seriously...about trying to learn to trust people, I mean." Tucker stopped, it was much too complicated to relay in a quick car phone conversation. He laughed deprecatingly. "I guess what I'm trying to say is, if my back ever goes out again, you'll be the first one I call."

The older man closed his eyes, recognizing immediately the lurch in his chest was simply his heart giving a little jump of joy. He was to remember the timeliness of Tucker's admission and his response for the rest of his days.

"You'd call me, eh?" He felt a strange misting in his eyes. "By God, son, you've just given me a tremendous compliment and I recognize it as such."

Tucker laughed, somewhat embarrassed but deeply touched by the response. "Well," he said, "life has certainly gotten more interesting since I took your advice and started trying to figure out how to go about listening to my...ah...

heart." It sounded so corny said out loud that Tucker wished desperately he could call back the words.

Tyler passed the back of his hand over his eyes. "By God, Tucker, you've just made my day," he said. Tucker could clearly hear the warmth and sincerity in the older man's voice. "Goodbye, now. Perhaps you'll tell me more about those interesting things tomorrow."

By the time Tucker had cradled the phone, he found he couldn't quite recall just why his boss had turned the calling of the ambassador over to him, but he was pleased with the responsibility.

Leaning back against the leather seats, Tyler admitted to himself that had he not, just minutes ago, experienced something that may very well have been a minor heart attack, this would be one of the most rewarding days in his life. *Yes, indeed! Tucker Jones is a fine employee and he seems to be working on becoming a real live, feeling human being!*

He decided to call Midge on her private line. He wanted to tell her of the conversation. *I was pretty hard on her about trying to fix that boy up with Dawn. Perhaps I was wrong.*

The phone rang hollowly and repetitively in his ear. *Where is she?* He looked at his watch and thought hard. *No, she should be home. Tomorrow is her S.O.S. meeting. Perhaps she's stepped out into the garden.*

Tucker, too, had tried to call Midge. He had been intending to call her for some time. He wanted to pin down what his role in helping computerize the cooking contest was to be. *Besides,* he thought, *it's been some time since we've had time to chat and exchange our usual verbal repartee. I've missed it.*

She was, he was certain, dying to know more about his relationship with Heather. He wouldn't share that, but he might let slip that he and Dawn had exchanged letters.

Disappointed when she did not answer, he let his mind linger on thoughts of Dawn. *Funny how most of my thoughts seem to center on her these days. I wonder if I'm becoming a bit obsessed.*

He also wondered how long it would take a letter to reach the West Coast. *Might she get it by Friday?* He retrieved her letter from his bedside table and compared

429

the postmark to the inside date. *Yes*, he decided, *she might have it on Friday.*

He pictured her opening it, tried to imagine her response. Would she, as he had done, memorize the careful lines? Would she be able to read between them and pick out that it was SHE he was interested in, NOT Heather Anderson...never Heather Anderson. He closed his eyes remembering the scene in the parking lot with distaste. *But what if that had been Dawn in my arms? What if it had been her lips, her breast under my hand?*

His eyes flew open and he again recognized a sudden stiffness in his shorts. He shook himself. He was, he admitted honestly, very confused by the sudden awakening of his sexual feelings. *There's one thing I'm sure of! I'm not going to be another notch in the belt of Heather Anderson, contrary to what Lola at the club reception desk, the fat man in the steam room, Harold and perhaps even Al, had evidently already assumed.* At least, after much thinking, that was what he realized all the innuendos of sly veiled looks and snide comments were about.

He shrugged and pulled out his recipe file. Kathryn was coming to his house for dinner and on a whim, first thing in the morning, he had also called and invited the Nelsons. His afternoon was all planned: Massage, bring Kathryn to look at the condo, a quick trip to the nursery of her choice to buy him some plants, home to start dinner. To make the timing work, he was bringing Kathryn home with him after the nursery visit and then taking her back at the end of the evening.

Tucker suddenly smacked himself on the head and looked at his watch. It was nearly 2:00 o'clock. He had almost forgotten to call to the ambassador. The thought that he had almost let Mr. Tyler down made him feel nauseous. He rushed to his phone to call Peggy for the ambassador's number.

Her voice was calm and professional as always and so Tucker was surprised when, after giving him the number, she said, "Tucker, may I ask you something?"

"Yes, of course." He answered, hoping his voice sounded as crisp as hers. "What is it?"

"Well, it's about Mr. Tyler. Is he ill?" She rushed on, "I know it's not my business, but I've been sitting here since

430

he left, worrying myself sick." Her voice faded and Tucker felt a sudden fear, quickly squelched. Slowly, he said, "I don't know, Peggy. What makes you think so?"

"Well, it's just that he has a doctor's appointment and then when he buzzed me today and I knocked on the door like I always do, he didn't answer. So I waited, knocked again and then when he didn't answer, I open the door and went in. And there he was, just sitting there. At first I thought he was just leaning back, thinking, but his color wasn't good and his eyes looked funny. It was almost as though they were unfocused."

"Did you ask him if he was feeling all right?" Tucker asked, fighting to keep his breathing even.

"Yes, I did. And truthfully, he sounded fine."

Tucker gave his practiced, gentle chuckle that sounded false even to him. "Then," said Tucker smoothly, "what do you say we put our worries on hold until we hear something specific. Goodbye, Peggy."

It took Tucker long minutes of drawing deep breaths, waiting for the nausea to subside before placing the call. He confirmed the Zitec team and then he and the ambassador chatted about other details regarding the economic and political climate of his own country. Finally, Tucker suggested faxing him several of the most informative articles. After listening to several minutes of gracious 'thank yous,' he was able to hang up and return to thinking about his dinner party, ignoring the nagging alarm he felt at Peggy's observation.

Since it was to be a cold buffet, already that morning he had made the Pâté Brisee. Now, he retrieved the dough from the refrigerator and turned the oven to 400°. While he waited for the dough to soften, he reread the menu: cold poached salmon, spinach salad, chilled new potatoes, dilled croissants and the desert he was in the process of making, Clafoutis aux Cerises. He still needed to pit the cherries for the clafoutis, boil the new potatoes and poach the salmon. It was time to hustle. But, even hurrying, he knew there would be some task left undone if he was to be on time for his massage.

Time to prioritize, he thought. He put two bottles of Pinot Noir Blanc in to chill. He put a check mark in the "done" column of his computer printout list. He did not allow himself to acknowledge or even remember the call from Peggy, although he did prioritize calling Mrs. T about the cooking contest.

By the time Tucker was ready to leave for his massage, a bouquet of odors befitting the kitchen of a good French restaurant filled his condo. *Unfortunately,* he thought as he once again tried Midge's number, *the trouble with a cold meal is that by the time the guests arrive, the odors are mostly gone.*

He stood and listened to the phone ring for long minutes, wishing again that Midge Tyler would either have Clarice or Charlie answer when she was out...or get an answering machine. In desperation, he called Charlie's line. But the cook didn't seem to know anything specific, only that she had left the house in a big hurry. Tucker thanked him for the information and asked that he tell her of his call and then rushed out the door.

On the drive to Kathryn's, Tucker decided that it was important that he not allow an unfounded, somewhat illogical concern for the Tylers to ruin his day. He would try calling them later, from the car phone if necessary. *They will be in for dinner or Charlie would have mentioned it.* With that thought for comfort, he allowed his mind to drift onto what Kathryn's response would be when he told her he'd had a massage at the club, albeit a shortened massage, due to Heather's competitive impatience. *It was a good idea,* he thought and then frowned, knowing he would always wonder about her opinion of his response to her angry name calling. "Checkmate and game definitely over," he said quietly to himself.

Kathryn, hose in hand, watched him coming up the walk, lost in thought, a smile tweaking at the corner of his mouth. "You've a good look about you, Tucker. Does that mean it's a day to trust your massage therapist enough to let her do the entire body?"

Tucker laughed. "I guess it is time, especially since I took both a steam bath and a massage at the club last night without a whimper." He waited, looking at her, enjoying the incredulous look that she gave him.

"No! You didn't? Tell me you aren't just pulling my leg?"

He nodded, smiling. "It's true. My back was a little stiff and I had a tennis game to play. So I walked to my club and had a bit of a going over by old Harold."

She looks suspicious. "Your whole body?"

"Oh no." Tucker said, trying to keep a serious tone. "That honor, such as it is, belongs to you."

Smiling with pleasure at his words, she said, putting her hands on her hips, "Well then, let's get to it, me bucko."

Feeling inordinately proud of himself, Tucker slipped out of his clothes and into the waiting steam cabinet and pulled the cover shut before calling to Kathryn. "At least come in and talk to me while I'm being parboiled. What do you hear from Sunny?"

She came in from the waiting room, dust rag in hand. "Allison is fine, but no talking until after the session. "I've lots of interesting things to tell you, but we've got the evening and now isn't the time." So saying, she tightened down the seal on the cover, turned a lever, pushed a button, patted him on the head, smiled and disappeared back through the door.

Tucker leaned back then and with practiced ease, cleared his mind until only the familiar white space remained while the swirl and hiss of steam opened his pores and extracted rivulets of perspiration. Hovering, mind suspended, it seemed like only seconds had passed before Kathryn was back, handing him a fresh towel and discreetly leaving the room.

Fumbling only slightly, he lay face down, on the table, towel in place. The steam cabinet had done its work. He felt rubbery, unfocused and relaxed. He closed his eyes as Kathryn draped him with a sheet and began to explain the procedure in detail.

"Other than to tell you what you need to do next or what I'm going to do next, there will be no talking," she said firmly. "Use this time to let your mind drift."

And he did. He was amazed at how easy tidbits of information, details, conversations, mind-pictures all seem to float on gentle waves through his head. Only vaguely did he seem to hear Kathryn's coaching. Only now and again was he really aware of the oil-warmed hands kneading a particularly tight group of muscles. And when finally her hand slowed and stopped, resting firmly on his chest to signify completion, he opened his eyes and found her grinning down at him.

"'Tis hard to believe 'twas only a month ago you were here ordering me about, gritting teeth, spitting out words like bad meat. You are definitely a changed man, Tucker Jones."

He blinked and tried to adjust himself to real time. The sensation was not a new one. Often, working on the computer, a similar time warp sensation would occur. He would look at his clock and find that hours had passed instead of minutes. Then he sighed. "Good job, Kathryn, old girl. But how in the world am I ever going to find the energy to get off this table, much less make dinner for you and the Nelsons?"

She laughed. "No doubt you'll manage. I'm going to go and find you some juice and then I'm going to change my clothes. So, don't hurry yourself, but meet me in the garden. One of the hostas has a new purple flower.

Tucker was finishing his juice, waiting for her in a chair. Jon Bon was in his lap purring loudly, kneading his trousers with gentle paws. He somehow felt honored.

Kathryn returned and nodded at the cat. "He's lonesome. He misses Allison's pestering."

He looked up at her. She was wearing a dirndl skirt, its fullness and bright colors rather accentuating the stockiness of her body, but the splashes of red, green and yellow on the blue background certainly gave her a festive air.

"You look like a party," he said grinning lazily up at her, feeling loath to move. "Shall we go see if we can find one?"

She gave a little twirl on her Birkenstock clad feet, "Pete brought me this, years ago. It's an Austrian peasant skirt and is one of Allison's favorite things for me to wear." Then she sat down quickly in the chair opposite and leaned forward, elbows on the table, fist under her chin. Her eyes were twinkling. Tucker waited and sipped his juice.

"Speaking of Allison...I talked to her last night. She's fine. Having a wonderful time and says to give you a big hug and that she misses you..." Katherine paused, sat back and stretched up her arms and laughed. "Then Pete got on the phone and after a wee bit of hemming and hawing, wanted to know 'just who in the hell is this Tucker Jones.'" She made her voice imitate the gruffness and somehow, the worry she had picked up from her ex-husband's voice. Tucker thought it remarkable mimicry, though he hadn't a clue as to what Pete really would sound like. They sat and grinned at each other. He could tell she was quite pleased.

"What did you tell him?"

She laughed and tossed her head. "Not a thing. I know my daughter well. She's described every detail of your fine head. Of course, if he ever meets you, he'll be expectin' the physique of Superman and the intelligence of Einstein."

She laughed again. Clearly she was enjoying the apparent jealousy. "He was telling me she took him to the library to check out a car book so she could show her grandparents what the chariot that carried her to and from the zoo looked like."

Tucker watched her eyes get a faraway look and sat quietly. Finally, she sighed. "I don't suppose I should be enjoying his discomfort quite so much. But it's nice to have the shoe on the other foot, with him doing a bit of worrying for a change."

Tucker stood up after gently transferring the gray bundle on his lap to the third chair.

"Well," he said, looking at his watch. "Sunny should be getting my letter today. That might add a bit of fuel to the fire, eh? Come on, my conniving friend, time to rescue my condo from its sterility."

She smiled. "Let me get my purse and put away these things... I've a present for the new mood we're creating."

435

Chapter Thirty-seven

Kathryn seemed quite relaxed as she waited for Tucker to open the passenger door of the Aston and chatted easily while he retrieved the basket from the trunk. Tucker, on the other hand, found, by the time they reached his front door, he had to clamp his teeth together to keep from calling the whole excursion off. Fortunately, she did not seem to sense his doubts and cheerfully plucked the basket from his arms and waited patiently for him to let her in.

Once inside, her chatter stopped and she gave full attention to the condo, finally saying simply, "Ah, Tucker, I see what you mean."

The Indonesian basket, almost too big for her arms, finely woven of tan, umber, black and rusty-brown rushes, was large enough to serve as a cachepot for something dramatic. After a quick look around the living room, she took it to the far, sunny corner, opposite the piano and set it there with a flourish. Even empty, it gave life to the space. "See how it picks up the black in the piano?" She said happily as if some matter were finally settled.

Tucker admitted to himself that it did. He decided to give in gracefully and accept the basket as intended--a gift from a friend. When she had first walked from her house carrying the enormous basket, he noted its value and had protested vehemently. She ignored him and said, "Please open the trunk. "This basket has been sittin' in my closet, serving as nothing more than a hamper. Surely it deserves more."

When he continued to protest, she finally agreed that she would take it back if it didn't suit the look of the condo. Now, seeing it in place, he simply nodded in response to her observation. "I give up, Kathryn. You are absolutely correct and I thank you. It is a splendid gift and it does look very attractive in that corner," he said formally.

Then he smiled at her fondly. "Now, let's go find a plant to put in it."

They not only found a huge fishtail palm to put in the basket, she talked him into getting crimson geraniums to nest at the base and hinted that the same red in sofa pillows or a throw might liven the living room a bit.

The bird's nest fern they found for the coffee table was a magnificent specimen, but the phalaenopsis, or what Ethan had called a moth orchid, was what Tucker picked out for himself. It now sat, in creamy splendor, anchoring the corner of his computer desk.

Kathryn volunteered to plant the geraniums and Tucker nodded without protest. He had looked at his watch. It was time to start dinner and he still needed to reach Mrs. T. He excused himself and pushed the telephone button.

Midge came on immediately and seemed very glad to hear his voice. After they talked about his role in the cooking contest, she casually mentioned her husband's doctor appointment and said so airily that Tucker could picture her waving a hand in the air, "They did various tests but we won't really know anything until the results are evaluated."

Her words sounded dismissive, as if everything was simply routine and Tucker found himself feeling great relief. Then suddenly, it came to him that Midge was behaving a bit oddly, abruptly changing from topic to topic without stopping for breath. He began to wonder if she was keeping something from him; though he couldn't quite put his finger on what made him feel that way. *Perhaps because she is changing subjects without even a segue. We've talked about the cooking contest, the waterfront announcement, his mother's role in the meeting, Charlie's delicious lunch and even Dawn.*

Midge seemed to be nearly babbling as she told him that because of the cooking contest, she had been talking with Dawn and her mother almost every day. As he listened, he became amused, noting that Dawn, in some way or another, came up in every conversation with her lately. "Did I tell you that, Tucker, dear?"

Impulsively, he decided to see if he could stop her in her tracks and quickly inserted into the slight pause at the end of her question, "I don't think you did, Mrs. T. Dawn didn't mention it in the letter she wrote."

He realized with satisfaction, as the silence grew, that once again he had surprised Midge Tyler to the point of speechlessness. Mission accomplished!

"Really? Didn't she? Mention it, I mean."

"No, not a word," he said firmly, feeling fully in command for the first time. He changed the subject back to his role in the computerizing of the cooking contest data, clearly signifying that was the only tidbit about Dawn he was going to drop. Much later he would realize that by the time he hung up the phone, he had totally blocked the discussion of his bosses' health.

Kathryn, just finishing the process of planting the geraniums at the foot of the fern, could not help but overhear the conversation and see the mischief in Tucker's eyes. He was smiling when he hung up the phone.

"My bosses' wife," he said in the way of explanation, "is a wonderful woman, but she does try to manipulate my social life. She has tried to fix me up with all her friends' daughters, but until Dawn, I couldn't seem to get interested."

Then he frowned, remembering how forced the conversation had felt. *It's not like Midge to be so secretive. About what?* Since he had unconsciously blocked his concern about Mr. Tyler's health so cleanly, that her worry could be related to his doctor's appointment did not come up.

He shrugged dismissively, pulled himself firmly from his reverie and nodded towards Kathryn. "You were absolutely correct about the geraniums. It makes a much stronger statement with the red. I hadn't realized how much my piano dominated the room. Thank you again for the basket...and for all your help. Now, I will finish preparing our feast, as your reward."

When Kathryn finished the planting, put the unused potting soil by the door and disposed of the plastic pots under his sink, she sat on a stool and talked to him, sipping wine and watching with some surprise how easily he moved about the kitchen. At her request, he handed her the bowl of cherries to pit. "Tell me about your other guests," she said companionably.

438

So, as he prepared the custard and poured it carefully over the cherries sitting in reddish-black splendor on the buttery-brown flan crust, he told her. As he talked, he realized, with a shock, how focused, but lonely he must've been.

"My professors all said I couldn't stay on the varsity tennis team and keep up with my coursework, but I did. That's where I met Greta and Greg. Actually, I didn't know them well, but then I didn't have any real friends at college. Greg and I played a lot of singles, gave each other quite a workout, but mixed-doubles was his preference and when the coach paired him with Greta you could almost feel the chemistry. They were really good...ARE really good. Even back then they..."

He stopped talking as he carried the clafoutis to the oven. Kathryn noted his total relaxation and concentration as he completed the simple task and set the timer. He was indeed a very handsome man and there was an unknown but definable innocence about him that made her believe his claims about not having had girlfriends.

When he finished, he turned and looked at her. "I'm glad it worked out so well for them," he said simply.

She nodded soberly, wishing it had worked out that well for her. And when she looked at Tucker, she could see he was reading her thoughts so she changed the subject. "Why weren't you interested in the young women this person, Midge, tried to line up for you?"

He raised his eyebrows in surprise and thought hard. "I guess it has to do with the wall. I didn't even let myself think about women, other than as someone who would find ME a fascinating companion. It wasn't in my vocabulary to ask myself how I felt about something. I centered every thought around how to make myself the most agreeable companion possible. It was part of my defense mechanism...you know, they could be crazy about me, and that fed my ego in some sick way...but I allowed myself no feelings about any of them. It was safer that way I guess."

Absently, he began chopping dill. "Actually, except for Dr. van Castle, you and Sunny are the only friends I've worked hard to be "real" with. You were sort of an experiment, and of course, I give credit to the garden.

439

Kathryn found his words had pricked her sentimental Irish heart as though it were the blade of his chef's knife. She raised her glass and said in a wavering voice, "Here's to friends! 'Tis an honor you think it's so. And the Lord bless my garden."

Then the doorbell announced that the Nelsons had arrived and there were several awkward moments while Tucker poured wine and everyone searched their minds for topics of conversation to seize upon. Kathryn, recognizing shyness when she saw it, took command. "So, Tucker tells me you positively knocked everyone's socks off last night at the tennis tournament. He says you played well enough in college to turn professional." She was stopped by the look the couple exchanged. Greta, slightly red of face, said softly. "We did try it for a while, but it's not for us." Greg laughed. "We're really the house-with-a-picket-fence type. We'd rather have children, a dog and a garden than a case full of trophies."

"Yes," said Kathryn nodding, "I know just what you mean."

"Speaking of gardens, you should see Kathryn's garden. It's amazing!" Tucker said as he plated the food.

The evening rolled on from there. When the time came, Greta and Greg had insisted on taking Kathryn with them. They were still thanking him as he walked with them to the elevator. Once on, Greta got back off and walked to where Tucker stood. She looked up, squinting with concentration. "I like THIS friend, Tucker," she said, giving him a peck on the cheek. Then, she turned and hopped back through the elevator doors to take her husband's hand.

For a moment Tucker wondered what she meant. *It can't be that I needed to be told she liked Kathryn. That was obvious and they confirmed it when they insisted on dropping her off.* "It's just minutes out of our way," Greg had assured him.

"Besides, I want to know where she lives," Greta admitted. "She has invited me to come and see her garden."

With sudden insight, Tucker realized Greta was talking about Heather. Her stress on the word THIS was a very subtle way of letting him know how she felt about

Heather. He shook his head. *Women, he* thought as he opened his front door, *need a special instruction manual to go with them.*

Tucker paused at the open door of his condo and let his eyes rove about the room. He was more than satisfied with the evening. The place had the look of a successful party. There were dishes in the sink, empty drinking glasses here and there, dessert and coffee cups still on the table. *My condo has never been so cluttered or looked so well,* he decided. *It looks...lived in...and much of that look has to do with the new foliage.*

As he rolled up his sleeves and began to gather dirty dishes, Tucker had to admit to himself that his dinner was all that he hoped it would be. He smiled as he pictured his mother's surprise when he called her to tell her about his first dinner party. "Without help, Tucker, dear?" she would ask.

The next morning, it was exactly what she did say. "How lovely, Tucker. What a wonderful menu! Now, you must tell me about each dish in detail so I can share with your father."

So, Tucker described every recallable detail, until she was satisfied. Then, she paused, as if still taking the extraordinary news in. "And you did it without any help, you say? How very brave of you. Did you use Grandmother's Limoges?"

He was still smiling when he hung up the phone. He used to think his mother was totally predictable...until she had accepted the challenge of judging the cooking contest. She had told him all about the Tuesday meeting and how Althea had scooped the paper and told everyone about the governor's plan to put low-cost housing and a training center in the middle of the worst slum on Front Street.

"And, Tucker, though I don't think this is for publication--that is why Midge is working so hard on this cooking contest. She wants to buy property in the area and build a park with S.O.S. funds. Isn't that a lovely idea?"

Tucker could clearly hear the excitement in his mother's voice. It seemed that she had taken the project on as her own. "Yes, it is mother. Is there land available?"

"Well, dear, actually, that is a bit of a problem perhaps..." And she went on to give Tucker a blow-by-blow, detailed description of the entire meeting. For the first time, he realized his ability to remember what was heard might have been an inherited thing.

He looked at his watch, loath to cut his mother short, but realizing with an internalized groan that he was going to spend the day hurrying once again.

"Mother, sorry to cut you short, but if I don't, I'll have to keep Mr. Tyler waiting."

She was immediately contrite. But Tucker laughed, "Actually, Mother, I think this whole land acquisition idea is fascinating and I think you might consider volunteering some time in addition to the judging."

"Why, Tucker, I hadn't ever thought...yes, I see what you mean. Thank you, dear. I will think about it and discuss it with your father. Goodbye. I hope I haven't made you rush."

But of course I'm rushing, thought Tucker as he stuffed computer printout files into his attaché case. Then on a whim, he picked up the computer printout of his letter to Dawn and put it in the inside pocket of his suit jacket. It would be nice to show Dr. van Castle that he had taken his advice when they met. Remembering that he had not given the photos to Heather, he took the time to retrieve them from his athletic bag before rushing out his front door.

Driving smoothly through the heavy traffic, his mind drifted back to his mother's conversation. *Front Street? What did he know about Front Street? Not much, other than its geographic location.* He wondered what Mr. Tyler knew about it...and an idea had planted itself firmly in his brain.

Mr. Tyler stood up when Tucker entered, which was uncharacteristic. He held out his hand. "Midge said you called the other evening to inquire after my health. Thank you, son." He shook Tucker's hand heartily. They looked at each other while Tucker scrambled to decipher the words. Only because his boss had prompted, could he even vaguely recall talking with Midge about the doctor's appointment...but he must have...Mr. Tyler seemed to think he knew about it. *What's the proper response? Why can't I remember?* He took the only course he could think of, his voice nearly breaking with brittleness as the old familiar feeling of nameless dread threatened. "And how are you today, sir?"

They walked to the table and sat, Tucker with his attaché case unopened, gripped in his hands below the table's edge. He worked hard to keep his breathing even and his face relaxed. He thought he knew what his boss was going to say next.

Tyler looked at Tucker sharply. He could see the lad was under some duress and came to a quick decision. "Aw, that little twinge I had yesterday was just enough to make me keep the doctor's appointment my mollycoddling wife had made. So when Hank and I get there, who is in the parking lot?" Without waiting for an answer, Tyler said, "You guessed it." He threw up his hands. "My darling wife, with a gleam in her eye...making me admit to it...and before I knew it, I was no longer having a simple physical. I was having an upper G.I., lower G.I., electrocardiogram, x-rays: the works! And today, they want me back to walk on a treadmill. I'm telling you, Midge had that doctor standing on his ear. Neither of us could calm her down and you know how she can get..." He grinned. "Fearsome woman when she gets her feathers fluffed. I thought she was going to hit me when I told her to stop being such a banty hen."

He stopped and scowled. "Those damn doctors don't tell you a thing! All they want to do is stick you with needles, poke things into you, tape things on you and have you fill out forms and answer questions. The doctor said, after the testing was done, that he would be able to tell us more. Secretive son-of-a-bitch! Even Midge couldn't dig anything out of him."

Tucker found he had been holding his breath, the old familiar feeling of panic still threatening, but loosening its hold as he accepted his bosses' words. He managed to say, "You certainly look fine sir."

"I am fine! Perfectly fine! Never felt better! Now let's get to work."

Without altering his expression, Tucker loosened the grip on his attaché case, quelled his queasy stomach and turned to the topic at hand. "As the email I wrote you said, I did talk with the ambassador. He's pleased that Clifton is to head the team. He said SOFOFA has narrowed the potential location to two sites and he would like an engineer

443

with Clifton's reputation to give an opinion. I faxed him some data."

"I know. He's already phoned me twice this morning. He's delighted with that map showing the increase in arable land projected from putting those wind machines in the passes. Show me the data on those two sites."

As Tucker opened his case, he heard his boss sigh. He looked up. There was a look of distaste on the older man's face. "The second phone call was to warn me that Zitec was probably going to receive the same negative lobbying by big business interests that it got when we went into Malaysia."

He drummed his fingers angrily. "Damn! Zitec International means just that...worldwide. I refuse to let pocket politicians deter me from foreign projects that might affect their precious constituents' profits and force me into projects only at home."

"Actually, sir, I was going to mention an idea for a project at home at the end of this meeting, if there is time. And I do mean at home, literally."

"Eh? What? All right, let's stay on task then. Sorry to bother you with the political claptrap. Show me the sites."

Tucker had warned Dr. van Castle that on Thursday, it was sometimes difficult for him to get away at lunch time and the doctor had promptly suggested they meet after work for a drink instead. It turned out to be a very good suggestion since Mr. Tyler was not completely satisfied that he understood the reasons textiles had been chosen for the manufacturing venture.

"These climate charts don't seem to indicate the ability to keep a large workforce busy in textiles, do they? Can a wind machine generating power make that much difference?"

"Not a single wind machine," Tucker corrected gently, "wind machines." And of course, the reservoirs. Remember, we almost declined to consider Chile because of its climate. But look at the map that excited Baraque. Now, superimpose this population density map. Notice how currently, 90% of the population is confined to the central and the northern areas of southern Chile. This land to the north is, for all intents and purposes, useless. There are no controlled water sources, thus no hydroelectric potential.

444

However there is an abundant and limitless supply of wind. SOFOFA thinks it can be harnessed. It means cheap electricity for the region."

Patiently and methodically Tucker explained, "Clifton and the team support the contention that the wind machines..."

Bit by bit, strand by strand, the pieces were pulled together so that by 10:30 Tyler sat back and stretched.

"Chile was the right choice and our original assumption still seems to be correct. We do have the technology to influence climatic changes. Damned exciting isn't it?"

Tucker smiled. "I'm looking forward to the findings of the team."

With a snort of what sounded like a cross between admiration and disgust, Mr. Tyler pushed back from the table. "There you go again, bursting my enthusiasm with your pin of logic. Do you have time for lunch after the meeting? I really would like to hear about a potential project, as you put it, 'close to home.'"

Tucker nodded. "I'd like that sir."

"It's also a celebration for putting this project together, as much as we can without the on-site visit and the signing of contracts." Tyler smiled ruefully. "We might have even taken the afternoon off for golf, if I didn't have to go walk on that damn treadmill. Do you still have your shoes in the trunk of your car?"

"Always!" said Tucker as he walked from the office. "One never knows when one's boss is going to call for the ultimate sacrifice. It wouldn't do to have one's shoes in Guilford."

Over lunch, Tucker thought his boss seemed very relaxed. He was extremely interested in hearing what Tucker's mother had learned at Tuesday's meeting with his wife and wondered why Midge hadn't shared those particular details about the cooking contest with him. He told Tucker that he had read about the governor's plan in the paper on the way to work, but had only skimmed it. He had too much else on his mind. Immediately, he caught the drift of Tucker's association.

"Yes, of course, there would be opportunity to revitalize the area with jobs, once the area is cleared up. It sounds to be a splendid idea," he boomed, causing several of the nearest diners to turn their heads curiously. Tyler smiled at them benignly. "Sorry," he said genially, mostly to the room at large. Then he took a long, reflective sip of coffee. "You know, Tucker, something isn't quite right here. I have a sixth sense that there is more going on in the guv's office than meets the eye. Also, I have a strong hunch that Midge knows more about it than either of us."

It was interesting to watch his boss turn from smiling congeniality to sharp, squint-eyed, political calculation, Tucker decided. He thought of his day at the zoo. *He's turned from otter to eagle,* he noted, watching the man's eyes as he sorted and shuffled his thoughts.

Tyler mused softly, almost as if to himself, "This is a big deal, especially since it's bound to be controversial. That's a bunch of money to allocate to one segment of the population in an election year." He suddenly looked at Tucker. "He's got the Republican votes, but he should have been milking this deal for all if it's worth if he wants to capture some of those liberal-assed Democratic votes...and it's just now we're hearing about it? Robert didn't even mention it on the boat, that I remember."

"He said nothing in my presence."

"Hmmm." Tyler said, speculatively. "I believe I'll call Robert when we get back to the office on the pretext of wanting to know more about the training facility and see what else I can pry out of him. You can bet cocktails at our house tonight will be interesting. Unless I miss my guess, Althea slipped some juicy confidential tidbit to my darling wife. Now tell me about Dawn."

The transition was so abrupt, that for a second the younger man sat blinking with astonishment, the words failing to compute.

"Midge told me you had a letter from Dawn, Tucker," the older man prompted as if speaking to someone having limited knowledge of English, enunciating each word. "How is she?"

"She's fine. It wasn't a long letter."

Clearly, Mr. Tyler expected more. He sat, giving his young employee full attention. Tucker felt his entire body flush and knew from Mr. Tyler's smirk that his face must be glowing. "I think she's a wonderful person," he stammered.

446

Mr. Tyler was looking at him strangely. "Yes, yes indeed she is. Midge and I still miss having her around. She quite spoiled us with her energy and enthusiasm in the two weeks she spent with us. We started looking forward to her return as soon as we put her on the plane."

Tucker felt his heart lurch. "Is she? Returning, I mean." He asked carefully.

Mr. Tyler waved his hand. "Of course she is. Midge told me that her mother said she was having a hard time settling back into her beach routine and that if Tufts didn't accept her, she'd apply elsewhere on the East Coast. But Tufts will accept her of course. We're expecting to hear any day. Besides, she has to come back this fall." Mr. Tyler looked hard at Tucker. "I understand Heather invited her to hike the Maine woods and she accepted."

Tucker looked puzzled. "What? Heather take Dawn hiking in Maine? That doesn't seem..."

Mr. Tyler interrupted to correct himself. "Not just Heather. Evidently, her invitation included you. She said something like, "would you like to join Tucker and me and hike... Deborah and Rob are included too."

Tucker, Tyler noted with disgust, seemed to be missing the point, concerned instead with trying to picture elegant Heather Anderson in hiking clothes, mud on her boots, swatting the occasional deer fly.

Tucker mumbled, "Heather just doesn't seem like the hiking type. Funny, everyone seems to know about this but me. It just doesn't make sense." But then, suddenly, Mr. Tyler could see that it did. Making a sound in his throat that sounded like, "Arugh!" Tucker pounded his forehead with a fist, totally unaware that his boss was watching him with gentle amusement, thinking that his wife would certainly be proud of his meddling. The boy was definitely rattled and the blush had been magnificent. *Yes, I have done my job. I can tell Midge that the chemistry is still bubbling.*

Tucker's mind was reeling. Now, Dawn's letter made sense. The pictures made sense. Everything made sense! Heather Anderson had probably been doing a number on Dawn the entire boat trip and he had unknowingly contributed to her plan. Into his mind flashed the picture of his putting an arm around Heather while Dawn snapped the picture. He put his head in the crook of his arm and

447

groaned, face down on the table. When he looked up at the blue eyes placidly studying him from across the table, he knew immediately that his boss had not asked about Dawn just to make conversation. He would bet money that the manipulative hand of Midge Tyler had help in restacking the deck.

He sighed and managed to grin. "Thank Midge for convincing you to tell me, I guess. Luckily, even without your prodding, I had written Dawn back, telling her how I felt."

Fortunately, Mr. Tyler had sense enough to let the matter drop. He raised a finger for the check. "Good!" he said. "Now, let's get back to the office."

Chapter Thirty-eight

Tucker sat in the coolness of his office and tried with superhuman effort to concentrate on his summaries. Each time he settled himself to remember what had gone on prior to the meeting in Mr. Tyler's office or at the management meeting, Dawn's face, the morning he handed her his cup and strode off seething with anger interfered. If it wasn't Dawn's face, it was Heather's as she snuggled up to him and placed his hand on her breast.

He finally jumped up from his desk and paced around the room. *This has never happened before. I've always been able to concentrate. What's going on? I'm going to have to call Mr. Tyler...*

Tucker stopped pacing, worry stilling his steps. *I can't call him. He's at his doctor's appointment.* He sat back down at his desk and stilled his mind as best he could. *I can't concentrate because I'm worried. I'm worried about having hurt Dawn, but I'm more worried about Mr. Tyler. I don't ever remember him leaving work to go to a doctor's appointment. He said he wasn't planning to be back this afternoon. These summaries can wait.*

Tucker realized he could go home, change out of his suit, have a quick shower and still have time to meet Dr. van Castle. *Maybe, after I hash this new obsession with women over with the doctor, I can regain my concentration.*

By the time Tucker sat down across from the doctor in the small, comfortable, slightly seedy bar he felt wooly in the head from thinking. He also felt the need to apologize. "I thought this was going to be a relaxed sort of a drink, but it's not. Do you mind?"

Dr. van Castle who had been a bit early and had already poured his second beer from the pitcher; looked across at the tall man who, contrary to his words, looked very relaxed as he leaned back against the wooden bench and crossed his hands behind his head.

449

"You don't look upset," he observed quietly, pushing an empty glass towards Tucker.

"Pure deception of the sort for which I'm famous," said Tucker with a languid smile.

Tobin leaned forward with interest, his beer forgotten. "Jesus, you ARE good! I am totally deceived. Do you care to tell me the source of your agitation?"

Tucker dropped his act, uncrossed his hands and leaned forward, allowing the doctor to read the anger in his face. "I just found out today that a friend of mine, a beautiful woman friend, mind you, has been quite untruthful by innuendo and outright deception."

Whoa! Thought the doctor, *There's the anger!*

Tucker looked down at his hands lying on the table and clenched them into tight fists. *Very good,* observed the doctor silently, *now that's an angry gesture.*

"One of the things she's been untruthful about is the nature of our relationship. She evidently made people think we are romantically involved." His face flushed. "And I'm totally embarrassed to say that I was too naïve to notice how I was being used."

Yes, thought the doctor with satisfaction, *he is truly emotionally engaged.*

Tucker, who had remembered to transfer the pictures and his letter to Dawn from his suit coat, reached a hand into his vee-neck sweater and pulled it from his shirt pocket. "The only good news is that I took your advice and wrote my feelings to Dawn. She might even have the letter as we speak."

Tobin looked first at the pictures, saying nothing. Then he read Tucker's letter, digested its contents and felt sick. He looked at the pictures again, trying to think how to proceed, wishing heartily that he hadn't had the second beer.

Finally, he looked at Tucker. "First of all, you're right. This woman is really good looking. Sometimes when women are that pretty, they don't have to be anything else, just pretty. Is she one of those?"

Tucker had the sudden comfortable feeling he was in good hands. He poured himself a beer. "No, not really. She is a fantastic tennis player, has a good mind, very good manners…actually, what I decided is that we are quite a lot alike. I think there was an initial attraction from that thought, but she uses her intelligence and her good looks to get what she wants without seeming to care about the cost to others."

"Ah," said the psychiatrist smiling, "a bitch."

"Yes, I think so," said Tucker seriously. "As you can imagine, figuring that out was a little scary for me, since trusting comes a bit hard."

"Tell me more about that," said the doctor.

Tucker grinned. "I knew you were going to say that. It's quite comforting to hear, actually."

Van Castle smiled and waited. Inside his head he was thinking: *What you don't know is that I am avoiding telling you what I think of your ghastly letter and am stalling for time while I think how to lead up to it.*

"Anyway, Heather isn't what she seems. I would guess, if you asked, most people would describe her using the same adjectives I did. They might add sophisticated, well-groomed, thoughtful, caring. It makes her sound like someone you can trust…but she isn't."

"Did you?" asked the doctor. "Trust her?"

Tucker thought for minute and then shook his head. "I started to say, 'yes,' but then I remembered thinking that our relationship was like a chess game. In fact," he blushed, "when I decided not to let her seduce me Tuesday night, I remember feeling very secure that it was the right move, even said the word out loud, 'checkmate!' I don't believe she would have liked that very much."

Tobin tried not to laugh and failed. "So," he said, eyes twinkling, "the game is over, eh? It seems to me that you do have some ability to consciously decide whether or not to trust people. This woman happened to be in the "don't trust" column."

Tucker looked surprised and then gratified. He thought for a moment. "Yes. Actually that might be true. In fact, now that my brain is again functioning, I'd have to say I have started to try trusting some of the people in my life."

"That sounds positive," said the doctor. "What exactly do you mean?"

"Well, I have another woman friend. She's my massage therapist. As a matter-of-fact, Doctor Beemers assigned me to her."

"Oh, Kathryn."

Tucker looked at him in surprise. "You know Kathryn?"

Van Castle shook his head. "Not well. Jeff recommended her once and after the massage, I took a long shot and asked her out. But, I think my reputation preceded me and she turned me down flat."

At Tucker's look of frank curiosity, he winked and waved a hand. "We can talk about me some other time. Right now, let's keep wrestling with this."

Tucker felt strangely reluctant to talk about Kathryn now that she was no longer anonymous. He fell silent and the psychiatrist sensed why.

"Sorry about that, Tucker. My fault. It was probably bound to happen as our lines of therapy, friendship and beer blur the path." The doctor's round face was troubled.

Tucker took a long pull at his beer and then nodded. "Probably. I'm trying to think why I'm uncomfortable now." He tipped his glass again, this time taking only a sip. "Maybe it's like talking behind her back since we both know her." He spread his hands, thinking. "Well, just let me say, when she asks me a personal question, I try to answer her honestly. We seem to tell each other things that matter, things one doesn't normally tell another, if you know what I mean."

The doctor nodded. "Yes, I'd say that is most certainly a measure of trust." Internally he sighed. It was time to get back to Dawn and the letter. "Now, about Dawn...do you think you might be able to trust her?"

Tucker didn't even pause to think. "Absolutely! She has personal integrity. She also has courage. I've thought a lot about her letter and how difficult it must've been for her to write."

Tobin watched his enthusiasm mount. "Really, what she was saying was, even though I was supposedly committed to Heather, she liked me enough to be friends."

"Why do you suppose she wrote that she liked being carried...how did she put it...in your arms?" The doctor cocked an eyebrow and waited.

"Well, that's pretty easy to figure out. She just told me what she felt, just like I told her what I felt."

Tobin sighed and closed his eyes, suddenly feeling very old and wondered if there was ever a time that he didn't try to second-guess what a woman thought or said. Then he opened his eyes. "And did you, Tucker? Did you tell her how you felt?"

Tucker sat and stared at the doctor as though he'd taken leave of his senses. "Yes!" he said, the ring of confidence clear in his voice. "You know I did! You read the letter."

Their eyes met in a steady gaze; Tucker's resentful; Tobin's patient. Tucker's eyes dropped first and he snatched the letter from the table where the doctor had left it and unfolded it with jerky haste. He stared at his words. They had seemed so perfect when he wrote them, seemed even more perfect every time he reread them. "Aw, no! Aw, Doctor...oh Christ!" His disgust with himself was palatable, his dejection complete.

Van Castle ran distracted fingers through his curls and concentrated on remaining silent. Finally, Tucker looked up. "How is it that I keep screwing up my chances with the one girl I am really interested in?"

Lack of practice! The words remained unsaid inside the doctor's head. Aloud he said, "I don't know, but now that you're thinking straight, what might you have said to her?"

Seemingly, the words rolled easily from Tucker's downturned mouth. "I should have told her that I think she is beautiful and that when I was around her I felt wonderful, funny, masculine, and protective. I should have apologized to her for being such a jerk and admitted to her it was because I was afraid she could see inside me and wouldn't like what she saw. I should've told her I can't get the odor of her perfume off my mind!" He finished in a whisper, his tone so sad and resigned that Tobin found himself reaching out a hand to Tucker's arm.

"Tucker," he said, "you appear completely distraught and I find myself wondering why. You haven't done anything that can't be fixed. All you have to do is call her and tell her the exact words you just told me."

Tucker's reaction was startling. He jumped from the bench as if it were burning. He looked horrified. "Call her? My God, doctor, I can barely stand to say those words to

453

you. There's no way in the world I can say them to Dawn over the telephone."

Tucker's breathing began to quicken, his dark eyes did not focus on the doctor, but darted instead about the dimly lit room and his hands clenched convulsively at his sides. A part of Tobin van Castle found it very difficult to sit quietly and watch his friend struggle for control. Another part of him--that of a trained researcher--was interested in watching the manifestation of a classic panic attack.

Fascinating from more than one standpoint, he thought wryly. His experiment of serving as mentor to Tucker Jones was definitely not going as smoothly as he had anticipated. Never in a million years, had Tucker been his client, would he have given such a directive. He might have said, "Have you considered what you might do to correct the situation?" But, certainly, he would have offered nothing more leading than that.

Van Castle noted that Tucker seemed to be conquering his desire to bolt blindly by grasping the back of the bench. "Deep slow breaths, remember?" The doctor said softly, but for a moment Tucker seemed not to have heard. Then he moaned softly and inhaled deeply. The doctor got up and put a gentle hand on his friend's back, quietly making a non-verbal connection, feeling the breathing deepen and steady in tempo. Tucker was gaining control. He turned slightly and dropped back onto the bench. He looked up at the doctor, who was still standing and drew a long wavering breath. "The real Tucker Jones," he said in a voice bowed down with wretchedness.

The doctor nodded without breaking the silence. Slowly he too sat back down. "Your description before was accurate. That was a full-blown panic attack. But this time you didn't run. Why didn't you?"

"I wanted to," said Tucker dully, not raising his head.

"Yes." The doctor persisted, "I could see that you did. But you didn't. I don't think it was because of me. You had already anchored yourself by grabbing the back of the bench before I reminded you about your breathing." To himself he thought, *maybe this mentor/friendship thing works after all. In all my work with Tucker in the past, I never saw him at this point of vulnerability.* He made a sudden decision.

454

"I think we're onto something very important here, Tucker. Let's take a walk and chew on it for a while."

Tucker raised his head, nodded his acquiescence and laboriously got to his feet. He felt as though he had taken a beating. Van Castle threw several bills on the table and they walked out into the warmth of the summer evening.

Simultaneously, they both drew deep breaths. "Lord!" Tobin stretched his arms over his head. "I used to love spending evenings drinking beer in cozy, smoky pubs. Now, I'm finding they make me feel a little claustrophobic. I think I'm getting old."

They began to walk, each wrapped in their own thoughts, toward the campus. After minutes of silence, Dr. van Castle said, "How much research did you do on anxiety?"

Tucker looked down at the doctor in surprise. "Funny," he said, "I was just going to say that perhaps one reason I didn't run out on you was that I'd read up on anxiety as a general condition and then specifically on panic attacks. One of the things that stuck in my mind was it may have been triggered by something entirely different than what we were talking about, at least that was one theory."

Tobin had the grace to look abashed. He nodded. "Now you know why it's called an 'inexact science.' Generally, no one seems to adhere exactly to anyone else's theory...but please go on."

"Well, I guess what Dollard and Miller had to say about the approach-avoidance conflict where the person soon represses all anxiety producing thoughts, used to fit me pretty well." He smiled down at the doctor whose eyebrows were raised. "Yes, I did look up repression."

Tobin smiled. "It's not that. It's your capacity for learning that amazes me. Even as a boy, you seemed to be able to repeat what others said to you verbatim. I was so impressed that I wrote a note in your chart about it and that's what triggered the significance of your not being able to remember the conversation with Dawn."

Tucker thought about the doctor's words, savored the admiration evident in his voice. Then he said, trying for a light tone, "A classic case of approach-avoidance, wouldn't you say?"

Tobin van Castle did not respond. He had stopped, lost in thought, hands in his pockets, looking as though he were memorizing the ground in front of him. Tucker turned and watched him quietly. Time passed. The doctor still stood. Tucker noticed a cement bench and went to sit on it. Still, the doctor thought.

Finally, as if coming out of a trance, he blinked and looked around for Tucker. He walked towards him shaking a finger. "Try this theory on for size." He paused, carefully selecting his words. "The problem is that the problem is NOT a single problem, there are two problems." He looked up at Tucker. "In your life, what would you say was the most traumatic event?"

Tucker knew immediately, but saying the words was difficult. The doctor watched him struggle. "Losing Ethan and Mary," he finally said.

"Exactly! I think it's possible that your tremendous control is masking the fact that your panic attacks are really caused by a fear of loss. You transfer the feeling to some small, but anxiety producing, event so you never have to deal with the fear of real loss."

The doctor went on. "That's why the attacks seem so illogical. For example, you might be asking yourself, 'How could I possibly go so berserk when I think about phoning a girl?'"

Tucker felt his senses sharpen. His mind reeled with the truth of Doctor van Castle's words. "If that is problem number one, what's problem number two?" he croaked.

The doctor shrugged. "We've already identified it...fear. Fear of allowing yourself to feel the spectrum of human emotions. When you shut down or repressed your feelings, you cut yourself off from access to the very data you needed to understand and solve your problems."

Tobin paused and there was wonder in his voice. "But for some reason, you aren't doing that anymore. I don't believe in miracles, of course," he smiled ruefully. "It goes against my training. The number two problem, in my professional opinion, is on its way to being solved. Now that you are calmer, you'll decide what you want to do about

Dawn...but I don't think that attack you just had was really about Dawn."

"No," said Tucker. "I mean...yes, I see what you mean. It wasn't logical. My stress over that situation allowed me to vent something else I've been repressing...is that what you're saying?"

The doctor plopped down on the seat beside Tucker, feeling as though he'd run a mile. His eyes were without twinkle. "It's a theory at least, one worth thinking and talking about."

They sat on the bench, not quite facing each other, looking pensive, each rolling the ramifications of the doctor's theory around in their heads.

Finally, Tucker sighed and looked at his watch. "I can't think about this anymore right now and I've certainly taken up most of your evening. Hopefully you didn't have other plans."

"No," the doctor smiled tiredly. "No other plans. Want to go for a bite to eat?"

Tucker sat up straight. "I may have just had a brilliant idea." He stood up and bowed slightly to the doctor. He suddenly felt the ghost of the same playfulness he had experienced with his boss the night of Dawn's rescue. "Sir, I would consider it an honor if you would join me at my club...a light bite, a massage, steam room, swim...whatever and in any order...what do you say?"

The twinkle came immediately back into Tobin's blue eyes. "I say it sounds quite wonderful."

"Fine," said Tucker. We'll call the club from my car phone and get things set up."

Chapter Thirty-nine

Tucker and Tobin were both famished and went straight to the dining room at the club. In unspoken agreement, both talked of things other than Tucker's issues. Over a good glass of Cabernet Sauvignon and small, rare, thick tenderloins, Tucker talked of how Kathryn's garden had been built from nothing into a place of lovely serenity and how surprised he had been to go through the plain wooden gate and into such a magical place. He talked too, of meeting first the cat, with the odd name, Jon Bon, and then the girl, Allison. Tobin noticed the warmth in his eyes and the humor in his tone. *This is really a very likeable young man,* he thought.

"So, Dr. van Castle," he heard Tucker say, "You said we could talk about you later. Is this later? I think you know a lot about me but I know little about you."

"Well, sure. However, please start calling me Tobin. That's what my friends call me." He looked Tucker in the eye. "I meant it when I said I wanted to be a mentor and a friend to you…not a therapist."

Tobin found Tucker to be an excellent listener. By the time they had finished their coffees and Tucker had signed the tab, he'd told the younger man about his boyhood in upstate-New York, his passion for snow skiing and his early decision, while in medical school, to study the mind.

As they walked towards the locker room, Tucker asked his only probing, personal question. "Did you ever find time to marry?"

Tobin laughed. "Ah, Tucker, what a great way to phrase that question! In truth I found the time, I just have never found the woman, at least not the one woman I'd want to settle down with for the rest of my life. I'm like Jeff Beemers, a confirmed bachelor, I guess."

Lola was again behind the desk outside the locker room. "Hey, Tucker," she said and pushed the sign-in book towards him.

"Hello, Lola, this is my friend, Tobin van Castle. Thank you for booking our massages.

"No problem. Glad to do it." She stood and reached over the counter, holding out her hand. "Very nice to meet you, Mr. van Castle," she said.

Tucker watched with some interest as Tobin smoothly captured her hand in a warm, two-handed shake and fastened his twinkling blue eyes on her. "It's a pleasure to meet you too, Lola, but please call me Tobin," he said engagingly, grinning his boyish grin.

It seemed to Tucker that the shake lasted a bit longer than it might have. He noticed that when Lola turned her attention back to him, she looked softer somehow; a slight blush on her cheeks.

"Cute friend, Tucker," she said as she handed him towels. "You have plenty of time for the steam room. Harold will come and get you. She turned back to Tobin. "And Marcella will come for you. She's fairly new, but I've heard good things."

"Lovely!" Tobin said, bouncing on his toes like a delighted boy. "This is quite a treat."

Once in the steam room, neither man talked. They sat, towel draped, feeling the heat begin to work its magic. Tucker was still somewhat amazed at the spontaneity of the evening; that he had thought to ask; and that Tobin was flexible enough to accept. His thoughts returned to Dawn and his reaction to the doctor's suggestion that he call her. *I'm just not brave enough, he decided.*

It was then that Tucker decided to write Dawn a second letter. This one would be an accurate description of his feelings, perhaps even giving some explanation of his rotten behavior, and sending it off Federal Express. He started to tell Tobin of his decision when Mr. Tyler's image floated into his consciousness. He sucked in his breath and sat up, wondering if the man was standing there, the image was so strong.

With a frown, he closed his eyes and lay back; feeling sated by the dinner, Tobin van Castle's excellent company and the conversation. Lazily he thought of Lola's reaction to his friend and could feel a smile lifting the corners of his mouth. *I'll bet he was really what my father would call, 'a ladies' man' in his day. In fact, if Lola is an indicator, he might still be.*

Tucker gathered his wandering thoughts and tried to recall Tobin's theory of his problem being two pronged. *So, if it wasn't calling Dawn that caused me to trip out, what was it?* Immediately, the image of his boss floated into sharp focus again behind his closed lids. He jerked himself into a sitting position, feeling his breathing start to quicken. *Here it is. Here's the cause of my nameless dread. It's Mr. Tyler.*

The feeling of a truth clanged like a bell in his mind. He glanced to where Tobin was sitting, slumped, eyes closed, and fought to control his breathing. He struggled to keep his mind focused on his discovery. *Why? What am I repressing about Mr. Tyler?* He felt the sudden elevation of his heart rate but he grabbed the bench and tried with all his might to hold the thought. *Fear of loss? That's Tobin's theory. Lose Mr. Tyler? Wait, let me think. Why am I worried about that? The doctor's appointment? Midge's reference to his health? Peggy's reference to his paleness and shortness of breath?*

Suddenly, in the swamp-heat of the steam room, Tucker felt cold to the core. *Don't give into this Tucker. Think! Think! Are you being rational? Do you really know if anything is wrong with Mr. Tyler's health? Think!* A groan escaped through clenched teeth. It caused the doctor to open his eyes.

"Holy shit! What's up, Tucker? What's going on?" He grabbed his towel and crossed the room to sit by Tucker. "Breathe man, breathe! Slow and steady now, or you're liable to pass out in this heat."

Tucker lifted his head, looked at the doctor and panted, "You were right, Dr. van Castle. I think this panic attack has to do with my boss."

True to form, Tobin said gently, "Tell me why you think that, Tucker."

"There could be something really wrong with his health, only I haven't let myself really know it until now. Every time someone brings up the worry, I've immediately either blocked or discounted it. I even asked how he felt, but was very careful not to listen to the answer."

Tucker could tell that saying the words had somehow reduced his agitation. "In a way, it certainly fits your theory."

Tobin nodded, agreeing. Aloud, he said, "It looks like you're starting to handle it. Let's get you out of here."

In the locker room, Tobin made Tucker sit on a bench while he tightened his towel went to get water from Lola. Immediately, she noticed the seriousness of his expression. "Is everything all right?"

"Yes, I think so. We should have thought to drink this water before we went into the steam room." As he walked back towards the locker room, he thought, *This poor kid has had one helluva therapeutic day. I hope he survives it.*

When he got back to the locker room and opened the door, a wiry, older man was sitting beside Tucker. He heard Tucker say, "I'm fine now, Harold. It's just that every now and again, I have a panic attack."

Well I'll be damned! What a class act. No brushing the dirt under the carpet for this kid. If I were writing a chart note, I'd say, Tucker Jones is on his way...and for him, the sky is the limit. He walked on in, smiling at his own clichés. He handed Tucker a bottle of water. Then he put out his hand. "You must be Harold. I'm Tobin. Tucker tells me you're good at what you do."

Tucker looked back and forth between the two men and saw concern and kindness written on their faces. "Listen, Harold. I have to make a phone call. I might have to cancel my massage."

He looked at Tobin. "I need to call the Tylers."

Tobin nodded and gave Tucker a ghost of his impish grin. "It would seem the logical thing to do."

Harold gestured towards the small room behind him that served as the towel room and his office. "You can use the phone in the cubby if you'd like."

Tucker nodded his thanks, noting that both men were standing as near to him as possible without being obtrusive as he hitched his towel and took his first steps.

Midge Tyler's usual cheerful voice immediately filled his ear. "Hello, Tyler's residence."

Tucker covered his eyes with a hand and drew a ragged breath. The silence grew as his mind registered that nothing could be very wrong with his boss if his wife's voice sounded so normal. He cleared his throat. "Hello Mrs. T, This is Tucker."

"Tucker? My goodness dear. You don't sound like yourself. Are you all right?"

"Yes, I'm fine." He strove mightily for the usual gentle bantering tone he used with her. "I called to ask how Mr. Tyler is doing."

Midge immediately picked up on the real note of concern in Tucker's carefully casual voice. "How nice of you to call, Tucker," she said, thinking once again that her husband was wrong in his opinion of this boy...although she thought he might be starting to reconsider. "Actually, we don't know for sure. We go in tomorrow morning for our appointment with the doctor to discuss all the findings. James says he feels fine and I for one am quite relieved that he has finally had a thorough physical. Would you like to speak with to him?"

Tucker considered. "No thank you, Mrs. T. I don't want to disturb him, but I'm glad he is fine. I hope I didn't interrupt anything important."

"Of Course you didn't, dear. In fact, I was just thinking about you earlier. Our committee met today and I do need to put your computer to work. May I call you tomorrow?"

"Certainly," said Tucker, infinitely glad that she was not in the mood to talk details at this moment. "I'll be home until about 2:30. Call me anytime."

"Oh, good! I'll get myself organized and call you after we go in for the consultation."

Tucker gently replaced the phone receiver in its cradle and stood up. He turned and looked through the doorway at the men waiting patiently at a discreet distance. "He seems to be fine," he said as he walked towards them. The relief coursing through his body was evident in his voice. "He and his wife go in for the results of all the testing in the morning, but she said he's feeling just fine."

A small warning bell rang in the psychiatrist's brain and he opened his mouth to sound a cautionary note and then closed it. *It is possible that optimism isn't warranted since the results have not yet been interpreted for them, but on the other hand what possible good could it do for this already over-wrought young man to have his fears reactivated?* Instead, he smiled warmly at Tucker and said, "Great! I'm glad you called to get that off your mind."

Tucker looked at him and thought for a moment. Then he smiled. "I think I hear what you're implying, Doctor. I'd already made up my mind in the steam room to write to Dawn when I get home. I'll Federal Express it in the morning." He turned to Harold. "Now how about that massage?"

Harold nodded and then turned to Tobin, "Marcella will be here in a jiffy. Tell her I said to take good care of you."

Midge was smiling when she walked back into where James was sitting, feet up, reading Forbes magazine. "That was Tucker inquiring after your health."

James looked up. "He did, eh? That seems a little funny. The several times it's come up in our conversation he has seemed totally disinterested, even bored. In fact, once today he changed the subject on me. And the other day, I could've sworn, though he made a polite response, that he didn't really hear me at all," he said flatly and returned to his reading.

Midge smiled down at the top of his gray head. "Perhaps he was hiding his worry. He sounded genuinely concerned on the phone."

James grunted without raising his eyes. "Perhaps," he said.

Dawn sat at her desk, fully aware that she was having a pity-party. Tucker's letter, fully memorized lay, tear-splotched, in front of her. As usual, she was trying to scold herself out of self-pity. *I set myself up. What did I expect? I should be glad he agreed.* "Shit!" Not swearing except in times of major stress, the word had been ringing steadily in her head since she first read the letter several hours ago. *What's wrong with me?*

Dawn had become so incredibly bored with the beach scene that she had stopped going. She couldn't seem to fit back into her California life at all. She was doing

463

what was required of her, but inside she felt like a piece of wormy wood. The only time she seemed to get relief from her self-pity was when she was running, or when she allowed herself to fantasize about Tucker Jones.

She gave a cross between a sob and a laugh and reached for yet another tissue. What hadn't she done with Tucker Jones in her fantasies? *What I need to do is cross out my image and insert Heather's into those erotic scenes. It's time to accept reality and get on with life!*

She and her mother had already talked about plan B in case she didn't get accepted at Tufts. More self-castigation. *Why didn't I explore other universities while I was with the Tylers?* Looking in the back of her *Webster's New World Dictionary*, at the list of colleges and universities, she found the whole geographic area around the Tyler's was absolutely dotted with good schools.

She had totally ignored her mother's gentle reminder that she really couldn't expect to hear from Tufts so soon. She had submitted her final application less than a month ago. "The wheels of bureaucracy turn slowly, Dawn. You know that." Her mother had chided her gently and wondered to herself what could be done to help heal her daughter's first broken heart. She certainly wasn't finding solace in her friends, in fact, was avoiding them. She did her volunteer work dutifully, but without her usual enthusiasm. She was working diligently on the barbecue and had actually been of great help in her willingness to do any task mentioned, no matter how trivial. But her willingness seemed more an effort to stay busy and isolated than from the sense of purpose she usually got from doing a good deed.

Barbara sighed. *Perhaps I should talk to Charles about sending Dawn back east to explore other schools. Watching her suffer is driving me crazy. And, maybe I'll call Midge in the morning and get her advice.*

But, Barbara, who had indeed talked the problem over with her husband, until late into the night, did not get the chance to pick her friend's brain.

At 6:30 the next morning the phone rang. She watched sleepily as her husband rolled over, looked at the clock and raised an eyebrow at her before lifting the receiver. She saw him come instantly and fully awake. "Yes, Midge. She's right here. Just hang on."

Barbara took the thrusted receiver, and expecting the worst said, "Oh Midge…"

Charles watched his wife's face and tried to follow the conversation. "Oh darling!" Then… "What a miracle! When will you know?"

He could hear the indistinguishable but rapid voice that seem to be drifting out the side of Barbara's head, but could not catch the gist. His wife finally looked up at him and mouthed the words, "Whip has had a heart attack," before returning her entire attention back to the receiver. "Of course! In fact, Charles and I were discussing whether we should send her east again just last night. She isn't doing well here. She got this very proper letter from Tucker mentioning Heather, but acquiescing to her offer of friendship yesterday, and she's been in a tailspin since. Just a moment, I'll have Charles go and get her."

Charles, for the most part, now able to follow the conversation, immediately got out of bed. His wife nodded and he hurried out their bedroom door to get Dawn, still hearing his wife's gentle voice. "No, dear. No, you sound fine. Yes, I'm certain I can spare her. Don't give it another thought."

Dawn flew in, wide-eyed, her hand clutched her throat and, with a distraught look at her mother, waited impatiently to be handed the receiver. As soon as she heard Midge's voice, she started to cry.

"Now, darling," Midge's voice came calmly over the phone line, "I need your help, so don't cry. The crisis really has passed. He is lying, quietly sedated, in his hospital bed, not in any pain."

Dawn snuffled on. "Dawn, darling, pull yourself together," Midge said, somewhat sternly. "Do what I did and concentrate on the miracle that he had the attack while we were sitting in the doctor's office. Can you believe it?"

Dawn realized that her mother was giving her a, "you'll have to do better than this," look. She gulped and said, "Just a minute, Midge." Grabbing a tissue from Barbara's nightstand she gave her nose a healthy blow and then said tremulously into the phone, "Okay, sorry, Midge. What did you say about needing my help?"

465

Barbara watched her daughter's face closely and when Dawn's eyes flew up, asking for permission to go, she smiled and nodded.

"Yes. Yes, I will. Tell James that I love him very much....And I love you to-o-o." Dawn's voice, which seemed to have finally steadied, broke into a wail.

Barbara gently retrieved the receiver from her hand. "Listen, Midge," she said, "she'll be fine. We'll get the plane reservations made and she'll be on her way. We will have you both in our prayers. Do give James our love. Goodbye, you amazing woman."

The three Simpsons looked at each other, each feeling various shades of déjà vu. "Why don't we make a pot of coffee and go out on the deck," Charles suggested.

"No!" said Dawn still wiping ineffectually at her eyes. "I'll go make a pot of coffee, wake the kids, then we can all five sit in bed and drink it...just like in the old days."

Her parents laughed. "All right," Charles agreed, "coffee and kids in bed, just like the old days. Have at it."

On her way down the stairs, Dawn poked her head into the bedrooms of her brother and sister. "Coffee in bed with the folks this morning...up and at 'em if you're interested," she said it each doorway.

In the kitchen, she ground the beans and started the coffee, then went to open the house to let the coolness of the early morning air blow out the afternoon stale heat. She also heated cream mixed with sugar and a bit of cinnamon in the microwave. Coffee for Cal and Lisa Ann was still half-sweetened cream and half coffee, something she had given up only when she graduated from high school.

She recognized that she was feeling far more light-hearted than she should have, with the knowledge that James could, but for the sake of lucky timing, have lost his life. *But,* she rationalized, *I am going to help them. Just like Mom did when they lost Scotty...only this has had a happy outcome. I'll be able to help entertain James during his recovery and at the same time help Midge with her cooking contest.*

Not once in her musings, did she allow herself to consider that a part of her feeling of elation had to do with the fact that very soon a plane would be flying her east towards Tucker Jones.

466

Chapter Forty

Tucker had just finished arranging the new red wool throw over the back of his sofa and was feeling quite pleased with the effect, as well as with himself, when the phone rang. He looked at his watch and smiled. He'd made it! He had hurried a bit through the things he had to do because he wanted to be at home when Midge called.

Already this morning he had sent the letter to Dawn by Fed-ex. He had also stopped at the Irish import shop in the mall, hoping to find just the right throw for his sofa.

He hurried to the phone feeling only the smallest pang of anxiety over Mr. Tyler's test results prick him as he picked up the receiver. The prick turned into a stab the moment he heard her voice. "Tucker, darling, I'm afraid I have some rather shocking news."

She first assured him that her husband was not in danger and then went on to tell him what had happened in, at least to Tucker, horrifying detail. "The doctor knew immediately what was happening. He leaped from behind his desk where he'd been calmly telling us that James did actually have some arterial occlusion and might want to consider angioplasty, where they clean out the arteries. Or he could go ahead with open heart surgery, which is far more invasive but would be a better fix, especially for one living our lifestyle. He was being a bit facetious, I believe. But when James grabbed his chest, moaned and began gasping for breath, he hit some button, filled a syringe with something or other, and had it in James's arm before the nurse made it to the door to say the ambulance was on its way."

Tucker, until months later, could only recall two pieces of information from the entire call. The first was that the doctors were now recommending that Mr. Tyler be scheduled for immediate open-heart surgery and the second was the startling request that he picked Dawn up at the airport that very night.

"It would be a great favor, dear. I really feel the need to keep Hank at my beck and call. I am much too distracted to drive myself and I know how much it would mean to Dawn to see a familiar face when she gets off the plane. Would you do it?"

I must've agreed, he thought later, since he had written the time and the flight number down on his phone pad and was still carrying it around in his hand. But, at the time, he had been too intent on getting the details about Mr. Tyler. He forced his mind to concentrate and not block the information. "Mrs. T," he said, the panic threatening. "It sounds to me as if you are about to say goodbye. Please don't hang up!"

There was a slight pause as Midge catalogued his distress. "Well, all right Tucker, I won't." She heard his heartfelt sigh of relief and waited quietly.

"Is he? I mean, is he going to have the surgery today?" Tucker was gripping the phone with white knuckles, trying not to let the tentacles of roiling fear engulfed him.

"Why, yes, Tucker. Didn't I say that? I'm so sorry. It's scheduled for 3:00 o'clock." Her voice was bright to the point of being brittle and through his own despair; Tucker was able to recognize hers.

He needed to know, was desperate to know, what the odds of success were for open-heart surgery. But he knew he could not ask her; she was not allowing herself to even consider such a painful thought; whereas Tucker could think of nothing else.

"Mrs. T," he choked, "may I come to the hospital? Would it be possible to see Mr. Tyler for even a moment?"

"I don't know, Tucker," she said thoughtfully. "I believe it's families only."

"Mrs. T," he said desperately, "please let me come. Tell them I'm your... son."

Amazingly, he heard her famous tinkling laugh. "What a splendid idea. Do come. He's sedated so he is not very good at conversation, but I know it would mean a great deal to James to see you."

She gave him the hospital name and the room number and even before his receiver was properly cradled,

Tucker was booting his computer. He scanned quickly through the databases available and selected one called Medi-chek.

Quickly, doing the Boolean logic in his head, he punched in the descriptors: heart attack, surgery, success ratio. Immediately, there on his screen were the titles of abstracts. Within seconds of scrolling, the words leaped out at him: factors determining the success of open-heart surgery include the following... He scanned to the next screen and there was the chart he was hoping for. He activated the printer and there was the data in black-and-white. He groaned to himself. 80% chance of success... 90% in a relatively undamaged heart. *Is Mr. Tyler's heart relatively undamaged?* He didn't know. He leaped from the chair for his car keys and then stopped himself. *No! No, this won't do.* "One," he counted to himself, drawing in a great draught of air, "two...three..." Still concentrating on slow, steady breathing, he walked to the sofa and sat down, his eyes resting on his beloved picture of Ethan and Mary. The dual strategy seemed to be working. He felt calmer. "Four..." His mind began to function. *What is it that I need to do before going to the hospital? I might not be back tonight,* he thought with surprise. *Not if I'm picking Dawn up at the airport.* He looked with some curiosity at the pad in his hand and wondered how it got there. *I probably should pack some clothes and call and cancel my afternoon appointment with Kathryn.*

He, of course, got her answering machine. "Kathryn, this is Tucker. I am terribly sorry, but I have to cancel my appointment. My boss has had a..." He couldn't force out the word heart attack. "He's... er, having surgery and I want to be at the hospital. I'll call you when things are a little less crazy and apologize in person. Thank you again for your help and for coming to dinner. If you talk to Sunny, tell her hello for me. I got her letter yesterday. It was delightful..." Tucker realized that he was trying to tell Kathryn all the things he had been saving to tell her that afternoon and rather abruptly, hung up the phone.

At the nurse's station on the fourth floor of the Yale-New Haven Hospital, Tucker presented himself, per

469

Midge's instructions and smiled engagingly. "Hello, I'm Tucker, the Tyler's son."

The young, black-haired nurse looked up casually and then her eyes widened a bit and she smiled. Tucker was wearing a soft blue, vee-necked sweater over a snowy Oxford shirt that was open at the neck, showing just a touch of chest with its whisper of golden hair. She looked her fill before answering. "Oh yes, Mrs. Tyler told us you were coming. Try to get her to go and have a cup of coffee or something, would you? She's awfully strung out." She smiled and Tucker nodded, his eyes flicking around, sorting out the room numbers and then looked back at the nurse.

She said, as she pointed, "Thataway, Tucker." As he thanked her and walked away, she let out a soft sigh, wondering to whom such a gorgeous man could belong.

Midge was sitting on a chair by the hospital bed, reading, when Tucker knocked softly and opened the door. She rose and put her hand to her throat in a gesture that reminded him of his mother. They both turned and looked at the drowsing man. Tucker felt his heart plummet. He returned his gaze to Midge and in a flash, she saw into his soul. Naked in his eyes was love, pain and for some reason, great fear. Unknowingly, he groaned and she turned toward him and opened her arms. They stood rocking, holding onto each other for dear life. A sob rose and caught in Tucker's throat as Midge pleaded, "Oh don't, Tucker. Please don't. I must be strong... We must be strong for James's sake." Her wiry arms surrounded him, propped him up, comforted him, but still she did not let go. "Listen, you big oaf," she gave him a shake as best she could, "do you really think the Lord would allow my husband to have his heart attack in a doctor's office if he planned to take him from his earth?" She loosened her arms and stepped back, peering up into his stricken face. "Well, do you?" Her tone carried a touch of anger or disgust.

He shook his head, recognizing some bizarre logic in her words and mutely walked toward the bed. The tentacles of fear loosened themselves from the death grip they had been holding in his stomach just enough that he could look fully at his boss.

Midge came and stood by his side, holding his hand and it did indeed feel to her as though she was holding the

470

hand of her son. *How could my husband not feel the love in this young man?* she thought. *How could I have doubted it?*

The sedated man, perhaps sensing the presence of the two, opened his eyes, focused for a moment, a smile touched his face and he tried to raise a hand in greeting and then dropped it.

"Sleepy." He mumbled.

Tucker sank into the chair, clasped the dropped hand in both his and gave into the fear buried and held in too long to be denied. "Please, please, don't die. Promise me you won't die!" The sob that had been stuck in his throat tore loose and came tumbling out as he bent his head to rest on the entwined hands.

With great effort, the older man disengaged his hand and lifted it to rest momentarily on Tucker's bowed head and said weakly, "Promise."

The words were a blessing and a benediction. Gradually, Tucker's tears subsided but he still lay with his forehead on the firmness of the hospital bed, not thinking, simply feeling...realizing that some great weight had been removed from his spirit.

Midge had watched the tableau through the blur of her own tears. She too had heard the whispered promise and it lodged itself in her heart. For the first time, she allowed herself to fully feel her own fears.

"Tucker," she advanced and put her hands on his back, "dear, we love you very much. I...I can't thank you enough for being here...I didn't think I wanted anyone here. I told even Althea no...but...I am so glad you came. You are like a son to us you know."

Tucker lifted his head, turned in his chair and buried his head just below Midge's breast and put his arms around her. With a deep and wavering sigh she patted his back and they stayed that way, each feeling unwilling to break the closeness of the bond. Midge's hand strayed to the usually neat brown hair and smoothed back a few of the tousled strands.

"Don't be worried because he is so drowsy," she finally whispered. And Tucker wondered if she had been reading his mind. "The doctors gave him something to make him sleep. It will start to wear off soon, but they wanted him completely rested and alert before he was

471

prepped for surgery." Tucker nodded into her midriff to signify he understood. The feeling of having been somehow set free was still with him.

When finally he lifted his eyes and looked at Midge, she was gratified to see that only the love remained in their soft brown depths. The fear and the pain were gone. She smiled at him and said, "Let's go and sit in the chairs by the window."

He nodded and stood slowly. The tears had dried themselves and he cleared his throat gently. "It feels as though I've cried more this past week than I have in my entire life," he said softly. Then, as they walked toward the sitting area, Tucker remembered the words of the nurse.

"First, before we sit, I'm going to insist that you go and get a cup of coffee. Go outside and have a sniff of the day, stretch your legs. It's the nurse's orders," he added when she looked doubtful. "And when you come bouncing back, bring a cup of coffee to me...and something from the cafeteria." He grinned his engaging grin. "I guess I was so upset I forgot to eat."

Though Tucker hadn't intentionally planned it that way, his request for food worked like magic on the woman who was about to refuse to leave her husband's side. He saw her considering--looking at him. He grinned again and she sighed. "I suppose you're right. A break would do me good." She reached up on tip-toe to kiss his cheek and even then he had to bend down so she could properly plant it. "I'll be right back," she said sternly, collecting her purse. "Keep an eye on him."

Dawn looked at her watch and for the umpteenth time, calculated the time difference. Two o'clock on the East Coast. Mr. Tyler still had a whole hour until his surgery. "Please, dear God," she prayed, "keep him safe."

She was not particularly a religious person, but she had heard what her mother said on the phone to Midge and somehow felt she needed to do her part. She felt helpless and trapped by the confines of the airplane. Unfortunately the flight was full, so there was not really room to move around. She had gotten off in Denver and had at least done some fast stretching, oblivious to the admiring glances of other deplaning passengers as she, as her mother used to say, "Got rid of her ants."

Now, the book in her lap lay unread. Her mind was either with the Tylers, or, though she tried to prevent it, Tucker. Last night she had slept only fitfully until she made a deal with herself to repeat three sentences to herself each time she thought of Tucker. As the deal went, after she repeated the three sentences, she would consciously think of something else. She grimaced. *I am s-o-o-o tired of those particular three sentences!* The first sentence: Tucker Jones is a fantasy. Second sentence: Tucker Jones is dating someone else. Third sentence: You do not try to steal another woman's boyfriend.

With resignation, Dawn put her book back in her purse, leaned back, closed her eyes and muttered under her breath once again, "Tucker Jones is a fantasy…"

Tucker waited with apparent nonchalance in the arrival area. Only that he occasionally checked his watch and looked at the reader board which showed United flight 237 was still running 20 minutes late, gave any indication that he might be waiting with some anticipation. The fact that he had arrived more than an hour early for a flight that was often late, was another. A *Wall Street Journal* lay folded and unread in the empty seat next to him as he tried to think of the things he wanted to say to Dawn.

He pictured her rushing into his arms and his giving her reassurance that Mr. Tyler was in recovery. It had not been as simple as it had first been supposed. Midge and he had waited for what seemed like days, though it was less than five hours, for the actual surgery to end. *But*, thought Tucker, *he's alive and the doctors assured us he was completely out of danger;* though he would need to stay in the hospital for one to two weeks and at home convalescing for another three.

He sighed, thinking how he would feel if he were Dawn--strapped in an uncomfortable seat, not an inkling as to the outcome of the operation. His mind pictured her agitation. She would likely be very tense when she got off the airplane. The first thing she would want would be assurances that Mr. Tyler was fine. *Then what?* This was the point he always got to and saw them rushing into each other's arms. But the logical part of his brain knew that scenario wouldn't be very likely. *Not after that damned letter. I should probably do the safe thing and offer her my hand to shake.*

Speaking of tense... He stretched his back, recognizing his own tenseness. But, then his mind reverted back to its circular thinking and continued until suddenly the loudspeaker broke into his reverie announcing the flight.

He stood, unable to control his agitation for one second longer, and began to pace. All traces of the seemingly relaxed, almost bored, young man completely gone. Occasionally, he would allow himself to shoot a glance at the gate to see if the plane had yet disgorged its human cargo. He began to count his breathing but stopped when he saw he was drawing attention. *Damn! Why didn't I take Tobin's advice and simply call her? Then she wouldn't be on the East Coast and my letter heading towards, if not already on, the West Coast.*

Just when he thought his nerves could stand no more, the first of the passengers began to emerge. He drew a deep breath and with a nonchalance he did not in the least feel, went to lean against one of the pillars.

Dawn, as soon as she cleared the gate, began searching the crowd of happy people greeting each other, for Hank's face. Instead she saw Tucker Jones. He was looking straight at her, but at the distance she couldn't read his face. She dropped her eyes. *What is he doing here?* Suddenly, she realized she had stopped walking, was in fact blocking the gate and shuffled forward, making an effort to raise her eyes. The way he was leaning there against the pillar, it really looked to her as though he was put out for having to come and get her. *What on earth should I say?* Her nimble brain deserted her completely.

Tucker watched her come, saw the lag in her pace, the downcast eyes. His heart fell and turned into a lump of lead in the pit of his stomach. *She's wishing that it were anyone but me here to pick her up,* he thought wretchedly. *She probably detests me and I don't blame her. Her letter was simply good manners.* He had the sudden and almost uncontrollable urge to take to his heels. *I can't do this after these last two days,* was his fleeting thought as he suddenly realized that he was looking at the top of her bowed head with its familiar carefully wrought French braid. The wonderful, nostalgic scent of spicy lemon filled his nostrils so that they quivered. He realized then, that he only had one option…the option that had worked for years.

With casual deliberation, he straightened from the pillar and reached out a hand. "Hello, Dawn. How was your flight?" His voice was mellow, affable and engaging.

With a shudder, Dawn lifted her head, showing hollowed, distraught eyes. "How is Mr. Tyler?" She asked.

The sentences of conversation they shared on the way from the airport to the hospital were forced. The topics, after they covered James's heart attack and the fact that Midge had called Dawn to come and help her with the cooking contest and to keep her husband entertained in his convalescence, dried up.

Though inside her head, Dawn phrased how she would brightly ask after Heather's welfare, she found she couldn't actually bring herself to say the words. Both sighed with relief when the Aston came to a halt in the visitors' parking lot at the hospital. Wordlessly, Tucker got out and came around to help Dawn out and then went to the trunk to retrieve her bags. She would be going home with Midge; he would be going back to his condo. *Now that Dawn is here,* he thought, *Midge doesn't need me hanging around anymore.*

He looked around the parking lot, spotted the Mercedes with Hank at the wheel and made a sudden decision.

"I believe it would be easier if we just put these in the trunk of the Mercedes now." He picked up a bag in either hand and strode toward the big car. Hank saw them and after exchanging a joyful greeting with Dawn, helped Tucker stow the bags.

"It's a great day, that's what I got to say. The Missus came down and let me come up and have a peek in at 'em. He waved and called me by name. It's a bloody miracle, that's what." Hank appeared to be dashing a tear from his eye. Dawn bent forward and put her arms around him and that was just too much for Tucker.

Abruptly he said, "Tell you what Hank, since you know the way, perhaps you wouldn't mind showing Dawn to Mr. Tyler's room and I'll just be off for home." With those words, he turned abruptly and fled to the Aston. It felt as though his heart had fallen to the soles of his feet and he was walking on it.

Dawn watched him go, feeling numb but also glad to be free of the pressure of being with him. She turned hollow eyes on Hank and tried for a smile. "Take me to him, my friend. I also need to see the man with my own eyes."

The first person Dawn saw when she got off the elevator was Clarice and when her eyes adjusted to the dimness of the waiting room, she saw Charlie. Then she burst into tears and was folded into Clarice's ample bosom. "No cause to cry, child. Things be fine. De good Lord, he be in charge of dis whole thing." Clarice soothed her braid. "This be a celebration. I say to John, 'I ain't missin' this celebration. I's borrowin' my car back from Carter'…he's one of my fool sons…'and Charlie and I are going to the hospital.' So here we are!" Clarice kept up the gentle patter until Dawn seemed more in control. Then she held her at arm's length. "Just look at her, Charlie. Ain't she somethin'? Mmm. Mmm."

Charlie, who had been waiting serenely for Dawn's attention, got it more suddenly than he had anticipated and found himself enveloped in a bear hug. "Gosh, but I've missed you two! I think you spoiled me way too much when I was here. California seemed awfully lonesome without you."

Charlie smiled and bowed. "Good art not spoiled by admiration." He said and then smiled again. "Missee Dawn complete safe journey?"

"Yes, yes, I certainly did."

If either Charlie or Clarice noticed the absence of Tucker, both were too polite to mention it, Dawn thought. She asked, "Do you know when I can see Mr. Tyler?"

Charlie nodded. "Knock on door. Mam inside waiting for honorable presence. You come…we all get one more peek. All go home. Charlie make one big pot of tea."

Dawn hurried to do as she was told. At her knock, the door opened, as if Midge had been waiting on the other side. "I thought I heard something out there," she said in a bright whisper as she clasped the tall girl in her arms. "Hello, my dear. James has already been awake and was asking for his sunshine girl before he dropped off again."

Midge led Dawn to the bed where a James Tyler Dawn scarcely recognized lay quietly sleeping, drawing the long easy breaths of drug induced sleep. Midge smiled. "I think we could all be in here peering down at him, jabbering away, and he would sleep right through it," she said softly.

Dawn took a deep breath and tried to think of something to say. The only time she had ever seen this man he'd had been vibrant, absolutely generating his own steam plant of energy. This was not that man. This man was sallow, much smaller, hair grayer...and she thought sadly, much older. She clasped Midge's hand and decided to say nothing.

As she stood in the background watching, Clarice, Charlie and Hank trooped into the room and stood silently around the bed, paying homage to their boss, lost in their own thoughts. Hank crossed himself and Clarice murmured a prayer. Charlie did nothing, said nothing, but his strength and serene goodwill bathed the room. They all felt the comfort of it.

When they turned to go, Midge left last. She put her hand to her husband's forehead and gave a butterfly brush of lips to his cheek.

When they got in the car, Midge tucked her hand into Dawn's. "Are you exhausted, dear?" She asked.

Dawn shook her head. "Not at all. For some reason I have plenty of energy, but I'll bet you are just about to the end of your string."

She was rewarded for her comment by a small sound of bell-like laughter. "You sound just like your mother." Midge said comfortably. Then she sat up and turned to look at Dawn, frowning. "What happened to Tucker? I've just realized that he isn't with us."

Dawn shrugged and feigned nonchalance, though her heart had gone lumpy at his name. "He turned me over to Hank and went home."

"He what? Good heavens, I believe I forgot to ask him to stay. I suppose I just made the assumption that he would. I know he was looking forward to seeing you."

Dawn snorted. "Well if he was, he sure had a funny way of showing. He couldn't wait to get rid of me."

Midge looked at Dawn, wishing there were more than the flickering lights of the streetlamps coming through

477

the windows of the car to read her face. "Oh dear!" she said.

Barbara set her alarm clock for 5:00 A.M. and looked again at the envelope propped by her bedside. Her husband grinned over at her and pulled the cord of the telephone so that he could transfer it to her side of the bed. "I don't want to talk, but I do want to listen," he said, grinning. "Federal Express! My curiosity is absolutely killing me!"

Barbara frowned. "You don't think 8:00 o'clock is too early for them do you? I can't believe I couldn't get a single person to answer the phone all evening long. And to think I was too stupid to get the name of the hospital when Midge called this afternoon." She groaned. "Why couldn't that Fed Ex man have come just 15 minutes earlier...then I could've told Midge, who could've told Dawn...and then I wouldn't be going through all this."

This time, her husband, propped comfortably in bed, his reading glasses perched securely on the end of his nose, laughed. "Open it," he said.

"What? I'd never..." Indignation colored her voice and then was replaced by impishness. "But don't think I haven't thought about it." She pumped her pillow. "Good night, dear. I'm going to try to go to sleep now so 5:00 A.M. comes faster."

Midge was already up and pattering down to the kitchen for coffee when the phone rang. Feeling a pang of dread, since no one, absolutely no one, called at 8:00 o'clock on a Saturday morning, she rushed to punch her line into the kitchen telephone.

With a sigh of relief, she recognized Barbara's excited voice. "Yes. James is just fine," she said. Then a pause, and..."What?" Midge laughed. "He did? How wonderful! Just a minute, I'll go get her."

Laughing over her shoulder at Charlie, she turned to rush from the room, saying, "Tucker has Fed-Exed a letter to Dawn, only she was on her way here and missed it. Her mother is on the phone."

Midge knew what she was going to do was very improper. Dawn could easily take the call in the privacy of their bedroom or James's office instead of coming to the more public phone in the kitchen, but she didn't care. She said, gently shaking Dawn's shoulder, "Wake up dear, your mother is on the phone in the kitchen."

Dawn was immediately awake. "My mom?" She kicked back the covers. "Is something wrong?" Dawn was on her way down the stairs. Midge, snatching the satiny pink robe from the bedpost, hurried after, calling, "Don't worry, dear. Everything is perfect!"

Reaching the kitchen, slightly out of breath, Midge cast the robe around Dawn's shoulders, caught Charlie's eye and they both busied themselves, pretending only a little, for the sake of good manners, not to listen. Later, they would admit to themselves what a joy it was to watch as Dawn slowly understood what her mother was saying.

"From Tucker? You're sure?" Suddenly, from within, a light seem to turn on. Standing there, the satin robe perched precariously on her shoulders, the sole of one barefoot braced against the inside of her knee, one hand idly twisting a strand of golden hair, she looked for the world like a Rockwell illustration for the cover of *The Saturday Evening Post.*

They both watched as hope flickered, dimmed and then continued to glow steadily on her face. "Well, Mom, open it and read it to me!" Excitement rang in her voice. Then, she paused and waited. Midge found she was holding her breath. Dawn's eyes, full of suppressed hope, caught Midge's just for a second and then her attention turned back to the telephone.

On the other end of the line, Barbara unfolded the neatly typed, letter and began to read in a steady, warm voice:

TylerDear Dawn,

You would do me a favor if you threw that last letter away.
This letter says what that letter was intended to say. I don't even know how to apologize for my rude behavior towards you. Perhaps a start is to tell you that it was rooted in the fact that from the beginning,

*when I first saw you, with sticks in your hair
and blood running down your leg, I was
attracted to you.*

*I think those feelings frightened me. Until
recently, I have not allowed people to get
close to me, but all that is too long to talk
about in a letter.*

Barbara paused to swallow. Her husband sat
propped beside her, mesmerized. She reached for his
hand. "Sorry," she said to her daughter, "I had to swallow a
lump in my throat, darling…but I expect you're still there."

"M-o-t-h-e-r!"

Even Charles, on his side of the bed, could hear the
wail. He grinned. "Meanie," he whispered, "don't torture
her." She smiled mistily at her husband and continued:

*I can understand why you are confused
about Heather. She is rather a confusing
person. But let me say, unequivocally, that I
am not at all interested in Heather; no matter
what she may have said. I am, however,
very much interested in getting to know you.
But I think you should know some things
about me before you can consider whether
you might return the interest. They, too, are
things better said in person, and if you do not
intend to come to the East Coast, I would
come west, if invited.*

*In closing, I think you are beautiful,
exciting, feminine and have the capacity for
being a wonderful friend. Besides that, I am
crazy about your perfume. Its scent haunts
me still; though the memory grows faint.
When can I see you? I would very much like
for us to go for a run.*

Barbara paused, reading the line above the
signature and thought, *This young man does* indeed *have
class.* Then she said quickly, "The line before
the signature says:

480

Until I have some indication that this letter is not offensive to you, I will simply sign my name without embellishments or endearments. Please know that they are in my head.

Tucker Jones

Barbara wished fervently that she could see her daughter's face and wondered if Midge could. She would so like the two of them to be able to really live this wonderful moment together. She waited quietly on her end of the line.

"Oh, Mom!" came the voice, suffused with absolute joy. "Oh, Mom! Read it again!"

Barbara heard the unmistakable, bell-like, tinkling laugh in the background of Dawn's phone line and smiled. *Good old Midge, eavesdropping as usual.... Thank goodness!*

"No!" She laughed. "I am not going to read it again. You heard the whole thing. He sounds quite wonderful to me. Now, go do something about it!"

Midge came on the line, laughing. In the background she could hear her daughter's joyful voice and bumping sounds, but Barbara couldn't make out the words. Midge interpreted. "She's dancing Charlie around the kitchen and now, Clarice has come in and Dawn had dropped Charlie and is concentrating on getting Clarice to drop her bags and dance too. She's singing, "I think he loves me." Midge was shouting to be heard above the din. "Barbara, I'll call you back and update you in a bit. We all send our love. Goodbye!"

Once the phone was in the cradle, Midge turned and enjoyed the scene. Now, Dawn was dancing alone, hugging herself, twirling, throwing up her hands, and looking quite magnificent in her pink satin sleep shirt; the robe had long since hit the floor. "Yay!" She shouted, "Yahoo!" Then, with the speed of a tornado, she gave each of them a hug and bolted from the room, leaving the swinging doors rocking on their hinges. But even before the astounded people remaining could draw breath, she was back. "Midge, is there any chance I could borrow the Rover?"

481

Midge laughed. "Even better than that dear, you can borrow Hank. I'd already planned to drive myself today."

Dawn's smiled increased its already magnificent candlepower. "Perfect! Absolutely perfect! Please call him for me, because I'm outta here!"

And with that, she turned and rushed for the stairs, long legs flashing, as she took them three at a time.

The kitchen seemed suddenly to have lost both its audio and energy source. The three adults stood smiling foolishly at each other, realizing they would never again, personally experience, anything close to the power of those joyful feelings of first love. Finally, Clarice broke the silence. "Dat Tucker Jones is one lucky man!"

When Dawn next came into the kitchen, she was wearing her running togs with a blue sweatshirt over her tank top. Her back pack, stuffed to bursting, was over one shoulder. She looked freshly laundered and very beautiful. Hank, who had been there only minutes and had just taken his first sip of coffee, immediately got to his feet. Dawn smiled at him and he too caught the full radiance. It took his breath. "Sit a minute," she said magnanimously and then she turned to Midge, her eyes glowing. "Would you please braid my hair like you did the night of my fall? I think it brought me luck."

While Midge worked to plait the golden strands, Dawn told her admiring audience of her plan. "…and you'll know if it works," she said, "because Tucker and I will be showing up at the hospital to see Mr. Tyler together…and if it doesn't, Hank will bring me, alone, with my tail between my legs."

No one in the room, even for a second, believed that the second scenario presented was even a remote possibility.

Tucker had spent a miserable, sleepless night. He had been sleeping rather well of late and it had become a fond habit. Now, he sat groggily up in bed, feeling stale, sore, and, as he remembered the past evening, he groaned and closed his eyes. His eyelids felt gritty and his mouth tasted foul. He lay back thinking. *I have done more emotionally wrenching things this week than I have done in my entire life. I have shed copious tears, taken tremendous risks to share real parts of myself...but put me in the same dark car with Dawn Simpson and I revert to being a walled-in zombie.* He turned over on his stomach and punched his pillow with a clenched fist.

"Damn!" He shouted with frustration. "Damn you, Tucker Jones, for being such a bloody coward!"

As the echoes of his temper tantrum faded, he heard the doorbell ring. He looked at his clock. It was 9:45. He guessed it was a reasonable time for someone to ring the doorbell on a Saturday morning, but he had no idea who it could possibly be. He reached for his robe. *Well, whoever it is, they are going to see the worst of Tucker Jones, that's for sure,* he thought as he brushed his hand along the stubble of his jaw and made an idle pass to smooth his hair.

The bell rang again, more persistently this time. He looked through the peep hole. "Arugh!"

There she stood...the woman of his dreams. He turned to rush for the bathroom thinking wildly that he could perhaps get his teeth brushed and his hair combed, but no. Dawn had her finger jammed on the buzzer now. He gave up and rushed to open the door, fumbling the lock in his haste.

Dawn stood quietly, a smile on her face, backpack over her shoulder. She looked indescribably fresh and wholesome. *She really is beautiful,* he thought as he leaned, speechlessly, against the doorframe and looked his fill.

Immediately, Dawn saw the warmth and hope alive in his brown eyes.

"Hello, Tucker," she smiled her California girl, Ipana toothpaste smile and walked past him into the condo. "I've come to collect my run."

Epilogue
New Haven, Connecticut
Fall, 1999

Tucker gently laid his three-year-old daughter in the crib that had once been his. She did not stir. It was well past her naptime and she would probably continue to sleep for several hours. Her five-year-old brother, Clayton, was still at the Waterfront Park being shepherded by Sunny while Dawn and Kathryn helped the S.O.S. ladies clean up after the now famous, *Boat Food Cook-Off*. He picked up one of two baby monitors and tip-toed from the room to go in search of his mother, whistling quietly to himself.

He found his mother, as expected, relaxing on a chaise lounge in the garden; a copy of *Bon Appetit* lying unopened on her lap. She smiled a tired smile at him. "Thank you for bringing Nell and me home, dear. I confess, though I wouldn't miss judging the contest with Charlie for the world, it does seem to tire me these days."

"Not at all, Mother, it works well for all of us." He handed her the baby monitor. "I don't think you'll hear a peep from Nell. She absolutely exhausted herself on the playground equipment." He leaned forward and brushed her forehead with a kiss. "We'll see you in a couple of hours."

As Tucker pulled his Lincoln Navigator from its spot in front of the remodeled cottage where he now lived with Dawn and the children, he found he was still whistling. He allowed his mind to roll back the years. Except for the death of his father, due to pancreatic cancer--they had been the happiest and most productive years of his life. *It's Dawn, really.* When Tucker thought of the woman he had married, he realized, once again, how differently his life might have gone without her loving, steadfastness. *I'd still be a total robot-workaholic.* He grimaced in distaste at the thought and pulled his thinking back to life events.

A lot has happened these last ten years, starting at the point when I started dealing with my issues. Then, about that time, while I was falling in love and the S.O.S.

ladies we're trying to buy the tenement, I suggested to Mr. Tyler that some good deed at home in the U.S.A. might deflect those in Washington, D.C., intent on sabotaging his efforts to kick-start energy production and hence the textile industry in Chile.

Fortunately, his boss had jumped at the idea of starting his own charitable trust foundation. *Talk about serendipity! Only because he moved so quickly, was he positioned correctly to throw some serious muscle and money at the city of New Haven when it came to the land swap the S.O.S. ladies had been working on.*

Tucker grinned, remembering. *At the time the ladies were still in shock over the amount of money they were raising, thanks to that first cooking contest. Then, though he didn't yet know it, the old slumlord, Khalif Nubar, was about to sell them his rat-infested tenement to avoid bad publicity.*

The shoreline property owned by the city had been originally designated for low-income housing. However, the land fit the mission of S.O.S. perfectly and one of the most exciting discoveries had been when Tucker's city planning and development codes research for the ladies had shown a possibility of exchanging the tenement property for the waterfront land. "I think the city will go for it, Mrs. T," he had advised. "The cost for developing your site is going to be far less. The tenement already has existing power, water and road infrastructure, but it also has approved environmental and geological studies for large residential complexes. Think of the red tape they can avoid."

The end result, thanks in part to his newly energized boss, was that the tenement was razed and well-designed low-income housing had replaced it. The city-owned industrial site on the river, once a blighted area, became a huge waterfront park with a restored, natural riparian edge for the enjoyment of the housing project residents and the general public. It was now where the cook-off was held.

Even his wife of eight years, had been able to leave her mark on the new park. Her master's thesis from Tufts had been to design natural history themed playground equipment, much to the delight of the S.O.S. ladies. *It's amazing, really...how much we accomplished.*

He thought fondly of his big, gruff boss. After his foundation was up and running, he shocked everyone at

Zitec by announcing Clifton Eldridge had been named the new CEO and that, though he would remain as Chairman of the Board, he planned to devote most of his time to his new love: The James and Michelle Tyler Charitable Trust Foundation.

"Further," he announced, "Tucker Jones will remain here at Zitec in the same capacity; working with Clifton as he did for me." He beetled his brows so fiercely at that announcement that none dared ask exactly what that capacity might be.

After the announcement, Clifton looked down the table and nodded at Tucker, a smile dancing in his eyes. Tucker nodded back, feeling some of Charlie's famous serenity steal over him. He still enjoyed his work at Zitec and his current job description gave him a flex schedule that others could only wish for. He didn't yearn for leadership or the power it gave; his family was far too important.

Yes, thought Tucker, *it's been a great decade and even Mrs. T is happy now that she has Tobin to cluck over.* He chuckled to himself as he parked the SUV. *Well, she's got her work cut out for her if she thinks she can manipulate that fellow into settling down with a wife.*